THE INHERITANCE

Recent Titles by Claire Rayner from Severn House

THE INHERITANCE

Claire Rayner

This title first published in Great Britain 1998 by
SEVERN HOUSE PUBLISHERS LTD of
9–15 High Street, Sutton, Surrey SM1 1DF.
Originally published 1981 as one volume
under the title *The Running Years*.
This title first published in the U.S.A. 1998 by
SEVERN HOUSE PUBLISHERS INC of
595 Madison Avenue, New York, NY 10022.

British Library Cataloguing in Publication Data

Rayner, Claire, 1931-
    The Inheritance
    1.   Jews – Fiction 2. Domestic fiction
    I.   Title
    823.9'14 [F]

    ISBN 0-7278-5356-2

Printed and bound in Great Britain by
MPG Books Ltd, Bodmin, Cornwall.

For Max and Muriel
With love and with gratitude
for just being there.

ACKNOWLEDGEMENTS

The author wishes to thank the following for their help with the research: The Hebrew University of Jerusalem; The Israel Museum, Jerusalem; Eli Ben-Gal, Curator, Beth Hatefutsoth (Museum of the Diaspora), Tel Aviv; Tirtsah Levie, Curator, Joods Historisch Museum (Jewish Historical Museum), Amsterdam; The Curator, Anne Frank House, Prinsengracht 263, Amsterdam; The Imperial War Museum, London; The National Maritime Museum, London; Jewish Board of Guardians, London; Jewish Welfare Board, London; Education Department of the Jewish National Fund, London; Information Committee, Board of Deputies of British Jews; William J. Fishman, Historian, Morley College, London; Rabbi Michael Stanfield, Middlesex New Synagogue, Harrow, Middlesex; Dora Elliott, Debè Elliott, Alex Elliott, Rose Lee, Mary Moss, Minnie Guttenberg, the late Ronnie Elliott; Ben and Gertie Rosen, Brian Buckman, Max and Muriel Berk and many others too numerous to mention for their invaluable help with folk history.

And the Lord will scatter you among all peoples, from one end of the earth to the other; and there you shall serve other gods, of wood and stone, which neither you nor your fathers have known. And among these nations you shall find no ease, and there shall be no rest for the sole of your foot; but the Lord will give you there a trembling heart, and failing eyes, and a languishing soul; your life shall hang in doubt before you; night and day you shall be in dread, and have no assurance of your life. In the morning you shall say, 'Would it were evening!' and at evening you shall say, 'Would it were morning!' because of the dread which your heart shall fear, and the sights which your eyes shall see.

Deuteronomy xxviii, 64–7

The Dispersion
(from 72 AD)

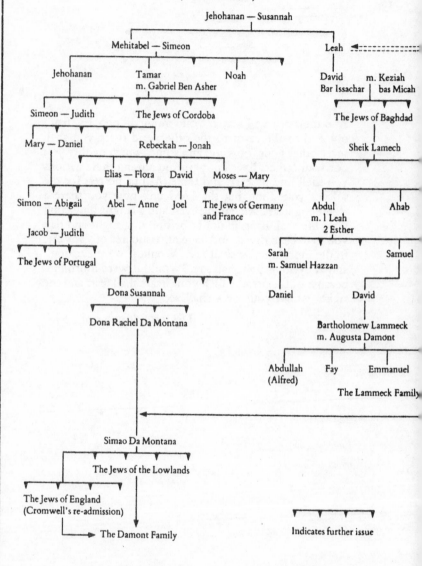

Jehohanan — Susannah

Mehitabel — Simeon

Leah ◄┄┄┄┄┄┄

Jehohanan

Tamar
m. Gabriel Ben Asher

Noah

David
Bar Issachar   m. Keziah
bas Micah

Simeon — Judith

The Jews of Cordoba

The Jews of Baghdad

Mary — Daniel

Rebeckah — Jonah

Sheik Lamech

Elias — Flora   David

Moses — Mary

Simon — Abigail

Abel — Anne   Joel

The Jews of Germany
and France

Abdul
m. 1 Leah
2 Esther

Ahab

Jacob — Judith

Sarah
m. Samuel Hazzan

Samuel

The Jews of Portugal

Daniel

David

Dona Susannah

Bartholomew Lammeck
m. Augusta Damont

Dona Rachel Da Montana

Abdullah
(Alfred)

Fay

Emmanuel

The Lammeck Family

Simao Da Montana

The Jews of the Lowlands

The Jews of England
(Cromwell's re-admission)

→ The Damont Family

Indicates further issue

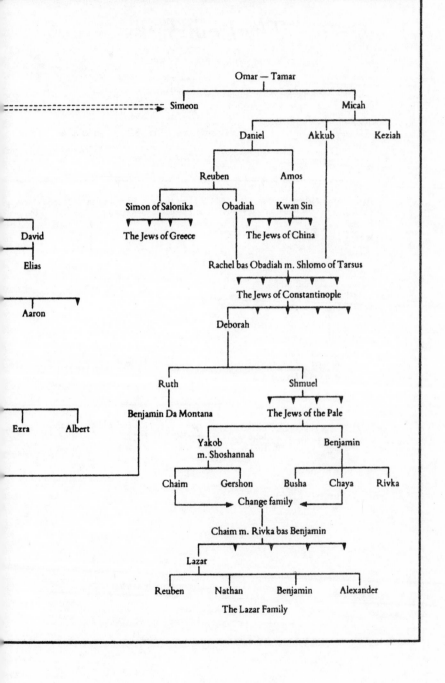

The Lammecks

(London from 1859)

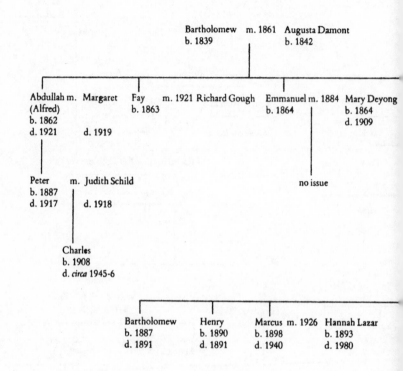

Bartholomew m. 1861 Augusta Damont
b. 1839   b. 1842

Abdullah m. Margaret   Fay   m. 1921 Richard Gough   Emmanuel m. 1884 Mary Deyong
(Alfred)   b. 1863   b. 1864   b. 1864
b. 1862   d. 1909
d. 1921   d. 1919

Peter   m.   Judith Schild   no issue
b. 1887
d. 1917   d. 1918

Charles
b. 1908
d. *circa* 1945-6

Bartholomew   Henry   Marcus m. 1926 Hannah Lazar
b. 1887   b. 1890   b. 1898   b. 1893
d. 1891   d. 1891   d. 1940   d. 1980

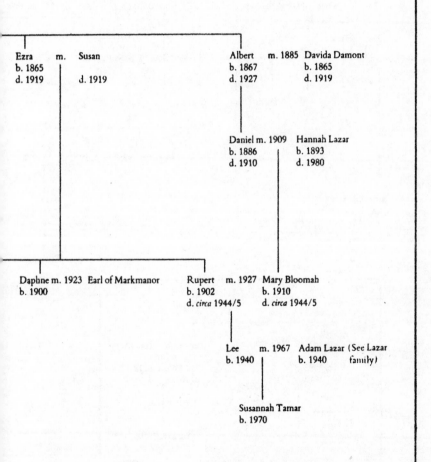

Ezra   m.   Susan
b. 1865
d. 1919   d. 1919

Albert   m. 1885   Davida Damont
b. 1867   b. 1865
d. 1927   d. 1919

Daniel m. 1909   Hannah Lazar
b. 1886   b. 1893
d. 1910   d. 1980

Daphne m. 1923   Earl of Markmanor
b. 1900

Rupert   m. 1927   Mary Bloomah
b. 1902   b. 1910
d. *circa* 1944/5   d. *circa* 1944/5

Lee   m. 1967   Adam Lazar (See Lazar
b. 1940   b. 1940   family)

Susannah Tamar
b. 1970

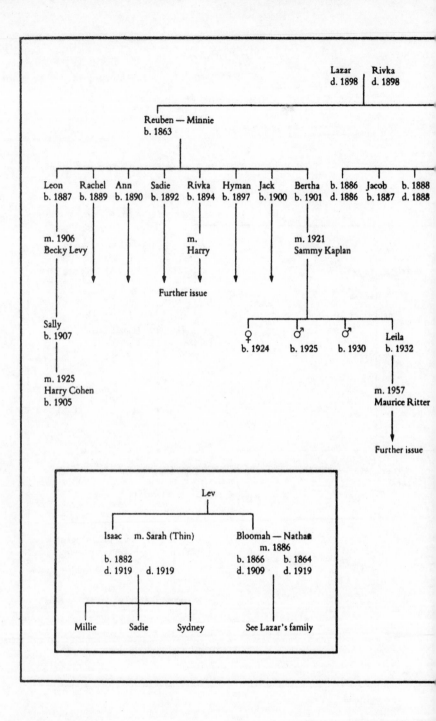

Lazar
d. 1898

Rivka
d. 1898

Reuben — Minnie
b. 1863

Leon
b. 1887

Rachel
b. 1889

Ann
b. 1890

Sadie
b. 1892

Rivka
b. 1894

Hyman
b. 1897

Jack
b. 1900

Bertha
b. 1901

b. 1886
d. 1886

Jacob
b. 1887

b. 1888
d. 1888

m. 1906
Becky Levy

m.
Harry

m. 1921
Sammy Kaplan

Further issue

Sally
b. 1907

♀
b. 1924

♂
b. 1925

♂
b. 1930

Leila
b. 1932

m. 1925
Harry Cohen
b. 1905

m. 1957
Maurice Ritter

Further issue

Lev

Isaac   m. Sarah (Thin)

b. 1882
d. 1919   d. 1919

Bloomah — Nathan
m. 1886

b. 1866
d. 1909

b. 1864
d. 1919

Millie   Sadie   Sydney

See Lazar's family

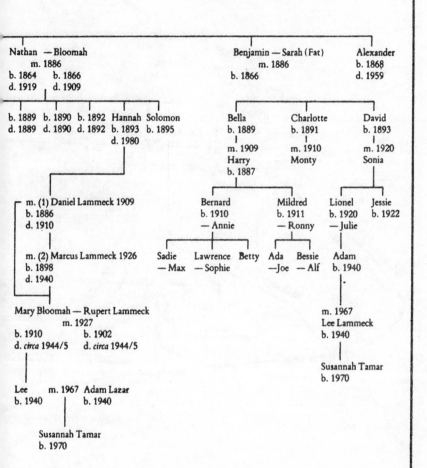

Nathan — Bloomah
m. 1886
b. 1864   b. 1866
d. 1919   d. 1909

Benjamin — Sarah (Fat)
m. 1886
b. 1866

Alexander
b. 1868
d. 1959

b. 1889   b. 1890   b. 1892   Hannah   Solomon
d. 1889   d. 1890   d. 1892   b. 1893   b. 1895
                              d. 1980

Bella
b. 1889

m. 1909
Harry
b. 1887

Charlotte
b. 1891

m. 1910
Monty

David
b. 1893

m. 1920
Sonia

m. (1) Daniel Lammeck 1909
b. 1886
d. 1910

Bernard
b. 1910
— Annie

Mildred
b. 1911
— Ronny

Lionel
b. 1920
— Julie

Jessie
b. 1922

m. (2) Marcus Lammeck 1926
b. 1898
d. 1940

Sadie
— Max

Lawrence   Betty
— Sophie

Ada
—Joe

Bessie
— Alf

Adam
b. 1940
.

Mary Bloomah — Rupert Lammeck
        m. 1927
b. 1910   b. 1902
d. *circa* 1944/5   d. *circa* 1944/5

m. 1967
Lee Lammeck
b. 1940

Lee
b. 1940

m. 1967   Adam Lazar
          b. 1940

Susannah Tamar
b. 1970

Susannah Tamar
b. 1970

Lazar's Family

(London from 1900)

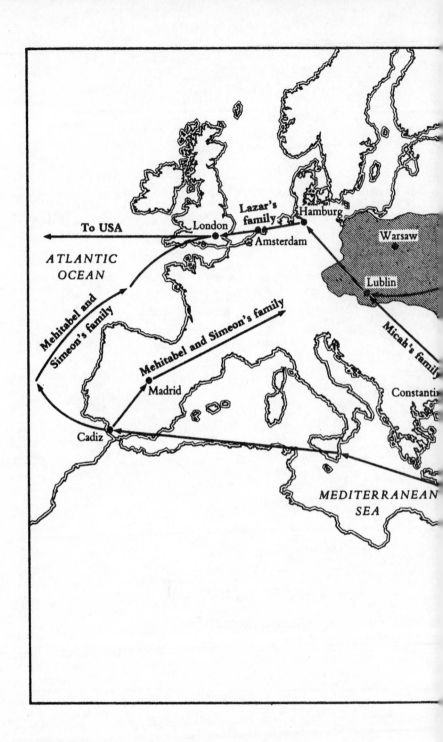

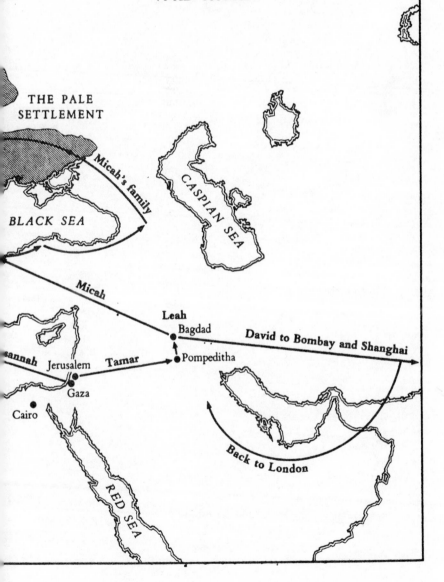

The Running Years

Travels of the children of Susannah and Tamar
70 AD–1881 AD

THE PALE
SETTLEMENT

Micah's family

BLACK SEA

CASPIAN SEA

Micah

Leah
Bagdad

David to Bombay and Shanghai

Susannah   Jerusalem   Tamar   Pompeditha

Gaza

Cairo

Back to London

RED SEA

BOOK ONE

Changing

1

The man sitting beside Hannah in the swaying crowded train was sucking his teeth mournfully as he read his newspaper. Hannah tried not to listen but even the rattle of the train could not drown the repulsive sound. She tried to read the headlines over his shoulder as a distraction, but that did not help because they were all about the gas attacks at Hill 60 and the Second Battle of Ypres. The War dominated everything as it was; to start reading casualty lists at eight in the morning was more than could be asked of even the most patriotic citizens.

She turned her head to stare out of the grimy window at the black walls of the tunnel, at the way the cables swooped and curved as the train rocketed by them, and made herself think of more pleasant things. Mary Bee this morning, for example, crawling into bed with her and making a great tangle of bedclothes and lace trimmed nightdress and demanding biscuits from the tea tray that Florrie had brought at six o'clock, and kicking her heels with fury when she was told they would spoil her breakfast. Little monkey! Hannah thought fondly. She had of course got her biscuits. I suppose I do spoil her a little but who can blame me? She's so very adorable, all red curls and wide blue eyes and a skin as firm and downy as a peach. And anyway, she only has me. No one but me.

That was an ever recurring theme in her thoughts about Mary Bee, her debt to her. She had tried, heavens, how she had tried, not to feel guilt about her daughter's fatherless state, tried to tell herself it was not a fault in her, Hannah, that had left Mary Bee to grow through her baby years to her sturdy almost five-year-old self without a father to care for her, but in a sense it *was* her fault.

Again she wrenched her thoughts away and remembered the previous evening instead. That had been fun, even though

3

it had been quite unlike the old days, before the War – was that only eighteen months ago? – when going to the theatre had been an event of high fashion. Last night they had groped their way there through the blackout, taking a bus to the Gaiety rather than the car, and had worn just ordinary frocks, she and Judith, while Peter had been in his office suit, all stuffy grey and sober tie. But they had laughed a lot for the play was fun and the music delicious, with George Grossmith as handsome as ever and the comedian Leslie Henson with his odd croaking voice exceedingly funny. She hummed the tune she had liked so much under her breath; ' . . . they'll never believe me – they'll never believe me . . . that from this great big world you've chosen me . . . '

The train slowed, came into Mansion House Station and the crowded seats heaved like a field of corn in a wind as passengers, looking tired even before the day's work had begun, got out and more came piling in. She relaxed. Not far now to Liverpool Street and the day's work.

Last night. Judith and Peter. Better not to think about last night with Peter sitting there between them. She and Judith had laughed and chatted during the intervals as they always did, yet she had been so aware of Peter's physical presence beside her, of the warmth of his body as his arm touched hers, of the way he looked at her sometimes in the dimness and how his eyes glinted with shared delight in what was happening on the stage. Don't think about that.

Peter and Judith. What would she have done without them these past four years? It had been Judith who had got Mary Bee Couturiere off the ground. She had listened to Hannah's tentative plans to make her living with the only real skill she had, her needle, and had sent so many of her fashionable friends trekking out to Paultons Square that for the first year of the business's existence Hannah had no time for anything but measuring and cutting and sewing and fitting, and of course looking after her daughter. As Judith had said, the two Mary Bees would be too much for anyone but Hannah Lammeck, who, she told everyone she met from Park Lane tea parties to East End suffragette meetings, was the hardest working woman she knew. In her loving generosity Judith filled her own wardrobe with Mary Bee frocks and cloaks and lingerie, and saw to it that everyone else she knew did the same.

4

And Peter. It had been he who had opened up the other half of her business, the factory in Artillery Lane to which the train was now carrying her. As soon as the War had started on that sweltering August afternoon, he had said, 'They'll need uniforms. Lots of uniforms. Find yourself premises, Hannah, get yourself some workers, I'll see to it you get the contracts.' In the past fifteen months since the factory had first switched on the banks of lights over the sewing machines and set the great goose-irons over the hissing gas jets, they had turned out more than fifty thousand VAD uniforms for the government, making money at a rate she would never have thought possible.

It worried her, the prosperity this hateful war had brought with it. The three years of struggle with Mary Bee Couturiere had been rewarded much less handsomely, in spite of demanding twice the effort, and still brought in a much smaller income though she still spent a good deal of time looking after it. But Peter had shaken his head at her in that dry way of his when she had said as much to him and told her shortly not to be so silly.

'There's no crime in being prosperous,' he said. 'If you did bad work, skimped on the contracts, I'd be as hard on you as anyone else. But you do good work. That's why you're paid so well. Enjoy it.'

Hard working Peter, growing more and more tired in his job in Whitehall, controlling so much of the government's war effort, handling so many contracts for war production; Lammeck Alley must miss him badly. They had only Marcus now to hold the fort, with the senior partners getting older and more inflexible with so many of the Lammeck and Damont nephews and cousins and in-laws in the army and navy. There were rumours that Marcus Lammeck too was getting restless and was talking of joining the Royal Flying Corps. Not that she cared about what happened at Lammeck Alley. Hannah Lammeck she may be, but not one of them cared for her or ever gave her a thought, apart from Peter and Judith, so why should she care? Yet she was, she had to admit, a little interested.

Liverpool Street at last, and, relieved, she joined the river of humanity that poured out of the stuffy train, walking with long easy strides for she was wearing one of her own 1914 creations but without the hobble underskirt that had been such a stylish feature then. She had ripped it out and now wore only the over-tunic which reached just below mid calf, and gave her legs ample room to move. Fashion was totally irrelevant in wartime, of course, but she had been pleased with the idea when it came to her, liking the look of the neat attenuated skirt with the pretty flare and been even more pleased when more and more women followed suit. Now she was surrounded by busy females wearing sensible tailor-mades and tunic dresses. Some of them were even hatless, here in the City, though most, like herself, still felt naked without at least a small head hugger. No need for feathers now of course; that sort of frivolity belonged to the lost world of 1913 and before.

She breathed more deeply now, looking up at the milky blue April sky, and the sparrows that swooped so busily. There were fewer easy pickings for them these days, with so many horses gone to the Front; the hordes of chattering small birds that used to feed so richly under the noses of great dray animals who sent clouds of grain flying from their nosebags. Now, the sparrows had to seek elsewhere for sustenance.

She passed the tea shop on the corner of Bishopsgate, and glanced inside, smiling at the steamy walls and crowded marble-topped tables and the bustling waitresses. Uncle Alex had prospered too, for he had had the good sense to open his shops (now more than forty of them, exactly like this one, scattered about London) from six in the morning till midnight. That way the people who worked the nightshifts in munitions factories could get their dinners, and the people who worked during the day, starting too early for landladies to bother to put themselves out, got their breakfasts too. But he was doing his bit for the War effort as well. Each week he spent a large amount of time in Whitehall, sitting on committees that planned the victualling of the army at the Front and the feeding of vast numbers of soldiers in training at home. He had become an expert in mass catering, all because of a now vanished coffee stall outside the Yiddish theatre in Whitechapel. It was an amusing thought, and Hannah's lips quirked as she crossed the road, dodging open topped buses and the hooting vans and cabs.

Uncle Alex. He had saved her sanity in those dreadful days after Daniel's death, seeing her through the hell of the

6

inquest, protecting her from Albert and Davida's wrath, when they had both turned on her on that awful day, accusing her of hounding their beloved only child to his early death. He sat beside her protectively as she sat *shivah* for Daniel for the full week, alone because Albert and Davida insisted on sitting their mourning days without her, at Park Lane. Albert's rejection of her had hurt, for she had thought he had become fond of her, but she understood it, dimly. He had to consider Davida, after all. Even at the cost of losing contact with his grandchild. So Uncle Alex had helped her through that dreadful week, and later it had been he who had finally pulled her out of her desperate misery when she had come so close to despair that she had contemplated, quite seriously, following her Daniel into whatever oblivion he now inhabited.

'Listen, dolly,' Uncle Alex had said to her that evening, five years before. 'You got to stop all this, you hear me? It's wicked, that's what it is. Wicked.'

'Wicked?' She had peered up at him through swollen eyelids. 'Wicked? I don't know what you mean.'

'Who do you think you are, dolly?' he had said earnestly, sitting facing her with his knees spread wide to accommodate his burgeoning belly. 'Eh? Who do you think you are? Some fancy lady that don't have to suffer on account she's some sort of special creation God made to amuse himself? That you ain't, dolly! I'll tell you who you are. You're Bloomah's daughter. You're my mother Rivka's granddaughter. They had troubles too, believe me, they had troubles. My Momma Rivka *Aleva ha-shalom* had to pick up everything she ever had to call her own to come and live in the stinkin' East End of a city that didn't want her or hers with people whose language she couldn't understand and who despised her and spat on her, and start again. Bloomah, God rest her soul, had to live in a lousy couple of rooms with a feckless husband who was as much use as a bloody sick headache to her, and work her *kishkas* out for her children. What satisfaction did she ever have in her life? And the women before them had it bad, just as bad. Worse, some of them. They really knew what *tsorus* was. There was one of the grandmothers, I don't know who, but I was told when I was a boy, one of the old *boobahs* in the family, had to give her baby boy away to relations to stop the Tsar getting him for his army. There was others who got themselves burned out by lousy Cossacks on account they'd committed the terrible crime of being Jews. There was some that was raped and killed – why else did they run the way they did and bring us all here, hey? So that you could live and your baby Mary Bee could live and keep us all going, till next time and the time after. Because the times keep coming, the bad times. They always have, and me, I reckon they always will. Right now the *goyim* are treating us fair enough, not too much hating, just a bit of nagging on account of some *meshugganeh* anarchists. But they'll start again, you see if they don't. They always have, and then there'll be work for you to do, and for Mary Bee and for all of us. Who are you now to fold up under your private trouble? Sure I know, you're suffering, oh God, but you're suffering. But that's what Jews is for, dolly. You got to suffer and try again, you hear me? And not only try again, but do better than anyone else. On account that's the only way we've got to show them what we're all about. Not just surviving but winning. Beating the lot of them.'

He leaned even further forwards to pinch her thin cheek. 'Like me, dolly, like me. You got to do the same. So cry a *bissel*, lie in your bed at night and cry a *bissel*, and then get up in the morning and get on with living.'

Somehow she had. She looked at his broad face and gleaming eyes, almost hidden now in the folds of expensively fed flesh and felt the strength and love in him and nodded and held onto him and cried bitterly for a long time. But it had been the last time that she had cried during the day. She wept at night, night after night, crying herself to her lonely sleep, but never again during the day did anyone see tears on her cheeks. They saw only concentration and seriousness, and then, as the months grew into years, sometimes laughter. Even now, after almost five years, she still wept at night occasionally, but it was less painful now, more a melancholy remembering of missed joys than the angry bitterness of the early years. She had filled her days with work, right from that evening when Uncle Alex had picked her up and dusted her off and set her on the road again.

Not at the tea shops. She had suggested that, but he had shaken his head.

'Dolly, would I ever like to have you! I tell you, I could make you the best bloody tea shop manageress the business

8

ever had, you should forgive the language. But that would be good for me, not for you. What you got to have is something of your own. And, love you as I do and care about you as I do, there ain't no way anyone owns Alex Lazar's business but Alex Lazar. Not even you, dolly. Anyway, you *need* something of your own. I'm here to tell you that there ain't no satisfaction in this world like your own business. You take your own hands and your own head and you use 'em to build something that wasn't never there before. Me, I got my tea shops, and my artiste's agency, and a couple o' this and few o' that besides, and I look at the offices and at the books and I say to myself, Alex Lazar, I says, that's *creation*. God you ain't, but you got that spark he gave you, and you've used it right. You got to do the same, dolly. You got to love Hannah Lammeck the way I love Alex Lazar, you understand me? Even if you don't understand it don't matter. You will one of these days.'

So Mary Bee Couturiere had been born, and thrived. The business made enough to pay the cost of running the house (at least she owned that, her only inheritance from her brief marriage) and to pay Florrie and Bet and later the girls who came to sit and sew beside her. To pay for the sewing machine and pressing table and materials which she put in the red walled dining room now her workshop, she sold her dining room furniture and that first year she had made enough to pay back to Uncle Alex his initial investment.

He stood and looked at her holding out the cheque to him, her chin up a little, and for one dreadful moment, she was afraid he was going to refuse it. If he had, the whole edifice would have crumbled, for she knew now the truth of what he had told her that April evening. That the full ownership of her own business had to be hers, that any feeling that he still had a share in it would somehow have diminished her achievement. She had fought back and won, and he had to take his money back to prove that she had. He understood. He took the cheque and solemnly gave her a receipt, and then took her out to dinner at Keppner's restaurant, and fed her on quantities of salt beef and apple strudel, and made her laugh a lot.

Now Mary Bee Couturiere operated smoothly and was still keeping busy in spite of the shortage of silks and satins and feathers and beads and sequins, and in spite of the guilty consciences of the fashionable women which kept them away from their dressmakers. And there was also Artillery Lane.

She stopped on the front step and looked up at the blank faced building and took a deep breath. The war was hateful. The fact they had to make uniforms for girls who would spend their time in them dealing with men who had been shot at and bayonetted or gassed by other men was sickening. But the hard fact could not be denied: Hannah Lammeck now owned her own factory, and employed fifty people in it and had a thickening bank balance to cushion the future for Mary Bee, safe at home now with Bet and Florrie to look after her. It was a warming thought.

'You're early, Hannah!' Cissie Weiss came thumping up the stairs behind her, panting a little. She'd put on weight since she'd agreed with joy to come and work for Hannah instead of Isaac Levson, but it suited her. She looked regal in her handsome green suit and with her mass of black hair pinned up. 'Bleedin' kid – you think I could get him out of bed this morning? Not Lennie Weiss! He reckons he's old enough to do what the hell he likes, and going to school ain't what he likes. I said to Joe Cohen at the paper shop this morning, I told him, that kid'll be enough to make me take him at his word one of these days and marry him. Maybe with a father to beat the *tochus* off him, we'd get somewhere. Seen the papers?'

'No thanks, Cissie,' Hannah said. They went together into the cluttered little office at the back of the factory, Hannah switching on the lights as she went. 'I've got enough to worry about. The more I read the papers, the worse I feel. Look, if that girl – what's her name, Jessie Cantor – if she's late again she'll have to go. I know it's hard to get people who're any good, but she's a bad 'influence.'

Cissie hung up her coat and pinned on her supervisor's overall. 'Glad to give that one the push,' she said with relish. 'She's a trouble maker. And I've got a couple of girls from down my street might do as fellin' hands, if I give 'em a bit of training. Listen, last night there was seventeen bolts of serge came in – I checked 'em and three of 'em's faulty. Bad dye errors. So, what do I do? Try and run 'em in on the cut and hope they don't show too much, or send 'em back? Thing is, if we do that, we'll run out of work for the third bench of machines, and they're on piece work and won't take it kindly.'

'Damn.' Hannah said. 'I knew I shouldn't have left early. If I'd have been here I could have sent them back right away. Look, I'll call the dyers. See what they can do to replace them. Three pieces, you say? It's a lot, and the next delivery not due till – ' She ruffled through the papers on her cluttered desk. 'Next Wednesday. Not good. I might have to send one of the men over – '

'Be better if you call Mr Lammeck, wouldn't it?' Cissie said. 'He gets them moving faster'n any of 'em. Or shall I?'

Hannah kept her head down, staring at the delivery note in her hand. Call Peter. She could say thank you again for last night as well as ask his help to sort out the bad delivery. Calling Peter would be a very agreeable thing to do, which was a very good reason why she should not do it.

All the same, as soon as the big clock on the far wall showed nine o'clock and she could count on him being there in his office, she closed her office door against the roar of the machines and the workers' chattering voices, and asked the operator to put her through to the Ministry of Supply.

2

'Dearest Hannah,' Judith said, 'I am utterly and totally exhausted. I can't tell you how it's been this past week – I've had every morning at Aunt Susan's, rolling bandages. You should just *see* them all, the old ones, solemnly dressed up in vast white aprons and nurses' white veils, every inch the ladies of the lamp, sitting there with the maids bringing in tea and cakes every five minutes to restore their strength, and moaning all the time about how frightful it is with all the butlers and footmen gone off to the army! I can't tell you how difficult it is to keep a straight face, but for all that it *is* hard work. They make me do all the really difficult bits like cutting the gauze and then humping the boxes of finished bandages away. Then in the afternoons if it isn't slipper-making at my revered Mama-in-law, it's sewing pillow cases at the Goldsmiths' or packing chocolates and cigarettes into

11

parcels for the Front at the Willem Damonts. And then I've been out three evenings this week at fund-raising balls. Truly darling, I am positively wrung out!'

She didn't look it. She sat opposite Hannah at the corner table at Uncle Alex's Bishopsgate tea shop eating her poached eggs on toast with every evidence of enjoyment, and looking very beautiful indeed. Even though she had done all she could to look 'ordinary', regarding it as immoral to look expensively dressed in wartime, removing every piece of trimming from her blue hand tailored suit, it still looked what it was, superbly cut and made of the most costly fabric Paris could provide. Her hair was as luxuriant as ever and her skin as unblemished and warmly coloured. It was small wonder that so many of the tired workers eating their frugal lunches watched her covertly over the rims of their tea cups.

'So, darling,' Judith finished her poached eggs and reached with gusto for her currant bun, 'I can't *tell* you how grateful I am that you have time to take care of my poor Peter. The poor angel works so hard all day he's entitled to a little relaxation in the evening and with me so busy on war work and organizing the fund-raising balls and all, I'm no pleasure to be with for he so *loathes* the social scene. And the darling does so enjoy his stuffy old music! It's so sweet of you to go with him and sit through it.'

'But I like Elgar,' Hannah bent her head over her own tea cup. This was awful. Her weekly visits with Peter to the Queen's Hall in Langham Place were a rainbow of colour in a world that was grey. To be thanked by Peter's wife for doing the thing she most wanted to do, which was to be alone with him, was beyond bearing.

'Really, Judith,' she said now, almost desperately. 'I love the music. It's been no hardship. But I won't be able to any more.'

'Oh, darling, why not?' Judith opened her eyes wide. 'He'll be quite *desolé*! He told me, you're much nicer to go to concerts with than I am. I chatter so much I spoil his enjoyment, and you, he said, are positively tranquil. You mustn't stop going, you mustn't. If you'd said you loathed the music of course it would be different, though even then I'd beg you to go on, as though it were war work, don't you know!' She laughed with great merriment. 'Indeed, I insist that you do. It *is* your war work. Well, I know the factory is

12

too, of course, but – well, you need the rest, and so does Peter, and you both enjoy it, so that is that!'

She gathered up her gloves and pushed back her chair. 'Dear heart, I must go! I promised Charles that I would take him to the Zoo this afternoon. I'll tell you what! I'll go along and collect Mary Bee, too, and take her. I'm sure she'll adore it, little wretch that she is, and then we can go to tea at Gunter's and I shall give them masses of cakes and ices and make them thoroughly sick and we shall all have a blissful time! Then you need not fret about rushing home to Mary Bee, you can go straight to meet Peter in Whitehall and have some dinner before you go to the concert! There, it's all arranged, and I must go. Thank you for lunch, sweet one. Too, too delicious.'

Hannah watched her go, and gave up fighting her conscience. Perhaps she was being foolish, after all. Peter seemed to see no threat in their evenings spent without Judith, so why should she? Clearly he did not recognize the electricity in her that she felt in him, so all she had to do was control her own reactions, and just go on being the Peter Lammecks' dear cousin Hannah, their good old friend, and not make any unnecessary problems.

It's probably all my own fault, she told herself as she paid her bill and walked back to the factory. I've been alone too long and I see things that aren't there and want things I shouldn't.

And the concerts *were* a delight. A haze of delight. He'd been so matter of fact about it that first evening, as indeed he was on every other succeeding one. 'I have tickets for the eight o'clock performance, and Judith as usual is gadding about on one of her things, so you shall come and hear it with me,' as though it were the most natural thing in the world. She had let the music wrap her in its comfort and sing its shapes into her tired brain and been totally content in a way she could never remember being, even when Daniel had been alive. There was a placidity in Peter, a still centre that sent waves of peace out to her, and quelled the anxiety that was so much a part of her now that she did not even realize it was there, until Peter dispelled it with his presence.

He had sent her home in a cab before going home himself that evening, and he said, almost as an afterthought as he closed the door on her, 'Next Monday. I'll meet you here, at

13

half past seven. Then we'll have time for a glass of sherry before they start. It's rather light and pleasant next week. Pomp and Circumstance, inter alia. Very patriotic of course. Never mind. We'll still enjoy it. Goodnight.'

She enjoyed it as he'd said she would, and gone the next Monday and the Monday after that too, as they drifted into a pattern, a drink before the concert at the Langham Hotel, watching the khaki clad figures of young officers on leave being fêted by the usual clusters of eager girls, and then the music, and afterwards back to the hotel for a little late supper. They ate little, for usually both of them were too tired to bother much about food by the end of the day, and both had busy days to face on the morrow. The long social evenings and self indulgence that led to fuddled weary mornings were long since lost, though the roistering officers and their friends did their best to carry on the old traditions. Peter would watch them sombrely and then catch her eye and smile a little wryly, and say nothing.

Perhaps tonight he would be a little more cheerful than he had been last week? He had shown his usual calm face to her, but she had been aware of tension, of uncertainty of some kind inside him and had fretted all week about it. Tonight, perhaps, he would feel better, be himself again?

They listened to the music as usual and then went on to the Langham, not talking much at all until they ordered their meal. Then, one soldier in particular caught their eye, a tall young man who laughed a lot with a great deal of exuberance and was particularly noisy, and seemed, too, to be more than a little drunk. Certainly he was exceedingly clumsy and knocked things from the table and laughed uproariously when his companions fielded them for him. They seemed less elated than he was, and after a while Hannah said quietly, 'I think he's blind, you know.'

They watched for a little longer and then Peter bent his head sharply, not wanting to watch any more.

'Yes,' he said. 'He's blind. That's quite a performance he's putting on.'

'They're really incredible, these boys. That's all they are, most of them, children. I feel sick sometimes. I dare not think about what's happening, it's so ugly. I keep saying to myself, just finish today. That's all. Tomorrow can take care of itself. Just finish today.'

14

'But it can't take care of itself,' he said. 'It's got to be looked after. That boy's looked after some of the tomorrows. That's why he's here now, blind as a mole and fumbling in the dark and laughing his head off so that we can sit here and think that he's drunk.' His voice sounded harsher than it usually did. She looked at him and tried to see what lay behind his words, but his face was, as usual, unreadable.

'There's nothing more we can do than we're doing,' she said, almost defensively. 'I'm working as hard as I ever have, and so are you. Though it worries me that I make so much money out of it.'

He made a little gesture, almost literally brushing that aside. 'That's not important. It's only money. Not important. There's more to be done than we're doing.'

He looked at her, and she could see for the first time some tension in the muscles round his eyes. 'I sit at a desk with a telephone growing out of the end of my hand and I move thousands of yards of cloth and buttons and thread and tape and needles and tailor's chalk and out of the other end of the machine which I am comes uniforms and uniforms and uniforms. But it's not good enough.'

'Not good enough? What more can you do, for heaven's sake?' She let her voice rise a little. 'You're already doing an enormous job.'

'I should be wearing one,' he said, and bent his head again to contemplate the untouched food on his plate. 'I should be there at Hill 60 listening to that barrage and up to my knees in mud. I should be falling asleep not knowing if I'll ever wake up again. I should be taking the same chances they are.'

'Why?' She wanted to reach out and hold on to him physically. The war had alarmed her from the day it had started and she had spoken no more than the truth when she said that it made her sick to think about it. But so far it had not touched her personally. No one who was close to her had put on khaki and gone to be killed at Ypres. No one she cared about was facing German bombs and torpedoes at sea. She had to deal with nothing worse than shortages of familiar goods, and hard work, and making money. But now she was frightened, filled with plain cold terror that made her shoulders ache and the back of her neck feel as though a great weight had been put on it.

'Why, Peter? I can understand the boys getting excited and

needing to go. They've sat in schoolrooms waiting to grow up and for them it's a marvellous adventure. And the people who never do anything worth doing, who have no real use at home except for ordinary things, they're the ones the recruiting posters are after. Not you! You're doing an important job, Peter. If you left the Ministry who else could run the department the way you do? It's like oiled silk, the way things work. I know you're doing a vital job, and so do you if you think about it. Don't be infected by war fever, please. You're needed here.'

'There are any number of people who could do my job,' he said, still with his head down, staring at his hands on the table cloth in front of him. He was kneading small pieces of bread into grey bomb-shaped pellets. 'Old people. People who'd be no use at the Front, in the way I would be. Established people. Not Jews.'

She leaned back, chilled suddenly by the edge on his voice. 'Jews? What has that got to do with anything?'

Now he did look at her. 'You have to ask that? You? Don't you know what the people who came here before you put up with? Your parents, all their relations, all their friends, they came here like locusts, and they moved in, and they stayed. And my people, not my parents, I know, but a little further back, though not that much further back, it was the same with them. Old Bartholomew Lammeck came here from India, a funny little man wearing a proper suit of clothes for the first time in his life, more used to a turban than a top hat, he came here, and they let him come and stay, and now London's full of us. My people and your people. Hordes of us.'

'Well?' she said, 'What of it?'

'We have to do something about it. *Now.*' He shook his head and managed to smile a little. 'I suppose I do sound like a story out of the "Boys' Own Paper", but there it is. I'm grateful, you see. I feel I owe this country more than I can repay. That's one bit of it. And there's the selfish bit, too, of course. They don't like us, really, you know, the English – not yet. They're a funny lot, you see. They let us come and stay and looked at us sideways and didn't say much, but they didn't really take to us, and though we've been here long enough now to look like them – well, not all that different – and to talk like them and live like them, we're still that bit

16

different and they don't really like or trust us. We make them uneasy. But if enough of us stand up and fight with them in this war, well, maybe they'll like us better. I've got roots here, Hannah. They don't go as deep yet as I'd like them to. Not deep enough to be really safe. I want to push them further in, and the only way I can do that is by putting on one of my own damned uniforms and going to that mess in France.'

She felt her eyes get hot as she watched his fingers, long flexible fingers, go on kneading the bread, making bomb after bomb, piling them neatly beside his plate. She didn't know what to say. She knew what he meant of course; she was as aware as he was of how unstable their hold was in the city of their birth. She had heard the gibes of 'Jewgirl!' shouted after her in the street. She had heard Judith making her light mocking jokes about the times she had been snubbed at fashionable parties because she was 'one of the Chosen, my dear, these Hebrews get in everywhere ... ' Had bitten her tongue when even Florrie who she knew was devoted to her personally made unthinking references to 'That there grocer, 'e's a right villain, always jewin' you down.' Only last month, there had been that fuss about Sir Edward Speyer. He'd been running the London underground train system for years, had made a superb job of it, but a whispering campaign had started, accusing him of being a spy, just because he was a Jew, and he'd had to resign. Peter was right. They did have to justify their presence in this country, had to prove themselves entitled to be here. Born here, but not belonging.

But that didn't help her dispel the sick fear she felt at the thought of Peter going to France. Let someone else go for you, she wanted to shout at him. Stay here and be safe and give me a reason for going on as I do. Let someone else go, not you.

That was precisely what she couldn't say, because that was precisely what he felt so strongly about; the fact that other people were going, taking risks that he was not. It was inevitable that he should feel so; people in general behaved so badly to apparently able-bodied men dressed in civilian clothes. There were girls who drew themselves aside with ostentatious disdain when such a man passed them in the street, others who spoke loudly and slightingly of 'shirkers';

17

and yet others, so she had heard, who gave white feathers to civilian men, as a label of cowardice. In such a fever of patriotism and recruiting posters and swaggering soldiers home on leave filling the streets, only the most insensitive could fail to be made uneasy. And Peter was far from insensitive.

She leaned forwards now and after a moment put her hand on his, wanting to stop the unceasing movement of his fingers.

'Peter. Please don't do anything hasty, will you? I think I know what you mean. I don't think you're right, but I know what you mean. Please take your time.'

'That's half my problem,' he said. 'I always do. I think everything through logically. It's an appalling habit. Makes you quite useless. Waiter! The bill, please.'

It didn't help that the waiter proved to be a middle aged woman, very neat and pleased with herself in frilly white cap and apron. More and more men's jobs were being filled by women. She felt the woman's slightly contemptuous stare at Peter as sharply as though the woman had actually spoken her thoughts aloud. *Oh, God, please stop him from going, please God.*

They came out into the street, pushing their way through the heavy blackout curtain and stood on the pavement trying to get used to the dark.

'Close your eyes,' he said. 'Keep them shut for a minute and then open them again. Then you'll be able to see.'

She obeyed. When she opened her eyes he was standing beside her, his face just a glimmer in the night for the moon had not yet risen. Without thinking, she put her hand on his arm and said, 'Peter, I do need you here so much. I know I'm selfish, but I do so not want you to go.' She felt her face go hot in the darkness. Mercifully, he couldn't see. He just said noncommittally, 'I know. Look, there aren't taxis anywhere, as far as I can see. Can you walk as far as Oxford Circus with me? I think we might do better there.'

She fell into step beside him, biting her lips with rage at herself. These Monday concert visits would have to stop if she couldn't trust her tongue better than this. It just wasn't safe. And maybe they'd stop anyway, if he acted as he was threatening to act. *Oh, God, please don't let him, don't let him.*

When it started it sounded as though it came from inside

18

her own head, it was so thin, so remote a ringing, and then it got louder and all at once there was a great rattle as a klaxon sounded nearby. She shrank back against the side of the building they were passing as footsteps went thundering by, seeming to come from all directions at once.

'What is it?' Peter was shouting, grabbing at someone as he ran by.

'Don't know, guv,' the man said breathlessly, and ran on as the wailing sound became louder and then louder still, and then, someone else passed them and shouted, 'Zeppelin raid! Come on, it's them bleedin' great airships, droppin' bleedin' great bombs! Come on and take cover!'

3

They discovered fairly soon that there was no need to be frightened after all, not there at Oxford Circus. They found a policeman who seemed slightly better informed than the passersby from whom Peter had tried to get some sort of coherent story, who told them that a Zeppelin had been seen at Stoke Newington and had dropped a fire bomb.

'Just by the railway station it was, sir,' the policeman said with relish, needing someone to whom to display his superior knowledge. 'Come up from Wanstead way, seemingly – no one saw 'er, seein' the moon ain't up, but they saw the fire right enough, and set off the alarms everywhere. 'My sarge, 'e says there's no need for no one 'round 'ere to get excited.' He sounded a little regretful, peering up at the black sky. ''E says it's all over to the East that there Zeppelin's going, and no one 'ere in the West End'll come to an atom of trouble on its account.'

'The East?' Hannah said, alarmed. 'Where in the East?'

'Last I heard, it was over to Hoxton way, Shoreditch like . . .'

'The factory,' Hannah said, and took a deep breath. 'Peter, the factory, there's no one there. No night watchman to put fires out. and we had a huge delivery on Friday, remember? I've got thousands of yards there.'

He stood in the darkness beside her, very still. She looked

19

at his profile and thought confusedly of what a stupid waste it would be if he took himself to France to be buried in mud, and what a waste it would be if the Zeppelin fired her factory with the cloth that Peter's office had sent to her, and what a waste it was to love someone else's husband as much as she loved Peter. It all boiled up together inside her to make her suddenly angry, and she took his arm and shook it and cried,'Peter, don't just stand there like an idiot! Do something! Come to the factory. If they drop a fire bomb on it it'll be ... Peter!'

He looked down at her and said nothing, and then turned away to the kerb. Traffic had started to move again now that the panicky sirens and klaxons had stopped their din. After a moment he lifted his hand and waved, and out of the blackness a taxi cab with its flag up moved to his side.

'Come on,' he said shortly. She climbed in, shaky now and ashamed of herself. There had been no need to be so hateful to him, but she had been so frightened, and so much in need of reassurance. She turned her head to look at him in the dimness of the taxi and moved her hand to touch him but there was something very unapproachable about him now as he sat in his corner staring out of the window. She put her hand in her coat pocket and turned to stare out of her own window, as the taxi crawled through the darkness of London, up New Oxford Street to Holborn, and then on over the viaduct past St Pauls and through the City to London Wall and Liverpool Street.

She became more tense as the journey dragged on, listening to the chug of the taxi's noisy engine and peering upwards, trying to see signs of the dreaded Zeppelin, expecting at any moment to see the fat silvery maggot come creeping out from behind a cloud. But there was no sign of anything, only the newly risen moon, round and full just over the horizon.

When they reached Artillery Lane and she stepped out into the street she could smell it, and her chest constricted with sudden fear at the scent of charring timber and paint and something more sinister and chemical that she could not put a name to. She pulled her coat about her and without waiting for Peter, who was paying the cabman, ran down to the factory half way along the street.

He came after her, running along the pavement with loud

echoing footsteps as the taxi's engine throb revved and faded away in the distance, and stood beside her in the empty street.

'Looks all right,' he said. 'Though there's been – I can smell it.'

'Yes,' she said. 'And it's so quiet here, no one about at all. There are people living here, there ought to be some sound.'

Almost as though it were on cue, a ringing began, far away and then more loudly. Peter said almost casually, 'Fire engines.' They stood and listened as the noise drew a little closer and then sheered away north and east of them. 'Not all that close, after all.'

'Where is everybody?' she said, almost fretfully. 'Surely there ought to be someone about.'

'Sheltering, probably. Hiding under stairs. Shall we go in?'

She stood hesitantly on the pavement, feeling rather foolish. It was clear now that there had been no need to come at all, that she had panicked and been childishly rude to Peter all for nothing. She said awkwardly. 'No point now, I suppose. There's nothing happening.'

There was a sound of footsteps running from the Bishopsgate end of the street and someone came rushing up towards them. Peter whirled and shouted, but the man didn't stop, calling back over his shoulder as he went, 'Fire in Fashion Street, 'nother in Princelet Street and Pear Street, and the bugger's still at it.' And he was gone, still running full tilt.

'We'd better go inside,' Peter said then, and took her elbow. 'We can go up to the roof, see what's going on. Then we'll know if there's any need to worry about a fire here. You've got the keys?'

She fumbled in her bag. 'Yes, I came straight to the Langham from here tonight. Here they are.'

He led the way in, and she was glad to defer to his authority. Even though this was her factory, her business, it seemed right, somehow, to let him take charge. She followed him through the heavy door, and waited just inside as he swept his hand along the wall, looking for the light switch. The single naked bulb sprang into life above the stair well, and she looked about her at the familiar shabby green and cream paint, the flaking lino on the stairs and the cobwebbed corners and took a deep breath of the smell of machine oil and new cloth and dust. It was shabby and ugly and it had all the comfort of home, as much as Paultons Square with its

21

fresh white paint and light curtains and familiar furniture.

He led the way up the stairs and unlocked the inner doors and switched on the single overhead light. The factory stretched there in front of her, the four banks of sewing machines shadowed and silent, the big pressing tables looming menacingly behind them.

'How can we get to the roof?' His voice sounded loud in the echoing space and she jumped a little.

'There's a fire escape out towards the back.' She led the way now, walking up an aisle between the machines. Ahead of her there was a rustle as mice scuttled away, but because he was there behind her she didn't mind. The fire escape door was bolted and had twisted a little, but it swung open after a moment's struggle and then they were out on the narrow iron stairway that led up to the roof and down to the yard below.

The roof had a small flat area bounded by a low brick parapet, and it looked eastwards towards the flats of the Lea river. She stood beside the parapet with her hands thrust deep in her pockets against the night air, which was chill even though it was now early summer, and stared out. He moved to stand behind her looking over her head.

The sky was very thick against the light of the moon, now lifting itself well over the horizon, and the rooftops beneath looked stark in the contrasts thrown by the shadows, gun metal grey and hard edged on the tiles. There were a few clouds, moving slowly away towards the west, and the air smelled both cold and sour, for the chemical odour of the fires was thicker here.

'Look,' Peter said quietly. 'Over there.' He pointed, his arm coming over her shoulder so that his hand brushed her cheek. 'Can you see?'

There was a glow where he was pointing, flickering a little against the dark sky. As her eyes became more accustomed to the light, she could see the drifts of smoke that were rising above it, curving elegantly against the light breeze.

'That must be on the other side of Commercial Street,' she said, trying to ignore the way her face held the memory of his touch. This was crazy, and getting crazier. 'Or further, maybe Brick Lane?'

'And there's another,' he said. Again she followed his pointing finger and saw, further away beyond the tangle of

22

chimneys, another glow, leaping higher this time and licking the sky with yellow fingers of flame. 'That must be beyond Aldgate East Station. It looks as though they're moving away from here.'

'Yes,' she said. 'Maybe it's safe here after all. We can go.' But she didn't move and neither did he.

'They might curve back, of course,' he said after a moment. 'Isn't that what happened when they bombed Yarmouth? Went over the town and then came back and dropped more bombs after everyone thought they'd gone. I think we'd better wait and see. We're here now, after all.'

'What's the time?' she asked and he peered at his watch.

'Getting on for twelve.'

'So late? You'll be exhausted in the morning. You need your sleep,' she said, and turned to look at him. 'You work too hard to do without rest. We'll take the chance and go. It looks as though the excitement's over for tonight.'

Below them the sound started again, the frenetic shrieking of fire bells as an engine raced from Bishopsgate going east. He shook his head at her.

'No. Not quite. And what was it that man said, Fashion Street and Princelet Street? That's quite near here.'

'Just across the other side of Commercial Street.' She turned her head to try to peer northwards, on the other side of the chimney stack that lay to their left. Though she could see nothing there because of the bulk of the buildings in the way, the smell still came in gusts as the night breezes lifted and strengthened.

'The way the wind's blowing it could spread this way. Flying sparks. We'd better sit tight. Just a little longer, now we're here. Where's the fabric stock?'

'On the far side of the factory.' She shivered a little as she indicated the fire escape steps going down into the darkness below. 'It's filled the corner beyond my office, you know where I mean? It's the only space I have, but it's not a good place. Right near the door that leads to the stairs. If it ever went up, it'd block the way out.'

'Let me see,' he said. 'We might as well use the time we've got, and it's cold out here. Come on.' He led the way down the fire escape, moving slowly so that she could follow him safely.

Inside, the factory felt warm and stuffy in comparison with

23

the air on the roof, but after a moment she felt the cold again, and in spite of herself shivered again. The cloth bay loomed ahead of them beyond the little glass enclosed office and she went to switch on the light in there, but he shook his head.

'No need to unlock the office just to put the light on,' he said. 'And you'd need to put up blackout shutters. I can see well enough. It's not ideal to keep cloth here, I suppose, but I'm not sure you can put it anywhere else.'

He moved away from her, walking all round the factory, down one aisle and then another. She watched him in the thin light of the moon, at the way his narrow shoulders moved and his back held its erectness and thought, he's walking like a soldier already. *Please don't let him go.* I don't want him to be anywhere but where I can be near him – and then she turned away deliberately, forbidding herself to look at him, sitting down on a bolt of cloth and leaning back against the bulwark of piled bolts that lay behind it.

'Nowhere else you could put it,' he said as he came back. 'Hannah? Oh, there you are. You look like a frightened child in a haystack. Hiding.'

She shook her head. 'It's just somewhere to sit,' she said. 'I'm not hiding.'

'But you are frightened, aren't you?' He sat down beside her, and she pulled herself into as small a space as she could, tightening her muscles against him.

'Frightened? No, of course not. What have I got to be frightened of?' How could he not frighten her, she asked herself, screaming inside her own head. All I'm frightened of is that he might go away.

'I am,' he said. 'Air raids, even small ones, are very frightening indeed. Thinking of a man, just an ordinary man like me, sitting in an airship over my head where the moon and the clouds are and deliberately aiming explosives and firebombs at me, I find that very frightening indeed.'

She blinked and then shook her head at herself. She had actually, just for a moment, quite forgotten why they were here. An air raid. It seemed somehow unimportant now that she had seen how far from her factory the fires were. Now that she was sitting here in a cocoon of bolts of cloth with his body warm and close beside her.

'I suppose so. War is frightening. Every bit of it,' she said and then felt the words dragged out of her, much as she wanted to keep them back. 'People one cares about going away to fight. Casualty lists in the papers.'

'I haven't gone yet,' he said. 'That's my problem. I haven't gone yet, though there's that man sitting up there over my head throwing bombs at me. Mad, isn't it? There he is and here I am, and there are men I know in France – quite mad.'

She couldn't help it, then. The threat seemed too big for her to contain her own need for him another moment, and his face was so close to hers in the thin light. 'Peter ... please, Peter. Don't go.' Her eyes were filling with tears and she couldn't stop them. 'Please, my dear, I do need you so.'

'Oh, God,' he said. 'Oh, God.' He bent his head and kissed her, his mouth feeling cold on hers, and she stopped thinking at all, stopped being angry with herself for her own lack of control over her thoughts, and let go completely. There was just now, and his closeness, and her own body screaming its need into her mind. She clung to him, feeling her curved fingers digging into the cloth of his coat.

For almost five years it had been corked down, that sensuousness that Daniel had first unstoppered, and far from dwindling in those lonely arid years it had flowered and come to a richness that, once released, could not be contained. She did not know what his feeling was, what his needs might be, and didn't even stop to consider them. She cared only for herself and just held onto him, and threw herself into their kisses and let time flow past her.

The cold didn't seem to matter as it struck her skin. Her coat and then her dress were there crumpled on the floor at her feet, and she could feel the roughness of the bolts of cloth against her bare shoulders, and then she was tugging at his clothes, feeling his skin warm under her fingers, his thighs and knees hard and bony against her softness, and they were together in one sudden urgent movement that came simultaneously from both of them, as far as she could tell. Yet even as she felt the excitement rising ever higher, felt her own hunger driving her further and further to satisfaction, she was watching herself, seeing herself on a blue green counterpane in a blue green hotel room, rolling and crying and hurting, but that was Daniel and this was Peter, and as at last the climax of her excitement came, hurling her breathlessly over the peak, she cried aloud, 'Peter!' And the image of Daniel

shattered and glittered inside her head and died in the glow
that burned behind her eyes as she lay, panting, his weight on
top of her.

4

'Oh, my dear one, what *can* I do? Not a thing. I mean I've
talked till I'm blue, and he just listens the way he does, you
know, and then carries on as though I had said nothing. My
mother-in-law is in such a state of rage, I cannot tell you.
And Alfred, he has tried all *he* can, even talking to the King's
equerry. You know the man, Major thingummy. No, well,
perhaps you don't, but he is quite a powerful sort of fellow,
got the ear of the War Office Papa says. He spoke to Peter
who made him agree not to interfere, and was really quite
bucked that Peter is so patriotic.' Judith laughed a little, a
tinkling sound that was painfully false. 'For my part, I have
to say it is of course frightfully good that he is such a patriot.'
She looked at Hannah sideways and smiled, but there was a
bleakness in her face that made Hannah want to cry.

She didn't cry, only put her hand out and took Judith's and
said, 'I'm sorry. I'm truly sorry.'

'It was such a shock, you see. France! I thought he'd just
stay at the War Office. Such a surprise,' Judith said. 'No,
Charles, my precious lamb, you'll spill your paint if you –
there! I knew you would. Let me help. There, like that.'

She fussed a little over Charles and Mary Bee who were
both enveloped in blue holland overalls and facing each other
over the nursery table, painting books spread in front of
them. Hannah watched her mopping the spilled water and
scolding Charles lovingly, and then looked at Mary Bee,
absorbed and silent for once as she spread crimson lake and
burnt umber happily, and her mother tried to pretend that
nothing had changed in her life and that everything was as it
had always been, work and Mary Bee and –

And Judith and Peter. She wrenched her thoughts away,
and looked now at Charles, standing there beside the table
with his head bent a little, watching his mother's deft hands
as she tried to repair the damage the water had done to his

painting. He had sleek dark hair on a head that looked too large for his slender neck. The curve of the nape of that neck seemed to Hannah suddenly very touching, making her eyes fill with tears. And then she realized it was not just the defenceless small-boy look that had so pierced her, it was his likeness to Peter. He looked up then and caught her eye, and she stared at him, at his wide dark eyes and thin little face, and the way that same lock of hair that Peter had to control so carefully on his own adult head flopped over Charles' childish forehead, and she wanted to get up and turn and run away.

'Mamma,' Charles said. 'Is it true? Is Papa going to be a soldier in France?' But it was Hannah he stared at as he asked the question.

Judith's hands stopped moving and then started again. 'Yes, darling, I think so.' Her voice was rather loud. 'There! Now you can start your picture again.'

'Will he be killed, Mamma?'

'Charles, darling!' Judith stared at him wide eyed and then at Hannah and she laughed again, that same tinkling false laugh. 'Such questions these small people do ask! One hardly knows – dearest Charles, do get on with your painting. I'm sure it will be a perfectly beautiful one, and then Papa can put it up on the wall of his study, and be madly proud of you. Hannah, my angel, I must fly, I really must. Bless you for having Charles tonight. Say thank you to Aunt Hannah, my sweet. Nanny shall fetch him first thing in the morning. I couldn't refuse her the night off...' She faltered and swallowed and looked up at Hannah, her eyes very bright and smiling. 'Dear Nanny! Her fiancé, you see, off to France in the morning. Now, Charles, mind your manners.' She kissed his cheek and then Mary Bee's and Hannah's in a flurry of furs and scent and was gone, leaving the three of them to sit in silence listening to the sound of the engine as her car purred away.

'Will he be killed, Aunt Hannah?' Charles asked again after a while as though nothing had happened since he had first asked. He was still standing beside the table, his legs thin and bony under his blue holland overall, and his socks crumpled about his ankles. She put her arms out to him and said simply, 'Oh, dear Charles, I don't know. We none of us know what happens when there's a war on.'

27

But he did not come to her as he usually did. They had always been close, for she loved him as dearly as she did her own Mary Bee, and he was as comfortable curled up on Aunt Hannah's lap as he was on his mother's. But not this afternoon. He just looked at her and then climbed back on his chair and picked up his paintbrush again.

'My picture's better than yours!' Mary Bee said shrilly, leaning back to admire the confection of colour that she had created, but Charles, who could usually be trusted to rise to such taunts, said nothing but went on with his painting. Mary Bee, content to have established, however temporarily, her superiority over him, returned to her painting too. Silence slid into the room.

Hannah tried to relax into familiar comforts. The same old clock ticked loudly and with a faint whirr on the high mantelpiece, the battered wooden table in the middle of the room looked as solid and comfortable as it always had, the worn red carpet on the floor was littered as always with Mary Bee's toys and books and the place, as ever, spelled peace and comfort as no other room in the house could. Yet she could not be comfortable, not now that she knew it was inevitable. He was to go.

She leaned forwards and put some more coal on the fire. It was still early September but it was getting chilly already, and it was pleasant to have the fire glowing in the nursery these evenings, as the sun slanted its late golden glow across the square.

He was to go. He had at last said so, to everyone. The sword that had been hanging over her head these past ten weeks had fallen, and curiously, she felt less badly than she had feared she would − or at least was able to behave as though she did.

It had been a very painful time, as the heavy summer months dragged past, day succeeding effortful day so slowly that sometimes she felt as though the world had stopped turning on its axis. Every moment of that night at the beginning of June was carved into her memory. She had long since stopped trying not to think about it. She had to think of it; there was nothing else that mattered half so much. So she often sat and remembered, looking back on every detail, from the concert with the strains of Elgar wrapping her round and the laughing blind soldier and the ridiculous way they had reacted to the Zeppelin (ridiculous because that had been so minor a raid, compared with the ones that had come later) to that incredible hour they had spent among the bolts of cloth in the factory. She thought sometimes of that cloth, and the uniforms it had gone to make. Had any of the passion that had so filled them both when they had used the cloth as their couch imbued those stiff folds with emotion? Did any of those VADs scampering so busily about their wards ever find their spirits stirring at the sight of the men they were caring for, the way hers had that dark night in Artillery Lane? It was a stupid thought, but it somehow gave her peace of mind, for it made the episode seem governed by fate, something over which she had no control at all.

Though of course she had, and once they had emerged from their hour of madness she had exercised it with adamantine determination. She had refused to allow him to put her in a taxi, insisting on going alone to Bishopsgate station to find a late driver there. She had refused to speak to him on the telephone the next day, the day after that, or indeed on any day at all. She had contented herself with writing only one letter to his office, short and crisp, asking him – indeed demanding – that they remain always apart, and that nothing, absolutely nothing, be done to distress Judith.

She had prevailed. Telephone calls stopped. All her dealings with the Ministry of Supply were taken over by Peter's deputy, James Chesterton, and Peter was never available to join in on those evenings when she could not refuse Judith's invitations.

Judith had seemed unaware of the change in their social life. She exclaimed, of course, over how much busier darling Peter was these days, and how long he had to work at his dismal office, and so often, just as she exclaimed over the fact that Hannah too was over-working, often staying at her factory until almost midnight to get urgent orders out, and going in on Saturdays and Sundays too to cope with all the paper work. More and more now, though, she sat amid the machinists, pushing the heavy fabric under the bouncing iron foot as the wheels whirled, losing herself in the drudgery of boring repetitive labour.

The worst part had been the loneliness, not just the loneliness that came from not seeing Peter any more, but the loneliness that came from the barrier that she had erected between herself and Judith. She had vowed to herself, with all the fervour of which she was capable, that nothing she ever did would hurt Judith. She poured every scrap of energy she had into being the same as she had always been when they met. The burden of guilt that she bore with her made it difficult, but in a way more satisfying. The harder it was to keep Judith unaware of her own unhappiness the more virtue there was in succeeding.

And so the weeks went on, as Judith chattered about her fund-raising and bandage rolling and the children and poor dear overworked Peter, and Hannah listened and sympathized and said nothing significant at all, though she began to wonder, painfully, whether all her efforts to keep Judith happy had been wasted after all, for Judith changed, became edgy and nervous and brighter, more the chatterbox than ever. As June gave way to July and the war news became gloomier, she broke down at last and told Hannah of the real cause of her distress, the fact that Peter was determined to join the army in France.

Week after week it had gone on, Hannah having to listen to Judith talking about the arguments that were going on in every Lammeck and Damont household in London in anxious attempts to convince Peter that his sacrifice was unnecessary. It was not entirely selfishness on the part of the family either, as Judith was at pains to point out. Peter was doing a valuable job, as well as spending much of what little spare time he had in family affairs. With only Marcus to run the complexities of Lammeck Alley, Peter was a vital cog in the family wheel, but just as vital in Whitehall. Hannah listened and said nothing, for she knew all too well that she had no right to say anything. The last thing Peter had said to her was, 'I shall be joining the army, Hannah. I have to. But don't think, please, that this evening has anything to do with it.' Of course she was immediately convinced that it had. He had been talking of joining but would he have done so if she hadn't behaved as she had? Of course not, she told herself, listening to Judith. Of course not. Now, because of my treachery, our treachery, he feels he has to go. She hated herself with a dreary misery that made the days creep by even more slowly.

And today it was a fait accompli. Judith had discovered this morning that he had been going to training sessions on

30

weekends when she had thought he was working in Whitehall. He was to go to France next Thursday.

Next Thursday. That evening as she helped Florrie put the children to bed she thought about it. The next day as she supervised their breakfast and settled the day's household tasks she thought about it. All that day and the next as she busied herself at the factory she thought about it, and on Thursday afternoon, she could contain herself no longer. She had to see him go, not speak to him, but just see him. She had to.

Victoria Station was a wash of khaki and steam and noise. She stood just inside the great concourse staring into the hubbub and her heart slipped in her chest and she thought, I can't. But then a girl near her asked one of the harassed station staff where the embarkation trains were going from and he waved her towards the thickest part of the crowd, and almost without volition Hannah followed her as she went plunging into the melée.

The feeling of the place was extraordinary. It seemed almost as though they were going on cheerful holidays, these khaki clad men with great packs on their backs, shouting and laughing and roaring their jokes at each other as if the whole expedition was some great lark. But that was only the surface of the layered scene. Just below the level of joking men there were women smiling and nodding and chattering, but they stood with their shoulders very closely hunched as though a cold wind were blowing through the station; it was fear, not cold, that lifted the muscles into that tension and tightened the smiles on their faces. And then there were children, some carried on their soldier fathers' backs. Hannah saw small face after small face as she pushed her way along the edge of the crowd towards platform seven, and none of them were smiling. They looked peaky and solemn, their eyes wide and somehow blank.

Here and there she could see the glimpses of the bottom layer of all, people in tears of fear and horror and foreknowledge. A middle aged woman, wearing a very smart hat over a sable coat, was clutching a brown paper bag full of fruit. As someone pushed past her the bag broke and apples went tumbling about the platform and she stood there making no effort to pick them up, letting tears of acute distress run down her cheeks. Hannah stared at her and the young man standing helpless and embarrassed beside her in the clean and polished uniform of the very new officer, and she felt a stab of the same pain the woman was feeling. They were all so helpless in the face of the madness which had overtaken their world, the madness that was turning France into a pandemonium of bloody mud, that all they could do was weep at the tragedy of fallen apples.

The crowd behind her pushed her onwards, and she began to panic, afraid suddenly that they would see her, Judith and Peter. She didn't want to be seen by him, and she certainly did not want to observe their parting. She had been mad to come, and couldn't think why she had. She turned against the pushing tide behind her and began to battle her way back.

As she pushed her way at last out of the thickest part of the crowd, coming out by Smith's bookstall at the front of the concourse, she heard Judith's voice high and clear above the hubbub, and so determinedly bright it had the quality of polished glass. It might have shattered at a touch.

'Darling Hannah, I knew you would come! I just knew you could not let him go without being here. Peter, my angel, here she is, come to scold you for being so wilful as to go, and to wish you well. Aren't you, Hannah?'

They were standing side by side at the bookstall, where Judith had just brought a sheaf of magazines for him. He looked at her and nodded, his face quite still.

'Hallo, Hannah. Thank you for coming.'

Judith moved away to the chocolate stall to buy the most expensive boxes they had and Hannah looked at her briefly and said, 'I didn't mean to come. I don't know why I did. I shouldn't have. Let me go, now. I wish you well, and – oh, God, I must go.'

'No,' He put out one hand and held onto her. 'You can't. Judith would be bitterly hurt. She needs you. Stay.'

She looked at him, at the way the peak of his flat khaki cap sat so neatly on his forehead, at his shining buttons and the polished Sam Browne and the neat luggage at his side and could not see him at all, somehow. He was like every other soldier in this maelstrom of officers and men; just another chess piece in khaki, like the embarrassed youth with the mother who was weeping over her apples, like the nearby

32

corporal in boots so bright they could mirror the face of the child he had perched on his shoulder, like every single one of them. She stared at him, her forehead creased. Who was he? Why was she here?

Judith came back and began to cram the magazines and chocolate into Peter's side pack. He said nothing, letting her do it, and then as she stood up he said gently, 'It will be all right, my love. It will be all right. Whatever happens. We'll be *all right.*'

She looked at him, her eyes wide and sparkling. She was as beautiful as ever, as elegantly dressed as ever, as perfectly head-turning as ever, and every line of her body spoke of the misery that was in her. Hannah stepped back, feeling sick with shame. This girl was her friend and she had used her so badly, and she wanted to blurt it all out, wanted to tell her what had happened that night in June in Artillery Lane, anything to shift the guilt from her own back, to let someone else suffer it. She bit her tongue so hard that she tasted salt blood.

'Remember what I told you,' Peter was saying, softly but so clearly that even above all the noise around them Hannah heard every word. 'Whatever happens, we two will be all right.'

He turned then and looked at Hannah and smiled. For a moment it was the Peter of the Monday concerts again, the Peter who had been her beloved friend these past five years, the Peter she loved and needed so much.

'Take care of her, Hannah. And of Charles. And they'll take care of you.' He bent and picked up his bags and his side pack and looked again at Judith, who was standing very still and straight. He bobbed his head and then turned and went, pushing his way into the crowd and disappearing into the sea of khaki. Judith and Hannah stood side by side and watched him go, and went on watching the crowd long after they knew his train had steamed out of the vast station, leaving wreaths of grey smoke tendrils to float about the iron tracery of the roof far over their heads.

5

If I can bear it for three weeks, it will be all right, Hannah would tell herself. Just for three weeks. And then would feel sick at the reason for feeling so.

It had been Cissie who had put the notion into her head, Cissie all unknowing and cheerfully chattering to the finishers as they worked late over a batch of uniforms due to be shipped out to Etaples on the midnight train to the coast.

'Three weeks,' Cissie had said. 'That's what they say, you know, three weeks is all anyone lasts out on the Front now. Wounded or worse they are, inside o' three weeks.'

Hannah, who had been sitting in her office with the door open, checking delivery notes, felt her throat tighten so that she almost retched. She got up and pushed the door closed and then tried to concentrate on the delivery notes again: seventy-five yard bolts of blue serge, width forty-eight inches, quantity fifteen; hundred yard bolts blue striped white calico width thirty-six inches, quantity thirty-five; fifty yard bolts scarlet flannel width forty-eight inches, quantity fifteen, dammit, that meant they'd be short of red flannel for the capes, and she'd have to spend another hour on the phone. Three weeks? She'd read that too, somewhere, but had managed to forget it till now. Three weeks was the life expectancy of men at the front now that the battle of Loos had begun. Three weeks if they were lucky. Three weeks before they were sprawled in the mud or hanging over the barbed wire staring blank-eyed at the squalor of no-man's-land, or weeping with pain in the casualty clearing stations behind the lines, waiting to be shipped home, if they survived long enough, to be patched up ready to be sent back to start all over again.

The words kept repeating themselves in her head as she went about the day's work, checking the cut of the capes and the dresses, watching over the stitching of the aprons and caps, thinking, *three weeks, three weeks, three weeks.* If I can stop myself saying anything for three weeks, it will be all right.

It was a crazy thought, a totally illogical idea, but it sustained her. Each evening she went home to find Judith waiting there for her, for she had surrendered her control entirely with Hannah. With everyone else she was her old self, chattering, bright, full of busyness and excitement. The bandage rolling ladies of the West End commented to each other admiringly on how brave darling Judith Lammeck was, and how she was an example to all young wives, or more waspishly told each other it was remarkable how unmoved she seemed about her dear husband's absence; these days, young women were all hard selfishness, were they not? But to Hannah, Judith displayed her distress in all its rawness.

She would manage, somehow, to get herself to Paultons Square every evening in time to collect Charles to take him home, or sometimes, more and more often now, to kiss him goodnight as he curled up in the spare bed in Mary Bee's nursery. The two children were becoming inseparable, for now that Judith's nanny had gone to make munitions, leaving the house staffed only by maids who were not bright enough to be of much use doing war work, it was better for Charles and easier for Judith to let him spend his days with Florrie and Bet. There had been some desultory talk of Florrie going off to a factory but Bet had coaxed her out of it, and Florrie knew herself to be indispensable to Hannah's war work, and so stayed put. More and more Charles regarded Paultons Square as his second home and, inevitably, so did Judith.

Perhaps that was one of the reasons she was so unguarded with Hannah, or perhaps it was an awareness that Hannah shared her sense of loss. It would never have occurred to her that Hannah felt anything but cousinly affection for Peter; Hannah knew that, and it made her own situation that much more poignant, her guilt a greater weight on her mind. It was not eased by looking at Judith's exhausted little face, the eyes shadowed and dull.

They spent many evenings together – for Judith could not bring herself to go to fund-raising balls while Peter was at the Front. They sat facing each other on each side of the fireplace in the pretty white drawing room with its Heal's furniture and its sinuous shapes, often knitting, sometimes sewing, frequently just staring at the dull embers in the grate. It was almost as though they were an elderly married couple,

Hannah thought, and almost said as much to Judith, and then, as ever, did not. More and more Hannah was learning that superficial chatter was the only safe talk there was. She became, despite Judith's frequent company, more and more lonely.

Chanukah, the festival of lights, came and Judith's spirits lifted for a while. She hurled herself into planning entertainment for the children, giving them their daily gifts for the eight days of the holiday (which made them both tell Florrie and Bet, happily decorating their small tree in the kitchen, that Christmas might be all right, but it wasn't a patch on Chanukah, which went on for days and days and *days*) and being everything a mother and aunt should be. Hannah did all she could to be as eager, but it was becoming harder to dissimulate.

The three weeks she had so feared had long gone, and still Peter survived. He wrote long letters to Judith, and equally long ones to Hannah, filled with friendship but with no hint that there was anything more than that between them, and seemed well enough; he was acting as a supply officer behind the lines, but went up to the trenches quite often, he said, to ensure that all the men needed was getting through. Hannah would take a deep breath, trying to control the fear that rose in her as she read his words, reminding herself that by the time the letter reached her he had moved on, and would agree brightly with Judith that 'he seemed to be his old darling self, did he not?'

By the end of January she was beginning to feel better. As the memory of that June night receded, so did some of the guilt; it had happened, and that was that. It had not been premeditated, and clearly it had done no harm to anyone but herself. She was suffering, but Judith was obviously not. Letters came with punctilious regularity; Judith relaxed and became less fearful, more cheerful in the evenings in Paultons Square. Hannah was feeling better too, for had Peter not survived the horrors of the trenches for four months now? He might even get some leave soon. And then she would feel that stab of fear again and would think wildly, 'If he does, I'll have to go away – not see him. Take Mary Bee to the seaside perhaps.' She shook her head at her own idiocy, for who went to the seaside in the depths of winter?

In early February, Uncle Alex came to see her, for the first time in some weeks. He had been, he told her with not a little self importance, hectically busy.

'I tell you, dolly, feedin' that lot – it's like pushing mountains down the Commercial Road. Running forty restaurants is a pushover compared with it on account people're prepared to pay for what they get in a tea shop. But dealing with the army, it's like selling apples to a man with no teeth. They don't eat the stuff themselves, the officers that do the buying. So they don't see that the cost of it has to be what it is and they keep cuttin' back. So there's me with the farmers on one side screaming for top rates and the complaints about the bully beef and plum and apple jam from the soldiers on the other, and the officers in between – I tell you, I feel like a nut between two sets of crackers.'

But he was obviously in his element, busy and content, and he beamed at her over his still burgeoning belly and lit another cigar. He might look like the sort of war profiteer so many of the nastier current jokes were about, but he was working hard, and he clearly took pride in his contribution.

'I'll tell you why I come, dolly,' he said after a moment. 'It's Solly.'

She frowned sharply. 'Solly? What's the matter? He's not ill?'

He shook his head and grinned. 'Ill, that one? Tough as a pair of old boots. No dolly. It's just that he says he wants to join the army.'

She closed her eyes for a moment. 'Solly? But he's so young.' She herself was almost twenty-four and Solly twenty, but somehow when she thought of him she still saw the cheeky small boy with the grubby clothes and the watchful sideways look in his round eyes, not the weedy youth that he had become.

'I thought they'd turn him down, he's so scrawny, but they're not so fussy as they was, the recruiters. They said they'd take him. Trouble is, your father. Since Jake went up to Scotland on that training camp job there's only been Solly to take care of your father – I mean, Aunt Sarah really does it all, but you know what I mean. Nathan's got to think it's his own life and his own boys – he don't take no help from relations if he can help it. If he knows it – you know what I mean?'

'I know what you mean.' She was silent for a while.

'What do I do?'

'I did what I could. Asked Nathan if he'd bury the hatchet, now you're a widow. I thought, if he's got you maybe he'll let Solly go. And Solly, he's getting very upset, stuck at home. Four times some stupid bitch gives him a white feather in the street, he feels it, the boy.'

'What did Poppa say?' She had felt a moment of lifting pleasure. Could they pick up the old threads again, she and Nathan? But Uncle Alex shook his head.

'That one! O' course he won't. So, all I can do is try to get some sort of army job for young Solly that don't take him to France. London's full of bleedin' officers in fancy uniforms that don't never get mud on their boots. So I thought these officers, they got to have batmen, drivers and that, eh? I got my contacts, but I used 'em a lot already to get favours, got three o' the boys from the gym into the regiments they wanted that way, Jews though they are, and I can't keep on pullin' the same bits o' string without breakin' 'em. So I thought, maybe you could ask your father-in-law. That *ferstinkeneh mumser*'s done little enough for you and his granddaughter. So maybe he can do something for her uncle, hey?'

She shook her head, reddening. 'Dear Uncle Alex, you can't mean it: They haven't spoken to me for five years. Not since Daniel died. His mother took it into her head that I'd – that it was something I did that made him ... that ... ' She shook her head. 'Please, I can't. It's not that I don't want to help. You know I do. But not that way.'

He made a small grimace, and finished his cup of tea. 'Well, if you can't you can't. I'll pull on my own bits of string again. But I ain't too hopeful, I tell you.'

'I could ask Judith,' she said after a moment. 'Her father-in-law, Alfred, he might. He's got some sort of pull at the War Office. He tried to keep Peter away from France that way, but Peter wouldn't have it of course.' She tilted her chin with a moment of pride, and Uncle Alex looked at her sharply.

'Is that a fact? All these people with consciences, what's the sense of it? You don't have to go to France to get yourself spitted to be useful. I reckon you do a better job bein' a bit less heroic and a lot more practical,' he said. 'You think that Alfred'd do something for young Solly? It's not just for your father, you know. I know the recruiters took him, but you only got to look at the boy to know he wouldn't last five minutes out there.'

'I'll ask Judith,' Hannah felt the weight of hopelessness settle on her again. It had been easing as the weeks went by, but now this. Solly at the Front to worry about as well as Peter? It had been a small comfort that Jake had been selected for a job as a training corporal in the north when he had joined the army; she had thought then that for once God had been on her side. But now Solly – '

'I'll ask,' she repeated.

Being asked seemed to help Judith in a most remarkable way. She listened to Hannah's explanation of the problem and caught fire, just as the old Judith would have done.

'Of course we'll have to arrange it!' she said, and went chattering on about whom she would call and how it could be done, and left in a flurry of furs and plans.

For the next two weeks she was almost her old self again, busy, sparkling, seeming happy in her hard work, bustling from Whitehall office to rich house to Paultons Square and back again.

Charles seemed more content too, not waking in tears in the middle of the night as he had been doing, and Hannah, putting the children to bed one night, thought, it's all going to be all right. We can manage. I think we can manage. She hugged Charles and settled him on one side of her lap and Mary Bee on the other and began to read them their bedtime story.

It was one of those soft muggy evenings in February when mist thickened over the London chimney pots and the streets smelled of people's suppers and horses and the promise, some time soon, of spring when snowdrops and crocuses would appear in the sooty little front gardens of Chelsea. The children were warm and scented from their baths, and sleepy as they listened to her reading with slightly glazed eyes, both with their thumbs in their mouths, and Hannah felt a lift of sheer pleasure as she sat there, murmuring her story of Peter Rabbit and Flopsy, Mopsy and Cottontail. She heard the telephone ring below, heard Florrie's footsteps come toiling up from the kitchen to answer it, still reading and with no sense of anxiety in her. For weeks now every knock on the door, every ring of the telephone had made her stomach lurch but tonight the sound did not. Even when Florrie's footsteps came up the stairs, and the door opened she felt no sense of doom. She just hugged the children and said, 'That's all for tonight, my darlings. Tomorrow we'll finish it. Now let Florrie tuck you in while I go and talk to whoever it is. Florrie?'

'It's that there Mildred, mum,' Florrie said. 'From Mrs Lammeck's 'ouse.' She looked at Hannah uneasily, but Hannah just smiled back, still a little dreamy herself from the story telling and the soft warm children. 'Sounds a bit put out, she does. I'll tuck 'em in, mum, while you go to talk to her. Come on you two, up the wooden hill to Bedfordshire.'

Mary Bee giggled and said shrilly, 'Soppy Florrie! We're already upstairs!' and Florrie laughed and Hannah went away leaving the warmth of the nursery behind her with a small pang. Mary Bee was growing so sturdy and tall; it was such a little time since she had been just an armful of hungry baby.

'Oh, mum,' Mildred's thin voice crackled at the end of the telephone. 'Oh, mum, what do we do? 'Ere's a telegram come for Missus and Cook's 'avin' the vapours cos she says she knows it's the master dead and mangled in that there 'orrible trench and what shall we do, mum, on account of Madam ain't 'ere, and I thought she might be there, and would want to know right away, wouldn't she, mum?'

6

Bereavement this time came easier because there was so much around her. There was Charles's still white face, determinedly showing no feeling at all as he went about the day's play and lessons with Miss Porteous, the visiting governess Hannah had employed for the children. There were Florrie and Bet looking drawn and streaked with tears. Above all, there was Judith, who had come to stay with Hannah and now sat in the big chair beside the nursery fire all day and stared at the embers and said nothing. Looking after Judith, coaxing her to eat and drink, urging her to go to bed at night and persuading her to get up again in the morning, above all dealing with the commiserating telephone calls and letters that came for her, gave Hannah little time to explore her own distress.

But it sat low in her belly, an amalgam of memories of the way she had felt when Daniel had died, her own still smouldering guilt about her relationship with Peter, her sadness for the disappearance of Judith's sparkle – for that had vanished at the moment the telegram had been put into her hands – and finally her private sense of confusion over the loss of Peter himself. When Daniel had died he had seemed to her to be snuffed out. There had been no lingering consciousness of his existence. It was as though he had never been. But then there had been all the trappings of death, a funeral, a *shivah*, to make it all real. For Peter there was just a piece of paper; no funeral, no special rites to mourn his passing (for Judith, showing her only spark of will, had refused to go to her parents-in-law's home to sit and mourn there, and certainly Hannah could hot visit them). So he seemed to linger on in her world, shadowy, but with so strong a sense of his presence that sometimes she actually found herself looking up to see him. I'm going mad, she thought one night, frightened.

But she did not go mad. She just went doggedly on, working at the factory and dealing at home with the restructuring of their lives.

It was not easy, for Judith was so pliable. Whatever Hannah said she acquiesced. Hannah thought Judith should move into Paultons Square for a while? Then Judith would. Hannah thought that Judith should start sewing for something to do as the days crept by? Then Judith obediently took up her needle. Hannah thought Judith should eat and drink and bathe? Then Judith would. But she did nothing of her own will, and the weight of her became ever greater, until at last Hannah decided that she needed help. It was not right that there should be just herself looking after Judith and Charles; they needed contact with Peter's family.

Was it because they were themselves so stunned that they remained aloof? Certainly none of the Lammecks made any attempt to contact Judith at Hannah's house, though plenty of caring messages came from her friends and her own cousins. But her in-laws were silent, and because of her own remoteness from the clan it was difficult for Hannah to know how to cope.

41

She asked Uncle Alex what she should do. He sat over coffee with Hannah after Judith had gone to bed, his lips pursed as he considered.

'I tell you, it's crazy,' he said at length. 'How come people can behave so strange? Here's a man, his only son gets killed in the trenches, he don't make no effort to get in touch with his grandson, and his grandson's mother? Me, I ain't got no sons and I ain't got no grandsons, but believe me, dolly, if I'd lost the one there'd be nothing in this world'd keep me away. I can't understand it. These English Jews, I just can't fathom 'em.'

She smiled a little at that. 'What do you mean, English Jews? What are we but English Jews?'

He shook his head. 'We're different, dolly. We came from the shtetls with *gornicht mit gornicht*, with nothing in our pockets to call our own. All we had was each other, you know? You won't remember how it was, but I tell you, it was beautiful. A person arrives, got nothing but a few kopecks in his pockets, and the clothes on his back, and what does he do? He looks for his landsleit, the people from his shtetl in the old country, and when he finds them in Spital-fields or down the Commercial Road, Stepney way, they look after him. He gets married? They look after his wife and children God forbid trouble should come to him. And they're still doing it, though it's twenty, thirty years or more since some of 'em came here. All over the East End now there's people lookin' after soldiers' widows and children like they've always looked after widows and children. But these English Jews, these rich men in their big fancy houses who call kings and lords *their* landsleit, they leave their young widows like ... ' His voice trailed off in hopeless fury. 'I tell you I don't understand them. They make me sick!'

'They're upset themselves, I suppose,' Hannah said, feeling oddly impelled to defend the Lammecks and Damonts, thought they had used her in her time of loss as badly as they were using Judith now, and even though Judith was one of them in a way she, Hannah, had never been. 'Peter was special. I mean, everyone is, especially someone's only son, but there was more than that. He was special ... '

Her voice dwindled away a little and Alex shot her a sharp knowing little glance.

'But what do I do about Judith?' Hannah said. 'It worries

me – I mean suppose she gets ill? Or … '

She stopped, unable to give voice to her deeper fears, but as usual, Uncle Alex knew.

'That's a lot of nonsense,' he said sharply. 'I don't know the girl like I know you, but you treat her like she's a real friend, more than a relation, you know? That extra bit, which means she's a sensible girl like you. You didn't do nothing stupid after Daniel died, and neither will she. Believe me.'

She did, grateful to have his strength on which to hold, but she still felt it was necessary to do something about the fracture that had seemed to appear between Judith and her in-laws. Eventually, Uncle Alex agreed with her.

'They don't deserve no-one should go to so much trouble for them, the *shprauncy mumserim* they are, but you're right, I suppose. Listen, dolly, you got enough on your plate. I'll go see this Alfred myself, all right? I'll tell him you're worried, see what he's going to do.'

'Bless you,' she said and took a deep breath of relief. Having Uncle Alex there always on the edge of her life ready to be turned to in such moments of anxiety as this made all the difference to her. It was not that she called on him all that often, perhaps because he was there and available; it was just knowing that she could.

Alex came back two weeks later with his face thunderous with anger, and a sort of shame, and stomped into the dining room where she was sitting sewing a dress for Mary Bee with Judith sitting on the other side of the table sorting buttons. It was one of those monotonous and therefore comforting jobs that Hannah had learned to give to Judith, and sitting there in the dull heaviness of a March Sunday afternoon there was satisfaction for her too in listening to the click of the buttons as Judith dropped them into their boxes.

'Uncle Alex!' Hannah said, and looked at Judith. 'How nice to see you! Shall we go upstairs?' She indicated Judith's bent head with a glance but he seemed too angry to be aware of her concern.

'I tell you, Hannah, those *ferstinkeneh* Lammeck relations of yours! May the good God bring down on their stinkin' lousy heads the sort of *tsorus* they been askin' for, the selfish, stupid – '

'Uncle Alex, please!' Hannah said. 'We'll talk upstairs.' But to her amazement Judith looked up and said dully, 'It doesn't

43

matter, Hannah. Let him tell you.'

'Tell me what?' She looked at Judith and then shook her head. 'No need, Judith, is there?'

Judith managed a smile. 'Dear Hannah. Always expecting the best of people aren't you? I never did. Still don't. I know my in-laws better than you do, and I expected nothing from them.' She looked at Alex. 'Why did you go to see them?'

He hesitated, for the first time aware of having blundered. 'I'm a *shlemiel*, Mrs Lammeck, you know that? I wasn't thinking. You should forgive me. I went to see your in-laws on account of Hannah here thought it would be a good idea.'

Judith turned her dull gaze on Hannah, and Hannah shook her head irritably. 'Darling, I had to! There's the future to think about, yours and Charles's. You can't just ignore your family. Charles is their grandson.'

Judith bent her head to her buttons again, her fingers moving slowly among the mother-of-pearl and bone and glass. 'They know that. They'll have made sure his money is all right. You don't need to worry about that.'

Hannah reddened. 'I wasn't even thinking about money!' she said sharply. 'I was thinking about *him*. I know how you feel, Judith, but since Peter died, it's been as though Charles was forgotten. His father's dead and you, well, you might as well be in some ways, you've been so lost. I know you can't help it ... But he needs his family, his grandparents.'

Judith didn't raise her head. 'He's got you, Hannah. That's why I can indulge myself the way I have been this past six weeks.'

Almost sick with contrition Hannah ran round the table to kneel beside her. 'Oh, dear, *dear* Judith, I didn't mean that the way it must have sounded. I truly didn't. I just – you're so stricken, darling, and Charles is so small and helpless and there's only me, and I can't ... Peter asked me to look after you and I will, all my life I will, but I thought that looking after you meant making sure you had others, not only me. Charles's grandparents.'

'Grandparents!' Alex, sat down on the other side of the table. 'They ain't like other people, those Lammecks. Some grandparents.'

'What happened, then?' Hannah said, and looked at him, her hand still on Judith's arm, and then, even as the words came out, she shook her head at Alex and turned back to

Judith. 'Please, Judith, can you understand why I asked Uncle Alex to talk to them? It was for you, really, to ... to give you someone safe to look after you. Mary Bee and I – we've got Uncle Alex and I don't think we could have survived without him. I *know* we couldn't have. I want you to have someone as strong for yourself and Charles. That was why. Not because of *money*. I can always make a living for us. I know that now. It was Uncle Alex who showed me how. And Peter. But there's more to surviving than money.'

'It goes a long way to keeping body and soul together,' Uncle Alex said dryly and, incredibly, Judith laughed.

'Of course it does. And it matters a lot, but darling Hannah, you needn't give it a thought. I've a little of my own that my father left me. It's in trust for Charles, of course, and all Peter's money is mine while I live, and then Charles's, and I dare say that my parents-in-law have made sure Charles gets his fair share of the family trust. They always look after things like that because money's so easy. Charles is probably very rich, you see. One day I'll find out and let you know so that you needn't worry ... ' She stopped fiddling with buttons then and turned her head to look at Hannah. 'Dear Hannah, you needn't have sent your uncle to find someone for me to lean on. There's no one I need more than you. You've got enough strength for yourself and me and a hundred others besides. Don't you know that? You don't even need him. Does she?' She looked across at Uncle Alex.

'D'you have to tell her that?' he said gruffly. 'You think I don't know? She don't, but while she thinks she needs me, it makes me feel good.' He grinned crookedly at Hannah and suddenly she found she was crying. Then Judith was crying too, her arms hot around Hannah's neck. It was as though someone had opened the flood gates to let the held-back emotion out. And the two of them clung to each other with their faces wet and for the first time since the telegram had come allowed themselves the luxury of shared tears.

When at last Hannah lifted her head and dried her eyes she saw that Alex too was crying, sitting there with his hands set on each knee. She managed a watery smile and said, 'She said you were the strong one.'

'So I am,' he said and sniffed lusciously. 'Believe me, it takes a strong man to cry, and you two are enough to break anyone's heart. Such people, these Lammecks, that they deny

45

themselves not to see such lovely girls as you two.' He wiped his eyes on a large white handkerchief.

'What did happen?' Judith asked then and Uncle Alex settled down to one of his long dissertations, his delight in talking never more apparent, even though the subject matter clearly angered him.

'I'll tell you,' he said. 'I got there, right to their fancy house in Belgrave Square. There's three men working there, you know that? A butler, two footmen. I saw 'em and I thought, why ain't they in the army like my nebbish Solly who's so scrawny you could tie a knot in each leg? And then I see the butler's limping, so I feel bad on account the man's a cripple and I been thinking rotten things, and you know how that makes a man irritable, so I suppose – ' He looked like a child who had been caught stealing. ' – I suppose I come on a bit strong, you know? There's him sitting there, that Alfred, at his desk looking busy, and I just land into him. I know I shouldn't, I know I made it bad, but I don't know, there was such an atmosphere there, you know what I mean? Cold and, *English*.' He said it as though it was a bad word and Hannah said, 'But what else should there be? The family isn't like ours – it's been here a very long time.'

'I know, I know, but at the time I was, well, I was angry. I have a go at him, he tells me to mind my own business, gets me shown out. Says he'll deal in his own way with his grandson and that's that.' He stopped and then said, 'I can't blame him.'

'It doesn't matter,' Judith said. 'Honestly, it doesn't matter. He'll come round when he's ready. Once I've gone home to my own house.'

Hannah looked at her sharply. 'Is it because you're here that he's kept away?' she said, her voice edged with anger.

'Yes,' Judith said. 'They're all like that about you. They went on and on at me because I was your friend. I told them it was none of their concern. But . . . ' She shrugged. 'They'll come to see me once I go back to my own house. Don't worry, Hannah.' She looked at Hannah's face then and closed her eyes in distress for a moment. 'Oh, darling, I didn't mean that! I didn't want you ever to know. I did what I wanted, you see, and told them to go jump in the Serpentine, but I'd have bitten my tongue off before I told you. Oh, I'm sorry!'

Hannah shook her head. 'It doesn't matter,' she said. 'I've

always known they hated me. It's just – it's being told, I suppose.'

'It's Davida. She's been like this about you ever since Daniel, you see. They all are, now. I mean they don't know you, do they? So they believed Davida and blame you for what happened to Daniel because it makes them feel better. They wouldn't if they knew you the way I do, of course. But they don't, so ... ' She put her hand out to touch Hannah. 'They aren't worth fretting over, darling. And don't fret over Charles either. Once I go home to my own house, they'll soon be coming to see him, I know that. They'll start agitating about what school they'll want to send him to, how he should be reared to go into the business as soon as he's old enough.'

Hannah sat back, contemplating her hands in her lap. She saw not her hands but Daniel, bored and spoiled, his face reflecting his discontent, going each day to Lammeck Alley. She saw how he had looked the night he came back from Shanghai. She saw the desiccated face of Young Levy who had given his whole life to serving Lammecks, and her own father-in-law's lined and yet unexpressive face, a face born to dissimulate in the business world bounded by Lammeck Alley. And she thought of Charles, small and thin, his socks crumpled about his ankles and his eyes dark and watchful under that lock of hair that so stubbornly refused to behave itself, Charles with the curving nape to his neck that made her eyes melt with love when she looked at it. She thought of the way he would sit on her lap with his thumb in his mouth listening when she read stories to him and to her own Mary Bee, and how the two children played together and squabbled together and grew together.

She lifted her head and said very deliberately to Judith, 'Don't go back to your house, Judith. Sell it. Come and live here with me and Mary Bee and Charles and Florrie and Bet. Never go back to the Lammecks again. We'll be the new Lammecks, you and I and the babies. Will you?'

Judith looked at her and then at Uncle Alex and without a moment's hesitation said calmly, 'Of course. I was so afraid you wouldn't ask me.'

7

It was remarkable how happy they were. The small house was filled to bursting with them all. The dining room continued to be the home of Mary Bee Couturiere, small business though it was doing these days as the demands the factory made on Hannah increased steadily, and the drawing room on the floor above, which had once been so cool and pretty became cluttered, for Judith brought some of her own furniture with her when she sold her house. But none of the clutter mattered to Hannah, because somehow it all felt so *right*.

She tried to work out what it was about the new arrangement that comforted her so and came to the rather surprising conclusion that it was because it was like the East End. Antcliff Street had been mean and narrow, where Paultons Square was wide and pretty; the flat that Nathan and Bloomah and she and her brothers had lived in had been shabby and ill furnished and dreadfully cramped, whereas Number 22 Paultons Square was solid and spacious, but it had been home in a very special way. When she remembered her distant childhood now it was an amalgam of smells of food and drying laundry and carbolic soap but particularly human bustle and purpose that she recalled, and it was that same feeling that now filled Paultons Square. They did not feel their neighbours on each side and in the street outside pressing in on them in the same way they had in Antcliff Street; but still it felt the same. Warm and human and reassuring.

It was decided that the children should go to school together, now that Mary Bee was gone six and Charles was nine. Each day they went, accompanied by Florrie, along the King's Road to a small private school. Each afternoon Florrie went to fetch them home again and then each evening all of them, the two mothers and the children and Florrie and Bet, would sit down together at the big scrubbed wooden table in the basement kitchen to eat the main meal of the day. Hannah had been adamant about that; the days were long since gone, she told Florrie and Bet firmly, when they could lead separate lives.

'Having servants rushing around and waiting on people who can do things for themselves doesn't make sense in wartime,' she said. 'We'll eat the same meals at the same time. We're a partnership, now.' This startled Judith at first, for she had always inhabited a world where servants were ever present but never considered as people like herself. But she was now so completely dependent on Hannah that she did not demur.

Hannah continued to run the factory and the remnants of her couturiere business, while Judith, feeling quite freed from any involvement with her past interests, chose to start work at the munitions factory in Woolwich, travelling each day on crowded workmen's trains and returning white faced with exhaustion to Chelsea each evening.

The change in Judith worried Hannah dreadfully at first. That she should grieve for the loss of Peter was inevitable, but that she should so totally reject her past self as well as her in-laws seemed strange, even mad, and that was very alarming. Then, dimly, Hannah realized what Judith was trying to do. She was trying to retain her hold on the future by killing the past. The Judith that Peter had known was to die as surely as Peter himself had died. The chattering, sparkling creature who had fluttered so gaily around the rich drawing rooms of the West End had to go, leaving behind a different person, just as the death of a caterpillar gave birth to a butterfly. But in Judith's case it was a reversal of that metamorphosis; the butterfly had given way to the dullest and most dogged of caterpillars.

Once she understood, Hannah stopped worrying. She had genuinely feared that Judith might, in her despair, destroy her own life, but now that she saw Judith had destroyed only part of it, Hannah felt they were safe. With Jake still safely busy in his Scottish training camp, and with Solly strutting triumphantly in his neat khaki uniform as the driver to a colonel at the War Office (the last favour Judith had ever asked of any of her Lammeck relations having been granted), they could relax. The worst had happened with Peter's death. They had nothing more to dread.

Or so Hannah thought. But just as the war was coming to an end the next blow fell. Years later, when Hannah looked

49

back, she would marvel at how casually it had started.

She had spent a busy afternoon at the factory joyously supervising a change-over of machinery to handle lighter peacetime goods, for she had decided that once the war was over she would expand Mary Bee Couturiere into a wholesale manufacturing house. Once the war was over, she told herself shrewdly, every woman in the country would be yearning for new feminine clothes; she had to be ready for a deluge of orders.

She had gone home by taxi, indulging herself a little, for she felt more tired than she usually did and had a mild headache. It surprised her to feel so low. That she, who had gone home with enough energy to spare for playing with Mary Bee and Charles after the hardest days at the height of the war and her grief, should feel tired now surprised her. What surprised her even more was how much worse she felt by the time she reached Paultons Square. Her headache was thumping in her ears, her back and legs ached abominably, and she felt shivery though it was a sunny early October afternoon and she dragged herself up the front steps and put her key in the door feeling wretched.

Florrie took one look at her and bustled her off to bed. 'Depend on it, mum, it's this 'ere Spanish 'flu,' she said. 'I'm a'callin' of the doctor, that I am. The things I've 'eard said about it, it won't do to neglect it. Turns into the consumption overnight it does, if you don't watch it.'

'Nonsense,' Hannah said, dazed, and then, as she moved her head and a sharp pain shot through it, added weakly, 'Well, maybe bed would be ... Spanish 'flu? What's that?'

'Ain't you been reading the papers?' Florrie had her upstairs now, and was busy turning back the bed, and setting a match to the paper and sticks laid ready in the fireplace. 'They says that there's ever such a lot of it about, started in Spain it did, been going all over the place, like anything. India's terrible, really terrible, it said in my paper. People fallin' over in the streets.' She shot a look at Hannah who was swaying a little as she tried to unbutton her dress and prudently said no more. To tell her that the papers had said that Indian peasants were dying in their hundreds and thousands would hardly make her employer feel any better.

The next few days were a blur for Hannah. Her temperature shot up, and she became delirious, calling for Daniel, and even, once or twice, for Peter. She was to remember, afterwards, seeing Florrie's worried face looming over her distorted and huge, and Judith's too, and the doctor's, and then slipping away into the hot red darkness of the aches that filled her. She would wake in the night and stare wildly about her at the lamp burning low on the table beside Judith, who was dozing in the arm chair, and shout suddenly and Judith would hurry to her and bathe her forehead with cold water and murmur soothingly and she would fall asleep again to dream terrifying visions of great animals chasing her and huge towers built of glass bricks which changed colours horrifyingly and then collapsed about her in thundering roars of noise. And everywhere she hurt, her eyes, her ears, her very bones.

Then, one morning, she woke to the drumming sound of rain on her window and looked about her and was puzzled. The fire was burning low and the room smelled odd, sulphurous and heavy, and there was an armchair beside the table with someone asleep in it. She blinked and looked and said, 'Judith?' in a puzzled way and was surprised because her voice came out in a small croak.

Judith woke at once and came to the bedside and peered down at her and set her hand on her forehead and then smiled, her face lifting from thin tiredness to relief.

'Oh, he was right, thank God, he was right. The doctor said you'd be all right this morning. The crisis was last night and we were so frantic about you, darling, you've been so *ill*. I'm so glad you're better.'

Hannah blinked and tried to sit up. Her muscles felt like cotton wool and she could hardly move, but blessedly they did not hurt; it was just an all pervading weakness.

'Ill?' Her voice was a little stronger, but still husky. 'I – I remember, I think. Florrie said it was influenza.'

Judith was busy now, fetching the washbowl from the marble topped washstand in the window, and bathing her face with cool water. It felt marvellous and Hannah was grateful, suddenly aware of how sourly she smelled, of illness and sweat and fever.

'It's been awful,' Judith said. 'Quite awful. You'd got pneumonia, you see, on top of the influenza and the doctor said it was very grave, but there was no help he could get us

51

for you because all the nurses are so busy. We sent the children away, of course.'

'Away?' Hannah peered up at her, suddenly feeling tearful. 'Away? Mary Bee? Where is Mary Bee?'

'Now, don't fret,' Judith said soothingly. 'It's all right. It was just that we were so worried about you, and you've been ill for almost two weeks, you know, darling, and the doctor said we should get the children somewhere safe because the epidemic is spreading quite dreadfully. Bet had it and – '

'Bet?' Hannah closed her eyes weakly, and now tears did run down her cheeks and she could not stop them.

'The children have gone to Bet's sister Jessie, the one who lives at Thorpe Bay. She's got a seaside lodging house there, you remember? And with all her summer people gone she's got room. They're better there, I promise you. Charles writes the most delicious letters every day, I'll show you.'

Judith was helping her into a fresh nightgown now, and Hannah said in a muffled voice, 'Bet?'

Judith laughed at that. 'She's as tough as they come, our Bet. She was over it and up and about in a couple of days. Doctor says she had it very mildly.'

'And Florrie? And you?' Hannah was lying back on her pillows now, feeling much more comfortable. She coughed a little, trying to clear her voice, but it remained stubbornly husky. 'Are you all right? You look so tired. Have you been here with me all the time?'

Judith laughed lightly. 'I was bored on my own,' she said, but Hannah stared at her, and felt the ready tears of the invalid come bubbling up again. Judith looked pale and very tired. Her hair was dragged up to a rough knot on the top of her head and looked thin and lifeless, and her cheeks were shadowed deeply, as were the hollows of her throat. 'Florrie's fine. She's helped marvellously.'

'Please don't get ill, Judith,' Hannah said weakly and made no attempt to dry her tears. 'I couldn't bear it. Please be well, Judith.'

'Of course I'm all right,' Judith said, and then shook her head suddenly and almost as though the words spoke themselves, said 'It's because I'd rather not be that I am.'

'Rather not be?'

'It doesn't matter, my darling. I'm going to fetch you some breakfast. Sleep a little, and when I come back I'll bring you in the children's letters.'

It was to be a long time before they came home again. Although Hannah improved steadily from that morning on, recovering more and more of her strength each day, the pestilence reached out and touched them again.

By the middle of October, the papers told them, the death rate from the infection was up to three thousand a week in England alone, the toll more than taking the place of the casualty lists that had been so much a part of the newspapers' daily offerings for so long. No one was exempt. When Florrie showed the too familiar early symptoms and Bet rushed to fetch the doctor to her, they were told the doctor had died himself of the 'flu the day before, worn out by weeks of incessant night calls. There was no other doctor they could find to help, and anyway there seemed little a doctor could do. Everyone knew the only answer was bed and hope, though they tried various nostrums. The chemists' shops everywhere did a brisk trade in sulphur candles, used in pathetic attempts to keep the infection at bay, and cough mixtures and steam kettles for the pneumonia cases, and tonics to restore the tissues of those left weak and miserable as the tide of the disease receded and left them behind.

Fortunately Florrie, who like Bet and Hannah herself had been reared in the crowded infection-ridden streets of London, seemed to have the same sort of resilience Bet had. She recovered within a few days, and by the end of the week was creeping about the house again, weak but determined to do her usual day's work. But Judith was of quite a different order. When the 'flu touched her at last, its hot, greedy fingers probed deeply.

Hannah thought sometimes, as she sat in the same armchair that Judith had used to watch over her own fever-filled delirious days, that Judith had by sheer effort of will refused to succumb while Hannah had needed her. Now she lay against the white pillows, her face looking like that of a painted Dutch doll, the skin white and pinched around the high spots of colour in each cheek and with her eyes half open so that the whites showed, sickeningly, and with her breathing rasping in her taut throat. She seemed to Hannah to have gone somewhere far, far away. Hannah would call to her sometimes, when in the dark early morning hours her own residue of weakness built fear in her, calling her name urgently and tugging on her damp, hot hands, and after a while Judith would open her eyes unwillingly and stare, unfocused, at her and then close them again, wordless, untouched by Hannah's urgency, or by her love and fear and tears. It was as though she had already died.

So that when she did die quietly, one dark afternoon when the first of the winter fogs had come drifting stealthily over the roof tops, her skin almost mauve with lack of oxygen, it came as no shock. It was to Hannah as though it was something Judith had wanted, something she had planned from the very day that the telegram had come telling her that her life was over, lost in the mud of Verdun. All through the succeeding weeks, as she tried to pick up the pieces of life yet again, once more having to contemplate the pattern of bereavement, she comforted herself that way. She told herself that Judith was happy now. That she had been loaned to Hannah for just a little while, to help her make her own life livable, and now, her self-appointed task done, had thankfully gone home.

Usually Hannah would not have thought so confusedly, so sentimentally, for later, much later, when she was free of the deadening depression her own 'flu had left behind in her and had recovered from the shock of all the other losses that she was to sustain, she realized that she had been sentimental and foolish. But it helped her when she most needed help, and she was grateful for that.

For not only Judith died. Less than a fortnight after Judith's death the message came from Solly, garbled and frantic but clear enough. Nathan was in the London Hospital, in the adjoining ward to the one in which Bloomah had died a decade before him, delirious and ranting hoarsely as the pneumonia that followed the influenza virus into his racked lungs consumed him.

She stood and stared at the telegram in her hand and knew that this was the end. If the disease had killed Judith, how could it fail to collect Nathan, too, a man so much older, so much less able to withstand the strain of illness after his long suffering years? Though she had known he could not survive, might already be dead by the time she got there, she set out for the hospital, greatly to Florrie and Bet's despair, for she was still weak and fragile. She travelled there in a cold rattling cab behind a wheezing old horse for she could not find a motor cab to take her, so desperately hit were the drivers by the same virus that was killing everyone else. It was a long and tedious and miserable journey through grey wintry streets and all the way she tried to think of Nathan as she had known and loved him when she was small, not as the bad tempered worn out sick old man he had become and whom she was afraid to see again. But she need not have distressed herself so through the long ride, for by the time she reached the ward he was dead and his body long since removed.

She stood at the ward door as the sister told her shortly, for she was too rushed to be anything but perfunctory, that Bed Seventeen's son had removed him, and no, sister did not have any idea where the body had been taken.

Hannah went back to Paultons Square, huddled in the corner of the cold cab, trying as hard as she could to remember her father with some sort of feeling, but she could not. He was dead, and somewhere inside herself she felt dead, too. No Judith, no Nathan, not much of herself; and what did any of it matter anyway? Her 'flu-born depression settled over her like a thick wet blanket.

Worse was to come. Uncle Isaac, Bloomah's only brother and his tired wife, thin Sarah, joined Nathan in the cemetery, though their children managed to emerge alive and shaken from their attacks of the infection. Davida and Ezra and Margaret Lammeck died too, and many more. Spanish influenza had shown no special signs of favour to the rich well-fed and well-cared-for. If thousands died in the East End slums, hundreds died in West End mansions. When the end of it all had come, when Armistice night with its frenetic celebrations and fireworks and tears was over, when the third and final wave of the influenza spluttered out in the spring of 1919 and the totals were counted, they found that more people had died as the result of that invisible virus than had succumbed to all the soldiers' bullets and shells in the muddy squalor of France.

Not that Hannah cared about comparisons. Her two Apocalyptic horsemen, war and pestilence, had taken from her a mere handful of people, not millions, but she was to mourn them bitterly for a very long time. She was not left without comfort, for she had her Mary Bee, and also Charles. The Lammeck relations argued and shouted and set lawyers to work, but there was nothing they could do. Judith had left a watertight will, appointing Hannah as Charles's legal guardian with full control of all his finances and his education and his life. Judith, in dying, had given Peter's son to be Hannah's own as surely as if she had borne him of her own body.

And so another child moved from one side to the other of the family descended from Susannah and Tamar of Jerusalem.

BOOK TWO

Fighting

8

'My God, just *look* at them, will you? Honestly, Mother, they're – '

'Mary Bee, if you say another word, I'll – '

'And if you call me that, I'll just walk out, I swear I will. You promised me you wouldn't.'

'All right, all *right*. Marie, then. If you say another word about what anyone else does or is wearing or says, then not a penny of next month's allowance do you get, you hear me?'

'I don't care; I shall go to Gramps and tell him. He'll give it to me.'

'Oh, no, you won't, young lady! And you'll find out what happens if you try such a trick. Now be quiet and behave. For heaven's sake, child, it's only for a few hours! Is it so difficult to be polite to a few people just for a little while? To please me? I know you only came to do me a favour, but don't ruin it, darling, please!'

I'm doing it again, Hannah thought, staring at Mary Bee's sulky little face. I try to be firm and I end up cajoling. Oh, damn, damn, damn. And she looks so lovely and can be so sweet when she wants to be, I want them all to see her at her best, not sulking like this.

'Darling, listen,' she said then. 'Just be sweet and charming to everyone for an hour or two, and then as soon as I can I'll cry off with headache or something and we can go home. How will that be?'

'Can we go to a nightclub afterwards, then? On the way home?' Mary Bee's chin lifted and her lips curved so that the dimple that punctuated one corner of her mouth showed very clearly. Hannah closed her eyes in exasperation and said, 'No! Are you mad! You're fifteen years old, and people of fifteen do not go to nightclubs. So stop this nonsense and behave yourself.'

The music changed, swinging into the newest Charleston

rhythm, and Charles, on Hannah's other side, got to his feet.

'Come on, fishface,' he said. 'Come and show 'em how it ought to be done.' He took Mary Bee's hand and pulled her onto the dance floor, winking briefly at Hannah over her shoulder, and Hannah smiled her gratitude at him and leaned back in the little gilt chair, aching to kick off her shoes but knowing it would hurt more to put them back on again.

It had been an exhausting day. When the invitation to Sally Lazar's wedding had come, a massive creation of thick imitation deckle-edged vellum and semi-opaque paper and gilt print and white satin ribbons, her own heart had sunk at the prospect. She had looked at the invitation and then at Mary Bee and said as brightly as she could, 'Darling! Such fun. One of our cousins is getting married.'

Mary Bee looked up from her breakfast and said hopefully, 'A Lammeck cousin? Or one of the Damonts?'

'No,' Hannah had said, her smile brighter than ever. 'My cousin Leon Lazar's daughter Sally.'

'Oh, God, Mother, not one of those awful East End crew! You can't be serious. You're not *going*, are you?'

'Not going? Not going? How come, not going?' Jake looked up from his own breakfast, a sizeable plateful of bagels which he bought in the East End, since no King's Road Baker had ever heard of such things. 'Whoever don't go to weddings?'

Mary Bee ignored him, as she usually did ignore her uncles. They had lived in her mother's house for six years, but she had steadfastly refused to treat them with anything but the coolest of disdain.

'It's up to you, I suppose, Mother,' she said, returning to her oranges. 'They're your family, I suppose.'

'The invitation is to all of us. You and Charles as well as me and your uncles.'

'Me? Are you mad?' Mary Bee stared at her. 'Me, go to that sort of vulgar brawl? I remember the last one you dragged me to, and I swore I'd never go to such a thing again as long as I live.'

'Pitchi putchi!' Jake said cheerfully. 'So what's so terrible about it? You'd go soon enough if it was madam the Earl's missus inviting you, so why not for Sally, the presser's daughter, hey?' He laughed fatly at his own wit and started on another bagel.

Mary Bee threw him a withering look. 'Earls' wives are called countesses,' she said coldly, unable to resist answering this time. 'And if Daphne asked me to something it wouldn't be a vulgar brawl.'

Hannah was staring at her, her brows tight. 'What do you mean, Daphne? How long have you been on first name terms with her?'

Mary Bee reddened a little. Her very white skin showed the changes in her emotions more clearly than she liked, for it made it difficult to hide all she wanted to hide, especially from her mother.

'Oh, we met at a party,' she said with a fine nonchalance. 'At the Ritz – oh, don't stare at me like that, Ma! I wasn't doing anything I shouldn't. It was the one Charles took me to, his friend David Gubbay's party for his twenty- first. You said I could go, and she was there and she talked to me, and was very nice, and why shouldn't I call her by her first name? She's my cousin, isn't she? Even though if you had your way I'd never see any of my really nice relatives.'

'I've never stopped you from seeing anyone you want to, or who wants to see you,' Hannah said, wearily. This was an old argument. 'I've told you that over and over, so don't, please, launch on that again, Mary Bee.'

'Don't call me that!' She jumped to her feet and glared at Hannah across the table. 'I'm not your trade mark! I'm not going around like an advertisement for your wretched dresses! I want to be called Marie, and you said you would.' She began to wail, and then turned and ran out of the room, slamming the door behind her.

'The sooner young Charles comes home for the holidays the better.' Florrie, who had just come in with a fresh pot of tea slapped it down in front of Hannah. 'He's the only one can get her to behave proper these days. Honestly, fifteen!'

The row over Sally Lazar's wedding was indeed settled by Charles when he came home. Only when Charles was home from school for the holidays did the house seem to pull together. It was not that he pushed himself in any way, not that he actually tried to smooth the turbulent waters. He was just his own quiet self, smiling and friendly, with his dark hair brushed cruelly hard to his head in an attempt to control the curl, but, fortunately, quite failing, and his eyes that smiled easily. And that was enough. Just because he was

61

there, people around him relaxed. Hannah accepted the invitation for them all, praying that Mary Bee – no, Marie, damn it – would come round, and said no more about it.

Charles cheerfully dressed himself up in his best morning coat, and set out his white tie and tails ready for the midday change that was an inevitable part of the proceedings, and to Hannah's intense relief Marie followed suit. She had chosen one of the best of her mother's designs for the morning and came downstairs a vision in beige knitted silk jersey, her long legs resplendent in beige silk stockings, and with a beige cloche hat, neatly trimmed with a hint of chocolate, pulled down over her nose. Her shoes and gloves were beige too and she had carefully masked her face with beige poudre Tokay and smelled faintly of Chanel's latest perfume.

Hannah stared at her and for a moment wanted to send her upstairs to wash her face and put on something more suitable for her age, like the charming navy and white sailor dress she had made for her last year. Wisely, she bit her tongue and was glad she had when Charles said easily, 'Dear Marie! Feelin' a touch off, are you? Never mind. I'll walk you slowly to the car. That'll bring the colour back into your poor little face.' Marie pouted at him, but rubbed off some of the powder.

The long car journey to the East End with Charles driving rather proudly – this was a new skill for him – had been the best part, with the children chattering about his school affairs, for Marie was avid for Eton gossip.

Hannah had hesitated about sending her much loved Charles away to school, wanting to keep him near her, but her guilt about the way his family had rejected him because he was her ward had overcome her. If his surviving grand-parents and his dead parents' cousins wanted to pretend he was not a Lammeck, that was up to them; but she knew he was, and he was to be reared as his own parents would have wished. Which meant Eton, for all Lammeck and Damont sons went there. So, she had driven him to Windsor one September morning and settled him in his new school, a diminutive, forlorn figure in his high collared shirt and scrappy trousers under the classic jacket and top hat. She wept all the way home again, but it had been the making of him in many ways, training him up to be what he was now, easy going, relaxed and charming.

Listening to Charles and Mary Bee chatter as they drove

through the deserted City of London towards Aldgate and Commercial Street she smiled at the back of their heads, and felt a great wave of love for them both wash over her. The years had not been easy since the war had ended, what with the struggle to get the business back on its feet once the factory took over dress mass production, but the children had been there to help her feel there was a point in all her labours. She had no one else but them to love so uncomplicatedly, for her brothers' laziness filled her with exasperation and she felt guilt, still, about Nathan. Having the children had helped soothe the long lonely nights when she would lie awake trying not to remember Peter and behind him, in the shadows of her memory, Daniel. She had made up her mind to it that that sort of love was over for her. She had brought nothing to her men but cold death, and she was never going to take the risk of loving again. So thank God for the children.

Until Marie had stopped being just a wilful spoiled child and had become the wilful spoiled young woman she now was. A naughty ten-year-old can be scolded and put to bed early. A naughty fifteen-year-old, Hannah was finding, was quite another story. She refused flatly to go away to a stuffy old girls' school, and demanded the right to stay at home and have governesses, if she must have an education (for which she frankly saw no use at all) and insisted on going out and about unchaperoned, a demand to which Hannah had not yet acceded and which caused most of the fights between them.

The one thing they did not fight about was Marie's decision to seek out her Lammeck relations. She knew, for Hannah had told her so, that there had been a split in the family long ago, though not really why, and that her father's relations chose not to acknowledge her mother. In her young years she had been content to accept that. But when she was thirteen she had slipped out of the house one afternoon and with all the aplomb of a person twice her age had taken a taxi to the house of Albert Lammeck, having found his address in the telephone book, and there introduced herself as his granddaughter.

Old Albert, long alone now, forgot the hatred his poor dead Davida had felt for the child's mother and her refusal to have any contact with the child she had borne, and fell instantly in love with Marie. He refused to see her mother, which suited Marie well enough for she enjoyed having the old man to herself, and began to bestow outrageously lavish gifts on the child. And Hannah said nothing at all, bitterly hurtful though Marie's behaviour was. She felt she had no right to stand between her own child and her other relatives however much she mistrusted them. Only once did she intervene, and that was when the presents became too lavish altogether. She insisted that Marie return Albert's gift of a diamond ring and wrote a stiff letter to him demanding that the practice stop, pointing out that while the child was under twenty-one she, her mother and legal guardian, had every right to exert such control. The old man had muttered and complained and told Marie how cruel her mother was, and gave her presents of money secretly, a fact which Hannah well knew and could do nothing about. Marie, of course, was in her glory. When she had trouble with her mother she could always run to her Gramps. Indeed, being a good mother to Marie was a very difficult thing to be, Hannah told herself, even when Charles was home, for Marie, like everyone else, loved Charles and wanted to please him.

But not today. However well it had started, it soon decayed into another of Marie's squalls. They arrived at the house of cousin Leon, in a neat terrace at the Hackney end of Shoreditch High Street (for Leon had come up in the world and was doing well with a factory of his own) to find it in an uproar. The living room had been rearranged so that there were chairs all round the walls, under the many heavy pictures of which Leon's wife Rae was so proud, and a large sofa under the window had been covered with a white damask tablecloth. The bride, a large girl with a somewhat bewildered expression on her face, was sitting in the middle of it, her white lace dress with its uneven handkerchief hem mid-calf length (to show her thick legs in white silk stockings and white kid ankle strap shoes) carefully arranged to display the richness of the design which was fussy in the extreme. Hannah, whose own taste and therefore designs tended towards severe simplicity of line, could not help glancing at Marie and saw the faint sneer on her face and felt a little coldness form in her chest. Today was going to be bad, whatever Charles did to keep the peace. The rest of the bride's outfit was fussy too, with a headress plentifully sprinkled with large satin lilies of the valley and twinkling sequins and a veil spotted with more sequins, and a massive heavily beribboned bouquet of already wilting gardenias and camellias and arum lillies, and she could feel Marie's rising contempt as clearly as if she had given words to it.

The centre of the room was filled with the inevitable food-laden table, round which neighbours and friends and family milled and grabbed and grasped and chewed at the tops of their voices. The room smelled powerfully of gefillte fish and brandy and sweet cakes and moth balls and cigars and perfume, and already a hint of sweat, for it was a warm day although it was still early spring.

By the time they reached the synagogue and had been bombarded with the usual oohs and aahs over how much Marie had grown, and the service under the canopy had been chanted and wept through, Marie was in a towering sulk. Charles was as he always was, quiet and amused and interested in all that went on around him and unfailingly polite to everyone, but for once this seemed to make Marie worse.

After the ceremony they went on to the wedding breakfast at two o'clock, a vast meal. Marie picked ostentatiously at her plate and ate nothing, while Charles ploughed his way happily through a heaped plate, and even took second helpings, much to the approval of Aunt Sarah and Uncle Benjamin on each side of him, while Marie grew crosser and crosser.

At home, afterwards, where they had gone to change into evening clothes for the rest of the day's celebration, the Dinner and Ball, she had thrown a tantrum and sworn she would not go back, but somehow Charles had managed to mollify her. Back they trundled, now in evening dress, to the same hired hall with its trimmings of balloons and trailing smilax and flowers and the false sweep of staircase at the far side where the wedding group were photographed in half a hundred poses.

Now, the second colossal meal having been served and eaten, as though none of the guests had been fed for a week, the dancing had taken over. Another half hour, Hannah promised herself, and I'll tell Marie we can go. Thank God tomorrow is Monday, and I can lose myself at the factory, and the plans for Buckingham Palace Gate. She sank herself for a while in a little reverie about how she would arrange her splendid newly leased showrooms, and began to feel better.

The music pounded on and on, and she nodded and smiled at the aunts and uncles and cousins as they whirled past, glad no one had come to sit beside her and gossip. She was almost hoarse with a day of talking to them all, for they were clearly proud of her and her success and everyone in the family and the family's families by marriage had gone out of his way to come and say, 'Please God by your lovely daughter and your boy,' and 'God willing we should always meet on such simchas.'

The music stopped and the sound of voices rose to fill the gap. Somewhere across the big ballroom someone started shouting for a horah, and the band good naturedly followed the rhythm of their clapping hands and burst into one of the old tunes. For a moment Hannah felt as though she was five years old again, sitting beside her parents at a neighbour's house and listening to the singing voices and the thumping stomping feet of the dancers in a circle, heads bobbing and knees bending as they went through the ancient rhythm. *Ha va nagilah, ha va nagilah ...*

She was watching indulgently as one after another they all joined in until the place was bursting with the noise of singing and stamping, and enjoying it in a slightly dazed way, when Charles came pushing through the hubbub looking a little crumpled but happy enough.

'Hello!' Hannah grinned at him. 'I thought you'd be trying this one!'

'No such luck, I'm afraid,' he said, and not for the first time she was startled by the deep note of his voice. Would she ever get used to that baritone sound? Surely she should have by now; he was seventeen after all. 'I'm just not clever enough to learn it. Where's Marie?'

She jerked her chin up at him. 'Marie? She was with you!'

'Oh, blast her!' Charles said softly and then shook his head, irritated. 'I told her not to be so silly and to come and sit with you. She was in one of her tempers over someone accidentally kicking her. I'll go and find her. She really is getting tiresome, Aunt Hannah. You'll have to do something – send her away to school, I reckon. It does me all the good in the world, you know.' And he went ploughing into the still stamping shouting dancers to look for Marie.

But Hannah knew he wouldn't find her. The wretched

child had made up her mind to leave, and leave she had. Her peach silk coat with its chinchilla fur collar had vanished from the cloakroom, and the tired part-time commissionaire at the door of the hall thought, though he wouldn't like to swear to it mind, that he'd seen the young lady goin' off down the Commercial Road. Looked very nice she did, he thought, when she put her coat on, and he'd said as much and had his head bitten off for his pains, so he didn't exactly look to see where she'd gone when she'd went off, I mean, what man would? But he thought she'd gone off down the Commercial Road, all the same ...

9

'I'll find her,' Charles said soothingly. 'Don't worry, Aunt Hannah, I'll *find* her. She's probably gone to the Bag o' Nails or somewhere like that.'

'Bag o' Nails?' Hannah stared at him. She felt sick with fright; it was silly for her to be so alarmed, for Mary Bee – Marie – wasn't a baby after all; she'd be all right, surely? But she is a baby, a secret voice somewhere deep inside her whispered. Only fifteen. A baby. 'What's that?'

'A night club,' Charles said briefly, shrugging into his coat. 'She's developed a passion for the wretched place. A dead bore, if you ask me, but there, our Marie never really asks anyone, does she? I'll find her, I promise. Don't worry. Go home, darling, and leave it to me.'

It was Uncle Alex who took her home. He had a gift for appearing at just the right moment, and now he came out into the little lobby, his thumbs hooked into the pockets of his white waistcoat and his head wreathed in smoke from the cigar clamped between his teeth, and grinned at her.

'Having fun, dolly? Where's that little girl of yours? Not a dance have I had with her, and I've got to do that before the night's over.'

As Charles explained, Alex's face lengthened. He shook his head at Hannah. 'I've told you, dolly, that little puss wants her *tochus* smacked. You spoil her, you always have. Listen, Charles, you go look. Make sure she ain't out in the streets, on account it's not a good time. There's been some trouble,'

'Trouble?' Hannah said sharply.

'Ah, nothin' new! The local *shaygetzes* got nothin' better to do, they roam around, pick on nice Yiddisher boys, beat 'em up. I've got an arrangement with the gym, they're gettin' a few of our boys together to keep an eye out, you know? But they're not out tonight and I'm told there was a bit of trouble over towards Arbour Square. So watch out for yourself, Charles, you dressed like that, they'll get funny if they see you. Take one of the others with you.'

'Oh, really Uncle Alex, no need!' Charles was at the door, his hand on the knob. 'She's probably picked up a taxi and gone to a night club. That's her latest craze.'

'Look in the streets first,' Alex said. 'Taxis there ain't a lot of around these parts.' Charles went, smiling reassuringly at Hannah over his shoulder. 'Come on, dolly. I'll take you home,' Alex said. 'I got the car round the corner.'

'Ours is here too,' Hannah said distractedly. 'I can't leave it here.'

'I'll deal with it,' Alex said soothingly. 'Relax. One of the boys'll drive it home for you. Don't worry, Charles'll find her, you'll give her a spanking, it's finished! You're tired, dolly, that's why you're worrying.'

But when they had been at home in Paultons Square more than an hour and there was still no sign of either Marie or Charles, he stopped being so soothing. Hannah sat hunched in the armchair beside the long dead fire and Alex stood at the window staring out and smoking steadily so that the room greyed with wreaths of tobacco mist.

'I'm going to call the police,' Hannah said at last, unable to bear it any longer. 'Something awful must have happened. We can't wait any longer.'

'Not police,' Alex said. 'That makes dramas, and please God, there ain't no need for dramas. Listen, where's this place he said she might have gone? I'll phone, see if anyone's seen her.'

'It's one in the morning!' Hannah said. 'You can't phone now.'

'Night clubs I can phone,' Alex said grimly. 'I don't go to them much, but that for them one o'clock in the morning ain't no time to worry about, that I know.'

The operator took some time to answer. Hannah sat on the

68

edge of her chair, watching Alex jiggle the earpiece rest, and wanting to shake him to hurry him up and knowing she was unjust for feeling so. Fear was building in her so that she felt as though her skin was stretched tightly over the maelstrom of feeling within and would burst at any moment and leave her a screaming wreck. She had to clench her fists to control herself. She was so intent on Alex's struggles with the telephone that she did not hear the front door open and close. Not until the drawing room door opened did she realize the wait was over. Hannah whirled and stared and Alex stood open-mouthed and then very quickly cradled the earpiece on the telephone and started forwards.

'My God, what happened? Bloody hell, the lousy *mumserim*. Hannah, call a doctor!'

'No,'·Charles said, his voice husky. 'No. It's not as bad as it looks. Not as bad as it looks.' He stared at Hannah and shook his head. 'Believe me, Aunt Hannah, not as bad as it looks.'

His coat was torn and thick with mud. His white tie had disappeared from his collar which had sprung open and his shirt was smeared with mud and blood, most of which seemed to have come from his nose. His right cheek had a graze that ran from the corner of his eye to his jawline, and one eye was swollen and bruised. His hair was ruffled and had sprung back into its childish curliness, and the combination of that and his attempt to smile reassuringly at her was too much for Hannah. She felt the tears spill over and she held her hands out to him and almost wailed his name.

They helped him out of his coat and settled him in a chair, and Hannah ran to fetch water and a towel and gently cleaned his face as he sat patiently, trying not to wince. As he had said, it looked worse than it was. When she had finished it was clear that apart from a black eye and the graze no damage was done. His nose had bled ferociously, but was now staunched and had not been broken, and the graze was superficial, like those on his knuckles.

'I gave them as good as I got,' he said contemplating his own fists, and then looked up at Alex. 'Uncle Alex, for God's sake, *why*? I did nothing to them! I was just walking, looking for Marie.'

'What happened?' Alex said and sat on the arm of Charles' chair.

'I don't know.' Charles leaned back, tiredness in his voice

69

now. 'Five of 'em – thin fellows, no brawn on them at all. Looked half starved, to tell the truth. But there were five of them. They just jumped me, you know? I wasn't doing a thing. They were shouting first, standing at a coffee stall, and when I went by they shouted "sheenie" and "yid" at me and I took no notice. I just walked past but then they started again and I stared at 'em. Dammit, who wouldn't? And that seemed to do it, because they came all at once, the five of them. And that damned coffee stall man and the other people around, there were enough of 'em, they watched and they cheered them on. It was the most sickening unfair thing you can imagine. They *watched*! And they shouted too – "Kill the bloody sheenie! Kill the bloody sheenie!".'

He closed his eyes and Hannah suddenly saw the small six year old Charles standing beside the nursery table with his paint brush in his hand and his thin legs sticking out beneath his blue holland overall. 'Is Papa going to be killed?' he had asked, and he had looked just like this; young and serious and remote.

'Did you find Marie?' Alex said after a moment. He turned his head and stared at Hannah and shook his head lightly at her. She took a deep breath and pushed down the new wave of fear that his question had created in her.

Charles shook his head. 'I think she must have got her taxi. I'd been walking around for ages before this happened. In fact, I was sure she'd got away from the district and I was looking for a taxi myself, walking along Whitechapel Road, you know? I don't know where she is, but I'm sure she's not in the East End. At a nightclub probably, safe and sound.' Charles opened his eyes and stared at Alex. 'Why, Uncle Alex? What did I do to make them do that to me? Or me to them? I beat them, you know. The five of them – they went off in the end, and one of them got a fair old pasting from me, I promise you. I've been boxing at school. And one of them, I think I broke his nose. I felt it go, and that was awful because it was only a fight – I mean, I didn't want to do anything like that, but what could I do? There was only me and those other people were cheering them on, and no one shouted for me or helped, so what could I do? I just hit him as hard as I could, and I felt his nose crunch. *Why*? That's what I can't understand. I was just walking past.... '

There was a little silence. Alex put his hand on Charles'

70

head for one brief moment, then took it away. 'You're a Jew, my boy. A yid, a sheenie, a Jew. That's what you did. That was the insult.'

'Insult? How can it be an insult just to *be*? I know I was better dressed than they were, and that's a bit insulting, I suppose, if you can't dress up yourself. But it was a wedding, wasn't it? A wedding, people always dress up for weddings.'

'Especially Jews,' Alex said heavily, and got to his feet. 'Especially Jews. Whatever we do, we do bigger than other people and they don't always like it. And we're foreigners, remember? Lousy foreigners.'

Charles stared at him, and then grinned, a lopsided grin that made his eye twitch with pain as his grazed skin stretched. 'Me, a foreigner? How can I be a foreigner? Dammit, I can't even learn a foreign language! You must have heard what old Barnsley said about my French, and my Latin isn't much better. Me a foreigner? I'm English.'

Alex shook his head. 'You're a Jew, my boy. And they'll never forget it, even if you do.'

The front door opened again, making a muffled sound beyond the drawing room. All three of them lifted their heads at the same moment like birds in a field, startled and alert.

Marie came in and stood just inside the drawing room door, her head down as she watched herself peel off her gloves.

'Really, this is too absurd!' she said in a high drawling voice, very artificial and controlled. 'Waiting around for me like this. I just decided to go on, that was all! Too absurd.'

She lifted her head and stared at them all, and they stared back silently and then she saw Charles and her face blanked. She moved to peer more closely at his bruised eye.

'Charles? What's the matter? What is it?'

He looked at her and then at Hannah, and lifted his eyebrows in a mocking little grimace. 'What happened? I went looking for you, fish face, and got my own face pushed in for my pains.'

'You, looking for me? But I don't – '

'You heard what he said, Mary Bee.' Hannah stood behind Charles's chair, her hands on his shoulders. 'He went to look for you when you ran off that way and frightened me, and some hooligans set on him and did this. Because he was

71

looking for you.'

Marie was on her knees now in front of Charles, staring up at him. Her face crumpled and she began to cry, looking as she always did when she was distressed, more like a five-year-old than her almost grown-up self, but this time Hannah was not beguiled. For years Mary Bee had only had to cry to reduce Hannah to total compliance. It had always seemed to her that her child was uniquely disadvantaged in having no father, and she would do anything to protect her from unhappiness. But not this time.

'Take a good look, young lady,' she said now. 'Take a close look. You did this.' And Marie shook her head and wept even more bitterly, putting her face down on Charles's knees.

'Oh Lor!' Charles said lightly, and pushed her head away, grinning at her lopsidedly because of his sore face. 'What a carry on! Do stop, ducky. You'll have all the crease out of my trousers. No need to make such a fuss. I'm all right. Bit shattered is all. And I'm not sorry it happened.'

'Not sorry?' Hannah said, and bent her head and set her cheek against his undamaged one. 'That's taking good heartedness too far.'

'No, it's not – oh, Marie, shut up for the love of Mike!' Mary Bee sniffed and wiped her face with the back of her hand, looking very woebegone. 'I mean – it was interesting,' Charles said.

'Interesting!' Alex gave a little snort of laughter. 'Interesting, the *shlemeil* says! Maybe they mashed his brains, eh? Interesting, he says!'

Charles stared up at the ceiling, speaking in a rather flat voice, almost to himself. 'It's this sheenie business. I've never had it, you see. No one ever said anything like that to me. It makes you think, doesn't it? It's interesting. . . . '

'No one at that school of yours never made no cracks about you, Charles? You amaze me,' Alex said dryly. 'You really do. I get around, my boy, and the places I go to, I find the same sort of people as your coffee stall heroes. Only they don't always act so honest and direct. It's a bit more on the side when you get to some of the high places. Like, they make arrangements for entertainments that don't include you, by goin' to the sort of clubs that don't admit Jews. Or they organize things that you ought to be part of on Friday evenings or the High Holy Days, so that you got to be left out. And they stop talking when you come by and look at you sideways and grin and nod and borrow your money and sneer at you. Oh, I tell you, Charles, sometimes I'd rather have the coffee stall *shaygetzes* and their fists. With them you know where you are. With the polite *mumserim*, you can't get hold of nothing. And you never noticed that at your school?'

'I never look for it,' Charles said. 'And I think that sort of thing you have to look for. But people with fists, thin people who look as though they'd break in a high wind because they're so scrawny, going for a chap like me with their fists, that's *important*. Isn't it?'

'What's important now is getting you to bed, darling,' Hannah said. 'You'll feel like death in the morning if you don't get some sleep. Come on.'

'Charles, Mama,' Marie said in a husky voice. 'Please. I'm sorry. I didn't mean it. I'm truly sorry.'

Hannah looked down at her and then managed a small smile. 'No, love, I don't suppose you did. You never do, do you? Go to bed, too. It's almost two in the morning. And tomorrow's a working day for me, if not for you.'

'Me too,' Alex said, and stood up. 'I'll be on my way. Listen, Charles, my boy, keep out of trouble, you hear me? No more going alone to the East End. Even if this *meshuggenah* madam here goes adrift again. Let *her* be beaten up next time. It'll be her turn.' He shook his head at Mary Bee, but there was no real anger in it. No one was ever angry with her for long, and she looked very crestfallen indeed as she watched Charles get to his feet a little stiffly.

'Of course I'm going back,' Charles said. 'I've got to.'

'You've got to do nothing of the kind,' Hannah said sharply. 'You're not the sort to go in for revenge, Charles, for heaven's sake.'

He stared at her, his forehead creased. 'Revenge, Aunt Hannah? Of course not! I've done that. I mean, I gave them worse than they gave me. I told you, I broke that poor devil's nose! It's not that. It's just that I've got to find out. Uncle Alex said this sort of thing happens all the time. But I'm seventeen and it's never happened to me, and I've got to find out why and – well, just *why*. So I've got to go back.'

'Charles, don't be a *shlemeil!*' Alex said. 'You're one of the lucky ones, one of the golden ones. You never got spat at in the street? Great. You never got a cold shoulder? Better still. You don't have to go looking. Just be grateful you're sitting where you sit, and stay there. Only an idiot goes looking for trouble.'

'I'm not looking for trouble,' Charles said. There was a stubborn note in his voice now. 'Just information. I have to know *why*.'

'Bed,' Hannah said authoritatively. 'Bed for everyone, and especially you. You're worn out and you can't think straight when you're worn out. Come on.'

As she was falling asleep at last, an hour later, after seeing both the young ones settled in bed, and having hugged a contrite Mary Bee back to peace of mind, she thought suddenly, 'How did she get home again? She didn't have enough money with her to pay for two taxis. How did she get home?'

10

Something would have to be done about Marie. Even as she thought it, sitting alone at her early breakfast the next morning, Hannah made a wry little grimace. The child had won over her name, just as she won over everything. It wasn't good for her. She was becoming more than wilful; she was a danger to herself, and knowing it was largely her own fault that Marie was the way she was didn't help Hannah feel any better.

She went first to the factory in Artillery Lane to spend an hour with Cissie, who was still managing that complex operation with ever increasing efficiency, and then went on to Buckingham Palace Gate to check the new workshops and showrooms there. The ready-to-wear side of her business was thriving and was the source of the family's security. As long as women wanted cheap and cheerful dresses Artillery Lane would make a comfortable living for Hannah and the children as well as Cissie and Florrie and Bet and all the workers who spent their days with their heads bent over the machines and pressing tables. But it was the couture side of her activities that most satisfied Hannah, and always would.

74

To design beautiful garments for rich and beautiful people was a source of real joy to her, and not because her clients were rich and beautiful. She found a complex pleasure in taking handsome tweeds and luscious silks and frothy chiffons and converting them into new objects of clean shape and elegant line and harmonious colour. When she made her Mary Bee garments she was creating as any artist would, and she knew it. When she made her Artillery Lane garments, which didn't even have a trade mark (the shops that bought them put on their own labels) she was simply making a living.

The difference was important to her even though the couturiere business had made her once again an unwilling part of the clan upon which she had turned her back. Her customers included many of the established English aristocracy, but the merely rich came to her too, and that included Lammecks and Damonts and Gubbays and Rothschilds and all the rest of the great Jewish houses; and her attitude to them could not help but be coloured by her past experiences at the hands of Davida and Albert Lammeck. When a new customer heard her surname and was surprised and started asking questions about her connections with the Lammecks, she was evasive; polite but unforthcoming, though she knew they soon found out from each other and gossiped. She needed to remain remote.

But she had to admit they were a particular joy to dress, these connections of hers, with their lazy good looks and elegant bodies and the carriage that came from years of wealth and security and contentment. English beauties with their pallid fairness and their delicate skins faintly flushed with rose were subtle and interesting, but these Jewish women with their splendid complexions and large dark eyes and lustrous skins, still carrying, many of them, the hint of rich colour that Bartholomew had brought to England from the East all those long years ago, looked magnificent in Mary Bee creations. She would stand back and watch them preening and know that they were special and be angry with herself for admiring them the way she did. She ought to be as cool with them as she was with the English roses, just a couturiere, a creator to whom they turned for self-adornment and no more than that. But because she tried so hard to be the same with her Jewish clients as she was with the others, she

75

only succeeded in being even more remote and abrupt. She did not know it, but she had a reputation among many of her clients for 'difficultness'. Not that it mattered; it added to her distinction in their eyes. Having Hannah Lammeck ignore you showed you were being dressed in the most fashionable way possible.

Buckingham Palace Gate looked particularly satisfying this morning. The workmen she had set to rearranging and decorating the rooms had nearly finished. She stood in the marble entrance hall staring at the great curving staircase and feeling good, in spite of her fatigue. Her eyes were sandy with lack of sleep, for she had only dozed for a bare four hours or so, but still she felt good as she looked. The crimson carpet against the white marble of the stairs, the delicate curving iron balustrade, the little marble copies of Greek statuary in the staircase niches, it all looked exactly as she had visualized it. The great showroom, too, with its creamy wild silk covered walls and the massive crystal chandelier and the low white suede sofas and armchairs almost blending into the deep pile of the white carpet, all looked as muted and subtle and yet as exciting as she had planned. Her clothes would stand out magnificently against such a background and she felt a lift of sheer excitement as she imagined, for one brief moment, the first mannequin parade she would have, next month. The clothes were nearly ready, the invitations were out. It would be superb.

Then, even as she saw how the great showroom would look, another vision lifted itself against her eyes. Herself as a scrawny carrot-headed child crouching by a half dead fire in Antcliff Street drawing pictures of dresses on blue sugar bags. It was an odd experience, and she shook her head at herself, and went swiftly up the stairs to the workrooms and her office above.

By eleven o'clock her fatigue was forgotten. The workrooms were purring with activity, the women sitting at the big tables with their needles flashing busily as they made buttonholes and felled seams and set in hand-made shoulder pads. Hardly any machine work was done at all here, unlike Artillery Lane, and the noise and reek of machine oil that was so much a part of that establishment was quite absent. There was just the scent of new linen and the hiss of the modern gas fires and the breath of coffee from the corner where the most junior girl kept the pot bubbling to sustain busy fingers through the day. There were plenty of people working, for Hannah was now able to offer apprenticeships to selected girls, and there were several eager fourteen-year-olds being taught to sew fine seams as well as pick up pins and make coffee.

She was absorbed in her costing sheets when one of the little apprentices came breathlessly to tell her there was a gentleman please madam, and she'd told him as how madam was busy, but he said he wouldn't take long and please could he come in?

Hannah made a little face. There were always salesmen pestering her to buy cottons and needles and pins. She had opened her mouth to tell the child to send the man away when he appeared in the doorway behind the girl and nodded unsmilingly at her.

'Thank you, Rita,' Hannah said composedly, and Rita looked over her shoulder and bobbed at the visitor and then at Hannah and went scuttling away, leaving the two of them staring at each other.

She knew at once who he was. They had not met directly for many years, in fact the last time she had actually seen him had been half her life time ago, at an afternoon soiree Mary had given at Eaton Square, and then she had hardly noticed him. But he was so like his sister, with a wide mouth that looked as though it would move very easily with none of the stiffness about the upper lip that was so common among the men who came to her showrooms with their wives, and with those deep clefts in his cheeks, that he was unmistakeable. On Daphne, the Countess, that look gave a raffish air, a sly horsiness that had always made Hannah uncomfortable when she came to choose clothes, and which had coloured her reaction when she heard that Marie had met her. But in this man the look was quite different. It made him quite startlingly attractive and mature even though she knew he was five years younger than herself. He looked like a most interesting man, and one she would like to know better. No, she whispered deep inside herself. No, that's the last thing you want. Lammecks are trouble and never forget it.

'Mr Marcus Lammeck.' Her tone was frosty. 'What can I do for you?'

'Mrs Hannah Lammeck,' he said gravely and bent his head.

'Good of you to remember me. It's been a great many years since we actually saw each other. An At Home at my Uncle Emmanuel's house as I recall. I hadn't realized you'd noticed me at all. You, of course, were quite unmistakeable.'

I'm right, she thought. His mouth does move easily, curling around words in a most interesting way.

'I recognized you because you look like your family,' she said, still chilly. 'Your sister is a client of mine.'

'Ah,' he murmured. 'The Countess – tiresome wench, isn't she?'

'I really couldn't say.' Hannah lifted one eyebrow a little. 'What can I do for you, Mr Lammeck?'

'May I sit down?'

'By all means.' But she made no effort to indicate a chair. He fetched one from against the wall, and settled himself on the other side of her desk.

'I feel as though I'm asking for a job, sitting here like this. Would I be any use as a dressmaker, do you think? They tell me lots of men are involved with fashion these days, Captain Molyneux, and so forth.'

'I have a great deal to do this morning, Mr Lammeck,' she said, glancing at her watch pointedly and then at him. He stared back, and she became suddenly very aware of how she looked. She was wearing one of her favourite dresses, a soft green crêpe with pleats falling in panels from the low slung pockets and with long wide cuffed sleeves that showed her slender wrists and fingers. She had had her hair cut in the newest close shingle, and it shone with a particularly coppery glint in the sunshine pouring in through the high windows of her office, and despite her fatigue, she knew she was looking well. She needed little makeup and rarely used it, but this morning she had used some mascara to darken her lashes, as much to cheer herself as because she particularly wanted to impress anyone.

And now she was worrying about impressing this man! It was maddening. She tightened her lips and said again, 'I really do have a great deal to do this morning.'

'Then I'd better get to the point, and I don't want to,' he said, and unexpectedly smiled, a wide smile that deepened the clefts of his cheeks making him look, paradoxically, younger. 'I've come to meddle in your affairs, Mrs Lammeck. I loathe doing it, but I think I must.'

78

'Oh?'

'It's my sister's fault, I suppose,' he said, and leaned back in his chair. 'She has no more sense than a flea, frankly, and since she married her wretched earl she's lost what little she ever had. She's taken up with your daughter, I'm afraid.'

She raised her chin a little. 'I know. Marie told me.'

'She *told* you?' For the first time he lost some of his air of relaxation. His brows came down to form a straight line over his dark eyes. 'You know and you don't *care*?'

'I didn't say that,' she retorted. 'I said I knew. But I fail to see what affair it is of yours whether I know anything, or what interest my daughter's behaviour is to you.'

'She looks a nice child, at bottom,' he said reflectively, almost as though he were talking about the qualities of a new car. 'Basically nice manners, but a little spoiled, I suspect. It worries me to see her with a hard drinking set like my sister's. I've told her, of course, but Daphne is quite impossible since she married. If she'd done the sensible thing and settled down with the Goldsmid chap who fancied her, it would have been much better all round, and I told the family so at the time, but they were so dazzled by that damned earl business. So, she's lost what little sense she had, as I said, and I'm concerned to see a girl as young as yours hanging around with her lot. Very raffish, they are, Mrs Lammeck, very raffish. You ought to keep a closer eye on her.'

Hannah felt the muscles in her cheeks knot against her jaws, she was clenching her teeth so hard. To have this interesting looking man lecturing her made all her own anxieties about Marie even worse.

'I fail to see what concern it is of yours,' she said, her voice high and hard. 'I am well aware of my daughter's ... activities, and I don't need you or anyone else to come and tell me.'

'There! I said I loathed meddling in others' affairs.' He smiled again, friendly and relaxed. 'It does put people's backs up. But there are times when you must do what you must. And times when you have to take the risk of upsetting people. Take last night. There I was at the Manhattan, it's a most reprehensible place – Mrs Meyrick opened it last month after they let her out of prison, you know – and I wasn't too pleased to find myself there anyway. But a customer from Amsterdam wanted to go there, and what can we business people do? And almost the first person I recognize is your daughter. She looks very much as you did when I first saw you, you know. And I just had to do something. I walked up to the child, told her it's time she went home and put her in my own car. Daphne was past caring, frankly, and I dare say the party was getting a shade boring anyway, but really, the child shouldn't have agreed to go in a strange man's car so easily. I told her I was Daphne's brother, but there was no proof! She let me drive her home to your house, and swept out for all the world like a countess herself. She could teach Daphne a thing or two about aristocratic behaviour, I suspect, but I'm genuinely concerned about what Daphne might teach *her*. Do remember, won't you?'

He got to his feet. 'I'm fond of my sister, but I'm not stupid about her, and she's bad news for a girl as young as yours. So, there you are! I came to do my family duty, and now I've done it. I'm sure you'll keep a close watch on her in future and – '

'And you can get out!' Hannah said, luxuriating in lost temper. She felt the colour rising in her cheeks. 'How dare you come here and lecture me! Who do you think you are? The mere fact that I married your cousin and you run your family's business and lives doesn't give you any jurisdiction over me. Marie is my affair, and stays that way! I'll thank you to keep out of what doesn't concern you.'

'Oh, damn it,' he said quietly, so quietly that it stopped her in full flood. 'And I'd hoped I'd done it tactfully. Well, I suppose there's no way to be tactful in such a matter. I'm sorry, Mrs. Lammeck. I'd hoped we could become friends over this, but there it is. Good morning.' He turned and went quietly, closing the door behind him.

She spent the rest of the day in a blur, working smoothly but automatically, without giving her full mind to what she was doing. When the time came to go home she took a taxi instead of making her usual frugal journey by underground. It was not that she could not afford taxis; indeed she could, but there was a long memory of past penury in her and she hated to waste money unnecessarily.

This evening she sat at the back of the cab watching the traffic rush by and stared out unseeingly. That damned man!

As if she didn't know that Marie was a problem! Did he have to come and lecture her so? But he didn't, her secret voice whispered. He was really very charming about it, and it was a caring thing to do. Suppose it had been you in his position. Would you have gone to so much trouble for someone else's errant child? And instead of thanking him she'd chewed his head off. Oh damn, damn. Marie ought to be *spanked*.

But when she got home she forgot her rage because Marie was in such a state of anxiety.

'It's Charles, Mama!' Marie came rushing down the stairs to greet her as soon as she put her key in the lock. 'He's been gone all day, and I'm so worried!' She stood there with her eyes filled with ready tears and Hannah put one arm out and hugged her, almost automatically.

'Florrie!' she called, and Florrie came toiling up the stairs from the basement, wiping her hands on her apron.

'I've told her not to take on so, mum, but you know our Miss Marie, always works herself up, like she did when she was a baby. I told her, there'll be tears before bed if she don't stop it. No, don't you make faces at me, madam! No harm done, mum, I told him what you said, that he was to take it easy today, but he said he was right as a trivet and he had some business to see to and he was going out. He put some flour over his eye – he's a caution that one, but he was right, it did hide it real good! And off he went about eleven o'clock.'

'Where?'

'Back to that hateful East End,' Marie burst out and clutched at Hannah's dress rather dramatically. 'I told you it was an awful place, Mamma, and if we'd never gone to that horrible wedding, none of this would have happened.'

'Be quiet,' Hannah ordered. 'Florrie?'

'He said he had to see someone, and I asked who and he laughed and said not to worry, it wasn't no one as'd do any harm. Your cousin he said, but there, you've got a lot of them cousins, ain't you mum? And I couldn't say which it was, and with Mr Jake and Mr Solly not here there was no way I could work it out. But I wouldn't worry, mum, really I wouldn't and so I've been telling madam here all day. The way she's been goin' on! He's a good sensible boy, not like some I could mention as isn't a million miles away, and he'll come home safe and sound. He promised to be here for supper at seven and it's all Lombard Street to a China orange

81

he will. So you go and take your bath mum, and settle into your comfortables and I'll deal with you, Miss Marie. You can come and make the custard for dinner. Keep you occupied that will, and let Bet take the weight off her feet.'

At ten to seven Hannah heard his key in the door and came out of the drawing room to meet him. He was standing in the hall, unwinding his scarf from his neck. At first she couldn't see him properly, for he was standing with his back to the light that was coming through the glass panels of the front door. But then he turned to greet her and her chest seemed to lurch, for he looked so strange, so very unlike the Charles she had known and loved for so long. His usually neat hair was rumpled and his eyes, those sleepy smiling friendly eyes, were wide and seemed to have had a torch lit behind them. He looked as though he had been quite, quite changed, and she wasn't sure it was a change she liked.

11

'*Charles*, of all people,' Hannah said. 'How can such a thing happen to Charles? He's an intelligent boy, educated.' She shook her head. 'You're not helping, Uncle Alex,' she said with an edge to her voice. 'I asked you because you always know what's best, I've leaned on you for years and now you're just telling me there's nothing I can do? There's got to be.'

'For an intelligent woman you're being stupid,' Alex said, and leaned forwards across the vast expanse of his office desk. 'I'm telling you, the boy's been converted. Never mind that it's politics as much as religion – whatever it is, there ain't no way you can change the situation. Be glad it's no worse, is all.'

'No worse! He says he's leaving school! He wants to spend all his time in the East End with my cousin David, and when I get my hands on *him*, I'll – '

'You'll what?' Alex leaned back and shook his head at her. 'What can you do? The boy went to see him because he recognized the man's got a spirit in him. And so he has, one of the best Talmudic scholars this side of Omsk, got the

82

respect of more rabbis than I've had hot dinners.'

'And a bolshevik.'

'Listen, dolly, I don't know what he is, bolshevik, menshevik, all I know he's interested in the Russian ideas. And why shouldn't he be? What does a Talmudic scholar have to lose preaching revolution? *Gornisht*! So he can enjoy himself dreaming crazy dreams about how everyone can have what everyone else gets. When you're a businessman like me, you can't afford such notions. But I don't grudge David his dreams – they don't do him no harm.'

'They've done Charles harm!' Hannah flashed, and got up restlessly and moved over to the window to stare down into Pall Mall. Alex had bought one of the handsomest buildings London could produce for his offices, and worked as he lived, in luxury. But all she could see when she looked down was Charles's pale face and wide bright eyes and the air of suppressed excitement that had been so much a part of him since the evening he had come back from his day spent with David Lazar in Sidney Street.

'What harm?' Alex said reasonably. 'Just tell me what harm! So the boy wants to leave Eton? Is that so terrible? Place costs a fortune, and as far as I can see ain't doing him a ha'porth of good. If he'd ever said he wanted some special sort of career that he had to have Eton education for, it'd be different. But I've talked to him, and he always said he had no special ideas about what he wanted to do. Said he'd probably finish up in Lammeck Alley like all the others.'

Hannah turned and stared at him. 'He said that?'

'He said that. And looked content enough to say it. It fretted me, I'll tell you. It sounds so defeated, you know? No spirit in it. A nice boy, your Charles. Good hearted and – nice, you know? But he had no guts in him. Lazy, easy, nice boy. But now – ' He shook his head. 'I saw him, you know? Last night over at David's. And it was ... I don't know. It made me feel good.'

'It made you feel – Oh, Uncle Alex, you're as bad as he is! I can't talk sense to him, and now I can't talk sense to you – '

'Listen to yourself, Hannah! Just listen! *You're* not talking sense! You're just displaying your own prejudices! What does it all add up to? The boy says he reckons he's been a parasite all these years. That the Eton people are parasites and he's had enough of 'em. He wants to learn about his own roots, his own people, and he's going to go to David every day to learn Hebrew and a bit of Jewish history. Is that so terrible for a Jewish boy? Your David, he says he wants to be a *Jew*, a real Jew, not a parlour one. He says he got beaten up for the way he was, so he wants to have the game as well as the name. Be a *real* Jew. And you know something? That makes me feel good.'

'Why? Because it salves your conscience about your own behaviour?'

He grinned. 'Now you're using you kopf! Sure, I'm a lazy *mumser*. Never go to *shul* unless I must, and I forget the last time I prayed of a morning. So, it does me good to see someone else doing it for me.'

'It's not the religion I mind, Uncle Alex. I might not be a devout person myself – if anything, I suppose I'm not really sure I even believe in God. Why should I? But that's my business, just as Charles's beliefs are his. It's the rest of it that frightens me. He talks so wildly, how he's going to change the world, get rid of the poverty and the landlords and share all the money. It's such *nonsense*. He told me I'm at risk of being a capitalist, you know that? Because of the factory. I told him that without me a lot of people wouldn't have jobs at all, and people without jobs are people without food. And he said that would all change one day, that the time would come when the workers would own everything – that it was a future worth fighting for. On and on he went. It scared me.'

'No need to be scared, dolly,' Uncle Alex said comfortably. 'Believe me, no need to be scared. At his age he's entitled to change the world. Leave him alone, and thank God you don't need any of his earnings like parents did in the old days. You can indulge him while he gets it out of his system. And when the time comes and he's got to earn his living, I'll find a place for him. So don't be scared.'

She tried not to be, but the change in Charles was so dramatic that it affected all of them. The old laziness that had been so charming was gone. He was up before any of them each morning ('Praying,' Florrie told her in a low voice. 'With them leather straps and all that on his head and on his hands, real peculiar, he looks. I never meant to see him but he left his bedroom door open,') and refused to eat the sort of food they provided. Hannah had never bothered with kashrus; her mother had, of course, for all the East End people did, but Mary, in common with many of the richer

West End Jews, had been very lax about the biblical dietary laws, and Daniel had cared even less. Now, Charles demanded his own special china, and ate only vegetables and fruit and bread and cheese. He would eat no meat or fish for fear it was not kosher, and that ruffled Bet dreadfully. It ruffled Florrie too, and also, inevitably, Marie.

For days she crept about the house lackadaisically, doing all that her mother or Florrie and Bet asked of her. The only time Marie was so complaisant was when she was ill, and they watched her fearfully. But then, one evening, she burst into tears when Charles came home from the East End, where he now spent every day, and begged him to be as he had used to be, because she couldn't bear it.

'And it's all my fault,' she wept. 'If you hadn't had to go looking for me you wouldn't have had your head beaten by those horrible men and you wouldn't be acting so crazily now.'

Then it was Charles's turn to lose his temper. He told her she was an arrogant spoiled baby to take to herself the credit for what had happened to him. That she would do better to stop beating her breast and carrying on as though she were God himself, changing other people's lives, and set about changing her own by doing as he did, and learning something of her Jewish heritage.

'You're ignorant and stupid,' he said scathingly, and she went white at the scorn in his voice. 'When the revolution comes people like you will be – well, there'll be no place for you. You've got to change now before it's too late. And if you've got an atom of sense in that empty head of yours you will.'

Hannah lost her temper then, for Marie looked so stricken. She launched into him for his selfishness, and he went white too, and said in a clipped cold voice that he would leave the house and go and live where he belonged, among the real people of the East End.

They made it up, of course, for Hannah cooled as fast as she had boiled over, and managed to talk both the children down to calmness. In the end it was agreed that Charles would go on as he had chosen, attending David's East End Yeshivah each day, and going to his political meetings in the evenings, and that no one would criticize him for it; at home, however, he would stop criticizing Marie, or Hannah herself.

So an uneasy peace descended on Paultons Square. Marie spent her days with her governess, and her evenings drooping about the house or going to bed early with a book, while Hannah worked longer hours than ever getting everything ready for the first mannequin display of her new collection at Buckingham Palace Gate.

The night before the showing at Buckingham Palace Gate, she worked until almost midnight to make sure all was ready. She had known she would have that sort of day, and had asked Marie to come with her. 'I'd love you to see the dress rehearsal, darling,' she'd said. 'I'd value your opinion.' But Marie had pleaded a headache, and Hannah had gone without her.

She came home to find Florrie in a state of great confusion, standing in the hallway in her flannel wrapper and curling papers, and Marcus Lammeck in her drawing room, with Marie in her room refusing to talk to anyone.

'I've done it again,' Marcus Lammeck said, standing in the middle of the drawing room with his overcoat slung over one arm and his top hat gleaming in his hand. 'I had to.' He was wearing evening dress, and looked tired. She wanted to put her hand out to him, but she didn't. She stood by the door and said only, 'Marie?'

'Marie,' he said, then shook his head. 'I had no intention of ever meddling again, but damn it, the child was behaving appallingly. At my sister's house, I'm afraid. Half drunk, carrying on like a – well, you would have meddled yourself. So, I brought her home. Only this time she argued.'

He touched his cheek and for the first time Hannah saw that there was a scratch there. She closed her eyes for a moment.

'Oh, what *am* I to do?' She looked at him miserably. She was too tired to be angry, too distressed to be anything but honest. 'She's so unhappy and so am I, and since Charles ... I just don't know what to do.'

'Will you let me advise you?'

She stood very quietly there looking at him. He had not moved, still standing with his overcoat thrown over one arm and his hat dangling from the other hand, and she thought confusedly, such a nice face. So comfortable. A nice face.

Wearily she said, 'I'm not coping well on my own, am I? I thought I could, but she's almost defeated me. Advice would

86

be welcome.'

'Let me talk to her grandfather. He's a difficult man, I know, and he's behaved badly to you, but he's got some influence over Marie. I've found out that much. I think if *he* suggests to her that she should go away to school, somewhere that sounds exciting, like Paris, or Switzerland, she might go. She's at an age when she'll want to do things to upset you, you see, so if you suggest a school, she'll fuss. If my Uncle Albert does, however, she'll want it.'

She stared at him and then rubbed her face with one hand. It felt numb, she was so tired.

'You seem to understand her better than I do.'

He smiled then and the mobile mouth curled and the parallel clefts appeared in his cheeks. She thought again, nice face. Nice.

'That's because I don't love her too much,' he said. 'Which is why it's easy for me to see what she needs. You'll let me do it?'

'Yes please.' She managed a smile. 'And – ' She stopped and then shook her head.

'Yes?' He quirked his head at her, waiting.

'Nothing – I mean, would you care for some coffee, or a drink perhaps?'

He shook his head. 'You weren't going to say that, were you?'

'Yes, of course.'

'Try again.'

She made a little face. 'No, I wasn't. I was going to say I'm sorry. And thank you. And I hope you can forget how rude I was last time we met.'

He put his hat down very carefully on a small table, and threw his coat over the back of the chair beside the dead fire and sat down with a sigh of relief, stretching his legs out and throwing back his head against the chair back.

'Thank heaven for that,' he said. 'Now you come and sit down, and we'll start from the beginning again. It's the only place to start. And I'll have that drink you weren't going to offer. Whisky if you have it. You have something too. You need it.'

'Oh,' she said, a little blankly and then, with a spurt of irritation, 'Help yourself. The table in the corner.' She sat down in the other armchair, kicking off her shoes and throwing her own head back to rest as he had.

'Better and better,' he said, and went to fetch drinks. He brought her the same as his own, whisky with a splash of soda, and though she rarely drank anything so powerful, she took it gratefully.

'Now,' he said, coming back to his chair. 'Where shall we begin?'

'Where shall we – Don't talk riddles, please. I'm too tired.'

'We've a lot to learn about each other,' he said. 'Friends need to know a lot about each other, and if we're to be friends, then the sooner we fill in all the gaps the better. Shall I start telling you about me, or would you rather start telling me about you? I know a lot already, of course – '

'Like what?' She had taken very little of the whisky but already it was warming her, making her feel easier.

'Like you married my cousin and he left you a widow with a baby. Very stupid of him.'

'Stupid! That's a harsh word.'

'No, it isn't. I knew Daniel better than you might think. A charming chap, but not the most sensible of people. I hope you haven't gone on mourning him all these years?'

She looked at him over the rim of her glass, but said nothing. She should have been offended but somehow she wasn't. The whisky, she thought a little confusedly. Or tiredness?

'I've wondered why you haven't married again, you see,' he went on. 'I've kept an eye on you, as much as I could. When Judith left Charles to you, and everyone was in such an uproar, I told them then it would be all right, that I'd see no harm came to him, so I've had to watch out for you.'

She opened her eyes wider and stared at him then, her relaxation disappearing. 'You've been *spying* on me? Because of Charles?'

He laughed. 'Such a dramatic word! Not spying, just watching. Not that it was necessary. I told them all very early on that there was no need to worry over Charles. He's been better with you than he would have been with anyone else in the family. He's a lucky boy to have you for a mother.'

'I'd rather he'd had his own parents,' she said, and her voice was flat.

'I know,' he said gravely. 'They were special people. And Peter told me . . .'

There was a little silence.

'Peter told you what?' She sat very still, feeling a warmth growing deep inside her that she knew was not the whisky.

'That you were special,' Marcus said simply. 'That's all. That you were special. I knew anyway, of course.'

'That I'm special?' Her voice was a little unsteady, but she could do nothing about it.

'No. That I look forward to finding out for myself. I mean that he loved you, and you him.'

She felt the warmth rise higher and higher, filling her belly and then her chest, and then to her own fury felt it spill over into tears. She stared at him, holding her face as still as she could, and keeping her eyes wide open to prevent the tears from spilling out, and he looked back at her with that same grave look and said quietly, 'It's all right, you know. There's no need to feel bad about it. It helped him, I think. He loved Judith but he needed to love you too. It was inevitable. Just as his dying was. Those were bad times and you made them better for him. Hannah, will you believe me? It's all right. Don't look so . . . like that. Please. I need you to look happy. I really do.'

'Do you?' she said, and the tears that had hovered withdrew, leaving only the warmth behind. 'Why?'

He smiled then, that wide and easy smile that made him look so young. 'You'll find out,' he said. 'You'll find out. Now go to bed. You're exhausted. You look as though you need sleep more than anything else in the world. I'll see you tomorrow, after I've spoken to Uncle Albert. Tomorrow evening, over dinner. I'll call for you at Buckingham Palace Gate. Goodnight, Hannah.' And he was gone, leaving her sitting in her armchair and staring at the opposite one and trying to collect her thoughts into some sort of coherence.

12

In years to come Hannah was to look back on that summer of 1925 as though it had been preserved in golden amber. Though there were the children to worry about, especially Charles, it was a glorious time in every other way. The business was thriving; the first collection from the new showrooms caused a furore, and she found herself in demand in a way she had never been before. Women who regularly dressed in Paris, with Coco Chanel or Poiret, Lanvin or Worth, demanded Mary Bee clothes, and wore them everywhere. She was photographed wherever she went and bombarded with requests from the newspapers to write articles on What the Modern Girl Should Think, and What the Modern Woman Needs to Know, and a great many other things which had nothing whatsoever to do with her skill as dressmaker. Of course, she refused all such offers, having far too much to do to be interested in becoming any sort of journalist, but she was flattered and amused all the same, and found herself basking in her new found fame.

For the first time since she had moved into the house more than fifteen years before, Hannah agreed to make it over, and decorators and builders descended. The kitchens were equipped with the newest electrical equipment, including a refrigerator which made Bet's eyes open wide, and central heating was installed with radiators in every room, much to Florrie's gratification after fifteen years of hauling coal scuttles. The drawing room was stripped of its old fashioned art nouveau decor, somewhat to Hannah's regret, for she had always been particularly fond of it, and replaced with the newest rage in furnishings, which was cubist. There was square furniture upholstered in vividly coloured geometric patterns, piles of jazzy cushions, curtains which bedazzled the eye. Florrie was enchanted with it all, and no less enchanted with the dining room, which Hannah made as snowy as her showrooms, all in white and gleaming chrome and glass. Even her bedroom was done over in shimmering mauves and lilacs, and a new bathroom added in which she had a special shower built, all very daring and American. Jake's and Solly's rooms, too, were totally redecorated, since they had seized on an offer by Uncle Alex to spend some time in New York 'keeping an eye on his interests'. Hannah knew that Uncle Alex had created the job for them; and although she felt a certain amount of guilt about how relieved she was to have her house less crowded, she did not feel as badly about their departure as she might. She spent a great deal of money and enjoyed herself hugely, looking forward with glee to Jake's and Solly's exclamations when they returned from New

York and Marie's response to it all when she came home from Lausanne.

For Marcus had manipulated Albert exactly as he said he would. Marie, offered the chance of finishing school in Switzerland, was entranced with the idea. The word school on her mother's lips, she said, made her think of hockey sticks and long hikes in the country that gave you hideous muscles, but a Swiss finishing school, where she'd meet the most divine people and really learn about life and the world was something else. Hannah, suitably coached by Marcus, primmed her lips and looked doubtful, and allowed Marie to coax her into giving her consent.

Seeing her off had been misery, a hectic farewell at Victoria Station where Marie caught the boat train.

Hannah had been controlling her anxiety and distress at parting with her beloved only daughter so well that she had given no thought to where their final farewells must take place. When they actually arrived at the station in Uncle Alex's Hispano Suiza she felt her belly lurch in that all too familiar painful fashion. The station swarmed with fashionable people rushing to catch the boat trains or the Flèche d'Or through to Paris, but as she looked at it the scene seemed to float out of focus and a picture came over it of the way it had looked the first time she had seen a traveller off here, eight years before. Then it had been khaki, everywhere, under clouds of steam and children with crying faces and women with dry eyes and apples rolling on the ground ...

She jerked her thoughts away and helped Marie, who was flushed with the excitement of it all, to count her luggage, and soothed her when she announced dramatically that she had lost her dressing case and found it for her, and would not let herself remember.

At last Marie was ensconced in her first class compartment and the guard had been heavily tipped to take full care of the transfer of her luggage and her own safe conduct to the boat. As Hannah stood watching the train curve away down the line, she could control the memories no longer. She stood there, bereft, feeling the same sense of despair filling her as had filled her that last time, standing in this same station, with Judith at her side.

When she had turned to go, almost blinded by her own pain, he was standing there in what was becoming a familiar pose of his, his hands clasped together in front of him, his overcoat hanging over his arm and his hat in one hand.

'I thought you might be feeling it a bit,' he said. 'So I played hookey from Lammeck Alley. They can manage without me for a while, don't you think? Yes. So do I. Come on. We'll go and have a great big piggy tea at Gunter's and talk nonsense.'

And so they had, eating crumpets and jam and milles feuilles and licking their sticky fingers and laughing, so that she had gone home to Paultons Square calm and relaxed, genuinely happy that Marie was safely on her way.

Once Marie had gone, life with Charles became easier. He continued to be passionate about his new found beliefs, especially the political ones; he sat opposite her at meals, his elbows on the table, talking lucidly and with great excitement about his dream of a new world, and she sat and listened and watched his eager face, and began, slowly, to understand.

All her life she had known about poverty and hunger and misery. She had been born into it, and grown through it and out of it. Now she was comfortably off by means of her own talent and the pain of her deprived childhood had long since left her. Indeed, if she thought about it at all, it was to be glad that she had been so toughened in her early years. If she had not been so, would she have had the strength, the energy, the sheer application to have reached the point she now stood upon? Listening to Charles, she realized how different it was for him. Protected from his birth by the comfort of money and love, his world had been a good and caring place, marred only by the blind inevitability of war that had stolen his parents from him. Meeting for the first time in his eighteenth year, as he now had, the sight and smell of poverty, it had felled him. It had not been only his beating at the hands of those street boys which had affected his conversion; it had been his own later observations in those narrow mean streets that swarmed around Whitechapel Road and Commercial Road. And, now, talking to Hannah, he managed to communicate to her his anger and his passion and his solid determination to change it all.

'If I persuade just one man that he owns his own soul and the work of his hands, Aunt Hannah, it will be worth it. If I can fight and destroy just one of the men who steal their hearts from them as they steal their labour, then I shall have been born for something.' The high flown words were robbed of any banality by his sheer passion, his total conviction that he was right, and she listened and thought, and slowly stopped worrying about him. The way of life he had chosen might not be one she would have chosen for him, but it was his, and it filled him with satisfaction and striving. In his anger and distress and hunger for justice he was a very happy young man. What more could she want for a child she had always loved?

And all through that golden summer, while Charles learned and argued and listened to David and ranted at his meetings, and Marie danced and chattered with other girls in her Swiss school, and Florrie and Bet purred happily about the house in Paultons Square, Hannah fell more and more deeply in love.

She had never meant to. She was the woman who had made up her mind. She was the woman who was never going to love again. She was going to be celibate for the rest of her life, she had told herself; devoted to her work and her children. No man with a curling mouth and clefts in his cheeks was ever going to change that.

Was he?

But he made arrangements for her that were so irresistible that she could not demur, though she did try, often. But what was she to do when he announced he had such treasures as opening night tickets for the newest Noel Coward revue, 'On With The Dance!' Or when he arrived at Buckingham Palace Gate just as she was leaving at the end of the day, and drove her off to summer-warm Maidenhead to eat supper at Skindles, and then punt along the dark river while a gramophone played 'Poor Little Rich Girl' in the bow? Such treatment was irresistible and at last she gave up trying to resist. When she caught sight of his familiar figure standing in the hall waiting for her, his hands clasped in front of him, she let her stomach turn over and made no effort to control the excitement. When the telephone rang and she knew it was he, she hurried to answer it. He had slotted himself into her life as though a place had been carved out for him, long ago, and had just been waiting to be filled.

He never said anything about their relationship, even though they became closer and closer. They would talk about everything and anything – world news, the art shows, the newest ballets and plays and music and food and wine and books. They shared silly jokes and puns. They chattered about their acquaintances. Yet close as they became in friendship, still there remained a barrier between them, and that puzzled Hannah. She knew he cared about her, and found her exciting. She would see his eyes on her across a room and feel her skin redden at the unmistakable message that was in his glance; she would feel his hand on her arm as he led her to a theatre seat, and she knew the electricity that leapt in her at his touch communicated itself back to him. Yet he said nothing.

Until one night in late October. She was feeling depressed, for the summer holidays had been a disappointment to her. Hannah had been looking forward to Marie's return home with enormous excitement, and then, out of the blue, there had been a laconic telegram from Lausanne announcing that Marie had been invited to spend the holidays at the Riviera villa of Comte Hugo de Marechal, the father of her dearest friend at school, so she could not come to London after all. Hannah had managed with considerable difficulty to tele- phone her, waiting hours to get a line, and Marie had been cheerful and friendly, but clearly amazed that her mother could possibly expect her to come home to London when she had the chance to go to Cap Ferrat with such madly fashionable people.

'*Ma chère Maman*,' she had carolled in the thin crackling little whine that the telephone made of her voice. 'You said I could come here to be properly finished, and if you fuss over letting me take up the opportunities that come my way, how can I possibly benefit? *Tu comprends, Maman? C'est necessaire!*'

Hannah had comprehended and said no more. The child was happy, and that was what mattered, but Hannah had been disconsolate, and Charles had been of little help, absorbed as he was in his own doings. Hannah had tried talking to cousin David about him to see if he could persuade the boy to spend more time at home and with his old friends. It worried her that he was so intent on his new learning that he had no fun at all. 'A boy of eighteen,' she told David, 'ought to enjoy himself *some* of the time, surely. Tell him to come to the theatre with me sometimes, David, or to a party. He's looking so pale and so – oh, so *anxious* it worries me.' But she got as little satisfaction from him as she had from Marie.

'Listen, Hannah,' David had said, sitting at his kitchen table with his elbows on it, and the inevitable book between them. 'You've got your life to live and your boy Charles has got his. He came to me to be taught, and it's a *mitzvah* to teach such a boy. You wanted that I should refuse? Tell him he'd be better off dancing the Charleston? How could I? Sure I knew it would worry you, that his ideas and attitudes wouldn't be comfortable for you, but Hannah, that's your problem, not his. If you try to change him, all you'll do is drive him away. And I'll tell you this much, that boy is someone so special that I regard him as my brother. If he told me he wanted to come and live here with me, then the door would be open to him.'

And Hannah looked round the small crowded kitchen with its lines of washing drying on the racks overhead, and the toys that littered the corners and the shabby furniture and knew there was no more she could do. David and his young wife Sonia had enough to cope with, what with their two small babies and the struggle to live on the few shillings David earned as a Talmudic teacher; she could not allow them to burden themselves with her Charles. And she knew that if she leaned too hard on Charles that he would come here, unaware as only a rich boy could be unaware of the responsibility and expense he would be.

By that evening in late October, she was restless and aware of a dragging discontent somewhere deep inside her. Her friendship with Marcus mattered enormously to her, but it was not enough. The old needs were stirring in her, the old hungers that she had so rigorously repressed all these years. She would stand sometimes in her bathroom after her shower and stare at her own naked body, still beautiful, even though she was so far past her thirtieth birthday; she saw enough of the bodies of her clients when they were being fitted to know that her own shape was good. Her breasts were as firm as they had ever been, rich and full and smooth, and her waist had not thickened nor had her hips and buttocks sagged. Yet it was a beauty that was wasted, and that, for the first time since Peter's death, depressed her. She began to be angry with Marcus for awakening her hunger while doing nothing to satisfy it.

She dressed that evening particularly carefully, in a daringly cut copper coloured silk dress. She put on makeup too, more carefully than usual, so that her eyes looked startlingly blue against the dark lashes, and her skin shone as though someone had put a light behind it. When Marcus looked at her as she came down the stairs to meet him, his eyes widened a little, but his face remained quite expressionless.

She chattered with great vivacity as the car purred through the King's Road and on past Sloane Square to Knightsbridge. He said little and now again she looked at his profile, clear against the passing lights of the shops and the traffic, and redoubled her efforts. Dammit, she thought deep inside herself, dammit, I'll show him. But she didn't know what she was going to show him.

The dance given by one of the younger Rothschilds was a particularly fashionable one, well attended by Lammecks and Damonts as well as by an assortment of county English. There had been a time, early in her friendship with Marcus, when she had resisted going to such parties; were not these the people who had once snubbed her, misused her, followed Davida's lead into treating her like a guttersnipe? But she had overcome that, because she had realized how irrelevant it all was now. The ancient snobberies and slights had died with the generation which had displayed them. These younger Lammecks and Damonts had long since forgotten the old scandals. For Hannah to remember them, she told herself, would be stupid. And she was not stupid. So she buried the old hurts, and went to the parties with Marcus, and usually enjoyed them, gossiping with him about the people there, though usually objecting strenuously to being treated as a celebrity, as hostesses were wont to try to do.

But tonight, Hannah yielded to her hostess's determination to treat her so and allowed herself to be drawn into a group of chattering and exceedingly expensively dressed people. She went on as she had begun with Marcus; she was vivacious and sparkling and almost surprised herself with the wit that came bubbling out of her, and the way she made the people around her laugh. And all the time she was aware of Marcus near her, watching and listening, and redoubled her efforts.

That people liked what they saw and heard was undoubted. They laughed a lot, and the group she was in grew larger, as more people drifted over to be where the centre of interest so clearly was, and after a while Marcus spoke behind her. 'Hannah,' he said quietly. 'There is some-one who would like to meet you.' ·

She turned, feeling the group around her fall back a little, and looked at the man standing beside Marcus. He was rather short and had fair hair slicked fairly close to his head, and a face a little like Marcus's own, with deep clefts in the cheeks, but there was a petulance about his expression that was clearly all his own. He smiled, and that lifted the expression a little, and held out one hand.

'The Prince of Wales, Hannah,' Marcus murmured and she threw a glance at him and then to her own amazement, laughed. 'Do you know, I rather thought that was the case,' she said, and held out her own hand. 'You are not difficult to recognize, sir.'

The Prince looked a little blank, and there was a silence from the people behind her. Then he smiled again, and shook her hand warmly and laughed too. 'How do you do? I hope we shall be friends, Mrs Lammeck.'

'Hannah,' she said. 'My friends call me Hannah.'

'Ah, Hannah. How charming a name that is! Do you dance, Hannah?'

'Frequently,' she said, and he laughed again, as though she had been exquisitely witty, and as the music changed to a tango, stood back with one hand indicating the dance floor, so that she could lead the way.

All the time she was dancing she knew she was being watched and to her own amazement enjoyed the sensation, swooping and throwing back her head with all the elan she could muster. They moved through the staccato steps as though they had danced together many times, and he was indeed an elegant and adept dancer. She wanted to giggle and wished Marcus was near enough so that she could whisper some silly joke in his ear about the Prince pretending he was Rudolph Valentino and she behaving like Pola Negri. The idea was so absurd that she did laugh, and that seemed to please the Prince.

Afterwards, as the other dancers broke into a spatter of applause at the performance, he led the way back to the corner of the big room where there was a table at which he had been sitting, and insisted she join his party there, and she smiled brilliantly as the Prince introduced her to the various people sitting there.

'I have some champagne here, Hannah,' the Prince said. 'Or would you prefer a cocktail? Young Rothschild is quite disgusted with me, I have no doubt, for he's a noted wine bibber, but there, what can I do? I seem to have an affinity for gin, and I recommend the White Ladies. Rupert, do push that chap over there in this direction ... '

Hannah watched as the young man addressed as Rupert moved lazily away to fetch the waiter the Prince wanted and then, as he came back, felt her face redden. He was looking at her very directly with a sort of insolence in his expression, and she felt her lips tighten; he had no right to look at her so.

'And how is Marie, Mrs Lammeck?' he said in a high pitched and rather affected drawl as he came back to the table, followed by the waiter. 'Haven't seen her in an age, and she used to talk of you so much.'

'In Switzerland,' Hannah said sharply, and turned away, not wanting to talk to him, but he was not so easily put off.

'Such a charming daughter Mrs Lammeck has, sir,' he said, and his voice seemed higher than ever now. 'Prettiest little creature you ever set eyes on, very shapely. Not surprising of course, with so beautiful a mother.'

The Prince turned and looked at her. 'You have a grown daughter, Hannah? Bless me. I wouldn't have thought.'

'Indeed I have, sir. Perhaps you will let me present her one day. Now, if you will excuse me ... '

She got to her feet, suddenly tired of the silly game she had been playing. The people round this table were not her sort; they were either ten or more years her junior or pretending to be so, and the glossiness of them was no longer attractive and her head was beginning to ache a little. What had possessed her to put on so silly a performance on the dance floor as she had? She deserved to be reminded that she had an almost adult daughter, that she was too old for this sort of nonsense. Where was Marcus? She wanted to go home.

As though she had called his name aloud, he was there standing beside her shoulder. The Prince looked up and said, 'Ah, Lammeck, d'you know everyone?'

'How could he not?' Rupert said. 'My brother knows everyone in the world, sir, you know that! And disapproves of most of 'em! What ho, big brother! Going to tell me what a bad little boy I am? Or will that wait till later?'

'Depends on how bad a little boy you are,' Marcus said

98

equably. 'Hannah, my dear, you said that you had promised the Henriques we'd go on, and I rather think ... '

'What?' she said. 'Oh, yes, of course, the Henriques.'

'Oh, you can't take her away when I've only just met her!' the Prince said. 'Come, Hannah, do stay a little longer. I'm sure your friends will wait. Anyway they're probably here themselves – everyone *is* as far as I can see. Who was it did you say, Lammeck?'

'Some rather older people, sir,' Marcus said easily. 'Disapprove of the Charleston and cocktails, you know. We'd better go.'

'But we must meet again, Hannah.' The Prince stood up and took her hand and held it warmly. He was about her own height, and she was able to look him directly in the eye, which felt odd after being with Marcus who was several inches taller. 'I'm sure we could be very good friends, you and I,' he said, and his eyes crinkled with practised charm.

'I'm sure.' She nodded at the people at the table and moved away feeling safe and strong with Marcus at her side. 'Good night, sir.'

'I'm sorry about that,' Marcus said in a cold voice, as they approached the door. 'I'm truly sorry.'

'Actually I wanted to leave,' she said. 'I've got a headache. I'm glad to go.'

'I'm not apologizing for taking you away. I'm sorry because you had to meet those people.'

She laughed then. 'Meeting the Prince is supposed to be a special privilege, isn't it? I know when I met his grandfather people thought so. I don't imagine anything much has changed.'

Again she felt a wave of awareness of her age sweep over her. Thirty-three never used to feel so old, but now it did. She had met the Prince's grandfather and men she met at parties asked after her daughter.

'I hadn't met Rupert before,' she said then.

'And if I'd had my way you wouldn't have met him then,' Marcus said savagely. 'Oh, dammit, that's silly, I suppose. You'd have had to meet him sooner or later, if not at our wedding, but I didn't want you mixed up with that horrible lot there. It's all right for the Prince, he can hang around with any riff-raff he likes and get away with it, but for people like Rupert, they're a menace. There wasn't a woman at that table who hasn't had more lovers than she's had dinners, and most of 'em are – well, never mind ... '

They were standing now on the pavement outside the house while Marcus rummaged in his pockets for his car keys. She was staring at him, her face quite blank.

'What did you say?' she said after a moment. 'What did you say?'

'I said I'm sorry,' he said, 'and – '

'Our *wedding*?'

'Oh. That. Yes, I've been meaning to talk to you about that. Ah, here they are! Shall we go straight home, Hannah? Or would you like to go and eat supper somewhere else first?'

13

'I don't know why I won't,' she said again. 'I just won't. Can't.'

'But you're not a fool, Hannah! You're an intelligent woman with a good deal of commonsense, which is rare enough, God knows. You can't fob me off like that.'

She shook her head, and turned to stare out of the car window at the square outside, lying dark and ruffled in the October night. The wind was not high but it was enough to keep the yellowed leaves on the plane trees in constant uneasy movement, and the whispering seemed to echo her own uncertainty. She watched a few of the leaves go bowling along the gutter from pool of lamplight to pool of lamplight, straining her eyes a little to see them as they moved through the dark patches between.

'I'm not – ' she said, and turned her head to look at him. 'Listen, Marcus. Please listen. Don't interrupt or even think until I've finished, and I'll try the best I can to explain. I care a lot for you. You're the best friend I've got, I think, even better than Cissie at the factory, and you know how important she is to me. Since you arrived I've been happy. Excited, too. You're very exciting. I – damn, this bit's difficult. I got excited enough to be angry with you because you didn't do anything about it – no, don't *move*, I'm having enough problems. Just listen. I like you as a friend. I'm excited by you and I think you'd be a ... I think I want you as a lover. Dammit, I know I do. *No.* Keep still. But I don't want you as a husband. I've done that once. And ... well, I've done that once.'

Now he made no attempt to move, peering at her in the darkness. After a while he said carefully, 'Let me understand this. You're saying that the problem is not that you don't love me?'

'That's what I'm saying.'

'Then you do love me?'

She took a deep breath. 'I think – I'm not sure. That's part of the problem. I *want* you, I know that much. But I'm not sure I really love you. Enough.'

'Enough for what?' She felt him smile in the darkness and a spurt of anger lifted in her.

'Don't be indulgent at me! Enough not to make – not to make a mess of it. Look at my history, damn you, and then think again! I'm not just a silly girl you've picked up, someone who's young and inexperienced.'

'You're hardly old,' he said dryly.

'Almost thirty-four.'

'Hardly old.'

'I feel it, sometimes. Often. Marie is almost sixteen. She's a worry to me, the way almost grown daughters *are* worries to their mothers. I'm getting older.'

'Why should you be any different?'

'You're five years younger than I am.'

'So?'

'So, it worries me. I made a mess of two other men's lives, your own *cousins*, damn it. You should be glad I'm not about to rush headlong into doing the same for you.'

'Oh, come on, this is perfectly ridiculous!' He sounded genuinely angry. 'Just what do you see yourself as? Some sort of lethal black widow spider who destroys her mates?'

'You can laugh if you like, but it's true. Daniel ... ' She tried to go on, and she couldn't, feeling the tears tightening her throat and keeping the words dammed back.

'Hannah, listen to me. Please, my love, listen.' She could feel his breath warm on her cheek, but he did not touch her. 'I knew Daniel. Better than you did, for all you married him. He was a ... oh, he was a flawed person, I suppose. I know we all are, in some form or another, but in him it was

101

different. It ran so deep it had to destroy him. Really, my aunt had destroyed him long before he met you. I think you were the best thing that happened to him. If he'd done as my aunt wanted and married Leontine Damont do you think he'd have been any happier?'

'He'd be alive,' she said. Her voice sounded very loud in her own ears. 'He'd be alive.'

'Sometimes being alive is to get the worst of it,' he said. 'Easy to say when you're living, I know, but it wasn't your fault. You must believe that.'

'I've told myself that lots of times, Marcus. I used to lie awake at night and try to understand, to see whether it was my fault, or Mary Bee's for being conceived when she was, that Daniel . . . that it happened. And I'd tell myself I wasn't God, that Uncle Alex was right when he told me I wasn't to blame. But there's another part that doesn't listen. The guilty part.'

'Guilt! You and your guilts, Hannah! As long as I've known you I've felt that in you, that need to expiate all the time. What is it about you that makes you take everyone else's shame and fear the way you do?'

She managed to smile in the darkness. 'You sound like Uncle Alex. He says it's always been like that. That Jews used to be blamed for everything so much that now they blame themselves before anyone else gets the chance.' She imitated Alex's gruff tone. 'On account of we're quicker on the uptake. So he says.'

'He may be right. Don't change the subject, Hannah. I've asked you to marry me.'

She looked away from him then. 'I don't think I can. Marry you, that is . . . ' And deliberately, she left the end of her sentence open, fixing her eyes on his face now, trying to see the expression on it in the dark interior of the car.

He was silent for a long moment and then he said carefully, 'I think you'd better say it all clearly. Are you offering something different? I don't want to jump to any conclusions that might be – embarrassing.'

'It's not all that unusual,' she said, almost defensively. 'You said all those women at the Rothschild dance had them, more than they'd had dinners. Why not me?'

'Because you're not one of that crowd,' he said, and the contempt in his voice was icy. 'Promiscuous pieces of – of garbage! They're the richest most cossetted women there are in this whole damned country and they behave like pigs in straw. They'll do anything with anyone for no reason. They don't even have *need* to redeem them. They do it casually carelessly and – they're sickening. They've as much notion of love and loyalty and trust and – and decency as a dog. Less.'

'So!' She tried to sound light and relaxed, and managed to sound in her own ears only silly. 'It's clear you don't want to consider my offer.'

'I am offering you all I can which is everything. My love, my total concern for your happiness and welfare, my complete involvement in everything that matters to you. What are you offering in return? Just sex? That isn't enough, Hannah. Not for you, and certainly not for me. You demean yourself by suggesting it.'

'Demean myself?' She sounded very bitter then. 'There was a time when your family would have said that was impossible. That I was already so low I could go no lower.'

He was very still beside her, and then he said in a voice that was icy, 'I will not tolerate this. To refuse me as a husband because of what my older relations did would be an outrageous insult. I don't think you mean to offer *that*, whatever else you're offering.'

'I'm sorry,' she said after a moment. 'That was wrong of me, I suppose. But it still hurts. It still sits in my mind. I can't help it. They hated me. Perhaps some still do.'

He made an impatient gesture in the darkness, and she saw the glint of light on his hand. 'It's no reason to refuse me. No reason to suggest – whatever it is you're suggesting. Family connections mean nothing between us. There's just you and me. And what you seem to be suggesting is not an answer I can take. You must not speak to me in such terms.'

'You sound very biblical,' she said and took a deep breath. 'Very proper. I meant no wickedness, you know. I was trying only to be honest. There wasn't only Daniel, you see. There was Peter. But of course, in your eyes, that was – that was behaving like those women you so loathe, wasn't it? What was it you said? Pigs in straw? Like a dog? That was how it was with Peter and me, I suppose.'

'Oh, no, please stop, Hannah! This isn't what was supposed to happen! I love you! I want everything to be perfect for you, and I can't bear it that we've degenerated into this sort of horrible squabble. Please.'

'I'm sorry. I didn't mean to be unkind,' she said, a little dully. 'I only wanted to explain to you that I don't feel able to marry you. I'd be afraid. I've done enough harm to your cousins. To hurt you too would be ... I can't bear it.'

She struggled with the car door for a moment and then managed to get it open and tumbled out, and ran up the steps to the house, fumbling blindly in her bag for her key as she went.

He didn't follow her. And long after she was inside, sitting curled up in her new white armchair and staring blindly at the curtained window she heard the engine purr into life and the car go whispering away through the sound of the wind blown trees.

It could not be the same of course. It was not that he stayed away from her. He phoned her and told her there was a private viewing at a gallery of Sonia Delaunay's newest work from Paris, and could she come, and sent her flowers and saw to it that she was invited to the same dinner parties as he was; most London hostesses were fond of him, and willing to oblige him, even if they had their eyes on him for their own nieces or daughters. He invited her to theatres, to films, to concerts, just as he always had.

But it wasn't the same. The intimacy was gone, and she missed it dreadfully. Her sense of loss was not helped by her own anger at herself. She would lie in bed night after night unable to sleep, asking herself, why was I so stupid? Why didn't I say I'd marry him? Who do I think I am, that I'm afraid I'll hurt him if I marry him? He's not stupid; he can look after himself, and I want him! And he's right about the old feuds. They don't matter any more. It's him I want, not families, not revenge ...

And she would turn and bury her face in her pillow, trying to ignore the hunger that now bit so slyly at her whenever her guard was down. It had been a long time indeed since she had been so aware of her own sexuality, and it was not an awareness she enjoyed at all.

Marie came home for Christmas in a flurry of excitement, bringing with her a French girl and a German one, whom she introduced as her dearest chums in all the world. They spent

104

the four weeks of the vacation rushing about London shops and hotel thé dansants, and gossiping and giggling. Hannah was delighted to see Marie looking so happy, and was pleased she had such close friends to share her holiday with, but she felt a little bereft as well, for somehow there was no time for any talk between them at all. Marie was always fast asleep when Hannah left for Buckingham Palace Gate each morning and when Hannah came home at night she had already gone bustling off with her friends.

At first Hannah was anxious about the people the girls met, remembering all too painfully Marie's involvement with Marcus's sister, but then she discovered that the German girl, Mercedes von Aachen, had relatives at the German Embassy, who were entertaining the three girls a great deal.

'They are the cousins of my father,' she told Hannah in her prettily accented voice. 'And when they heard that Papa and Mama had to be away from Berlin during my holiday, they agreed that they would ensure I should be content here in London, which of course I am with you, Gnädige Frau. I have also been told by my aunt, the Baroness von Aachen, that I must meet some of her relatives here, since she is English, you know.'

'Oh?' Hannah said politely.

'Indeed. She was Fraulein Leontine Damont, of an excellent family here, I am told. She says to me I must visit some of her relations and she has given me some addresses.' Mercedes began to leaf through her notebook to show Hannah the people on whom she was to call.

Hannah said nothing, making no comment about the fact that she knew the names of all the people listed and was grateful that the French girl, Henrietta de la Tour, also had London connections, and was more clamorous about visiting them, so that the trio did not in fact visit Leontine's friends as much as they might have done.

'Not that it makes any difference to me,' Hannah would tell herself. 'Why should it? It's all so long ago now. It doesn't matter. And I'm glad Leontine married and is happy. I'm glad.' But it was difficult to believe herself.

Charles had chosen to go away for the Christmas holiday. He told Hannah bluntly that he could not bear the fuss that was made about it, with Florrie and Bet decorating a tree for themselves in the kitchen and insisting on distributing presents which of course Hannah reciprocated.

'It's all so *wrong*,' he told her earnestly. 'We're Jews, and anyway, it's a pagan fertility rite. I don't believe in God, you know – no, I know it sounds complicated but it isn't. The longer I study the Talmud and Hebrew the more I realize that what matters is the Jewish *people*, not the God they invented for themselves, and it's the people I care about. And because I do, I can't stand this Christmas rubbish. I'm going to go and stay with David in the East End. Please, Aunt Hannah. They've asked me, and it's what I want.'

She did not argue, but insisted he take a kosher food hamper with him as a Chanukah present ('Which they'll value if you don't,' she told him sharply) and made the best of the holiday that she could. She was, to her own distress, actually relieved when the four weeks were over and Marie returned cheerfully to Lausanne, leaving her with a casual kiss and never a backward look as she ran for her train at Victoria.

The year turned slowly through a biting winter to a chilly spring, and she worked harder and harder, and went out less and less. Marcus still telephoned occasionally, but she had made up her mind that she must wean herself from even his friendship. When she saw him she still felt that sickening leap of physical excitement and need, still had to bottle up her feelings behind a bland glass-smooth exterior. He called less frequently now, as the labour crisis had deepened and strikes began to loom on the horizon. Lammecks owned large blocks of shares in several coal mines as well as steel mills and other factory interests, and as labour unrest bubbled and heaved all through that dull spring of 1926, Marcus became busy as a mediator and spokesman for several of the owners. She read about him in *The Times* and listened to Florrie exclaiming over the things she had heard about him on the kitchen wireless and said nothing. She had set herself the task of forgetting Marcus Lammeck, and the best way to begin was never to talk to anyone about him.

When, on May 4, a General Strike was declared she decided to go on working and that any of her workers who could not get in because of the lack of buses and trains would still be paid. Cissie told her roundly that she was a fool, that most of the workers would take advantage of her goodwill, but she was stubborn.

106

And her stubbornness was justified. Many of them did struggle in, some walking the long grey miles from Hackney and Whitechapel to Buckingham Palace Gate as well as to the Artillery Lane factory, and Hannah felt a glow of pride. Other workers might be complaining bitterly of exploitation and bosses' greed, but hers saw the business as she did, as a co-operative venture that mattered to all of them, and supported her in spite of exhortations from pickets and street shouters to come out and stay out.

When the call came early on a Saturday morning she was at Artillery Lane, supervising the loading of a lorry she'd managed to borrow from Uncle Alex to deliver garments waiting for urgent despatch to Birmingham which couldn't go by train, as they usually did. The boy who came lurching into the back yard of the factory looked drunk at first and then she saw that in fact he was exhausted. His face was dirty and bloodstained, and he'd obviously been in a fight. She took him by the shoulder when she heard him asking one of the men loading the lorry for 'Charlie's Auntie Hannah'.

'What is it?' she said urgently with a sudden spurt of fear. 'Is Charles hurt? Is he ill?'

'He's bin beat up,' the boy said, and pulled away from her, and turned to go lurching on his way again. 'Made me promise I'd tell yer, so I did. In the London 'Ospital, under police guard. Got took there from the docks. Said I was to tell yer.'

14

The ward they sent her into was long and cluttered, with fireplaces at each end in which big coal fires burned, for it was a cold May. Nurses in blue print dresses and frilled lace caps and stiff starched aprons bustled by, rustling with every movement, and ignored her as she stood hovering between the big double doors. The ranks of beds on each side ran away to the far end in diminishing red blanketed oblongs, and the faces that lay on the pillows all looked the same, drawn and blank and ageless, hollow simulacra of men. The place smelled of soap and cold air and carbolic and a thicker ominous sweetness that stirred fear in her belly, and because she was afraid she lost her temper, and marched up to one of the nurses and took her by the elbow.

The girl reared back, offended by her touch, and stared at her frostily.

'I want to see Charles Lammeck,' Hannah said sharply. 'Immediately.'

'Visiting time this afternoon, two o'clock,' the nurse said. 'You'll have to come back then.'

'I was sent for, to see my son, my ward,' Hannah said. 'I was told he was injured. I insist on seeing him at once.'

'Insist?' the nurse said, and looked at her with a blank face. 'You can't insist. It's up to the doctor.'

'To hell with the doctor,' Hannah said. She turned and marched into the ward, looking from side to side at the beds she passed. The men in them stared back at her incuriously, as though she wasn't actually there. The nurse followed her, expostulating, but Hannah ignored her and marched on. As she reached the middle of the ward someone who was sitting beside one of the beds stood up and she stared and realized he was a policeman, though he looked odd, for he had his helmet in one hand so that his head looked naked and vulnerable.

'The young man says it's him you're looking for,' he said in a hoarse whisper, then reddened as the nurse stared at him with an icy glare, and Hannah thought absurdly, 'He's very young, scared.'

She came to stand at the foot of the bed and stared down at it, and at first she could not see anything but the glow of the red blanket and the whiteness of the pillow and then, slowly, she was able to focus more closely.

He was almost unrecognizable. One eye was completely closed as the tissues around it had swollen to such proportions that the skin seemed to be stretched as tight as the skin of a rubber balloon. It was almost as brightly coloured as a balloon, too, a blur of purple and red and blue, and the discoloration stretched right down one side of his face. His lips were blackened and cracked, and there was a streak of blood running from one corner of his mouth. His nose was swollen, looking as broad as a baby's, and she could see that it was blocked with cotton wool. One arm was encased in plaster, and lay awkwardly on the bed beside him as though

108

it was not part of him at all.

'Oh, my God.' Her voice sounded loud in the quiet ward. She felt rather than saw some of the men in the other beds turn to stare at her. 'Oh, my God. What happened?'

'Can't say, madam.' The young policeman sounded embarrassed. 'They sent me to stay with him till he could give me a statement, like, and they could charge him and all, they said, but they never said what the charges were. I only just got sent here, after the worst of the fight was over.' He looked down at the bed.

'Charles?' Hannah moved round the bed and crouched beside it so that her head was on a level with his. 'Charles, darling, what happened to you?'

He swivelled his one good eye towards her and his cracked lips seemed to lift a little. She felt tears rise in her. He was clearly trying to smile, though obviously it hurt him for he winced. Still he went on trying.

'I'll see the doctor, darling, find out what happened,' she said, and he took a sharp little breath and said in a cracked voice, 'No, he's mad at me. Don't ask him ... mad at me.'

'Mad at – what do you mean? A doctor looks after people. I'll find him and he can tell me. Oh, darling, I'm so – ' She bent her head and kissed his cheek, delicately, terrified of hurting him, but needing to have some sort of physical contact.

The nurse came back with a white coated man in tow. Hannah stood and stared at him with all the anger she had in her lifting her chin and said sharply, 'You are the doctor looking after my ward?'

'I am indeed,' he said and his voice was loud and heavy at the same time. 'And you have no right to come pushing your way here in this manner.'

'What has happened to him? I insist you tell me at once. He is under the age of twenty-one, and as his legal guardian, I insist on my right to be told all that pertains to his welfare.'

'Under twenty-one, is he?' the doctor said contemptuously. 'Then you, madam, should take better care of what he gets up to. The state he is in he frankly deserves to be in and I'm not afraid to tell you so! To come down here to the slums and try to meddle in matters that don't concern him, and then to fight with public spirited citizens who have come to try to keep this country going while those damned strikers try to destroy it! You should be ashamed to have a ward who behaves in so appalling a manner.'

An odd little sound came from the bed behind her. After a moment she realized that Charles was laughing.

'I told you he was mad at me,' Charles said in that rough hoarse little voice. 'Told you. Capitalist pig that he is.'

'Pah!' the doctor said, and suddenly Hannah wanted to laugh too for he looked so pompous and absurd in his white coat and with his face set in a scowl of disapproval. But she did not laugh, and looked instead at the policeman.

'Can I take him away from here to get proper medical care elsewhere?' she said. 'You mentioned charges – what charges?'

'Can't say, madam. Just charges in connection with an affray down the docks is all I know. And probably speaking out of turn to say that much.' He looked at her wretchedly, his smooth young face suffused with patchy red.

She turned back to the doctor. 'You will tell me the extent of his injuries, please. I will not discuss with you the manner in which they were sustained. I want only the *medical* information, so that I can arrange to have him cared for by my own physician.'

The doctor glared at her with his face reddening too, so that he was an older stouter parody of the young policeman, and she stared back at him, her eyes wide, using all the will she had to outface him. After a moment he said loudly, 'Fractured radius, three cracked ribs, superficial soft tissue injuries to the face, fractured nose, possible fractured skull. You move him at your own risk.' He flashed a contemptuous glance at Charles as though to say that for his part he could not care less what risk he was exposed to.

'Thank you. And the name of your superior? The specialist who is in charge of the case?'

The doctor reddened even more, opened his mouth as though to speak, then turned away, and said to the nurse sharply, 'If arrangements are made to remove this patient without my consent, see to it that this policeman's sergeant is called. He is not to be removed until I say so.' He went marching away down the avenue of beds with the nurse scurrying importantly behind him.

'Nice piece of work he is,' the policeman said in a low voice. 'Would you care to sit down here, madam? I can move away a bit – I mean, as long as I keep him in sight it'll be all right. I don't see why that doctor had to be so hard, that I

110

don't. There was lots o' these public school boys came down
the docks to do some work. Why pick on him like that?'

'Because he didn't come to strike break,' Hannah said, and
looked ruefully at Charles. 'Did you, my love? He came to
stand with the pickets, I imagine.' Charles looked at her with
his only available eye gleaming, and again tried to smile.

'Oh,' the policeman said blankly. 'Oh. Educated boy like
that? Standing with the pickets? That's a funny way to go on.'

'Not funny,' Hannah said. 'Just angry.' She looked at
Charles again and felt a surge of pride. A fighter. Not a
whiner who only talked and complained but a fighter too.
Her Charles. Wrong headed perhaps – and she wasn't sure of
that, to be honest – but a fighter.

'I'll be back,' she said to Charles and smiled briefly at the
policeman. 'I'll make arrangements, darling. Get it all sorted
out. Try to rest.' Again she kissed his cheek, and turned and
went, hurrying back down the ward and feeling the eyes of
the men in the beds on her back, and curiously, a wave of
approval, and she thought, 'They don't like that doctor
either. They're glad I argued with him.' She smiled as one of
the men she passed grinned at her and made a thumbs-up
signal.

She managed to find a sweetshop with a little sign outside
proclaiming, 'You may telephone from here,' and started to
try to arrange Charles's care. She began with her own family
doctor, in the King's Road, but he was away for the
weekend, she was told, and his housekeeper suggested
another. She called him only to be told that he was unable to
involve himself in a hospital case. 'And if the injuries are as
you say, he's better off where he is than at home,' the little
voice clacked in her ear. 'Not a case I can accept responsibility
for.' She called the factory in Artillery Lane, but Cissie had
gone, and she realized with a shock how late it was, after
eleven, and she had told Cissie she could close the factory
once the orders had been loaded and the lorries despatched.
She tried Alex next, but he was in Liverpool trying to sort
out the unloading of some of his more urgent tea supplies.
David? Perhaps David could help, she thought briefly though
she knew she was being absurd. What she needed was
someone who would scoop her Charles out of that horrible
huge ward full of hollow faced men, away from that
pompous doctor, away from the police, away from all the

111

trouble he was in. And David couldn't do that.

She held the phone in her hand, her forefinger hooked over the rest and the earpiece held against her chest, trying to understand why she was so unwilling to do what she knew was the only answer to her dilemma. The shop owner peered at her curiously over the piles of dummy boxes of chocolates and dusty toffee tins that cluttered the counter and sniffed mournfully at her. Hannah stared back and then released the rest. When the operator's voice answered she gave Marcus's number wearily. What else could she do? And why shouldn't she? Why be so upset at the idea? He would want to help, she knew that; indeed he would be bitterly distressed if he thought she had not sought his aid.

He was not at Lammeck Alley, but they found his secretary for her, a sensible young man she had talked to before, and she found herself spilling it all out. Charles was hurt, being badly cared for in the London Hospital, there was some problem with the police; 'He was involved with a picket line,' she said mendaciously, knowing the young man would assume as everyone else did that a well-off young man like Charles would inevitably be a strike-breaker rather than a supporter. At once the secretary was all concern: Mr Lammeck was at the airport at Waddon overseeing the delivery of gold bullion which had to be flown in because of the strike. The secretary would see to it that he met her at the hospital as soon as he returned. Three hours, he said apologetically, no more than that. She was to wait.

She paid for her calls and walked out into the street and stood there, her coat pulled up against her ears, for she was cold now in spite of the sunshine. Three hours. Three hours in this grey dingy road with its grey ugly people shuffling along the wide pavements, and the curious emptiness of the roadway, for there were none of the buses and lorries that usually thronged it, and few private cars either. The strike was now five days old and even the most eager of lift givers and parcel and letter deliverers had lost some of their heart. But there was nothing more she could do. No one but Marcus could help her extricate Charles from his bondage in that pile of carbolic smelling buildings. She would have to wait, and fill in the time somehow.

An old woman went by her, almost cannoning into her, and Hannah stepped back muttering an apology. The old woman looked up briefly, her eyes gleaming under the heavy fringe of her old fashioned wig and said automatically '*Gut shabbos.*' Hannah said '*Gut shabbos,*' equally automatically and then thought, almost surprised, 'It's Saturday. *Shabbos.* People in synagogues.' She realized this was one of the reasons for the emptiness of the street. She remembered how it used to be in Antcliff Street, long ago, when people put on their best clothes and went trooping off to the synagogue on the corner, peacocking a little if they had something new to wear, gossiping busily, cuffing the children as they skipped and squabbled, and how empty the street became after they had gone by. Sometimes, when he had been in one of his unusual moods of goodwill, Nathan would announce that he was going to *shul,* and anyone who wanted to come too was welcome, and then she would put on her coat and that hateful pancake of a black straw hat (she could almost feel its scratchy edge against her forehead now as she remembered) and go with him to sit in the gallery staring down at all that went on below and from which she was excluded. *Shul* in those days had been a sort of treat, a break in the dullness of the ordinary week, and she felt a great wave of nostalgia for it.

The wind blew a little gust, sending dust swirling around her ankles and again she shivered and looked at her watch. After a moment she pushed her hands deeper into her coat pockets and began to walk, down East Mount Street, then along Raven Row and into Sidney Street.

It wasn't too long a walk; along Sidney Street, through Sidney Square and then left into Commercial Road, and then there it was, looking just as it had when she was a child. But much smaller.

She stood outside for a moment. Two old men, long bearded and with their white hair in tight curls over their ears under wide brimmed black hats, and a few small boys in ill fitting clothes, stared at her. She smiled at them but they stared unsmilingly back. After a moment she pushed past them, for they made no effort to make way for her, and went in through the double doors she remembered so well.

She could hear them beyond the inner doors, that odd and interesting familiar combination of wailing and jubilation, the rise and fall of chanting voices with an undertow of chatter. She took a deep breath and then began to climb the rickety wooden staircase that led to the women's gallery.

It was not full; there were only a few little knots of women scattered about. Old ones with shawled heads and a little cluster of young ones in very modern cheap cloche hats, clearly a party come to hear a boy say his Barmitzvah portion, and a few small girls with their heads together whispering busily and giggling in stifled little shrieks which made their mothers turn and hiss at them. Hannah stood there for a moment as they all turned and stared at her and then moved down to the front row, picking up a prayer book as she went.

She turned the pages, enjoying the feel of the thin rustling paper beneath her fingers and letting her eyes slide over the heavy black symbols, as incomprehensible to her now as they had been almost thirty years ago when she had sat here in that horrible hat and heavy coat and painfully large boots, watching Poppa down there below with the men. He had laughed at her when she had asked why she couldn't learn Hebrew like Jake and Solly, and had told her it was enough a girl should learn about running a decent Jewish home and not to fill her head with such a thing as Hebrew lessons.

'Be happy,' she heard his voice come into the back of her mind. 'Be happy, Hannelah, don't worry about reading. What good did it ever do me, I want to know? Tell me one good thing ever came from all the hours I spent sweating over my *chumash* or studying the Siddur, and I'll let you suffer like I did, God forbid I ever should ...' She closed her eyes for a moment and then opened them and stared down into the synagogue below.

It was as though she had never grown up. There they were, packed together as close as they had always been, swaying and bobbing, their *tallus* clad shoulders making a pattern against the blackness of their suits. Row upon row of striped prayer shawls, row upon row of fringes, some long, some short, some hanging free, some flung back over the shoulders, row upon row of covered heads, yarmulkas and bowlers, homburgs and caps, and in the box in front of the Bimah on which the rabbi and cantor stood, three glossy top hats looking as full of pride as though they themselves were sentient beings.

The smell enveloped her, mothballs and oil from the heating stoves and cooking, for the old women near her reeked powerfully of the fish they had fried and the chicken soup they had prepared and the livers and onions they had chopped yesterday afternoon ready for the Sabbath. The sound wrapped around her too; women's voices whispering nearby, rich baritone and tenor voices singing below, old cracked voices praying. It was like crawling back into the past, and she took a deep breath and at last relaxed.

'Perhaps I should go to *shul* more often,' she thought after a while, almost dreamily, watching the men as the swaying went on. 'I've left too much of yesterday behind. I don't belong there where I am.' She thought of Paultons Square and Buckingham Palace Gate, trying to make them feel alien inside her head, but it didn't work. They *were* where she belonged and no amount of nostalgia, sitting here in the stuffy heat of a tiny East End synagogue, could alter that. She belonged in the West End as much as she had ever belonged here, more in fact. She had only spent ten years of her life here in the middle of the poverty and fervour that so filled this small rackety building, and almost a quarter of a century on the other side of London. How could she try to convince herself that this was what she needed, and what she missed? She was just being sentimental, she told herself, trying to rub off the dreaminess that still filled her.

The service went on and on, and she sat there, listening, watching, trying to clear her head, and then stopped trying. She just let it roll over her, the ancient rhythms and sounds. Somehow they did what it was she most needed done. They took the fear and doubt and loneliness they found there and wrapped it all in a silken shell of peace. All gone, she thought. All gone. I'm not frightened any more because it doesn't really matter any more. Charles will live as he must, and do what he must, and so will Marie, and I must do what I must and I know now that I want Marcus and it doesn't *matter* anyway – it's only me, today, and has no relevance. All this is about what happened yesterday, hundreds and thousands of yesterdays full of frightened anxious doubting people, and they lived and died while the music and rhythm and the chanting went on and here it still is. And tomorrow when we're all gone it will still be here, the swaying and that sound and that smell and these people. It just doesn't matter at all.

It was a very comfortable feeling to have.

15

Marcus arrived at the hospital almost half an hour before she had hoped he would, his car sliding to the curb just beyond where she stood waiting for him, huddled against the main doorway at the top of the flight of entrance steps.

'Where?' he said, offering no other greeting. She said nothing and led the way inside the building, and on towards the ward where Charles was.

Marcus stopped at the door of the small office beside the ward entrance and with silken courtesy asked a nurse to find Sister for him, smiled briefly at Hannah and said, 'Go and wait with him. I won't be long.' She went obediently. He was here, and she felt safe and free and almost elated, and somewhere deep underneath, intensely happy. To be happy in such a situation was both selfish and stupid, yet there it was, and she could do nothing about it. She did not try.

Charles was asleep and the young policeman beside him almost half asleep, but he alerted as she came in and tried to offer her his chair. She shook her head at him and perched on the edge of the locker beside Charles, and leaned there, glad to see he was resting.

He woke after a few minutes, turning his head to see her, almost as though he knew she would be there.

'Hello,' she said softly.

'Hello,' he said and his voice sounded less difficult now. She was relieved by that for he had sounded almost choked before. Now he sounded only rather thick, like a child with a cold in his nose. 'I ought to say I'm sorry. For worrying you.'

'No need to fret over that,' she said.

'I'm not sorry, though. For worrying you, of course. But not for the fight. It was a *marvellous* fight.' He moved his head on his pillow and grimaced a little at the discomfort and she said quickly, 'Please, don't upset yourself, darling. Just rest.'

'I want to talk!' He sounded petulant, like a tired child. 'They can bash me as much as they like but they can't do anything to the inside of my head, can they? And inside my head – ' he closed his one good eye for a moment, ' – it's

116

marvellous in there.'

The young policeman looked at her, his face troubled. 'I don't think as I'd encourage him to talk too much, madam,' he said a little diffidently. 'I mean, I ought to take down anything he says, I suppose.' He brightened then. 'Mind you, he hasn't been charged with anything yet, so maybe it don't matter.'

'Thank you,' she said, and smiled at him. A nice boy, she thought. Not all that much older than Charles, to look at him.

'Aunt Hannah,' Charles said suddenly. 'I saw some people from school.'

'School?'

'Eton,' he said irritably, and moved his head awkwardly again. 'Eton, of course. There was that chap Julian Lammeck, and the Gubbay twins, carrying on as though it was a great lark. Driving lorries and going onto the docks trying to run the pickets down. I climbed on the cab, and there they were, and I was so amazed I fell off. Why them, Aunt Hannah? They're Jews too, how can they try to break a legitimate strike like that?'

'Darling, please don't fret yourself,' she began but he stared at her with such ferocity that she stopped and took a deep breath. 'I don't see what difference it makes, their being Jewish,' she said carefully after a moment. 'I'm not sure what it is you mean.'

'How can they? Don't they know what it's like for these people? Don't they understand what poverty does to people? How Jews have suffered, are still suffering? And they come and drive lorries like all the rest of these damned capitalists –'

'Darling, they're ... what do you expect? Anyone who knows you've been in a fight involving pickets assumes that you've been fighting against them! Eton boys, it's natural. Try not to worry over it, please.'

'They ought to know,' he said, his voice rising fretfully. 'They ought to know. They're traitors, to behave so. I'm glad I hit them.'

'Was that how you got hurt?'

He lay still for a moment and then managed another of his painful smiles. 'Yes. Yes it was. Marvellous. They didn't know what hit them, *marvellous*. But then the others got involved.'

'Others?'

'People,' he said vaguely, 'and police,' and then looked at the young policeman at the other side of his bed and said no more, and the boy in uniform blinked and looked confused and then turned his head to stare pointedly down the ward.

They were quiet for a while, as Hannah too looked towards the ward doors to see if Marcus were coming. Then Charles said suddenly, 'I'm being Barmitzvah, Aunt Hannah.'

She stared down at him, amazed. 'Bar – but when you were at school, you flatly refused to have anything to do with it! I asked you, and people were very angry with me because I didn't insist when you said you didn't want it.'

She frowned, suddenly, remembering. 'Uncle Alex said you'd be sorry, if I let you have your own way, and he was right – '

'Yes,' Charles said and his voice sounded more tired now. 'He often is, isn't he? I'm sorry. I didn't know any better then. I was ashamed of being a Jew, you see. At school people didn't talk about it, so I thought it was a shameful thing. I knew so little, anyway, I didn't understand. Now I know. Now I understand, I'm going to be Barmitzvah. Not because of God, you see. Because of Jews. That's why David's arranging it. Soon.'

He closed his eyes and seemed to fall asleep as suddenly as a baby. She watched his chest rise and fall and the peace that had filled her since the hour she had spent at the synagogue began to dissipate and make way for the old familiar anxiety. Would he always confuse her like this?

At last Marcus came, walking quietly down the ward with a tall man in a neat dark suit beside him. He smiled reassuringly at her as he came up to the bed.

'Hannah, my dear, it's all arranged. Charles is to be transferred to a nursing home in Harley Street. An ambulance has been ordered. Dr Jaeger here is in charge of his care, and is happy to take him into his private clinic. Dr Jaeger, Mrs Lammeck.'

She bent her head in acknowledgement. The tall man smiled a little remotely and then moved to stand beside Charles, and took his wrist between his fingers to count his pulse.

'Constable,' Marcus said, and the policeman stood up. 'I

have been speaking to your Sergeant Forbes on the telephone. He's waiting for you to call in. You can return to your station, but speak to him first.'

'But I was told to stay here until I was relieved, sir, and –'

'I know,' Marcus said, still very soothing. 'And you're quite right to be unsure. That's why I arranged for your sergeant to speak to you on the telephone. You place the call yourself, and then you'll know it's all straightforward, won't you?' Though he still looked dubious the policeman yielded to the note of authority in Marcus's voice and did as he was bid.

'Solicitor's there already,' Marcus said briefly in response to Hannah's puzzled gaze. 'Young Peterson had alerted him, sensible chap, and he'd already done some investigating before I got here. It's all fine, my dear. You can stop looking so desperate. He's going to be all right.'

'I'm not desperate,' she said, but she felt the tightness in her face and knew he was right.

The transfer to Harley Street was uneventful, the ambulance moving through the half empty streets without hindrance, and once she saw Charles safely tucked into bed in a handsome single room, already bedecked with flowers and warm and scented, as unlike the bleakness of the London Hospital as it was possible for a room to be, she took a deep breath and realized just how tense she had been. The doctor assured her gravely that the boy was all right, bruised and a little battered but no worse harm done.

'His nose may have a certain – ha – shall we say characterful look about it henceforth. I set it as neatly as I could, but of course it isn't easy always to ensure a perfect cosmetic result. His skull is not broken, we've now had time to look carefully at his X-rays, so you can be reassured on that score. The fracture of the radius is a simple one and should heal without any dramatic problems. Try to keep him out of trouble once I send him home to you, in a few days, I think. And relax yourself, my dear lady.' He smiled that somewhat remote smile again and bowed her out. Marcus took her elbow in a warm grip and led her down to his car, and took her home.

Not until she sat in her own armchair beside her own fire, with an anxious faced Florrie bringing her tea, could she take in all that had happened. Marcus explained to her that there had been an intention of charging Charles with wilful obstruction of the police in the execution of their duty but that the Lammeck Alley solicitor, a much experienced man, had managed to persuade them that this was unnecessary since the boy was merely hot headed and infected with the current craziness. There would be no further problems, the solicitor had assured the police blandly – well brought up boy you know, and all that – and faced with the lawyer's authoritative superiority and the fact that his client was obviously very rich they had allowed themselves to be persuaded. Charges were dropped.

When he had finished his reassurances Hannah looked at Marcus and smiled, or tried to, but only managed a grimace as the tears exploded at last. He put his arms out and she crept into them and wept until she was exhausted.

'It's silly, isn't it?' he said after a while.

'What is?' By now she was sitting back in her own chair, her head thrown back against the cushions, feeling the puffiness around her eyes, aware of the tear stains on her cheeks and not caring, almost revelling in her exhaustion.

'You treat me like a husband,' he said. 'When there's trouble, you call me. You want me, and you need me, but you won't marry me.'

'I tried to do everything myself first – ' she began.

'And had to call me. Hannah, stop being so silly. Marry me. You know you'll have to eventually.'

'Yes,' she said, and let her eyes, tired as they were, move so that she could see him. 'I decided that this morning in the synagogue.'

He sat very still, only looking at her, and after a long moment opened his mouth to speak, but all he said was, 'The synagogue? Were you so frightened?'

'Perhaps. But I needed reminding. Who I am. What I am. I thought that there – ' She shrugged.

'And what you got was a revelation telling you to marry me?'

She smiled then. 'No. Not a revelation. I just realized that it's all so – that it's not important. What I do, what anyone does, it's all so temporary, I might as well do what I want. Does that sound selfish?'

'No, only sensible. Not very flattering to me, of course,

but sensible.'

'Then I'm being sensible.' She laughed then, a little unsteadily. 'Hell of a way to start a marriage.'

'It doesn't matter how it starts,' he said, and moved towards her for the first time, putting out a hand to take hers. 'It'll be how it goes on that will be important.'

They decided not to tell anyone yet of their plans. 'Let Charles get well,' she said. 'Let me see how things are with him, and then we'll see where we are. Please?' He agreed, content enough to do as she wanted. He seemed to be as he always was to outsiders, but she knew the difference in him. He was, she realized, incandescent with happiness. His calmness, his relaxed speech, everything about him bespoke a deeply happy man, and she felt humble and almost afraid of her own power since she had made him so, and could destroy his happiness as easily as she had created it. She was still unsure of herself, still confused by her own feelings, still feared at a very deep level that somehow she would destroy him as she had destroyed two of his cousins, men she had loved dearly too. She tried to believe that this was mere superstition, that it had no basis in any reality, as he continually assured her. It wasn't easy, but she managed it by letting go, by not trying, just as she had stopped trying that morning in the synagogue.

Charles came home at the end of the week, not long after the strike had ended, looking much better with his swollen eye almost healed and his scratches almost gone, though his nose was still rather puffy. He was dejected because the strike had, he assured them, failed.

'The bastards have won again,' he said passionately that evening over dinner to which Marcus had come. 'Those damned bosses have robbed the working man.'

'Not quite,' Marcus said quietly, and launched himself into an account of the issues raised by the strike, as seen from the side of the owners. Charles lifted his head and listened and then, pushing his plate to one side, leaned both elbows on the table and began to harangue Marcus about the evil of his ways. Marcus listened and now and again, when he could, interpolated a comment of his own, or a rebuttal, while Hannah sat and listened and curiously, gloried in it. Her boy, her Charles, was able to listen and learn as well as to defend his views, confused though some of them were, though his speech was adorned with a good deal of the sort of political claptrap she had heard spouted at Speakers' Corner many times and had read in newspapers. He had clearly come to no intellectual harm from his conversion to religious and political fervour, and though it was equally clear there would always be anxieties about him, that he would never spend his life in quiet safe backwaters, still, she had reared him well. He was becoming a successful person in his own eyes and therefore in hers. He had, she suddenly realized, watching him as he talked on and on in the light of that spring evening, almost finished his journey from childhood to manhood. The downiness on his cheeks was a sturdier growth; his voice was heavy with a new maturity and his body was as muscled and active as his mind. 'I'm free,' she thought. 'I can do what I choose. Marry as soon as I choose.'

Free except for Marie. She felt a pang of acute guilt as her daughter's name came slipping into her mind. Since she went away, all she had felt was relief at her absence. She knew she should miss her, but she didn't. And yet, in an odd way, she did.

'Marcus,' she said, when Charles, still tiring easily as convalescents do, had gone to bed early. 'I don't want to tell Marie of our plans in a letter. I want to tell her myself.'

'She'll be home for the holidays soon, though, won't she? Tell her then?'

Hannah shook her head. 'She's going to Berlin. To the Von Aachens. I can't say no, really. They're her close friends now.'

He sat silently for a while and then he said, easily, 'Then we'll go to Lausanne and tell her there. As soon as you feel happy about leaving Charles. We'll fly to Paris, shall we? And then take the Rome Express to Lausanne. And maybe, afterwards, go to Rome, just for a holiday. Would you like that, Hannah?'

She looked at him, facing her across her chrome and glass table in her white dining room, at the solidity of him and the sureness of him and felt the leap inside her that she had once been afraid of, even a little ashamed of, but now welcomed for its promise of joy to come.

'Yes please,' she said. 'And I rather think I'd like to be

122

married before we go, Marcus. Because I'm not sure I can wait much longer, and you won't – you want me to make an honest man of you, don't you? So, how soon can it be? I'm not asking Marie's permission to marry you, you see. I'm just telling her.'

16

It really was a silly plan in some ways; they both agreed that, yet still they did it. They would have a civil marriage at a Registry Office first, of which no one but Bet and Florrie who were to be witnesses would have an inkling, and then after returning from their journey to Lausanne, a 'proper wedding'. A synagogue wedding under a canopy, with all their friends and relations crowding round, and a noisy party afterwards. 'I like it,' Marcus said with relish. 'Honeymoon first, God's permission afterwards. It's got style.' Hannah laughed and accused him of being a hypocrite, since surely what they were doing made her as wicked in the eyes of religion as those women at the Rothschild's party, an argument into which he refused to enter. 'I have my standards,' he said with a heavy imitation of a pompous professor. 'And I don't need to defend them.'

She laughed again. They laughed a lot during those weeks while they waited for the formalities to be sorted out, though they both worked hard too. She organized the Artillery Lane factory as tightly as she could, giving Cissie reams of instructions to keep her going during Hannah's first holiday from the place, and at Buckingham Palace Gate arranged that there should be a close-down for most of the time she was away. It was the easiest way to do it, and had the added virtue of making her clients even more eager to place orders for later in the year. Hannah had discovered that being captious and masterful with her customers, far from driving them into the arms of other couturieres, made them cling to her even more closely.

Marcus too was busy, sorting out his complex Lammeck Alley activities, for now that the old uncles had retired he ran the business almost singlehanded, though the place was staffed as it always had been with young Lammeck and Damont cousins and nephews. He had not had a holiday for a very long time, so there was much to be done. But he found time in the middle of it all to arrange for Charles to go away for a while.

'You've had a rougher time than you realize, my boy,' he said, when broaching his idea to Charles. 'I think you need some time to catch your breath and the chance to learn a little more. We have an office in Amsterdam – it's run by a sensible chap, Piet Damont. His son, I'm told, is a considerable Talmudic scholar, very involved with the community there, and a bit of an historian. You're so interested in Jewish matters now I thought you'd like to stay with him for a while, and learn as well as relax. The boy's a couple of years older than you – Henk, they call him. I think you'll like him.'

To Hannah's relief, Charles agreed. She saw him off from Liverpool Street Station, on his way to Harwich and the boat for the Hook of Holland, with a warm hug and a supply of money which he tried to refuse, but which she insisted he take.

So, when the day came, in early June, for her civil wedding to Marcus, she was ready in every way she could be, or so she told herself. The factory and the workshop organized, Charles in Amsterdam, Marie safely in Lausanne where they would soon see her. She was ready.

Yet she sat at her dressing table that morning staring at herself in her mirror, trying to fight down an acute desire to run out of the house and away, away to anywhere except Caxton Hall in Westminster where Marcus was waiting for her. She wanted to abandon everything, not only the thought of being married again, but work and children and house and relations. But why? It's not that they're all that much of a burden, she told her reflection. Are they? Marie's so far away, and Charles, too, and even Jake and Solly, still in New York and apparently happy there, and Uncle Alex – what sort of a burden is Uncle Alex? It's the reverse, surely – he regards *me* as someone he has to worry about. And the aunts and uncles and cousins in the East End, do I worry over them? Of course I don't. So what am I on about, thinking of them as a burden I want to abandon?

Her reflection stared back at her, blankly, and she examined her face slowly, feature by feature, until she manage to slip out of her own body and become someone else. It was as though she were not the red headed woman with the blue eyes sitting in front of the mirror, but a totally alien being who stood behind the red headed woman and looked at her, mocking her, disliking her.

Florrie came bustling in with a tray of tea, looking exceedingly smart in a grey silk dress with a matching hat with a cockade up the side.

'Oh, mum,' she scolded. 'There's you sitting there and not half dressed and me and Bet ready this half hour. The car's already here, and the chauffeur's having his tea, so you get a move on do! I'll pour your tea – oh, I'm that excited, I can hardly breathe! Bet's as white as your shirt, she's so overtook by it all. You getting married, mum, it's wonderful, and high time and you should a' done it long ago, but never mind. The best always comes to them as waits, and Mr Lammeck he's really the best, and isn't it lovely you ain't changing your name, mum? Now there's your tea, and I'll just help you step into your costume, and it's as nice a piece of silk as I've ever set eyes on and no mistake.'

She chattered on, and Hannah obeyed her urging, putting on her new lime green suit, and thinking, you too. You and Bet, I have to please you two as well. What about me? Where do I fit in? What about what I want? And then felt fury at her own stupidity for she *did* want Marcus, she wanted him very much indeed. He was offering her the first chance of simple uncomplicated happiness she had ever had. No one in the background to spoil it or be hurt (Marie? No, not even Marie). No echoes of Davida's cruelty or Judith's pain. Why be so uncertain?

It went on, all through the journey to Westminster in Marcus's new car, a rakish Bentley in cream and chocolate with long sweeping mudguards and deep leather-upholstered seats into which she sank with a sense of great luxury, and even after she was climbing the steps, Bet and Florrie solemn-faced and rigid with excitement behind her.

Marcus was waiting and she looked at him consideringly, still the sharp-eyed mocking creature who had stared at her reflection in the mirror, not her own red headed, blue eyed self. Who was she? Who was he?

He did not smile, but took her hand gravely and that made it worse, somehow, for she was wearing gloves and he seemed remote through the thin fabric, a stranger. She took a deep breath and almost whispered it aloud. 'I'm going to run. I can't. Too many people to think about. I can't run.'

What happened then she could never remember. She had walked up the steps and Marcus had been there and taken her hand and then she had walked out, her hand tucked into his elbow and with a new ring on her finger and she was married, or so they told her, and she stood blinking in the sunshine as Florrie and Bet fluttered and giggled and wept, and she stared at them and thought, *why?* And did not know what she was questioning, let alone what the answer was.

They lunched at the Savoy, just the four of them, an idea of Marcus's, for he had told Hannah this was not their real wedding day and it would be a treat for Florrie and Bet, and she had agreed, grateful to him for being as aware of their importance in her life as she was. But then Florrie and Bet were in a taxi on their way back to Paultons Square, weeping happily and bidding her goodbye, and she and Marcus were driving out to Waddon to be flown to Paris. Once more strangeness swept in and she was lost in it. He seemed to understand, for he said little, holding her gloved hand lightly, and she was grateful. Time, she whispered in her head, give me time.

Paris, the drive from the airfield, the echoing steam filled railway station glowing in the dark of the evening like a miniature inferno. She shivered a little despite the warmth of the June night and he smiled briefly at her as the blue clad porters loaded their luggage into the train, and she tried to smile back. It was difficult.

They had their own first class wagon-lit, an elegant little compartment heavily panelled in walnut and full of chrome mirrors and little shelves and hooks and cupboards. They had their own adjoining bathroom too, for Marcus had used all Lammeck Alley's influence to obtain the compartment usually reserved for directors of the railroad. She undressed in there, slowly, very aware of him waiting for her in the compartment, and yet not excited. I wanted this, she told herself. Didn't I? I ached for him. I've wanted to go to bed with him for so long, yet now, I don't care. I'm tired. I just want to go to sleep. I'm numb. I don't want to. I don't want to ...

He was not in the sleeping compartment when she pushed

126

open the little swinging door, and she stood there as the train began to move to the accompaniment of a distant hiss of steam and the sound of the departure whistle and muffled shouts from the platform, feeling the train beneath her begin to pick up speed, standing in the swaying rattle listening, but all she could hear now was the wheels chattering over the rails as the train looped its stately way out through the Paris suburbs, going south-east towards Lausanne; diddly *dum*, diddly *dum*, diddly *dum*, diddly *dum*. It echoed madly in her head and she shook it irritably, and moved towards the bed the wagon-lit attendant had made ready for them, a handsome double sized bunk with crisp linen sheets and plump pillows, and slid in between the covers.

Marcus came in from the corridor, and she looked at him questioningly.

'I was smoking,' he said briefly and went into the bathroom, first turning off the light in the compartment, so that she lay there in the darkness trying to relax, trying to pretend to herself she was eager and hungry and ready for him, but the line of light around the bathroom door mocked her in the blackness, and she could not untie the knots in her belly.

The train rattled on, noisily sometimes, then more rhythmically for a while, and then chattered furiously again as a new tangle of points attacked the wheels and she tried not to listen because the interrupted rhythm irritated her, made her edgier than ever. Then the bathroom door opened and he came through and suddenly it was quite dark, as he switched off that light too.

She felt him move across the small compartment and then sit down beside her on the bunk, and after a moment he said, 'Shall I lie down, Hannah? Or would you be happier if I stretched out on the bench there on the other side? You're tired, I think.'

'Yes,' she said, and breathed in sharply through her nose so that she made a small hissing sound. 'Yes. Dreadfully tired.'

'Shall I, then?'

She was silent for a moment. 'No, Marcus, of course not. Come to bed. We'll sleep, and I'll be better. I'm just tired, that's all.'

'I know,' he said and she felt his hand on her cheek for a moment, as light as a breath. 'I know.'

He lay there beside her very still, his hands hooked

together behind his head, and she was filled with a great wash of gratitude to him, and then was more tense than ever because gratitude was not enough. What have I done, she shrieked silently into the blackness, what have I *done*? Why am I married? Marcus lay breathing quietly beside her and said nothing.

She must have dozed then, for the rhythm of the train changed and the swaying seemed to increase and she was rocking, lightly and easily, and it was a good safe feeling, a peaceful feeling and then, slowly and gradually, an exciting feeling. She was lying on a huge cloud of a cushion, a soft, silken cushion and she was being swayed from side to side so that there was a sweep of pleasure as she came down from one peak of the rocking, and then another as she rose again to the next and she was singing inside her head, and watching Marcus's face somewhere in the blackness above her, a smiling happy face.

The rhythm changed, became noisy and uneven and suddenly she was wide awake in the darkness of a moving train in the middle of France with Marcus there beside her, and she needed him then with all the urgency she had been suppressing for so long. She lifted herself on one elbow and tried to see him in the darkness and couldn't, and moved her head forward, searchingly, and felt his breath on her cheek.

'Marcus,' she said and felt his head turn towards her and find hers and she opened her mouth and reached for him with it and found his cheek, and then, still searching, his mouth, and clung to him, pushing her tongue against his greedily. For a moment he lay there and then she felt the surge of response in him as she moved even closer, but he pulled his head away and said questioningly, 'Hannah? Are you sure? Quite sure?'

She laughed then, a silly childish laugh, and put her hands on each side of his face and kissed him again and still he seemed uncertain, and she slid her hand down his neck and across his chest, and then on to his belly, pushing his silk pyjamas aside and then there was no doubt in either of them. They were rolling with the rhythm of the train, first against it and then with it, and the swaying of the bunk beneath them seemed to meld with the movements of their own bodies and then, somehow, they were part of the train as well as of each other. The whole world was movement and excitement and noise and great sweeping breathless drops and rises from peak to peak, and she laughed aloud again, a loud and breathless sound this time as at last the final doubts died, and with them the horrible mocking black creature who had dogged her all day. It was all *right*, at last. It could not be more right.

17

'Now this,' said Uncle Alex with huge satisfaction, 'is what I call a *wedding!*' He leaned back in his chair and hooked his thumbs into his waistcoat pockets and grinned at her. 'Real style, that's what it is, real style.'

She slid a glance at Marcus, mockingly, and he raised his eyebrows at her in a parody of husbandly reproof.

'To tell you the truth, Uncle Alex, I had remarkably little to do with it all,' Hannah said sweetly. 'Marie, and Marcus, were the ones who were most busy. He's a bit of a bully, you know.'

'She's lying in her teeth,' Marcus said. 'Ignore the woman – she's only my wife – and come and have another drink with me. You're looking a bit too sober for my liking.' The two men weaved their way across the crowded floor towards a bar which had been set up on the far side.

Hannah watched them go, smiling a little indulgently, happy to see them so comfortable together, and then smiled even more widely as Jake went swooping by with a Damont cousin in his arms, dancing with all the New York style he could muster. Since coming back from his eighteen months there with Solly, he'd been more American than the movies, something which had helped a lot with Marie. She had scorned her uncles while they were London East Enders, but New York East Siders were different – they had a special classiness of their own that made them socially acceptable to her, and she was very gracious with them these days.

Indeed, she was very gracious with everyone, Hannah thought happily, sweeping the crowded floor with her gaze, looking for her. It had been difficult, that meeting at Lausanne, over six months ago. Hannah had been afraid that

Marie would sulk and be difficult, or worse still refuse to accept Marcus as a stepfather, for their previous encounters had not been happy ones. But to her intense relief Marie had not only accepted him, she had been delighted with her mother's news.

'Does that make Daphne my aunt, then?' she demanded. 'I would like that, having a countess for an aunt, and you couldn't stop me from being friends with my own aunt, could you, Marcus!' She had laughed at that, giving him a wicked little sideways glance. 'I mean, you were madly annoyed with me for going to her parties, weren't you? And sent me home like a baby. But you couldn't do that if she were my aunt, could you?'

'You were younger then, my dear,' he had said gravely, 'and less aware of the ways of the world. Now you've been here to school and learned a little more, I think you'll understand more about how to behave, and also why I was so tiresome when last we met. I shan't be a nasty step-papa, I promise you.'

'I shouldn't let you be,' she had said airily, and for a moment Hannah had felt her belly lurch with apprehension, but then relaxed as she realized all would be well. Marcus would be tactful with her and Marie was genuinely pleased about their marriage, and threw herself with great delight into the business of planning the wedding. Hannah was glad to let her do so, for it gave the child something to keep her busy after her time at the school ended in September, and also to keep her mind off the change in her personal fortunes. For in August Albert died. He was not all that old, just reaching his sixtieth birthday, but he had chosen to retire from Lammeck Alley when his brothers did, though they were older than he and ready to do so, and somehow he had never really found his life worth living after that. He had left the bulk of his fortune to his granddaughter, Mary Bloomah Lammeck, to be hers absolutely when she reached her eighteenth birthday.

Hannah had been shocked by that. It was not that she did not want her child to be the heiress to such a sum (for Albert, although he had been a prodigal spender, had left a sizeable fortune). Any mother would want it for her daughter. But she knew her girl, and it frightened her to think of her having the use of so much at so young an age. Marcus shared her concern, and it was he who told Marie of her inheritance in such a way that she did not fully realize how much it was, nor that she could have control of it in just over a year's time.

'The less she knows the better,' Marcus said. 'I'll see to the investments, and we'll try to keep any fuss about it to a minimum. Let her have her head with the wedding, my love, and that will help.'

Marie had indeed shown a remarkable skill for one so young in planning a big party, and Hannah had greatly enjoyed watching her busy with her lists and her plans and her estimates and her suggested menus and her decoration schemes. It was all so like the way she had been herself all those years ago planning Mary's ball for the old King.

There had been one altercation to mar everyone's pleasure in the coming wedding, and that had been Hannah's insistence that all her East End relatives be invited. Marie's brow had darkened in the old childish way, and she had expostulated bitterly, but Hannah had been adamant. It had been Marcus who had managed to persuade Marie that having an invitation list that covered every sort of society was extremely chic. He pointed out the way his sister the countess filled her parties with crooners and jazz players and boxers, anyone who was fashionable, and managed to convince Marie that a party that included Uncle Reuben and Aunt Minnie's great brood with all their husbands and wives and in-laws and children would be as chic as any number of jazz players and boxers. Amazingly she believed him.

'I'd rather leave Daphne and Rupert out,' Marcus had said to Hannah over dinner at his flat that evening. 'How I ever came to have so disreputable a pair as my closest kin I'll never know. Someone up there must hate me. Mind you, they say the same about me – they think me intensely boring. Still, what can I do? They're my sister and brother and Marie would never forgive me if I didn't ask her wretched countess of a new aunt! You don't want that ice, do you Hannah, my darling? Say you don't and come to bed.'

That was the silliest part of that summer and autumn and early winter of 1926; their pretence that they were not yet married. It would have made no difference to anyone at all if they had chosen to set up house together as soon as they came home from Lausanne, indeed Florrie and Bet expected him to move in to Paultons Square. But, perversely, they chose to wait until the 'proper' wedding was over. So, all through those long months each of them lived in their own home, and worked at their own work. They made love whenever they could, either at Marcus's flat or at Paultons Square on the rare occasions when no one was at home to interrupt or disturb them. It was mad, but it was fun, and it also had another function; it gave Hannah the time she had so badly needed. Time to make the move from her old life to her new one, time to realize that she was not some sort of threat to Marcus, that she could be, eventually, the happy successful wife she so wanted to be.

And now, sitting here at her own wedding party at the Savoy Hotel, watching the great banqueting suite pulsating with people dancing to celebrate her happiness, she felt deeply content. The metamorphosis was complete, she told herself. She was happy, and she could go on being happy.

The music changed and the floor thinned out a little and she could see the children across on the other side of the room. 'I shouldn't call them that,' she thought, and smiled at herself. Children, with Charles, newly home from his prolonged stay in Amsterdam, so tall and handsome, and Marie so exquisitely grown up as she was! Seventeen now. It didn't seem possible.

They were standing side by side near the bar where Marcus was still talking to Uncle Alex, and there was something in the way Charles was hovering over Marie that made Hannah more watchful for a moment. He had been different somehow, since coming home, still besotted with his politics, of course, though less involved with religion. It seemed as though his long period of study with Henk Damont in Amsterdam had burned that passion out of him. He had been Barmitzvah as he had said he would be, shortly after returning to London, at a quiet service one very wet morning at a synagogue where none of the family was particularly well known, so that there was the minimum of fuss, and then had spent less and less time with David at his yeshivah, much to David's regret, though he did not question it. Charles no longer wished to study the word of God? All right, that was his affair and God's. He, David, would turn his attention to his own boy Lionel, a precocious lad of nearly seven. One day *he* would be David's great scholar, since Charles had decided to abdicate that role.

Charles instead began to work at a settlement, in Jubilee Street, not far from David's home, running a youth club for the local children and teaching them politics with every chance he got. But it was mostly in the evenings that he was really busy. His days were largely his own and once Marie had come home he had taken to spending more and more time with her, helping her with her planning, running errands for her willingly. Hannah had been delighted to see it. She had tried to rear them as happy brother and sister, and she had been sad when a split appeared between them as it had after he had left Eton. To see them so close again now was warming. But she watched them now across the ballroom floor and wondered. Brother and sister? Was it really like that? Or had it changed? There was something about Charles's posture as he stood watchfully beside Marie that made her dubious.

Marie was talking to a tall young man, and Hannah wondered who it was. She could not see clearly from this distance and he had his back to her. She got up, pushing aside the table bedecked with flowers at which she had been sitting, and began to move across towards the little group there by the bar.

But Marcus was back. He slid his hand under her elbow and bent his head and whispered, 'Isn't this exciting? Imagine, married! At last!'

'Idiot!' she said, and lifted her face and kissed him, and he grinned at her, cheerfully. 'Where were you heading so purposefully?'

'What? Oh, Marie. I thought – I wanted to tell her how lovely she looks. And how beautifully everything went. And how happy I was in the synagogue this morning. All those things.'

'And I thought you were going to scold her,' he said lightly. 'You had that mother-hen look on your face.'

'I suppose so,' she said consideringly, and then made a face. 'I was a bit bothered. Charles – ' She turned her head to look for them again. 'Look at him. He looks so ... I'm not sure. What do you think?'

The dancers who had been clustered in the way moved a little and she could see where the trio had been, but only Charles was there now and she frowned, for he was leaning against the bar looking, she thought, rather pale.

'I thought Marie was there,' she said, and began to move again towards Charles. Marcus followed her.

'Hello, my boy,' Marcus said. 'Why so pale, why so wan, alone and palely loitering? Has the Belle Dame – whoever she was – been at you?'

Charles looked up and made a little grimace. 'Do me a favour, Uncle Marcus, I can do without the gags. I'm just a bit bored, if you must know. I know it's your wedding, but really, all this – ' he swept his hand out in a comprehensive gesture. 'It's really obscene, isn't it?'

'Obscene?' Marcus said, interested. 'Where? Who's being obscene?'

Charles shook his head irritably. 'You know quite well what I mean, I've said it often enough.'

'Yes, you've said it. And you're right, up to a point. A lot of rich people stuffing themselves and drinking too much when half the world is starving. But there are other values as well as concern for the poor, you know.'

'I don't know of any,' Charles said harshly.

'Oh, family feeling, and giving pleasure to others, and rites of passage to make people happy about the way their experience changes – things like that! You can't make the poor any happier just by making the better off miserable.'

'That's a specious argument, and well you know it,' Charles began hotly, but Hannah moved between them and took each of them by the elbow. 'I'm damned if I'll have politics at my wedding,' she said lightly. 'Charles, my love, where's Marie? I wanted to tell her how clever and lovely and altogether splendid she – '

'Gone,' Charles said shortly.

Hannah's eyebrows snapped down. 'Gone? Where?'

He looked at her with a sharp little glance from dark eyes that seemed suddenly to be thick with tears, though he was quite dry eyed. 'She's got a tendency to slope off from weddings, hasn't she, our Marie? But no need for any worries, so don't look like that! She's gone with your brother, Marcus. He's taking her on to a party. Apparently the Prince of Wales will be there, no less, and you know our Marie. Can't resist a name and never could. Told me to tell you, so I'm telling you.' He pulled away from her a little abruptly and moved across the big room to sit beside David and his family and talk earnestly to them.

Hannah watched him go and frowned and then Marcus said softly, 'Oh dear,' and she turned and looked up at him, her forehead creased.

'I think I know what's happening to our Charles,' Marcus said. 'Bad enough the poor chap's been bitten by this wretched political bug. Add love on and he's really floundering.'

She turned to him and put her arms up so that they could dance, for the music had started again and she could see her cousin Leon moving purposefully towards her and she wanted to talk.

They moved through a few turns, dancing easily and comfortably as they always did, enjoying the contact with each other, and then she said abruptly, 'Do you really think that's what's happened? They grew up together. People who were children together don't fall in love, do they?'

'It's been known,' he said. 'And they've been apart a lot lately. She's changed a lot, you know. Since Lausanne. Much less petulant, and very – oh, I suppose poised is the word. I don't like it, sounds like a damned magazine, but it fits her. She's a very handsome young lady, your Marie, and very beguiling. I can see he'd be bowled over by the change in her.'

'Has he changed, too, then? I thought he had. He seems bigger, somehow, since he got back from Holland. And just as involved with his ideas, but less, well, childish about them than he was. They seem more a part of him. Will it be all right for him, Marcus? Will she see the change in him and be bowled over too?'

'Darling, I don't know.' He held her close as the music changed yet again, sliding into a very romantic waltz. 'And stop trying to be Mrs God. I know you'd like to run their lives for them and make it all cozy and tidy, but you can't. Leave them to sort out their own feelings, and concentrate on ours. Have you told me today how much you love me?'

'Can't you remember?'

'I don't choose to. Tell me now.'

She told him, and they danced closer still and she felt her cheek against his and his back strong and relaxed under her fingers and knew she was blessed. But even while she revelled in her own happiness, dancing at her own wedding, she watched Charles sitting alone now on the far side of the

135

room and staring down at his fingers and thought about her Marie, out somewhere with Rupert. It shouldn't worry her, for Rupert was a grown man, well able to take care of any girl he escorted. So why was she worried?

It's a habit, she told herself, and looked up at Marcus and kissed his cheek. A bad habit, worrying about Marie. High time I stopped it. She'll be fine.

18

'So, then what happens?' the Prince said, enthralled. Marcus looked across the room and caught Hannah's eye and she nearly exploded into laughter but somehow managed to keep her face straight.

'What happens?' Sadie said. 'I tell you, it's like nothing you never saw in your whole life! They go *meshuggah* – '

'*Meshuggah?*' murmured the Prince.

'Crazy! Mad!' Sadie made a face, twisting her cheeks and mouth into an extraordinary grimace and crossing her eyes ferociously and the Prince blinked. 'They carry on like there's never been no fish brought into the place before, they jump up and down, they holler, they swear, you should forgive me mentioning such vulgarity to such a person as yourself, they hit each other sometimes but mind you, no hard feelings. Business is business and when it looks like someone else is gettin' a barrel of herring you got a fancy for, and what you knows is the best, sure you get *broigus* and hit out a bit – '

'Broigus?'

'Oy, Your Majesty, imagine me giving you a lesson in Yiddish!' Sadie beamed hugely. '*Broigus* means annoyed, put out, not very pleased, you know?'

'I'm beginning to know,' the Prince said. 'Now, what was that other word you told me? *Maven*. One who knows. I trust I'm beginning to be a *maven* – and to help you be a *maven* – Mrs Lazar, may I explain to you that it isn't correct to address me as majesty. Sir will do.'

Marcus had moved across the room to stand beside Hannah. He murmured in her ear, 'I don't think I *believe* this. I know he fusses about democracy and getting to know the people, but finding out from Cousin Sadie how to run a fish shop in the Mile End Road is taking it to the outside edge of enough – she'll be offering to take him with her to Billingsgate next.'

'I tell you, sir, Your Majesty,' Sadie said with an even wider beam, leaning forwards to tap the Prince's arm with a large red hand much bedecked with garnets. 'I'll tell you what. You feel like getting up a bit early one morning? I'll take you down the market, show you the ropes! We'll buy the fish, you'll come back to my place, have a cupper coffee, an onion platsel maybe, and a nice bit fried halibut – '

'Too kind, but I rather think that will be difficult. Other demands you know, other demands, although it's all so interesting, Mrs Lazar, I truly regret it is not possible. But I wish your business every success in the future, indeed I do. I trust you will – er – always get the barrels of herrings that you fancy.'

'From your mouth to God's ears!' Sadie said and clasped her hands together prayerfully.

Someone on the other side of the room changed the record on the gramophone and the rhythms of the 'Black Bottom' scattered people into dancing couples and the Prince turned away to talk to Lady Ingham. Sadie sat and fanned herself happily, revelling at being at so smart a party. 'Although,' she later told her enthralled customers, 'it wasn't what you might call a proper catered affair. I mean, no food as you'd notice, just a few bits o' this and that on a plate, and more cocktails than I've had chicken soup, I tell you. Still, what do you expect of these fancy people?'

Hannah relaxed. She'd been doubtful about this party but Marcus had insisted and he had been right. He had become one of the Prince of Wales's most trusted advisers during the year they had been married, even though Marcus disapproved of some of the Prince's other friends, and was not afraid to say so, but the Prince respected his views and allowed him to say what he thought. They saw a great deal of him though usually within the same close circle of familiar people. But Marcus had told her the Prince wanted to know more about other people in his country, and it had been Marcus's idea that they give a party that mixed both sides of their family, to give the Prince the chance he wanted. So here were several of the Lazar clan, including David and his Sonia, together with the regular aristocratic crowd. It shouldn't have worked, but it did.

Later, as they undressed for bed they talked lazily and comfortably of how it had all gone, of what Lord Ingham had said to David Lazar and how well David had put him in his place when he had tried to condescend, of the splendour of Cissie's new dress – for she had been a particularly successful member of the party, quite captivating the Prince with her talk of life in Artillery Lane – and how well Florrie and Bet had managed.

'I wish the children had been here, though,' Hannah said. She was sitting at her dressing table cleaning her face with cream, and he laughed as he looked at her, for she had made a mask of the thick white stuff, and her eyes peered through like holes in snow.

'Children!' he said. 'You don't look more than a child yourself, like that! Do stop it, love. You try too hard with those two. They're all right.'

'Are they?' She wiped her face carefully with cotton swabs, watching him through the mirror all the time. 'Are you sure, Marcus? I wish I could be.'

He threw his hands in the air in mock despair and now it was her turn to laugh for he was wearing only his socks, neatly held in place with sock suspenders, and the effect was ludicrous. 'What more do you want, Hannah? They're engaged! Isn't that what you thought would be the best thing for both of them? Why do you go on worrying so much?'

'Put your dressing gown on, do. I can't talk sense while you're prancing around like that. I suppose you're right. It all seems well enough, but somehow I don't know. I still worry. And they weren't here tonight and ... oh, well.'

Long after he had fallen asleep and was snoring softly beside her, his head pushed into the curve of her neck as always, she lay awake still thinking about Charles and Marie. They had come bursting into the house on a hot June afternoon, their hair bedraggled and their clothes dripping wet, because, they had said, they had fallen in the Serpentine while having a boat battle with a crowd of friends. 'And,' announced Marie, all wide eyes and excitement, 'He positively saved my life, darling Charles, and I realized he wasn't just my big brother after all, and I'm going to marry him. So there!' Charles had stood there, his face white and rigid with joy and his dark eyes looking as though someone had switched on a light behind them, and Hannah had laughed and cried together, she was so delighted for them.

But that had been six months ago. As the summer went on and they went away, all four of them, to a villa in Mentone which belonged to Julian Damont and which most of the family borrowed from time to time, and came back to plunge into the business of their hectic working autumn, she had become chilled and anxious. Marie seemed happy enough, singing a great deal, and being cheerful and friendly with everyone, and behaving very affectionately towards Charles in front of them all, but Charles seemed less serene. Sometimes Hannah would notice him watching Marie with a brooding sort of stare and then, as he realized she was looking at him, would smile reassuringly and try to look unconcerned. And there were times when Charles, headlong into one of his favourite political discussions with Marcus, who was always willing to defend his own capitalist viewpoint cheerfully against Charles's passionate attacks, would redden and falter and give up when Marie yawned at him or seemed sulky and bored.

But as Marcus said, they seemed content enough, though they both slid off the subject when Hannah tried to discover what their future plans were: did they want to marry this year? Next? Where would they live? Would Charles continue with his settlement work, or had he thought of something else to do? Marie would sparkle and laugh and kiss Charles's cheek and hug him and say, 'Oh, Mother, dear one, do stop rushing us! We've lots of time yet, haven't we, my angel? I'm not eighteen yet, and Charles isn't all that much more. We'll get round to it. It's just so lovely being engaged, I want to enjoy that.' Charles would just look at her with his face devoid of expression and say nothing.

And of course Marie was right. They *were* both very young to marry. There *was* plenty of time. But surely, Hannah would ask herself, surely that isn't the way young people in love talk? They don't say sensible things like that. They want what they want when they want it. It's just not ringing right, somehow. Not ringing right at all.

She had stifled her anxiety and learned to stifle her questions too, and was a little rewarded when Charles started to work full time as a welfare officer for his settlement, dealing with the needs of the old and ill people as well as the young ones in the Jubilee Street area, becoming busier. He left the house each morning at the same time she and Marcus left for their respective work, leaving Marie to sleep until later, and came home long after they did, on some evenings working until almost midnight. But Marie seemed not to mind his absence too much, and filled her days with shopping and chattering on the telephone with her girlfriends and going to matinees and afternoon concerts. And on the evenings that Charles was working late, she announced she would go with him to his silly old settlement and work too.

'I might as well,' she said, pouting a little, 'Mightn't I, Charles?' She looked at him challengingly, her eyes very bright, and he glanced back and smiled briefly. 'I mean, if he insists on doing such a job what can I do, poor little creature that I am? Put up with it, I suppose!' She laughed, a very merry little sound and began to talk of the dreadfully exciting gossip about her friend's marvellous new fiancé, who was a film actor from California and given to violent attacks of jealousy which made him behave very excitingly indeed. 'She had a black eye yesterday when I saw her at Fortnum's,' she said with great relish. '*Too* marvellous.'

She had been invited to spend the Christmas holiday in Paris with Daphne. Marcus had not been very pleased with the idea. Since his marriage he had seen little of his sister or his brother Rupert, and though he and Hannah did not talk about them, she knew that he found their ways ever more distasteful. She read of Daphne's doings herself sometimes, in the gossip columns, and felt keenly for Marcus, for there was no question but that Daphne had become a very talked about lady indeed. She saw little of her husband and seemed to devote her time to spending her considerable fortune as fast as she could. Her mother, Susan, had persuaded her own father to leave the bulk of his money, made in diamond trading on the Amsterdam bourse, to his only granddaughter, since Susan had been of the opinion that her sons would be well provided for by their Lammeck connections but that her daughter needed extra care. She had died content in the knowledge that her dear Daphne was safe for life, although, Hannah sometimes told herself, she would spin in her grave if she knew the efforts Daphne seemed to be making to spend all she had before she was forty.

Rupert seemed to be no better. Because Marcus had shown himself from his earliest youth to be capable and hard working, while Rupert had been a lazy, butterfly-minded boy from his earliest school days, Ezra, their father, had in his wisdom seen fit to leave the bulk of his money to his younger son before dying in the same 'flu epidemic that had killed his wife. It had been inevitable that the three of them should have split as they had; Marcus had to earn his living. He had done so handsomely, and was now a major shareholder at Lammeck Alley in his own right. He had gained his security by his own efforts. Daphne and Rupert, however, were of a different metal entirely, living lavishly on their income and sometimes even dipping into capital, behaviour that shocked the financial side of Marcus severely. Rupert at least worked sometimes, which redeemed him a little in Marcus's eyes. As a Lammeck he had almost automatically inherited a job at Lammeck Alley, and did in fact come drifting into the office occasionally, to try his hand at being an assistant sales director. His work was of small value but at least he tried, so sometimes Marcus was still hopeful for him. But he still could not approve of his social activities, any more than he could approve of his sister's.

But Marie adored them both, and it was difficult to give her any good reason why she should not spend time with them. They were her stepfather's family, how could they be bad company? There had never been any obvious breach, nothing on which Hannah or Marcus could base an embargo, so dislike the situation though they did they said nothing.

'Better to leave her to get bored,' Marcus counselled. 'Or for them to get bored with her. And anyway, once she marries Charles it will be all right.'

She returned from Paris after Christmas, looking tired and a little drawn in spite of swearing she'd had a super, fantastic, marvellous, glory-making time, while Charles looked paler and thinner than ever. He had worked every night rather than just three or four a week, to keep himself busy while she was away.

Tonight, as she lay in bed beside her peacefully sleeping husband, Hannah tried yet again to convince herself that all was well with her much loved children. Since Christmas it had seemed better, with Marie a little quieter and not so bubbly and Charles less busy at the Settlement and spending

141

more time at home with them all. Hannah had felt better until tonight, when she had come downstairs to check all was ready for the party, to be told by Florrie that Miss Marie had gone out at seven o'clock and never said where she was going, and Charles had come in from his settlement just after, and when he had been told Marie was out, had gone right out again himself.

All through the evening that had nagged at the back of her mind; they had not said definitely that they would be at her special party, but both had known it was important for her and Marcus, a sort of social experiment. It had been taken for granted that the young Lammecks would be there beside the older ones to see it through.

Not a fair assumption, I suppose, she told herself now in the darkness. I shouldn't have taken it for granted. I'm sure they would have stayed in if I'd asked them to.

She slept at last, and woke to the uneasy light of heavy snow on the rooftops opposite her bedroom window. It made her restless, and even though it was still only seven thirty, and she usually did not get up until eight, she slid out of Marcus's sleeping grasp and showered and dressed.

As she came back into the bedroom to sit at the dressing table and put on a little makeup, he woke, and reached out to pinch her bottom approvingly as she passed the bed.

'You're early,' he said, yawning.

'I woke early – couldn't sleep.'

'You should have woken me. I'd have thought of something to keep us busy till breakfast.'

'That was why I didn't. I love you, my darling, but seven in the morning isn't exactly my best time of day ... Marcus ... '

'Mm?' He was out of bed now, padding into the bathroom.

'I've been thinking about Charles. I know there's no way he'll ever work with Lammecks in the office but maybe there's some sort of job you could suggest for him that would let him earn a little more and at the same time feel comfortable? He'll never go into any sort of business of course, but – I thought, this welfare job he does. Don't some of the Lammeck factories use people for jobs like that?'

'Yes, but I doubt he'd agree to take one, and anyway, I'm not sure that I would want him to work for us. We've done quite well with our plants, less trouble with the workers than most of our competitors and I want to keep it that way. Let Charles loose in among 'em and we'll start having unions and strikes and heaven knows what. I love you dearly, Hannah, and I care a lot for Charles, but I'm a business man, remember. There's a limit to what I can do, ought to do, to please you. Anyway, he's happy enough where he is. What difference would it make if he did get another job, anyway?'

'Maybe they could get married,' she said after a moment. 'I know he's got money of his own to live on, and of course Marie has hers, but I don't think Charles will agree to use it. I tried to talk to him about his own money once and he got furious, told me to give it away. As for Marie – ' she stopped. 'I suppose we'll have to tell her now. It's been six weeks since her birthday. She's got a lot of money. Have we any right not to let her know?'

He came back into the bedroom wrapped in his bathrobe, rubbing his newly washed head dry with a towel. 'There's no obligation to tell her,' he said. 'I've talked to Peterson and he agrees with us. The longer it is before she realizes how much she has, the better. And once she does know, Hannah, do you think that will help? If Charles won't live on his own inherited money when he gets married, you can be damned sure he won't live on his wife's.'

She got up and tweaked her skirt into place. 'I suppose you're right. Oh, damn, I wish I could stop fretting over them. It was just ... last night ... '

'I told you, darling. No point in worrying. If there is anything to worry about, you'll know soon enough. Go have breakfast, and read the papers, and stop being a mother hen. You make a better business woman, believe me.'

He was right about one thing. She'd find out soon enough if there was anything to worry about. She found out as soon as she got downstairs.

19

When Hannah came into the dining room Charles was sitting in the window embrasure, staring out at the snow. She blinked and she looked at him for the combination of white furnishings within and the icy glitter from outside dazzled her for a moment. He seemed to be surrounded by little points of light himself and she had to put her hand up to shade her eyes.

'Charles? Have you had your breakfast? No, that's silly of me, Florrie hasn't brought any yet. She shouldn't be long though. Do come and sit down, and tell me what sort of day you had. I haven't seen you since this time yesterday.' *I won't ask him where he was last night, I won't.* 'What happened to that old lady you were telling me about? Did you manage to get the eviction order changed?'

'She's gone,' he said, and his voice sounded flat and very ordinary. There was no special emotion in it, but there was an odd note all the same, and she looked at him sharply.

'Oh, I am sorry, Charles! After all you've done, too.'

Florrie came bustling in with her trolley and began to slap things on the table, toast and the coffee pot and boiled eggs in their neat little cups, complaining bitterly all the while about the coldness of the morning and the iciness of the back steps when she put her foot out to fetch in the milk. Hannah murmured a good morning. Charles said nothing until the door closed behind her. Then still sitting in the window embrasure and still using that same ordinary flat voice he said again, 'She's gone.'

'Yes, I heard you. And I'm sorry.' Hannah began to pour coffee. 'I know you were very worried about her, poor thing. Did you manage to find another room for her? Or did she have to go into the workhouse? I do hope not.'

'Not my old woman,' he said, a little impatient now. 'Marie.'

She put her coffee cup down with a little clatter. 'What did you say?'

'Marie. She's gone.'

144

'Gone? Where?' Absurdly, she looked around the room as though Marie were there somewhere hiding behind the furniture. 'I don't understand.'

He sighed, irritably, as though she were a wilful stupid child he was trying to teach the alphabet, and turned his head to look at her. 'Will Marcus be long? I don't want to have to go through this twice.'

Fear took hold of her, making her belly feel as cold as the street outside.

'Charles! Tell me at once what all this is.' But he ignored her and went to the door and opened it and called, 'Marcus!'

'Coming!' Marcus was already half way down the stairs. 'Good God, boy, no need to hustle me! What's the matter with everyone this morning? It's only quarter past eight, we're no later than we usually are. Earlier if anything. Morning, Charles. Florrie! Bring me some tea, can't cope with coffee this morning. Too much last night, indigestion. Hannah, love, where're the papers? I want to see *The Times*.'

'Marcus, Marie has gone,' Charles said loudly and Marcus stopped at once, standing still like a child playing a game of statues, half bent to sit down.

After a long moment, he sat down, and Hannah, moving automatically, poured a cup of coffee and pushed it at him. She did it every morning, and even though she knew he didn't want it this morning, had heard him ask for tea, she still did it.

'You'd better explain, I think,' Marcus said quietly. 'And Charles, you'll feel better if you come and sit down and have some coffee. Come on, boy.'

Surprisingly, he did, coming to sit in his usual chair between them, facing the empty one which was Marie's, on the rare occasions she took breakfast with them.

'I . . . last night,' he began and then stopped and shook his head. Marcus pushed the coffee cup at him and Charles drank thirstily, spilling the coffee a little on the table cloth, for his hand was shaking.

'I can't start with last night,' he said at length. 'That was just the end of it, really. I – look, I'll tell you all of it, but for Christ's sake, don't interrupt. I couldn't stand that. Questions when I've finished.'

Florrie came in with a teapot and extra toast for Marcus, and they sat in silence till she'd gone and then he started. His

145

voice remained as flat and commonplace as it had been all the time, but underneath it Hannah could feel the painful control in him, and it was that which distressed her almost as much as what he told them.

'It was all right, at first. Marvellous. Happy and all. Talked a lot, we did, about how it was when we were small, and about my mother. She remembered her as much as I did, you see, but different things, and it helped, having her telling me what she remembered. Made Mama more ... complete, you know? I remember her as shadowy bits. Like a jigsaw puzzle with some of the pieces lost. It spoils the picture. And Marie filled in a lot of the pieces for me. That was marvellous. And she let me talk about what mattered to me, about all the bad things there are in the world, and I thought she was learning and beginning to care properly and understand. About how destructive it was to be so rich and comfortable and, well, anyway, I thought she was as happy as I was. But then – '

He stopped and Hannah opened her mouth to say something but Marcus slid his hand under the table and grasped her knee hard, and she closed her mouth again, grateful to him.

'I suppose it was natural she'd get bored. I mean, the settlement work's great for me, but ... she's a girl. Different. And it's mucky sometimes. People smell, you know? They can't always help it and anyway, what does it matter? But it bothered Marie and she said she'd go out with her friends, that she wouldn't bore me having to see them because she knew I loathed 'em and she wouldn't inflict them on me, but that they were her friends and, well, it was a matter of ... of justice and equality, wasn't it? You can't believe things that matter about how people should be treated and not treat the people you love that way. I mean, equality and freedom isn't just for the masses, it's for individuals. Me and you, and Marie. So she wanted to see her friends and I didn't, so I said fine, and she started to go out in the evenings with them while I was working and she said it was great but not to be stuffy and tell you because you'd taken a hate to Rupert and would stop her seeing him just because of some stupid family feud. And I – ' He looked up at Marcus miserably. ' – I believed her.'

Marcus lifted his eyebrows at Charles, clearly asking permission to speak, and Charles nodded. 'No feud,' Marcus said, 'but I can't deny I'm not – I don't think he's a good friend for Marie.'

'Nor did I. I said so, and she said I was stuffy too and we argued ... and then we made it up.' He bent his head and his neck began to redden as a tide of colour rose and Hannah felt another wave of acute embarrassment. *I shouldn't be told this. It's not right I should know. It was something between them.*

'After that – I – what could I do? I'd behaved dreadfully, taking advantage of her. She said I hadn't, though.' He looked at Marcus and it clearly took some courage to do so. 'I – she said that, Marcus. Said that it was more her than me, and that it was only sex and to stop being so stuffy and stupid and old and anyway I – anyway I wasn't the only one who ... But I didn't know what to do. It was the first time for *me*, you see, and – ' He shook his head and then with a curiously childlike gesture rubbed his mouth.

'Well, after that, it was impossible. I couldn't say, don't do this, don't do that, could I? And I couldn't come and talk to you, though I wanted to. Not after what I'd done. I felt filthy. Wicked. Like an oppressor.'

'No,' Hannah said. She could not help it. He couldn't be allowed to go on like that, hating himself. If she had been there with them, seen what had happened, she couldn't have been more certain that he was in no way the instigator in whatever had been between them. 'No.'

He looked at her and for one brief moment managed to smile.

'That's how I felt, anyway. Which is why she's been going around with him these past three months, parties and all, and you thought she was with me. So there it is.'

There was a long silence and then Marcus said carefully, 'And now what? You say she's gone?'

'There's nothing you can do,' he said drearily. 'She married him, you see. In France at Christmas. I didn't know myself till last night. I knew something had happened, because she stopped – I mean, stopped caring whether I said anything to you or not. It helped a bit that. I mean, I'd felt before I was keeping quiet to please her. At least since Christmas it's been to please *you*. I didn't want to upset you, you see. And I couldn't see what difference it'd make if you did know she was going around with Rupert. Making you unhappy wouldn't make me any happier. I think I've known for weeks she wasn't going to marry me. But when she told me last night she'd married *him*, well, that was different.'

'Married,' Hannah said. 'Married. Rupert. Married.'

'In France?' Marcus said sharply. 'Are you sure about that? It was legal?'

'Oh, I think so. I'm sure it was. Daphne helped them, I gather. She's got an apartment there somewhere near the Rue St Denis, hasn't she? Oh, she let them say they lived there and that made it legal. Anyway, it's a proper marriage. They stayed together all through Christmas at the apartment and then ever since – she hasn't always slept at home, you see. It used to drive me wild!' He slammed his elbows on the table so that the dishes rattled and put his face in his hands. 'I knew she was up to something but it never occurred to me that – ' He took a deep breath and sat up again. 'Anyway last night, she got a message from Rupert, it seems, and ran off, and I got worried and went after her because Florrie told me she'd heard Marie tell the cab driver an address and I went there to have it out with her. I thought it was rotten of her to leave last night, you see, what with your party and all and I was going to tell her so. But that bastard Rupert was there, and that was how it all came out.'

'Hannah, I'll look more into this,' Marcus said and leaned over and took her hand in his. 'Please, darling, try not to panic. She's under age and – '

'But what's the point?' she said drearily. 'You heard what Charles said. They went through some sort of legal ceremony in France. And anyway, if it's what she wants, what can we do? What should we do? Charles, I'm truly truly sorry. She's treated you appallingly and I'm sick with shame.'

'No. Aunt Hannah, please don't cry. It isn't your fault! She's just – it's not even Marie's fault.' He was crouching beside her now. 'Please Aunt Hannah, don't cry or I shall too. It's all ... let it be. It's happened. Let it be.'

'What are they going to do?' Marcus asked, and Charles squeezed Hannah's hand and stood up.

'I don't know – well, not for sure. Last night she told me I could – she said she was going to stay with Rupert and I could do what I liked. Tell you or not. She's a married woman now and I can't do anything. So I came away. I walked around for hours. I couldn't come and interrupt your

148

party, could I?'

'*Bloody* party,' Hannah said violently. 'Of course you could. You're more important than any party.'

'Well, I couldn't. And when I did get in you'd gone to bed and your light was off and I thought, why wake you? News like this keeps, doesn't it?'

'Charles. I . . . thank you, Charles,' Marcus said. He put his arms around the boy's shoulders and held him close, hugging him, and after a rigid moment Charles bent his head and began to cry on Marcus's shoulder, silently and helplessly, his shoulders moving clumsily with the savageness of his tears.

Outside the snow began again. Hannah sat and stared out at it and thought of nothing at all but the falling flakes and the way they looped and danced and thudded silently against the glass of the window, and the weight of the grey sky looming over the eerie whiteness of the ground beneath.

'We'll have to go and see them, Hannah,' Marcus said, after Charles had agreed to go up to bed. He'd sat up all night apparently, just sitting and staring out into the square, and now he was exhausted. Hannah had told Florrie, of course; she had to and anyway Florrie had always been part of Marie's life. She had as much right to know as anyone else. She had primmed her mouth and said sharply, 'Well, there was no way she was ever going to do anything to please anyone but herself, mum, and there's an end of it, so don't you go blaming yourself, for no one never had a better upbringing.'

'I suppose so,' Hannah said and then closed her eyes. 'I feel so unnatural, Marcus! She's my daughter and I love her but all I feel is fury at the way she's treated Charles. How could she be so cruel? How could she? And why don't I care more about what she's done, and about her happiness? It's not right.'

'It's right and it's natural,' Marcus said firmly. 'And it's sensible. There's nothing you can do to change Marie. She is what she's always been, and I suspect it was to be. A totally self-centred person, beautiful and vivacious and charming and wholly selfish. It's just one of those things. But Charles is different. And never forget he's as much your child as she is. You may not have borne him, but he is your son.'

'Yes,' she said drearily. 'Yes. And I've got to go and see

Marie and remember she's my daughter. Whatever she's done, she's still my girl.'

'You won't forget,' he said. 'Come on, love. I'll have to go via Lammeck Alley I'm afraid. There are some early appointments I'll have to sort out.'

'And I'll have to call Artillery Lane too,' she said, and rubbed her face distractedly. 'Damn, there are three big deliveries I wanted to be there to see on their way.'

'Then we'll stop there too,' Marcus said calmly. 'Work has to go on, and I doubt she'll be out of bed anyway, much before eleven. She never is here so why should she be in her own home?'

'Her own home,' Hannah said and shook her head wonderingly. 'I can't imagine it.'

When the car drew up in front of the building Hannah sat very still for a moment and then, as Marcus took her gloved hand and squeezed it hard, took a deep breath and smiled at him, albeit a little tremulously, and got out. It was in Sloane Street, a block of modern flats, and a uniformed commissionaire led them through a heavily carpeted lobby towards the ornate gilded lift.

'Expensive,' murmured Marcus, as the lift purred upwards. 'Very expensive. I can't imagine these flats cost much under three hundred a year.'

'Three hundred – are you sure?' Her forehead creased. 'Charles seemed convinced that this was their own flat. Is Rupert that well off?'

'I don't know. He had a sizeable income, but he's been a free agent for a long time now. He's twenty-six, remember. It's been more than five years since I had any involvement in his financial affairs.'

The door was opened by a maid in a very chic French uniform, very lacy and tight and Hannah thought of Florrie in her commodious aprons and how she would sniff at so fancy a creature and was, momentarily, amused. The flat was luxurious. Wide windows overlooked the street, and there were heavy pile carpets, glass and chrome furniture, and very modern paintings on the walls. It was untidy, however, with cushions hurled on the floor and a litter of unwashed glasses and overflowing ashtrays scattered about, which the maid seemed to regard with distaste and an air of unconcern, as though whoever was going to clean up, it would certainly

150

not be she.

They waited in the stuffy room, which smelled of cocktails and stale cigarette smoke, for ten minutes before at last a door opened and Marie came out, her hair rumpled and her face streaked with stale makeup. She was wrapped in a man's dressing gown. She stood and stared at them both for a moment and then made a face.

'Rupert,' she shouted, and kicked the door behind her. 'You'd better come. Storm warning's gone up.'

'There's no need for that sort of attitude, young woman,' Marcus said strongly. 'Let's get that clear for a start. We've come to see if you are well, to sort out what has been happening, and to do so in a civilized manner. There are not going to be any storms of our making. I hope there will be none of yours. I've better things to do with my energy and so has your mother. Is that understood?'

She stood and stared at him for a moment, looking very young suddenly, like a child who has been playing with her mother's makeup. Then she said awkwardly, 'Well, all right, all right. It was just that I thought...'

The door opened again and Rupert came out. He was wearing only pyjama trousers in a heavily brocaded black satin and had a sweater tied by its sleeves round his shoulders. He had a cigarette between his lips and looked half asleep.

'Well,' he said awkwardly and then produced a cheeky grin, trying to look as though he couldn't care less. 'My in-laws, as I live and breathe! Little Boy Blue blew his horn then, did he? Sent you looking for your little Bo Peep?'

'Charles told us that you two are married, if that's what you mean,' Hannah said quietly.

'Damn him,' Marie said viciously. 'I didn't want to make any fuss yet. No need to go meddling.'

'Not a word about Charles, Marie,' Hannah said firmly. 'I won't listen. Now, what is all this? Is it true you're married?'

'Yup!' Rupert said. 'Thought we might as well. Madly romantic and madly wicked. Catholic Church in Paris! How's that going to get to the old biddies round the family, hmm? But it's right and tight and legal, I promise you. Went through all the right French channels, that we did. You can't overset it.'

'I don't intend to try,' Hannah said.

There was a little silence and then Marie said carefully,

151

'You don't? But I thought you'd be furious! Aren't you?'

'I'm hurt,' Hannah said after a moment. 'I didn't think I was so difficult that you had to be so hole-in-the-corner. I didn't think Marcus was so difficult a stepfather either – but angry? What would be the point?'

Marie ran then, like a child, trotting across the room with her face split from side to side with a huge grin. 'Oh, Mama, I do love you! I didn't want to upset you, honestly I didn't, but Rupert said ... Well, you know how you are about him and Daphne, and it was such a lark, and there was the money and all – '

'Money?' Marcus said sharply.

She looked over Hannah's shoulder at him, hugging Hannah hard all the time. 'Well, you didn't tell me, did you? There was I getting a lot from Gramps when I was eighteen, and if Rupert hadn't found out at Lammeck Alley I'd never have known. I thought ... Rupert thought ... '

She faltered and looked back over her shoulder almost fearfully. 'Rupert?' she said.

'Well?' He was leaning against the bedroom door, his arms folded over his bare chest.

'You said, didn't you, they'd try and stop us on account of the money?'

He tilted his head, and squinted at them over the smoke rising from the cigarette between his lips. 'It occurred to me that you might. Why keep it so close to your chest, I asked myself? Is it to make sure the family money stays in the family? To let little old almost-brother Charles get it? It occurred to me – '

Hannah hardly saw Marcus move, he was so fast. Suddenly, he was standing in front of Rupert, his shoulders rigid with fury. She heard the sound rather than saw his hand move, and then Rupert was standing there, one hand to his face and his cigarette smouldering on the carpet at his feet.

'You apologize at once for that,' Marcus said, his voice unrecognizable to Hannah. 'At once, you hear me?'

There was a long silence and then Rupert shrugged sulkily and moved his hand from his face. Hannah could see the red weals left by the contact of Marcus's fingers.

'Well, for Christ's sake, Marcus! We're bloody Lammecks, aren't we? People who go on and on about money all the time! Why should you be any different? If it wasn't so, then it

152

wasn't, and I'm sorry, but you don't have to make such a drama.'

'But I do,' Marcus said, and came back to stand beside Hannah. 'Now listen to me. You two are married. All right, you're married. We won't interfere and can only hope the pair of you can be happy. I'll see to it that Peterson sorts out Marie's finances in such a way that she's protected from you. No, don't you dare say a word! I know about the sort of extravagance you're capable of, and Marie has to be protected. There'll be settlements and arrangements made. I'll see to it that he advises you on finding somewhere better than this to live, where you won't spend such a fortune, and we'll do all we can to see you on the right road. But be warned, Rupert. If ever you do anything to make Marie anything but very happy, I personally will deal with you. Do you understand me?'

There was another silence and then Rupert shrugged and muttered, 'Okay, okay! Leave me alone, will you? I've got a headache. I'm going to take my bath. Stop playing the big brother. Do me a favour, and leave me alone.'

Marie drew back from Hannah then and went back to stand beside Rupert, tucking her hand into his arm.

'It's such fun!' she said and her voice was high and fluting. 'Too too ridiculous. I mean, Mama, you're my sister-in-law now, aren't you? Isn't it too too delicious?'

20

22 Paultons Square,
Chelsea

2 January 1931

Dear Edie,

Well, here I am at last finding a minute to say thank you for the lovely stockings which fitted perfectly, and just the right colour to go with my new gunmetal costume with the coney collar that Madam gave me specially made to measure just like she does every Christmas, as always being very thoughtful. I was glad to hear that Kenneth is well and has got over his whooping cough so nicely, I always said as he was the strongest boy of all your children and would be a credit to us all and so he seems to be turning out what with his scholarship and all. I am sorry to hear your George has been playing about but that's men isn't it, even the best of them though I must say as how our Mr Marcus seems to be a different sort, but for my part I am glad enough I never did marry for all you keep on having a go at me about being an old maid in your letters ha ha! Anyway no need to go on over all that old ground it doesn't make for happy families does it. We go on here much as we always have with You-Know-Who coming to dinner twice this past month and behaving as always very handsome to me and Florrie leaving a very nice gratuity on his way out and when he does get to be King then we'll all be very lucky though not a word of ill would I wish on his father of course but you know what I mean. I cooked him a lovely turbot in hollandaise sauce and an ice pudding and trimmed it all very fancy and Madam said I was the best cook in London and was very nice about how it all went. She looks better now, at last, though she was so peaky poor lady all last year and it wasn't only the way she was after she had come out of hospital having had her operation after that miscarriage, I think it was the sadness of her tragic loss that got to her for after all with her older one behaving so funny it's natural she should want a baby of her own again, but as Florrie says maybe it was for the best seeing as how she's getting on a bit and you do see these funny babies born to older women though Madam isn't only thirty-eight and looks very young with it. We've been very busy here seeing as how Mr Jake and Mr Solly who you will remember are Madam's brothers and keep coming and going have been here over Christmas and all but they are going back to America soon lucky them but they've got their interests there now and doing very nicely it seems, certainly they look very well dressed and fatter than ever they both got a tendency that way not to say I haven't too lately, but as time goes on what can you expect. They say it is all the food they eat in New York and they come into my kitchen sometimes and try to tell me about cheesecakes and such things but I don't pay no attention they are just like you and George great ones for having a go. Mr Solly tells me all the time about the people he meets and he talked to Al Jolson he said and well I was that surprised because Mr Solly says he is a very hard man but in his films he is so lovely. I saw Mammy last week at the Empire Leicester Square and it was lovely I cried and cried do go and see it when it gets to you there in Whitby though of course you'll have to wait a long time Whitby isn't exactly like London is it, my turn for a joke. I will write again soon and will tell them all at Thorpe Bay when I hear from you and do give the children my love and tell your George not to be so silly I will tell him myself when I come to you in the summer.

Your loving sister,
    Bet

Lammeck Alley

17 March 1931

Mr Rupert Lammeck
Sir,

I am in receipt of yours of the 13th inst. and have noted the contents carefully.

I must tell you, however, that your request is not one to which we can accede. As has been explained to you on sundry earlier occasions the Settlements involving your wife's monies cannot be altered in any way except at her request and then only in certain circumstances.

Lammeck Alley

27 March 1931

Mrs Rupert Lammeck
Madam,

I am in receipt of yours of the 19th inst. and have noted the contents carefully.

It is of course possible to do as you request, and arrange earlier remittance of such sums as are due to you in this calendar year, but would respectfully beg that you reconsider your request. You will recall that last year you had drawn all income due for the year before the end of April, and this caused great embarrassment to your Trustees who are loath to act in any way that will jeopardize your long-term interests.

The fact that they had to draw on capital for you to maintain you for the remainder of the year caused great

anxiety among the Trustees and we would sincerely trust
that such a situation will not arise again.

I also trust that your husband can be helped to understand
that matters to do with the Settlements are entirely a matter
between yourself and your Trustees and it is not helpful in
any way when he addresses somewhat vituperative letters to
individual Trustees as he has done in the past.

22 Paultons Square,
Chelsea

11 April 1931

Dear Henk,

Thank you indeed for the cigars – a most welcome
birthday present though I must say being twenty-three
makes me feel exceedingly old. So much to do and a constant
feeling of too little time in which to do it!

You ask about progress here – and I have to admit it is
slow. God knows times are hard enough – people ought to be
recruitable, for ever since the Wall Street debacle money has
become tighter and tighter in the East End. But however
much we talk to them we don't seem to be getting through.
Street meetings get only desultory attention, organized hall
meetings get even less, which leaves only door to door. We
aren't helped too much by the activities of a new breakaway
group from the Labour Party either. They're trying door to
door recruitment, too, and seem to have a certain appeal we
don't, probably because they don't have any connection with
the old Bolshevik scandals of the past which linger on in
people's minds here and frighten them. It's little use telling
them we're different, they just don't seem to believe us. So
Mosely's lot, that is the new group, seem to be making
headway. I'll be watching their development most carefully.

I've heard from my stepfather through some of his connections that a cousin of his, who married into a German
family (von Aachen they're called, do you know them?) has
become involved with the German National Socialists, and
that there is a possibility of their man Hitler getting support
from the industrialists. They mentioned someone called
Hugenberg. I'd be most interested to know of anything you
pick up.

No, I am *not* returning to Yeshivah. That was, I now

156

realize, just a stage in my political development. I needed it, but I no longer do. My commitment now is entirely to the Party, and that being so I cannot involve myself in Talmudic studies however intellectually seductive they may be. Indeed, the more seductive they are, the more important it is that I keep well away. There is work to be done, and it must be done soon. I can't indulge myself with religion. It's a false comfort and saps energy from what most matters. But we've been through all this before, Henk, my dear old friend. Please let us not be deflected by such arguments now. We're much too good friends for that, and are in step with so many other important issues. My love to Miep,

    Yours ever,
    Charles

                        Hotel Magnifique,
                        Ostend,
                        Belgium
                        24 August 1933

Dear Uncle Alex,

    Just a line to let you know what a marvellous time we are having. We've taken over almost a whole floor here, as you can imagine, and with people in and out of each other's rooms all the time we're getting known as the crazy Englesi among all these French and Germans and what have you! The children are having a lovely time on the beach every day and we are too and the weather though not marvellous is thank God not so bad we can't have a good time. Charlotte's Monty isn't too well still, but then he always was a bad traveller, you'll remember the first time you sent us all on holiday it was the same. I'm sending you a card with this letter showing you our rooms in the hotel. I've marked them all with crosses and names so you can see we're really getting value for money. Believe me, Uncle Alex, we're all very appreciative, and please God you'll be able to come with us next year.

    Much love from Charlotte and Monty and children, Bella and Harry and children, and of course from David and Lionel, as well as me,

    Your loving niece,
    Sonia

WESTERN UNION CABLEGRAM NEW YORK NY 165AT
LIONEL LAZAR SHOREDITCH TOWN HALL LONDON
ENGLAND NOVEMBER 17TH 1933 PREPAID

MAZELTOV ON YOUR BARMITZVAH STOP MAY YOUR
FUTURE BE ALL YOU WISH YOURSELF STOP SORRY
CANNOT BE WITH YOU STOP MUCH LOVE UNCLES
SOLLY STOP JAKE

GPO GREETINGS TELEGRAM DIDSBURY MANCHESTER
NOVEMBER 17TH 1933 LAZAR SHOREDITCH TOWN HALL

MAZELTOV AND LOVE TO YOU DAVID AND SONIA ON
THIS SPECIAL DAY STOP MAY YOUR LIONEL BE ALL A
SON SHOULD BE STOP REGRET CANNOT BE WITH YOU
ON YOUR SIMCHA STOP URGENT BUSINESS IMPOSSIBLE
STOP CHEQUE FOLLOWS STOP LOVE UNCLE ALEX

News Chronicle Gossip Column, 1 January 1935

The New Years Honours List published today includes the name of Marcus Lammeck, Managing Director and senior partner of the noted city firm of Lammeck and Sons. His knighthood is regarded as long overdue by many of his City colleagues who know him to be a man of great integrity and dedication. Sources close to the new Sir Marcus whisper that it is his friendship with the Prince of Wales that has made him unwilling to accept this long overdue mark of appreciation for his services to business for fear he would be marked down as a mere courtier. However, the Prince prevailed upon him we are told as did many of his friends, pointing out that no one who knows Sir Marcus can be in any doubt of his fitness for such an honour. Lady Lammeck, who is the noted couturiere Mary Bee, is said to be pleased for her husband but will not be using her title in her own business. The family is not new to titles, of course, for that vivacious and well-known lady-about-town, Countess of Markmanor, whose husband the Earl is currently wintering in Italy, is Sir Marcus' sister. Last night, interviewed at the Kitcat Club Lady Daphne, was in the company of Beverley La Vere, who is dazzling West End audiences with his neat footwork in the chorus of Cole Porter's 'Anything Goes' at the Palace Theatre . . .

Dear Edie,

Well, I am sorry not to have answered yours sooner, but you didn't have to write so sharp to me just because I had missed one letter. When you don't know what is happening then you can't really say can you and you made me very upset the way you wrote and I had to stop Florrie writing to you very sharp indeed she was that upset at the way you made me cry but never mind I am used to being misunderstood by you Edie and really it's time you stopped to think before sounding off like that. I will tell you what has been happening and then perhaps you will understand why I have had no time or heart for letter writing of my own though if you read the papers properly you would have seen something about it I am sure and would understand and not write nasty to me. Anyway it started when our Mr Charles got very upset about this here Spanish War and was all set to go and fight though as I said to Florrie what business it is of his I really don't know but Madam was upset and asked him please not to it was bad enough his Dad was killed in the Great War and to please her would he keep out of it and he said he would but it was clear as a window he was very upset and was going to go anyway sooner or later and as I said to Florrie better sooner I'm sure because I remember last time that those who went early and got small wounds didn't die the way the young ones as went later did as well I remember because of Sam Chambers as I was going out with in 1915 as you'd remember if you had any heart instead of twitting me about having old maid ideas. Anyway, that is neither here nor there because as I say Mr Charles stayed here at home but was fretting dreadful you couldn't help but see it though he was going out every night as usual to all his meetings in the East End though why he doesn't find a nice girl and settle down I can't say. Then there was this dreadful march in the East End all those blackshirts and we was all that upset well you can imagine. I know you say some nasty things about Jews but I say speak as you find and my Madam has always been as kind and thoughtful as anyone could be and as I say to Florrie many's the time she's the most Christian lady I ever had to do with, speaking of kindness and good manners and that, anyway I was very upset because even those cousins of Madam that come here and aren't all you might expect such a lady as her to have have always been good to me and live and let live I say, and why have marchers in the Mile End Road got to go making trouble like that? It was big trouble too because the young Jews took it bad as is natural and turned out and fought them and of course our Mr Charles was there and it was just like last time only worse, you'll remember all those years ago I told you what happened in the General Strike when he got so hit about and got his nose broken which quite spoiled his face he used to be such a beautiful baby. This time he got hit even harder and his wrist got broken and the trouble was it was policemen he got fighting with because he said they was making it easy for them blackshirts instead of understanding that peaceable Jews got a right to live in their homes like any other Englishmen and Englishmen they are I don't care what you say. So of course there was big trouble and he was arrested and come to court and you must have seen it in the papers they was full of it with the *Daily Mail* being very nasty on account he's got such rich relations and the *News Chronicle* taking his side, it was all very upsetting one way and another because we had all those reporters coming here like anything. And then when he got home from the hospital Miss Marie was here with her husband who I can't like, it's no good he really puts my back up but she loves him I suppose so what can you say, well, they was here because Miss Marie had had a fight with him, Rupert I mean, and come home to her mum as she always does when it happens and it happens a bit too often that I can tell you, but she always goes back to him more fool her. And he'd come here to get her because they'd made it up. Anyway home comes our Mr Charles and I made a lovely dinner to celebrate, a really beautiful rib roast with a Yorkshire pudding it really was one of my best as light as you can imagine and there they are as happy as can be I thought and all of a sudden there's such a noise from the dining room and me and Florrie goes rushing up and there they are fighting on the floor, Rupert and Charles and it was dreadful with Marie crying and Sir Marcus as white as I've ever seen him he was that angry and to cut a long story sideways young Mr Charles is going to Spain after all and Marie and Rupert is going to live in America because he says there's going to be big wars again in Europe and he wants to get away while he can and why don't we get out he says so you can see what a nasty object he is. I'm glad to see the back of him though Madam is very upset on account of losing her Marie as she sees it, but I said to her, it's not the end of the world exactly, and she'll come home and don't our Mr Jake and Mr Solly keep coming and going between here and America but she's still that upset ...

35 East Thirty-Fifth Street,
New York,
USA

1 November 1936

Dear Hannah,

Hope this finds you as it leaves me, in the pink. Don't worry about our Charles. He'll come out on top, he always has, hasn't he? I hope we can visit come the New Year. Jake thinks it's possible, business here is beginning to pick up with bigger takes though the real money's gone out of boxing, as I was telling Uncle Alex when he was last here. It was good to see him, he's looking very well, I thought. I enclose a cutting from a newspaper here, very interesting isn't it? Do tell me what Marcus says, seeing he's a friend of his and all. People here keep asking me because I'm English, but I say to them from where should I know? Still it would be nice to have a bit of news so do ask Marcus. I'll look forward to hearing from you.

Your loving brother,
Solly

New York Post Gossip Column, 20 October 1936

Royal circles in Britain are still in a great turmoil, a little bird tells me, over our Mrs Wallis Simpson and the Prince of Wales. Will she be Queen Wallis, everyone is asking themselves, though not of course the ordinary British people who are being kept totally in the dark ...

Hotel Bristol
Nice

12 December 1936

Darling,

I'll be leaving here tonight, train to Paris, to sort out some financial matters for David, and then should be home by the weekend. I miss you – he's coping well enough, and she seems to be calmer now. It's been a horrible business and I'd rather have had no part of it, but he asked me, and I'm sorry for the poor devil. If someone had tried to stop me from marrying you, I'd have done the same, of course, so who am I to judge him? But all the same I'm sick about it. Still, we managed to get him away well enough from Fort Belvedere and he was grateful. I got some news out of Spain, so this expedition was as good for me as it was for David, since I discovered that Charles is *fine*. He's been given a staff job because his wrist is still weak and that's something to be grateful for. He was in Madrid when the attack came – Moroccans and Foreign Legionaires mostly I gather – but they evacuated the rebel staff and he went with them so he's safe and looks to stay so. Try not to fret, my darling. I'll be home as soon as I can.

The Times, 27 February 1939

Today both Britain and France formally recognized General Franco's government in Madrid.

News Chronicle, 7 March 1939

British members of the International Brigade are seen in this picture returning from Madrid. Inset – wounded men accompanied by British VADs

28A Southbridge East,
Tiburon,
San Francisco, Calif.

3 January 1940

Darling Ma,

Yes I know I should have written sooner but really, life is too too hectic. We spend so much time driving up to Hollywood, and it takes all day and then some, but *such* fun, we see a fair bit of all sorts of interesting people. Met Cary Grant last week, too divine. I think you'd adore him, I know I do, and then there was a party with Claudette Colbert, lots of lovely gossip, which I'll write to you as soon as I have the time. Rupert's behaving rather well at the moment, because he really feels this is where we belong, you know, so much our sort of world and people are saying he could actually get some sort of work in films! He'd like that and I'd be green with envy, but there it is. Who wants a swollen pregnant female on their screens? Never mind, as soon as the baby's born I'll see what I can do – and do stop fussing, Ma! Of course I'll be all right. People have had babies before, though I can't imagine why they bother, it's so boring, isn't it? Hope you keep well and there's no bad war news. Rupert was right, wasn't he? We got out just in time.

21

'It feels so *ridiculous*,' Hannah said, staring down at the cable in her hand. 'I mean, I'm actually a grandmother! Knowing it was going to happen didn't mean much, but now it has I feel so odd.'

'Why should you be any different?' Cissie said comfortably. 'I got three o' the little *mumserim*, God bless 'em. Such lobbuses! My Lenny told me, last week, Stanley got sent home from school for selling aeroplanes.'

'Aeroplanes?' Hannah was diverted momentarily.

'Sure. Paper ones his sister made him. Sold 'em for tuppence each to the other kids and told 'em they'd protect 'em from the raids when they came. Right little villain he is.'

'He'll go far,' Hannah said absently and stared again at the cable. 'She doesn't say anything, just that it's a girl. No birth weight, no name, nothing.'

'Oh, Hannah, when'll you learn?' Cissie said. 'That Marie of yours, she's a naughty girl! Not a letter have you had from her for months and months, she just don't care. No good fretting over it. That's the way she is.'

'Yes,' Hannah said and tucked the cable in her pocket, smoothing it carefully first. 'I suppose so. Still, she let me know about the baby. That's something.'

They went on with the packing in silence, though Cissie coughed occasionally as the dust rose from the folds of fabric, and Hannah looked at her anxiously. She was looking haggard these days, every minute of her fifty years, and was a little thinner than she used to be, but she had refused to see a doctor and there was little Hannah could do to make her.

'That's it then.' Cissie straightened her back and looked around the empty showroom. 'They can take this as soon as they like. I'll do a check, shall I?'

'I'll come too,' Hannah said. Cissie looked at her sharply and said nothing, but nodded and together they came out of the workroom and began to go from floor to floor down through the old house.

It looked mournful in the June sunshine thrown through the tall windows, the pale patches on the walls where pictures had hung and bare boards on the stairs where once the thick pile carpets had been. Mirrors, drapes, everything had gone, packed up and sent for storage out to High Wycombe.

'Although,' Hannah had said, 'Why High Wycombe should be any safer than London, I don't know. They could as easily bomb there as here.' But they had gone on, systematically stripping the Buckingham Palace Gate house of every sign that Mary Bee Couturiere had filled it with busyness and work and purpose for fifteen years.

'That's it, then,' Cissie said when at last they stood on the steps. 'I'll be here in the morning with the keys to let the men pick the stuff up, and then I'll leave the keys at Artillery Lane. When will you be there?'

'As soon as I get through at Whitehall. It looks as though its going to be ATS uniforms, rather than WAAF ones.'

Cissie grimaced. 'Pity. I like blue better than khaki. That was one thing about the last do. Striped print and red and blue capes – it was a pleasure to work on, sort of. This time, all khaki – oh, well, *was machst du*? That's the way it is. *G'ey g'zint* Hannah. See you tomorrow.'

Hannah watched her go and thought again how ill she looked, and made up her mind to phone Lenny tonight. A good boy, Cissie's Lenny, successful and busy in his accountancy office, for Cissie had done him proud when it came to education, and living in great comfort in a handsome solid house in Willesden with his handsome solid wife and handsome solid children; a good boy who cared still about his mother, although his wife sniped at her a good deal, finding her East End voice and her raucous East End manners offensive to her sense of propriety. Nice Jewish women didn't behave like that, Lenny's wife thought, and was busy rearing her two daughters to be nice Jewish girls with a liking for silk underwear and respectable addresses and refined accents and disdain for their tough old grandmother.

Grandmother, Hannah thought now, as she turned and began to walk up towards the park. I'm a *grandmother*. It doesn't seem to bother Cissie, it never did, but maybe it's different when you actually see your own grandchild, hold her, know her.

She remembered herself suddenly, with the baby Mary Bloomah in her arms, sitting on a box in the ice cold dimness of the Antcliff Street house, feeding her, a memory so sharp she almost felt the small mouth pulling on her nipple, and she shivered, in spite of the warm sunshine, pulling her jacket across her chest and walking faster.

The park was lovely, alive with people on this hot afternoon, and she let the smell of hot crushed grass and roses and syringa drift into her, enjoying the way the heat came and went on her face as she moved under the trees with their great leaf carapaces. Even the busy squads of men toiling over the digging of trenches and the filling of earth bags couldn't detract from the loveliness of the afternoon; and she wouldn't let them. They had lived with doubt and fear and then let-down for almost a year now. They had steeled themselves for bombs that had not come, and for battles which had not erupted, and now all the preparations seemed rather pointless, and far from alarming.

Even when she was at Whitehall, sitting in those vast echoing offices with those polite murmuring men talking about the methods of supply and collection that would be used when she started her uniform making again, she could not believe in this war. It wasn't like last time, when the casualty lists and the constant flurry of wounded soldiers at the railway stations were a constant reminder of what was going on over the Channel. This time it was different, a nothing war, an empty war. They were getting ready for nothing, nothing at all.

But as she reached the far side of St James's Park and began to walk towards Admiralty Arch, she knew she was deluding herself, and she knew why. It was a real war. Germany had moved into Holland two months ago now, and since then there had been nothing. Silence, total silence and the only way she could cope with it was by pretending it wasn't so. Really, he wasn't there, her Charles. He had not gone there to see Henk and make plans for joining the left wing forces in Germany. He hadn't told her that he had heard of things happening to Jews in Germany that had to be taken seriously, had to be dealt with. It wasn't true, it couldn't be. She had told him that, passionately, when the first refugees had begun to arrive, filling people's heads with tales of persecution.

'I don't believe it,' she said. 'They look all right, well fed and dressed and, they aren't like the people I knew in the bad days, Charles! Then they hadn't clothes to call their own, hardly, when they arrived at Tilbury with just a bag of bits and pieces, and starving into the bargain! These are cultured people, well fed,' she repeated. 'It's not true, it's not *true*.'

But of course it was. The old fires were smouldering again just as they had when her father had been a boy, at home in the shtetl in the old Pale, so long ago. For months now, even before Hitler had marched into Poland, they had been busy, the Lammeck and Damont women, the Rothschilds and Sassoons and Abrahams, the rich and safe ones, collecting money, arranging for friends to be scooped up and brought out of Germany and Poland and Czechoslovakia and Lithuania and Estonia and wherever else they could. It was bad and might get worse yet.

'No,' she whispered into the trees above her head in St James' Park as she walked on, faster, ignoring the way the exercise beaded her upper lip with sweat. 'No. It's all right. He's going to be all right. He'll come home soon.'

She tried to see him, tried to imagine him coming up through Paultons Square towards number 22, his curly hair riffling in the breeze, his injured leg kicking out to the left as it had ever since the battle of Teruel in Spain, when his knee had been shattered by rifle fire and been left permanently stiff. At least that had brought him safe home then, and though she had wept for him she had been glad too, for it meant, she had told herself, an end to it all. He would stay here, be ready to admit he'd done enough, might even learn to forget Marie and be happy with someone nice, marry, have babies.

But of course it wasn't like that. He wasn't going to come home to Paultons Square for he was still there in Holland, had been there almost six months, and there had been a total silence from him since May 10th.

Germans in Amsterdam. Soldiers with rifles and heavy grey helmets and heavy grey uniforms and heavy grey faces in Amsterdam. She could not imagine it, and tried to distract herself from her fears by remembering the Amsterdam she had fallen in love with in the spring of 1935 when Marcus had taken her there for one of their rare holidays.

They had taken the car, the big Bentley, crossed the Channel at Dover and had driven briefly through the north of France and on through the Flemish countryside to the Netherlands and the bulb fields. She could still remember it, the sea of colour and the great waves of scent that had broken over their heads. She had been drunk with daffodils, giddied with hyacinths and tulips and jonquils and narcissus and by the time they had passed Rotterdam and the Hague and come rolling through the flatness into Amsterdam she had been giggling and silly and he too had been skittish, making dreadful puns and roaring with laughter at them.

They had gone on like that all the time they were there, behaving like silly children as they walked through the streets of Amsterdam, leaning over the canal bridges to watch the barges beneath. The bells of the Westerkerk, as they walked slowly along the Prinsengracht, had made her cry deliciously, not a sad crying, but a happy moist emotionalism that, he told her, laughing, was sheer chocolate-boxery and she had laughed as well as cried and told him he was absolutely right, and that she was full of tinsel too, and held his hand and walked on over the cobbles, deeply happy.

And now there were German soldiers in those tall thin houses with the bell gables and the hooks above to carry up goods to the high floors, and in the restaurants with the fat waiters who waddled everywhere, almost falling over their too-long white aprons, and at the herring stalls on the corners of the bridges and in the Dam Square and on Waterlooplein.

And in the tight narrow streets of the old city where the Jews lived. They had gone, she and Marcus, almost accidentally to a service at the Spanish and Portuguese synagogue at the Jonas Daniel Miejerplein, not because either of them was particularly anxious about synagogue attendance, but because they had happened to be walking there that Saturday morning and seen the people go in, dressed in their best hats

167

and shining with soap and virtue, and almost without consulting each other had followed them. They had parted, she to sit in the gallery above and he to sit below in a borrowed *tallis* and his very English bowler hat on his head, and listened dreamily to the singing and prayers and come out blinking into the noonday sunshine, responding happily to the nods and smiles of the other congregants, and gone to eat a vast Dutch lunch which was anything but kosher with no sense of guilt or embarrassment. It had all felt so right, so comfortable, so natural. As she walked now through St James's Park in London five years later, where men in khaki sweated over filling bags with earth ready to protect buildings when the German bombs came, she remembered those Dutch people in their half circle city of water and cobblestones and bells and tried to imagine it filled with German soldiers. And could not. It was as though her mind could not take hold of the vision of that water-shimmering city being anything but flower filled and carillon-echoing and happy in the sunshine, and she knew she felt so because of Charles. While Amsterdam remained in her mind a peaceful place it was possible to face the fact, the cold bitter fact, that Charles was there and had not sent word since May 10th.

She reached Whitehall in time to almost collide on the steps with Marcus, who had arranged to meet her there. They went together to the third floor of the War Office, where they were to settle the plans for turning Artillery Lane into a uniform factory again. He looked a little pale. She took his arm and held it close for a second, and he smiled at her reassuringly.

'Darling, I've had a cable,' she said.

'Marie?'

'A girl. That's all it says. Nothing else. It came from Los Angeles, not San Francisco, so you were right, they have moved. I wish they'd let me know!'

'She's still getting her money through all right,' Marcus said, and squeezed her hand. 'We'll hear soon enough if there's anything really wrong. At least they let us know about the baby, Grandma Hannah! Never mind, darling, I still love you.' He kissed her cheek briefly, somewhat to the shock of a passing clerk, and led the way into the office.

They went afterwards to one of Uncle Alex's tea shops in the Strand and sat opposite each other sipping the thick brown brew that had made so large a part of Uncle Alex's fortune. After a while she put her cup down and said, 'Marcus – I think we're going to have to move, don't you?'

He looked at her briefly and smiled. 'I knew if I waited you'd see it. It's not going to be easy if the bombing does start, and – well, it's a responsibility. I thought it might be better to try to fix a flat somewhere nearer the factory.'

She grinned at him. 'Psychic. As ever. I talked to Cissie about it. We can convert half the top floor into quite a neat flat, she says. Now's the time to do it while there are still some people around to do some work. Marcus, I'm not wrong, am I? It is going to get worse, isn't it?'

'Yes,' he said after a moment, and put down his cup. 'Yes. I've been talking to people, War Office and Defence. There's no question of it. Dunkirk was a bad business, bloody marvellous but bad. And Hitler's sure to follow it up. The ones in the know are getting ready for a big push. Quite what it'll be we don't know, but it'll be big. So, we've got to make plans accordingly. And being near the factory is a good plan.'

'Is it near enough for you? To Lammeck Alley, I mean?'

'I'll be spending more time in Whitehall than Lammeck Alley,' he said. 'I ... ' He looked at her sideways. 'I tried to join the air force but they wouldn't have me. I'm young enough, just, but they had another job for me.'

'Thank God,' she said and closed her eyes. 'Oh, Marcus, I'd have ... how could you without telling me? After last time, I – ' she shook her head, her throat filling with tears so that she couldn't speak.

'I know. That's why I had to try. As it is, I'm getting a uniformed job, but they'll never let me out of London, so don't panic. Army. They're putting me in as a major. Supply and munitions.'

He reached over the table and took her hand.

'If ... if they try to send you to France ... ' she shook her head again, still choked and this time he laughed, gently.

'Darling, it isn't that kind of war any more. No one's digging trenches in Flanders or round the Marne. They've pushed us out of France, and it's going to be a long time before we get back there. I'm certain of that. We won't sort the Germans out in mud baths this time. This time it'll be different, God help us all. And I'll stay in London, where I'll be safe, with you. As safe as any of us can be, I promise.'

22

'All right, all *right*,' Cissie said distractedly, and reached for a rag from the pile in the corner to wipe the woman's face and then hugged her briefly. 'I know what it's like, believe me I know. Mine went last week. But they're better off gone, believe me, better off.'

The woman sniffed again, thickly, and began to weep once more, the tears rolling down her face unchecked. Cissie looked at Hannah and grimaced.

'Let her go home,' Hannah said softly. 'She'll be better off there. Let Milly go with her.'

They sent the woman home, and the machines began to whirr again, but the pall of emotion still hung over the wide factory floor. It had been a dreadful morning, and Hannah shared the woman's misery even though she herself had not had a child involved in the exodus.

They had gone from Stepney Green station, the children, all those over five, with their big handwritten labels tied to their coats and their gas masks in cardboard boxes strung over their shoulders and bouncing on their bottoms as they walked and their suitcases and bags of food and sweets and apples clutched in their hands. They had looked bewildered, some of them, and a few had been crying but most of them were just as children always were, noisy, excited by the fuss going on around them, unaware of what it all meant, even the big ten- and eleven-year-olds. All was orderly until the evacuation officials herded the children off down to the platform and onto the trains and refused to let the mothers seeing them off come any further, when one by one the women burst into wailing. The children, looking back, saw then what was happening, and began to cry too, and then it was an inferno of noise, of sobs and shouts and tears, and a few children turned and ran back, dodging under the officials' arms, and found their mothers and clung to them and refused to go. Hannah saw one look at her child, a black-ringleted plump little girl of about seven, and then, sideways, at the other mothers around her and begin to back away out of the crowd, taking her child with her.

'I don't care!' she had cried shrilly as one of the evacuation officials came bustling up to try and take the child away from her. 'I don't care, they ain't sent no bombs yet, have they? So they won't send none now! And even if they do, it's better we should be together. A bomb's got your name on it, what difference you're here or you're in Devon? It's got your name on it! My Shirley's staying here with me.'

But there had been only two or three like that. The train had pulled out with its load of labelled children and the women had been left standing on the bridge watching the empty rails glinting in the sunshine and then, slowly, gone back to their homes or to their jobs. Hannah had been there to help transport the children of her workers from Spital-fields, and now she filled the car with the mothers who belonged to her and drove them back, silent, trying not to think of Marie and her baby, of Charles, of Cissie's three grandchildren now on their way to America, of all the other shattered families who were almost the first casualties of this war.

Life had become unbearably hectic as she tried to run the factory while reorganizing so many other aspects of daily living. The Paultons Square house had been closed. Bet had gone to live with her sister Edie and her husband in Whitby ('And I know it's a sin and a crime to say it, but I don't like her, I reely don't, not the way I like you and Florrie,' she had wept. 'But I got to go, because they can't run their business now the boys 've gone to the army and George's heart isn't what it was so I got no choice, but oh, Mum, I'm that miserable.') and Florrie had set to work to make the flat at the top of the factory habitable.

It was tiny, with just a small living room and a bedroom for Marcus and Hannah and a boxroom for Florrie to sleep in with a slip of a kitchen alongside. Florrie grumbled mightily about it all, but coped, somehow, and Hannah and Marcus had moved in one lunch hour, so that they would lose as little working time as possible. The furniture had been put into storage, and so had the silver and china and all the ornaments and paintings they had collected over the fourteen years of their marriage, leaving the flat spartan and cheerless; but they were there so rarely, only sleeping and eating, that they hardly noticed.

Hannah had put the factory on a three shift system in order to increase output and from five a.m., when the machines went on as the first workers arrived, until midnight, when they were switched off at the end of the third shift, she was there supervising the cutting, the distribution, the sewing and the finishing, as well as dealing with the usual office work. Cissie had tried to argue to say she would work longer hours but Hannah had been adamant.

'You know what the doctor said. You can keep out of a sanatorium if you promise to work only three hours a day. So that's all you're working.'

But it wasn't easy without her, for there was no one else so reliable, and Hannah went doggedly on, working all the hours she could, growing more and more tired. And it was not only the factory. There were the firewatching rotas too. Someone had to sit on the roof each night, wrapped in heavy blankets in the corrugated iron lean-to, dozing uneasily over flasks of tea, waiting for warnings to sound so that they could leap up and go to lean over the parapets and watch for the tell-tale gleams of smoke which showed where incendiaries had landed. Hannah took her own turn with Marcus, one night a week. And then there was the canteen, her bit of special war work, she called it, looking after the air raid wardens who spent the nights waiting for the warnings to go on.

And behind all that, the anxiety about the rest of the family. Not just Charles and Marie, but her brothers too. They had sent anxious letters and telegrams many times during the first months of the war, trying to decide whether to come home. Their barrage of doubts and questionings, going on and on, had been irritating for Marcus.

'If they want to stay put, they should stay and stop nagging us about it,' he had snapped one morning, when they had been awakened from their exhausted sleep at an unconscionably early hour by the ringing of the telephone, so that yet another of Solly's cables could be dictated by a bored operator. 'I'm damned if I'm going to salve their consciences for them. Talk to Uncle Alex about it, for God's sake, Hannah.'

She had, pushing her way into his office one Monday morning through crowds of chattering singers and dancers and actors. She had been startled to find him so besieged, and had said so, and he had laughed at her hugely, taking his cigar from his mouth with an expansive gesture, waving it about.

'ENSA, dolly! I got myself involved with ENSA, well, sort of ENSA. Last time round it was catering, right? And I tell you something, I reckon I taught them a thing or two at the War Office on account of this time they don't need that sort of help. They got it organized already. And anyway, I'm getting on a bit now! Why should I kill myself doing work that ain't no fun no more? Catering ain't no fun no more, but this business, show business, that's different! That I like. I tell you the truth, if it wasn't I got my seventieth birthday past me, I'd go back to the old song and dance bit myself. I wasn't so bad when I was a boychick! But fifty years ago and now – it's different. But I still got my theatre interests, ain't I? I got my health and strength, ain't I? I got my connections, ain't I? There ain't many people knows so many people as I do. I can put a show together overnight with such stars, such style, such artistry, I can't be touched! So I went along to Drury Lane, told Basil Dean what I reckoned I could do, so he got me going, said I could look after the civilian side. I sent three shows last week to factories in the North and Midlands, lovely little shows they was, a singer or two, coupla novelty acts. Now I'm working up another couple for the evacuees, come Christmas.'

She laughed, at his own pleasure in his accomplishments, happy for a moment. Whatever happened, wars and tragedies, wandering children, lost homes, whatever happened Uncle Alex remained unchanged, even though he was now past seventy. She went round his desk and hugged him and he grinned at her and patted her cheek and for a moment or two they clung together in a bubble of contentment, pleased with themselves and each other.

But when she told him of her anxiety about her brothers, he shook his head crossly.

'Such *schlemiels*! I tell you they got no more sense than a pair of babies! I sent 'em to New York originally to get 'em outa your hair, to set themselves up, and now look at 'em! Can't think for themselves. I'll send 'em some cables'll make their hair stand on end.'

'Saying what? Come home or stay put?'

'Stay put,' he said crisply. 'They got to be outa their bleedin' minds not to. What good will they be here, either of 'em?'

Yet still she was, deep down, distressed that was how it

had turned out. Of course it was better that Jake and Solly should stay in New York. She had no home to offer them, and as Alex said, what good would they be here? Both too old for the army, even Solly who was two years her junior. They would be an additional worry, yet she felt obscurely that it would be better if they were all together. The war was a bad one, was going to get worse; they all ought to be *together*.

It was not only Jake and Solly's absence that disturbed her; it was the distress of her aunts and uncles and cousins as the younger members of the family were scattered. Young Lionel, David's son, had joined the army; at nineteen he was a tall well set-up lad, full of energy and pride in himself, for had he not passed his matriculation with flying colours and started to study law at London University? First he would fight in the army, he had told David and Sonia and old grandfather Benjamin, and then come back to finish his studies and be the first judge in the Lazar family. Reuben and Minnie's children and grandchildren too, had scattered, some going to the army and some sent away as evacuees. The East End seemed to shrink as the young faces disappeared. There were just the very old, and all the women and the babies; it seemed to Hannah sometimes like a ghost of its former self, the streets too empty, too quiet.

But life went on, somehow, as they went about their day to day work, waiting for – what? Since Dunkirk people had been sure that invasion was inevitable. Hitler had taken so much already, Norway and Denmark following Holland and Poland and France and most of the rest of Europe into his bag; why should he stop now? Twenty-two miles of Channel was all there was between him and us, the wiseacres told each other in pubs and tea shops and factory canteens, why should that stop him?

But it seemed to as a blazing June became a heavy July. The news picked up a little, as British bombers began night attacks on Germany, and that cheered some people, though Marcus shook his head when Hannah repeated to him the talk of the factory floor. 'They'll hit back,' he said wearily. 'Soon. They know it at the War Office. Very soon.'

It seemed to start almost casually, one hot August night after another, with the sirens throwing their ululating cry into the dark sky just at the time, everyone grumbled, when people had gone to bed to try to get some sleep. They tumbled out into their shelters, wrapped in sheets, or, sometimes, fancy outfits especially made to be 'Chic in the Shelter' as exhorted by the women's magazines, made cups of tea over primus stoves and then went stumbling back to bed when the all clear sounded, complaining bitterly because there had been so little reason to get up in the first place. 'Nuisance raids,' the papers dubbed them and everyone agreed, coming to work bleary eyed for lack of sleep, 'all because of them bleedin' sirens, shan't pay no never mind to 'em again, I shan't,' the workers told Hannah, and she shook her head at them and told them firmly that they should.

And then, in September, it all burst over their heads. It was a hot Saturday afternoon when the factories had closed for the well earned weekend break and Hannah had twenty-four hours of relaxation to look forward to before she had to go off to the canteen for her Sunday night stint. She had undressed to bathe herself in the woefully tiny bathroom that had been rigged up for them in their stuffy rooftop flat, and had just tied the sash of her bathrobe when she heard the sound begin, that familiar whine, starting far away to the East and then, very swiftly, taken up nearer and nearer, until the siren based on the fire station around the corner began, almost deafening her.

For a moment she stood there, tempted to ignore it; just another damned nuisance raid, that was all it was, surely? But then she remembered Marcus's anger when someone in the factory had challenged his insistence that they always take shelter whenever the sirens went. She sighed, and dressed again, irritable and sweatier than ever. If only Marcus was here! But he had had to go to Whitehall for a specially convened meeting to do with aircraft production. Florrie was out too, on one of her rare jaunts to the West End, little enough though there seemed to be to buy these days. Hannah made her way out of the flat, on her way to the steps and the shelter, alone.

She stopped though, at the top of the stairs, her head tilted listening to the sounds; the distant rumble of guns, and behind it a deeper more even burring that was something new. She frowned sharply and after a moment turned and went running up the last flight of stairs to the roof, to stand and stare out over to the east at the warm afternoon sky shimmering with heat.

At first she could not believe what she saw, but then she took a deep breath and stood very still, for the sky was almost black with planes. Hundreds and hundreds of planes. German planes.

23

It seemed to go on for ever, although in fact it was only a week or two, that first really bad time, though there would be other bad weeks to follow, later. But all she knew then was the eternity of it. It seemed the most natural thing in the world that within a few days, almost, they accepted the pattern of the days and nights as normal. They became totally matter of fact about vanished buildings and the stench of high explosives and dust and burst sewers and gas mains and the squalor of streets littered with debris and houses with half a room left bare to the open sky and wardens with red tired eyes and reception centres full of dazed bombed out people. The shops she usually bought from disappeared or looked alien with boarded up windows and chalked signs reading 'business as usual'. And she hardly noticed. Landmarks she had never really been aware of until they were gone vanished from her memory as they vanished from real existence. The gas didn't pop when she tried to boil a kettle, because the mains had gone and she just shrugged; the electric light failed to come on and water to run in the flat and she didn't even frown. She went through the days as serenely as though nothing unusual was happening. The workmen got the electricity fixed somehow when it failed, so she opened the factory again, and they went on doggedly turning out their khaki shirts and skirts and greatcoats as though they had never stopped. The gas company men managed to reconnect the supply, so they had hot food again and she forgot she had been hungry; the water came back so they could bath and she said nothing. She just went on, unflurried by any of it.

Because of Marcus. As long as he was all right, she was. And he would be all right, for the meetings and eternity of planning sessions which filled his days were no longer held in the upper floor offices in Whitehall, but in safe, deep shelters underneath Horseguards' Parade. Once he left the flat in the morning to go to his job she could relax; he was safe, just as he had promised he would be. The danger from the raids was here in the East End of London, and in the City, both far from where he was, and that gave her all the peace of mind she needed.

He, on the other hand, was far from happy, for Artillery Lane sometimes seemed to be right in the centre of the German target. Bombs came down in great showers, night after night, to flatten the surrounding streets and factories into dust. Yet, somehow, the factory survived, and went on working, which made it impossible for Marcus to prevail when he tried, and he did, very hard indeed, to persuade her to leave London.

'I'll be fine here,' he told her, holding her close as they curled up in their small shelter one night, watching the oil lamp swaying on its post as the distant thudding of the guns sent vibrations through them. 'But I go through hell knowing you're here. Please Hannah, go to Daphne! I know you don't like her much, but she's safe there in the village. I'd sleep easier if you were with her.'

'And I'd never sleep at all,' she said, and tightened her grip on him, twining her legs around his into a Laocöon knot. 'Can you see me sitting in a tiny village in the middle of Herefordshire with nothing to do but drink gin with Daphne? Don't be crazy, Marcus! This is where I belong, right here. I'm not going anywhere. I'm going to be fine too – as long as you are. I can cope with anything, and knowing you're safe with the brass hats makes me feel marvellous!'

The heatwave went on which didn't help, and a minor epidemic of gastro-enteritis hit the factory workers, making it almost impossible to go on working. Somehow, she and Florrie overcame that, by humping bucket after bucket of water up from the street standpipe to the lavatories; that went on for three days. And then, late one Friday afternoon, just as she was coming back from the bank with cash to pay the workers, the mains that fed the standpipe fractured somewhere back down the Commercial Road and the last trickles of water disappeared.

She paid everyone with Florrie to help her, and sent them all away, and they went with relief to scurry fearfully through the littered streets back to the false security of home. It didn't matter what happened overhead; if you were in your own familiar shelter, that you had dressed up a bit with gingham tablecloths and cushions and even the odd plant or two, you could manage to keep your chin up. So they went, glad to be free, glad to have their money in their hands, glad it was Friday.

Hannah hesitated after they had gone, wondering whether to go to Whitehall and wait there for Marcus to be free. He had said she could do that any time she liked, giving her a special card that would get her in past the sentry, but she decided not to do that. It was now five o'clock, and Marcus had said he thought he could be away not much after half past.

'We'll pretend we're real people again,' he said. 'Get dressed in ordinary clothes and go up to the West End and find somewhere to get a meal. There're one or two places which are still not quite decrepit, I'm told, in Greek Street. Try to be ready, my love. Tonight we'll play at being human again.'

She dressed, wishing she could bathe, but settling for the clean up with her last precious bottle of skin cleansing milk which was all she could manage, and even put on a little make up. It was the least she could do, she told herself, peering in the mirror at her pale face.

'Florrie,' she said as she came into the tiny living room. 'Don't hang around here. You can't eat or anything – no water. So you'd be better off going to Uncle Alex's place in Golders Green. I know you don't like going, but tonight, what else can you do?'

Florrie grimaced, but went willingly enough and Hannah hugged her briefly as she saw her off, filled as always with gratitude. Florrie never changed, always did what had to be done, and went on as though the German attacks were no more than another tiresome domestic upheaval of the sort she had coped with so well in the old days at Paultons Square. Now she stumped off to Alex's big house to find a bed somewhere in its tangle of rooms, which wasn't always easy, for he had opened his doors to anyone of the family who wanted to flee there.

'We might even come out ourselves, later,' Hannah called after Florrie's retreating back. 'We'll see how it goes tonight. Tell Uncle Alex if he's there. He should be back from

Liverpool now.'

Quite why she chose to spend the remaining half hour before she could expect to hear Marcus's feet on the stairs going through the cloth supplies she didn't know. She was dressed in one of her favourite dresses from well before the war, an apple green crêpe de chine with a matching coatee, and it was hardly suitable for scrabbling among bolts of khaki serge, but still she had to do something and that was something that had to be done. She made her way to the back of the factory floor, where the cloth was stored and crouched down to begin her work, a ledger resting on one knee as she began to count the bolts. It was an awkward position, especially in her high heeled pre-war shoes. She thought briefly, I ought to take them off, but didn't for fear of ruining her stockings. Silk stockings were not easy to come by these days.

The sirens startled her when they began. This time it did not start from far away as a gentle little whine but sprang into first life at the neighbouring fire station, suddenly blasting her ears so that she jumped. Her ledger went flying and so did she, tumbling forwards awkwardly and hitting her head on a corner of a cloth bolt. She lay stunned for a second as the siren shrieked above her head, filling her with a sense of urgency and she shook her head to clear it and tried to get up, only to find her ankle was twisted under her. She couldn't move without agony. The siren went on and on, joined now by other sounds, klaxons and, most ominous of all, the deep throated burr of planes, pulsating so heavily that she knew at once they were almost overhead.

She began to drag herself across the floor, ignoring the way her precious crêpe de chine dress snagged against the rough floor boards or the way tears sprang into her stockings, desperately trying to make her way across the factory floor to the door that led to the stairs and to the shelter.

Marcus! He must be almost here, almost at the front door, maybe on the stairs already. She must get to the stairs and Marcus, she thought, and felt her face wet, almost with surprise. The pain in her ankle was excrutiating, and it was making her cry without knowing it. She sniffed and rubbed her wet face and eyes against her shoulder, lifting her arm awkwardly, trying to see through the blur of her own tears.

The burring noise got louder, and so did other noises, great bursts of explosions and the high pitched whistle of falling bombs and she stopped and tried to sit up and lifted her head and called, 'Marcus?' – absurdly because she couldn't even hear her own voice above the din. If he had been on the stairs, he could not have heard her.

It got worse, louder and louder and the building shook, the floor beneath her seeming to tilt, and she flung her hands out to catch at something alongside her to keep her straight, to help her on the way to the door and what seemed to be safety and reassurance and all she could feel above her head was the floor again, and she thought furiously – 'Stupid! It's supposed to be underneath me – ' And then the floor hit her on the head, a huge flat handed blow that made her eyes seem to burst into great circles of light. And then there was nothing at all.

A cold wet weight on her foot, as she tried to run, tried to rush along the platform to catch the train. But it wasn't a train she was running for but a taxi with its flag up, and as she ran it turned away and she couldn't run after it because of the cold wet weight on her foot. She opened her mouth to call after the taxi, furious at the driver for not seeing her here on the station platform.

It stopped being a station platform and became a flower market. Roses. The scent of roses. 'Roses, roses all the way and myrtle dropped in their path like mad,' she heard someone say and tried to turn her head to see who it was, but the pillows under her neck got in the way and she couldn't move at all.

'Hannah.'

The cold wet weight was worse now. She flexed the muscles of her thigh, trying to move her foot away to be free of it, but no matter how hard she tried she couldn't do it and she was angry then and wanted to shout, but all that came out were little whimpers and she wanted to say loudly, 'Be quiet! Such a stupid noise!'

'Hannah, dolly, it's all right. It's all right. Keep still, dolly. The nurses say you got to keep still.'

Another voice, not a warm friendly familiar one with bubbles in it somewhere, but a cold voice with trickles of ice water in it. 'Lady Lammeck, you must stop that! If you keep moving that way you'll pull the drip down and then where will we be? Do keep still!'

'Hannah, dolly, open your eyes. Please, Hannah.'

She thought about that for a moment. Open her eyes? A strange request, for they were open, weren't they? She was staring at the taxi on the train lines at the end of the platform in the flower market...

She experimented, trying to open her eyes that were not closed, and discovered that she was wrong. They had been closed, quite tightly, and now that she was opening them the light that came in was hurtful. She closed them again, looking for the reassuring familiarity of the train lines and the flowery platform, but all she could see now was light. Platforms and trains and taxis had disappeared.

'Try again, Hannah,' the familiar voice said, and obediently she did and stared at the source. Uncle Alex, his face so blessedly familiar that she felt warm everywhere except where her foot was; that was still cold and wet and so heavy.

'Uncle Alex,' she said. Her voice sounded very odd, thick and croaking, just like the voice that had been so silly about the roses and the myrtle. 'Uncle Alex.'

'*Gott se dank!*' She saw he was crying, the pouches under his eyes wet and gleaming in the lamp light. 'I thought you'd never talk again, and that's a fact, dolly. *Gott se dank.*'

She looked at him consideringly and then turned her head, carefully, almost surprised to find it obeyed her. A long white room warm with light, with patches of red in tidy patterns and flowers in a vase. She frowned, knowing that what she saw was familiar yet not able to identify it. She turned her head back to Uncle Alex, looking at him with hope. He would know. He always knew.

'Uncle Alex?' He took her hand in his and it felt so comfortable there that at once she knew where she was and said carefully, 'Hospital?'

'Yes, dolly. Hospital.'

She lay and thought about that for a while, staring up at the ceiling high above her, watching a cobweb in a corner swaying in a faint breeze. 'Hospital,' she said again, still carefully.

'In Letchworth,' Uncle Alex said and she frowned at the cobweb which shook itself more vigorously in the breeze and told her nothing. There was haziness around the edges of the

181

cobweb and she thought, 'I'm tired,' and closed her eyes, but felt a wave of fear come with the drowsiness.

When she opened them again she knew somehow that she had been asleep for all she had been afraid to, and turned her head to look for Uncle Alex, to apologize for being so rude. He was sitting there, his head slumped to his chest and she wanted to laugh. He had fallen asleep too, was as rude as she was. She felt a wave of tenderness for him lift in her and wanted to touch him, but she could not reach, and let her hand fall back. But he seemed aware of her movement and lifted his head with a jerk and stared at her, his face a little blank from his sleep.

'Hello,' she said, and managed to smile, though it hurt a little, for her face felt stiff. 'Tell me what happened, Uncle Alex. I'm all – muddled.'

You can't be that muddled, a small lucid part of her mind told her rather pompously. Not if you know you're muddled.

His face seemed to crease a little, and he looked at her hand on the counterpane and then reached for it, holding it tight in his fingers. She wanted to pull away because his grip was hurting her.

'Factory got a direct hit,' he said, and his voice seemed louder than it needed to be. 'They found you in the street. Thrown out by the blast, you were. Fractured ankle, three ribs cracked, bruises. Bit of concussion.'

'Oh,' she said. Her ankle, that was the cold wet weight, of course. She tried to squint down at her foot, but all she could see was a hump in the bedding.

'A cast,' he said following her gaze. 'Plaster, you know? Like a great big boot. Looks silly, really, but it'll cure your break.'

'That's good,' she said drowsily, and yawned, and felt her eyes closing gently as sleep stole over her. It was a good feeling, not alarming at all, as it had been before, and she was just letting it slide over her head when she realized what it was that she hadn't said to him.

'Marcus,' she murmured, and hardly opened her eyes as she spoke. 'When will he be here?'

There was no answer and the sleep began to roll back from her eyes. Slowly she opened them and looked at Uncle Alex, there in the chair beside her. She said again, 'Marcus. He'll be

182

here soon, won't he?'

He lifted his chin and looked at her and now the tears were there again on his pouched and lined cheeks and he stared at her for a moment and then shook his head, very definitely, from side to side like a clockwork doll. He looked so absurd she laughed, had to laugh.

'Dear Uncle Alex, don't be silly! When is he coming?'

'I ... he won't be coming,' Alex said, loud again. 'You might as well know now. I told 'em I'd be the one to tell you, and I got to. He was on the stairs, dolly, when the factory got hit. On the bloody stairs. They reckon he never knew what happened.'

24

For a long time she did not think about Marcus. She thought instead of unimportant things like her ankle, which refused to heal and which eventually needed operations to repair the damage that had been done, and about the fact that the doctors told her, regretfully, that she would never regain normal use of it, that it would always be stiff. That gave her something to sit and brood about, there in the small day room at the end of the long hospital ward, something she could encompass in her mind.

She thought, too, about her workers, worrying herself about them so that she needed sleeping pills night after night. Where would they all go now? Millie, who had been a finisher for her for twenty-five years, ever since the VAD uniform days, and Moishe the presser who had come to her as a club-footed boy of seventeen and was now working to keep his senile parents as well as a wife and a couple of children, and old Mrs Schneider whose efforts as a felling hand were of small value to production but who had been part of the place, the best tea maker, the one all the young girls relied on when they were worried about their boyfriends; who would emp-loy her now, a woman of almost seventy?

And Florrie, what about Florrie, treking out from London to see her day after day, making the tiresome journey into Hertfordshire on slow erratic trains, standing around for hours on windy station platforms uncomplaining and eternally patient, what about her?

She would tease and worry at her thoughts, obsessively, and knew it was all she could do, for how could she allow other thoughts of the greatest hurt of all to come into her mind? If she once allowed herself to think of Marcus, she would be lost forever. She knew that. Only by resolutely turning her back on the abyss of pain and despair that Marcus now was could she go on living at all.

And, extraordinarily, that mattered. In later years when she could allow herself to look back on the autumn and winter of 1940 and the early spring of 1941, she would marvel at how she had never once contemplated the possibility of just dying, as she should have done that Friday afternoon in Artillery Lane.

She had listened to what Uncle Alex had to tell her, his voice angry and loud with the misery of it, about how Marcus had told the people at the War Office that he was taking his wife for a night out, and they were to let him go early, how the driver of the official car he always used had tried to persuade him to take shelter as the sirens went just as they reached Artillery Lane, how he had gone tearing headlong down the street to the factory as soon as he had realized how close the raid was, and how the bomb – a comparatively small one, as it turned out – hit the roof dead centre just after he had gone rushing in. The driver had tried to hold him back, had himself been blasted into a hole on the far side of the street because he had not gone to take shelter himself, but he had not been able to save Marcus.

Once Hannah had been told all that, she closed her mind on the information, wrapping it in silence, hiding it away. Alex, her most constant visitor, seemed to understand, for he said no more about Marcus at all. Once, one afternoon during that first month, he leaned forwards and held her hands together, cradling them in both of his, and said quietly, 'Dolly, I'm proud of you. You're a credit to yourself, to your family, to all Yidden. You're well named, boobalah, you know that? Lammeck, *lamech*, strong, in the old Hebrew. That's you. Strong and quiet and good. I love you, dolly. Take care of yourself, and what you can't take care of I will.' He had kissed her on both cheeks had gone, walking down the ward with that slight swagger of his, his heavy checked

184

coat swinging and leaving a trail of cigar smoke behind him. She almost cried that afternoon, sitting in a hospital ward full of yellow and bronze chrysanthemums, watching him go and feeling dreadfully alone. But she did not. *Lamech*, strong, I must be strong.

They let her go home in early November, limping heavily and holding onto a thick ebony stick that Uncle Alex had brought her, because she had become too restless to stay. The orthopaedic surgeon, an elderly man with finicky ways and a passion for complex joint surgery, had wanted her to stay', so that he could operate again. 'Might be able to get more mobility back,' he had said, but she had refused. As long as she could get about at all, that was good enough. She had no need for more. She needed home and peace and comfort now.

Home. Florrie had lit up when Hannah had told her she was going to open up Paultons Square again.

'I don't care if they do bomb us there,' she had said. 'Anyway, they haven't so far, so maybe they won't. It seems to be mostly the East End and the City and the docks. Anyway, I don't care. But you should go away, Florrie. Go to Whitby with Bet. You know she'd love you to be with her.'

But Florrie of course had flatly refused and had a happy fortnight getting all the furniture out of storage and cleaning the house from top to bottom.

On the day Hannah came home, the weather was the sort that she and Marcus had both loved, cold and crisp but very sunny, with the last of the leaves on the trees whispering in the sharp breeze. The air smelled clean, with none of that thick explosive smokiness that had been so much a part of the atmosphere at Artillery Lane. Uncle Alex helped her out of the car wordlessly, supporting her with one hand under her elbow, but she disengaged herself gently and stood there, leaning on her stick and staring up at the house. It was important to her that she walk in unaided, and he seemed to understand and stood back as she made her way slowly and painfully to the steps.

As she reached the top step, her control as tight as she could keep it, refusing to think of Marcus here, the front door of the house next door opened and someone came out. She stopped as she saw Hannah and smiled widely.

'Hello, Lady Lammeck! I am glad you're back! Oh, have you been hurt? I am sorry! Fall, was it?'

Hannah stared at her, a tall buxom woman with iron grey hair, trying to remember. She had never been on particularly close terms with her neighbours, and this one had come to live at number twenty only a couple of months before the war started, all so long ago, so forgotten. She couldn't even recall her name.

'No, not exactly,' she said now. 'I – it's nice to be home.'

'Will you be starting up your dressmaking again, by any chance?' the woman said brightly. 'I was just going to start coming to you for some dresses and lo and behold you stopped for the war! But not for the duration, I hope! I've got some absolutely stunning silks my son brought home for me from Shanghai and I'm absolutely dying to have them made up! *Do* say you're going to start again!'

Hannah looked at her consideringly and after a moment nodded. 'I might,' she said. 'Let me see the silks, I'll see what I can do.'

'Marvellous! Couldn't be more marvellous! I'll pop in tomorrow, after seven, if that's all right? Must dash now, war work you know! Got a first aid detachment waiting to be taught bandaging. See you tomorrow!' And she went rushing importantly down the Square as Hannah stood on her step and watched her go.

That was how it was that she began to live again. The factory was gone and had to be forgotten, and Marcus had gone and was not to be thought of, but Mary Bee Couturiere was still there, waiting to be part of her life again. When Cissie came out of the sanatorium she had had to go to at the end of 1941, after an alarming haemorrhage, to find that her Hackney house had been bombed and was uninhabitable, she came to live in Paultons Square with Hannah, and together they picked up the threads of the old days. They made up the precious hoarded fabrics that women brought them and altered and refurbished old dresses from the halcyon days of the thirties, and, later, when illicit supplies of parachute silk came on the black market, found themselves sewing that extraordinary material too.

Florrie went on as she always had, looking after them, cleaning the house and cooking their meagre rations with as much skill as she could muster and, when they needed her, joined in the sewing. Much of it was hand work, for sewing machines were hard to come by, and the only battered one they had frequently broke down, so there was ample work for all of them.

And, oddly, they were happy. They would sit, the three women, with the wireless playing 'Music While You Work' and 'Workers' Playtime', Cissie sometimes singing along with the familiar tunes in her gruff alto, and talk a little of unimportant things like weather and films and the books they were reading. They never discussed the war, never listened to the war news on the wireless together, tacitly agreeing to shut it out of their shared lives as much as they could. Hannah would read the papers at night, after she had gone to bed, and for all she knew the others did too, but whether she worried about setbacks in North Africa or found hope in news of successful RAF raids on Germany, she never said a word about it to them any more than they did to her. It was as though they had all agreed that they had fought their war, and lost it. Now they would just struggle on, somehow, letting others carry their share of the rest of it.

Nor did Hannah ever speak to Cissie and Florrie of her other distress, the continuing silence from Holland and from America. Once she had asked Uncle Alex to do what he could, to see if he could find out anything about what was happening in Holland but he had come back after six weeks, miserable and angry because despite his many contacts in Government offices he had drawn a total blank. There were some refugees trickling out, occasional escaped prisoners of war who managed to get away by sea to England, but none of them, it seemed, knew anything much about what was happening there, and certainly nothing about one young English Jew who had disappeared into Amsterdam.

As for Marie, all Hannah knew was that she still drew her regular income from the bank as arranged by the lawyers at Lammeck Alley. Peterson had come to see her shortly after she had come home from hospital, to tell her of her own financial situation, and of what was happening with Marie's money.

'Sir Marcus was a major shareholder in Lammeck and Sons, as you know, Lady Lammeck,' he had told her. 'Business at present is, of course, virtually at a standstill, except for those factories which have been turned over to munitions or other war production. All our overseas interests have been frozen for the duration, and quite what will happen there we are not in a position to know. But you need not be concerned about money. You have a handsome competence, very handsome indeed, and once this tiresome war is over, you will, I am sure, be better off than you now are. However – '

'It doesn't matter,' Hannah said flatly.' It really doesn't matter. I've always earned my own living, and I still can if I must.'

'Your factory, of course, was insured, I've checked on the policies and enemy action was covered, so there will be money there, although it may be some time yet before we get it for you.'

'I've told you, it doesn't matter,' Hannah said more sharply. 'We've got enough, Florrie and Cissie and me. We've got the house and we get our rations. We're not likely to get involved in black market buying.'

'I should hope not!' Peterson said, his face a mask of horror, and Hannah wanted to laugh for a moment. His probity was such a comfort, so cosy a reminder of the long ago days when the world could afford luxuries like virtue and honour and polite behaviour.

'I'm more concerned about my daughter,' she said now. 'Mrs Rupert Lammeck. I've heard nothing from her since – since a cable to say her baby was born. Nothing. Is she – have you heard?'

He shook his head, not looking at her. 'I am sorry, Lady Lammeck, but no. Not directly. I can only tell you that the arrangements for drawing her money were changed from the USA side at her request. We were asked to allow for cash to be drawn on any branch of the British American Bank, and we did that. I can tell you that it has been drawn from, let me see . . . ' He consulted one of the mass of papers on his lap. 'Ah yes. San Diego. Seattle. Las Vegas. Ah – Chicago. Then San Diego again. Then New York and the last time, hum, Detroit.'

She frowned, puzzled, and he said gently, 'She seems to be moving about a good deal.'

'Yes. A good deal. And Rupert? Have you heard from him?'

'Nothing at all. We will have to make contact of course. His brother, your husband, has left him a small legacy. Carefully tied up, of course, but all the same...'

'Yes. Marcus would have done that,' she said, and sheered away from thoughts of Marcus again. 'Please, Mr Peterson, can you try to find out for me what has happened? I can't help being afraid. Maybe she's ill. I just can't understand the silence. Though if she were in trouble she'd be in touch, surely.'

'Surely,' Mr Peterson said dryly. 'Quite surely. I will of course do what I can. I will see to it that messages are left at every branch of the British American Bank to be delivered to Mrs Lammeck should she go to them. Then perhaps she will make contact.'

'Yes.'. She seized on that gratefully. 'Yes, please. Just ask them to tell her to cable me, or write to me or ... something. Anything. Just to know she's all right. She and the baby.'

'Your granddaughter, yes,' Mr Peterson said, and then coughed a little stiffly and said, 'I – I have not spoken to you since – since Sir Marcus...'

'Please, Mr Peterson, let's just take it as said, whatever it is. Please? I ... I appreciate your kindness, the kindness you've always shown me. Let's just stop there, shall we?'

'Of course,' he said, and began to pack his briefcase again. 'So, that is that. I am always available as you know. Just a telephone call or a letter and I will come at once to arrange anything you wish arranged. And as soon as I hear anything about Mrs Rupert Lammeck, I will of course let you know.'

But he never did, because there was silence still. All he could report as the months and then the years went by was that the income was being drawn regularly, and that was all. Clearly Marie was alive and well enough to go to her banks, wherever she was, and she certainly seemed to travel a lot, for the bank reports came from a bewildering number of places, but she was not, for some reason, prepared to communicate with her family in England. And there was nothing Hannah could do to make her.

She swallowed that distress too, sitting day after day quietly sewing in her dining room, while Cissie sat beside her singing under her breath, and thinking only of the stitches she was setting, of the length of a seam, the shape of a shoulder. She ate her meals and went occasionally to walk around the Square, wearing though it was, for her ankle still gave her a lot of pain. She listened to music on her wireless. Sometimes the family came to visit, brought in Uncle Alex's car, old Uncle Benjamin and David and Sonia, and whichever of Reuben and Minnie's vast brood was available, and they would drink tea and gossip of family matters and sometimes play solo among much badinage and arguments about who had played what card in the wrong way. It was, on the surface, a tranquil life, an oasis of peace in the middle of the conflagration of a terrible war. And no one looking at Hannah would have known the maelstrom that was beneath that quiet surface. Indeed, they told each other, all of them, Hannah was a marvel, a real marvel, taking her loss so well, not moaning like some would, and with both her children gone as well as her husband. *Nebbish*, a real *guteneh shumah* thinking only of others and not of herself, so good to Cissie and Florrie and her neighbours. And underneath it all she was in a turmoil.

A turmoil of guilt. What was it about her, Hannah would ask herself in the long dark nights, what was it about her that destroyed those she most loved? Daniel and Peter and Marcus, Marie and Charles, all gone, vanished into a past that existed only inside her head, that filled her with despair. What had she done to have earned so sharp a punishment? She had never been taught to believe in her God as a caring loving personage. Nathan had not been one who could give such a message to his children, consumed as he was with his own rage against the world and the God who had made it. No, God had never figured in her scheme of things, till now.

And the God she now found was an angry one, a vengeful one, paying her in hard coin for sins she could not know she had committed. So she would tell herself, trying to understand. What did I do? Why me? What did I do that made me so poisonous to those I love? Why do they die? Why do they go away?

She became more and more enmeshed in her view of herself as uniquely wicked, uniquely punished. The quieter and the more serene she was by day with other people, the more bitter and angry and hurt she was at night alone. And somehow, that helped. Whatever it was she had done, surely she was paying for it now? This cruel God could not do worse to her, could he?

It was a sort of comfort, for a little while. Until late one October evening in 1944.

25

It was an evening with a difference because Florrie and Cissie had gone out to the cinema on one of their rare expeditions. There had been a time when Florrie and Bet had gone to the pictures every Saturday night, but that had stopped in 1940, when Bet went away. After that it had seemed, Florrie said, unpatriotic to spend money on such rubbish when there was fighting going on. And anyway, not so much fun. But now, as the news of the war improved each day, and the end seemed actually to be a possibility, her doubts about the morality of such simple pleasures were eased, and she was willing to go, even though the flying bombs had started to make nuisances of themselves.

'They didn't get me the first time round when they was aiming their bombs right at me,' she had said firmly, putting on her hat and her sensible knitted gloves, for it was a cold evening, 'so they won't get me this time, sending them things off from the other side of the Channel like they do, and not knowing who they're going for. Stands to reason –'

They had tried to persuade Hannah to come too, but she would not. It was difficult to cope if her ankle caused her pain, as it so often did, when she was sitting in the middle of a crowded row and couldn't get out, she told them. She would stay home and listen to 'Saturday Night Theatre' on the wireless. 'You tell me all about it tomorrow, Florrie. And I'll have some cocoa ready for you when you get in.'

So she was alone, sitting in the drawing room, listening to the wireless in the dark. There was a pleasure in not curtaining the windows, in being able to see the faint moon haze out there. It was as though she were somehow defying the blackout.

The play was dull, and she had almost dozed off in her comfortable armchair when she heard the rattle of the knocker on the front door, and jumped in the darkness. After a moment it was repeated, and she sat there uneasily listening. Who would visit her so late on a Saturday evening? None of the family ever did. She began to be frightened, sitting there alone in the darkness. She got to her feet awkwardly to limp to the window and look out.

There was a tall figure on the doorstep. She could just see the silhouette as she craned her neck and as though he could see her, he turned and stared up at the window and she drew back, nervously.

He knocked again, and once more lifted his face to the window. As a rack of cloud moved away from the moon she could see him a little more clearly, a cadaverous face, with a lot of dark hair flopping over the forehead and very dark eyes that looked like blank hollows in that pallid skull. And she felt another lift of fear.

After a while she saw him put his hand in his pocket, and take out something and as she watched she realized he was writing, his head bent close over his hands so that he could see what he was doing. She heard the letter box rattle as he pushed something through and then he went walking slowly but purposefully down the steps. She watched him go and then slowly drew the curtains and switched on the lamp on the small occasional table before, almost unwillingly, going to the front door to see what he had pushed through.

It was the back of a cigarette packet. She stared down at the picture of the sailor with his heavy moustache, locked forever inside his rope entwined lifesaver, and the legend 'Players Please', and then turned it over, and read the heavy pencil scribble on the other side.

'I will return later, in the hope you are here. I have news of Charles and Henk.'

That was all. She stared blankly at it and then, sick with terror, scrabbled at the front door, dragging it open, limping out onto the steps as fast as she could, looking for him.

He had reached the far side of the Square, almost to the corner where the King's Road was, or someone had, for she could just see a moving figure – and she shouted at the top of her voice, 'Come back. Come back!' and stood there very still staring so hard that lights began to leap inside her straining eyes.

Miraculously he heard her, for he stopped and then turned and came back with the same slow walk, not seeming at all surprised to be so summoned, until he was standing at the foot of her steps looking up at her in the dimness.

'*Mevrouw* Lammeck?' he said. 'I beg your pardon, it should be, I think, Lady Lammeck.'

'Yes, no, it doesn't matter. You know Charles? You have news of Charles? Where is he? Is he coming?'

He was silent for a moment and then said again, 'I have news of Charles.'

'Please come in, come in and tell me. Oh, I am sorry I didn't answer sooner. I'm alone, you see. I was worried. Please, please come in.' She was gabbling in her excitement, and she reached forwards to seize him, to hurry him in, and almost tripped. He took her wrist in a firm grasp and steadied her, then led her into the house again.

'A drink, some cocoa. I have some whisky somewhere, maybe – '

'Nothing,' he said. 'Just some time. I have a message to give you. Then I must go.'

'Who are you? A friend of Charles? Oh, I can't tell you what hell it's been, all the time, so frightened, he's been gone so long, it's been over five years, you see. I've been so frightened, so – '

'Your husband?' the man said, and she looked at him, surprised he didn't know and then angry with herself for her own stupidity. Why should he know?

'He was killed in an air raid,' she said, stiffly, waiting for the words of commiseration that she so hated. But he only nodded and said, 'Ah,' calmly as though that were news he had expected.

'Then I need not wait to speak. I can tell you alone.'

'I don't understand.'

'It would have been better to tell you in company with him, but what is not possible cannot be possible.' He spoke perfect English but there was a precision about his speech and a purity of tone about his vowel sounds that made it clear he was not English. As though he heard her thoughts he bowed and said, 'I am Gerhard De Jongh, *Mevrouw* – Lady Lammeck. Of Amsterdam. Your servant, madam.'

'I ... Hannah,' she said. 'Call me Hannah.'

'It would not be proper,' he said gravely. 'I am younger than perhaps I seem. I am twenty-nine. Two years younger than Charles.'

'He's a friend? You know him well?'

193

'Friends, yes,' he said. 'Perhaps I sit down to speak to you?'

'Of course, I'm sorry, it's just that I'm ... this way, please.'

She led him to the drawing room and he sat down neatly in a chair beside the lamplit table. She could see him clearly now, a thin man with heavy lines on his cheeks and very deep set eyes. He was right, he did look much older than twenty-nine and she felt suddenly very sad for him, wanting to touch him, and comfort him. He looked cold and hungry and in need of care. But then he leaned back in the chair with an easy movement that made him seem so in command of the situation that she could not offer him the food she would have done.

'Mr De Jongh,' she said carefully, 'I am glad indeed to see you. Perhaps, now, you will tell me what it is you know of my Charles?'

He stared at her for a long moment and then said sharply, 'You seem very comfortable here.'

'I – what? Yes, I suppose so.' She looked round the room, at the neat richness of it, the handsome well kept furniture, the bowl of late dahlias from the garden Florrie had set on the mantelpiece, and saw it through his eyes for a moment. It looked wealthy and very comfortable and she said again, 'Yes, I suppose so.'

'You have enough food?'

She frowned sharply. 'We have our rations.'

'Ah, yes, rations. English rations. Enough to live on, I believe. The people I see in the streets do not look hungry.'

'Yes, I suppose – Look, what is this? You said you had news of Charles and – '

'Yes, I have. But I am interested to see how little you English suffer. You share the war, yet you have enough food while our people starve, our children starve. Your streets are not filled with soldiers with guns.'

'There are soldiers everywhere,' she cried, stung, and he laughed.

'Your own soldiers! Those, of course. But no Germans.'

'No,' she said. 'No Germans. You are right, we are fortunate. But please, tell me. What news have you for me?'

He leaned back in the chair and pulled his raincoat open and she saw he was wearing a heavy sweater underneath it. His hand was bony and rather dirty, and she felt suddenly

194

very old. He seemed so young for all he was so tired and drawn.

'I have so much to tell you I hardly know where to begin,' he said. 'So much. I think perhaps I will have that whisky after all.'

She fetched it for him, trying not to think. Everything about his manner was filling her with dread, and when she gave him his drink she thought wildly for a moment as he stared up at her with those deep dark eyes, 'He doesn't know Charles at all. He's a thief, a murderer, come to kill me while I'm alone, he doesn't know Charles at all.' But he said, 'Thank you, *Mevrouw*,' gravely and she knew she was being foolish.

'Well?' she said, and he took a deep draught of his drink and then put the glass down beside him.

'I have known Charles Lammeck for many years,' he said. 'Indeed, he recruited me.'

'Recruited?'

'To the Party.'

'I see. Politics.'

'Yes. Politics. It is what this war is about, *Mevrouw*.' She felt the anger in him and was ashamed at the note of asperity that had crept into her voice.

'So, he recruited you to the Party. And you are friends?'

'Yes. He and Henk and I. For a long time. We talk together, laugh together, chase girls together.'

Her head lifted suddenly. 'Girls? He had girl friends? Oh, I'm so glad.'

'Because of your daughter? Yes, do not look so surprised. I know of that matter. He took it hard, I know. He told me all, and I had sympathy. These spoiled over-rich Jewish girls are all of a type.'

She reddened. 'You know nothing of the matter!'

'Don't I? Well, it is not important. As I say, we are friends. And we work together against the Nazis, in Holland, then in Germany. When the trouble starts, we three get back to Amsterdam just in time. Underground, you understand.'

'I'm not sure I do.'

He sighed, irritably. 'We are Jews and Communists! Both! You think the Germans care for such as we to be walking about easy? Of course not. So, we hide. We get a room in a house on the Kaisersgracht and we stay there all day, come

195

out at night, go to meetings, try to organize the people. They will not be organized, many of them. Some, yes. But most are already too frightened. Still, we go on trying. And then it begins ... '

She did not ask him what had begun; she just sat there staring at him in the lamplight, waiting.

'First there were the rules of behaviour for Jews, where they may work, what they may do, the rules, the rules. And then the Dutch, some of them, not many but enough, began to buy their own safety by informing. They help the police collect the Jews to deport them. They help flush them out of houses where they hide. The old women, the children, the sick men, all of them. For a couple of guilders, another ration of potatoes.'

He took up his scotch again and drank thirstily and she took his glass from him and refilled it without a word. He took it with only a nod of thanks.

'We do what we can, Henk and Charles and I. Some we smuggle out. We get them to the little boats and we smuggle them out. Others we try, but we fail and Charles – oh, Charles becomes so angry. It is the most beautiful thing I have ever seen!' The deep eyes seemed to be alight. Whisky, she thought dully. I should have given him some food.

'What happened?' she said after a while, for he had stopped talking, sitting staring into his glass with his eyes very wide open.

'Hum? Oh, yes. What happened.' He drew one hand across his lips, a worried little small-boy sort of gesture. 'He went back to Germany.'

'Back to – but how? How could he do such a – '

'He said things were happening there that we did not know enough about. That we had to get news. That somehow we had to discover what they were doing with all the Jews who were being shifted out of Holland and why the Germans were doing it. It all seemed so ... he said it was a puzzle that must be cleared. We had heard of work camps, you see. We knew of those. But Charles said he believed something else was happening, and he wanted to know what it was. So, he went back to find out.'

'And how – I mean, what happened? Is he still there?'

'No.'

'Then where is he? For God's sake man, stop being so –

you're playing games with me and I want no more of it! If you have news, give it to me. No more of this. I can't take more of this.' She luxuriated in her anger, letting it wash over her, almost encouraging it. 'I've had more than enough of your ... your stupid sideways talk! Tell me what has happened to my Charles or go away! I have waited this long for news, I can wait longer. If you won't tell me, someone will, some time.'

'You want news? You want to know what he discovered? You want to hear how he got back to Amsterdam, last summer? How he looked? What he told me? Then, by God, you will. Every word of it. Every last word that I can tell you I will tell you, you comfortable English lady here in London where the Jews can live in their houses like other people and never be hurt. Where there are no German soldiers with guns in the streets!'

Later, much later, she tried to remember the actual words he had used. How he had explained to her in ordinary English in those precise tones of his the facts that Charles had collected, but she could not. All she could remember were the pictures inside her head, the pictures he had painted for her, sitting there in his raincoat in the armchair in her drawing room in Paultons Square.

She saw her Charles, thinner now, for he had been ill, buying forged papers with money he had begged from one of the Damont family before they all managed to leave Amsterdam to go to America, for the Willem Damonts were rich, very rich. She saw him travelling by roundabout routes to Berlin, posing as a Dutch schoolteacher with Nazi sympathies, looking for a connection of the Willem Damont who had given him the money he had needed. His sister, in fact. Leontine von Aachen.

Leontine Damont. Hannah sat and stared at him as the name came slipping off his tongue. Baroness Von Aachen, Daniel's Leontine. Marie's glamorous friend. Leontine von Aachen.

The story had gone on and on. How Charles had waited in Berlin cafés and walked in Berlin Streets, trying to find a chance to speak to her alone, working as a waiter, as a street sweeper, any work he could get, freed from service by the German authorities because of his tuberculosis.

'Tuberculosis?' she had whispered and Gerhard had looked

197

at her in irritated surprise at the interruption. Of course, tuberculosis. After two years in hiding in Amsterdam, half starved most of the time, bitterly cold, in damp rooms, no medical care, how else should it be? Did he not have it himself? Did not half Holland? Of course tuberculosis.

He had gone on then, as though she had not interrupted, telling how at last Charles had managed his objective which was to take the huge risk of speaking to the important Baroness von Aachen whose husband was such a pillar of the Third Reich, so busy a member of Adolf Hitler's advisory staff, and telling her that he knew her history, knew that her brother, her Jew brother of Amsterdam had gone safely to America, and that he, Charles, would, if necessary, denounce her for a Jew to the powers that be, unless she helped him.

Helped him. Such strange help it was that he wanted. To go to work in one of those camps to which the Jews of Holland were being sent. That was what he wanted, and she, terrified that the secret she had managed somehow to hide from the Nazis might be exposed, had been more than willing to help. So he had gone there, Gerhard said. Gone to a little village in Lower Saxony, not far from Celle. 'Belsen,' he said. 'A place called Belsen.'

She stared at him uncomprehendingly, and he had leaned back and laughed, then again, loudly, the whisky rattling in the sound.

'Well, it will be heard of soon enough,' he had said and then had gone on. And on and on, until she could bear it no longer and had tried to cover her ears, but he leaned forwards and pulled her hands away and made her listen.

She saw it all. The rows of huts, the people skeletally thin with eyes bigger and darker and even more remote than Gerhard's staring at her so burningly across her familiar drawing room. People who would kill each other for a crust. People who despaired so much that they threw themselves against the high tension wires that enclosed the place and burned with a reek of cooking flesh while soldiers in grey uniforms laughed and watched and made ribald jokes about feeding the remains to the watching blank-faced hordes in the compounds. About the stench from the high chimneys that belched their greasy black smoke into the soft skies of Lower Saxony while the local farm workers went serenely about their business and paid no attention at all. About the women screaming as they were dragged from their children and pushed towards the waiting buses which had pictures of happy people painted on the blacked out windows. About the young women who were taken to the camp hospitals and could not, would not, say what happened to them when they came out again grey faced and blank eyed.

It went on and on until she felt first numb, and then, suddenly, hugely angry.

'You're a liar,' she said, shouting it at him. 'Liar! It's not true. I don't know why you're here, why you're telling me this ... this filth, but it's not true, and I won't listen to it.'

'I said the same,' he said, and nodded at her, solemn as a child in school. 'I said the same to Charles when he came back. I did not believe it could be true, but he had been there and he had seen.'

'I don't *believe* you,' she shouted again. 'I don't believe you! How could he have come back to Holland to tell you? And how are you here? It's all a mad lie and I don't know who you are and why you've come to tell me all this wickedness but I won't listen.'

'Oh, you can warm yourself with disbelief if you choose,' he said, and now he sounded weary. 'I tried the same. I could not see how he could have made such discoveries and got away to come back to us, but Charles is Charles. Resourceful is I believe the English word. Resourceful. He worked there, you see. On the ovens. Would you believe, on the ovens? He wanted to cry out, he wanted to make the people there cry out, to fight back, but they weren't people any more. They could not fight back, and where would be the profit in dying with them? So he scratched inside his throat with a pin, he told me, and spat blood, and the village doctor said he must go away from there, so he did. Resourceful, my friend Charles. I want some more scotch.'

'No,' she said, but he just grinned at her and got up and went to the table in the corner and fetched it for himself. She could not stop him, for she was now too frightened to do anything at all. A madman, come to tell her mad lies. Cold terror filled her legs and weakened her knees and made movement impossible.

'Henk and I, still in Amsterdam, feeling good because the Dutch went on strike, you know that? They went on strike, our dull Dutch workers who only care for their bellies and their sacks of potatoes, they went on strike! The German soldiers shot some of them for their pains but they went on strike and Henk and I were in the middle of that, so proud, so hopeful, and then Charles came back. Back to Amsterdam, and told us it all and we said he lied. We too said he lied. And then the strikes ... the Germans came and took Henk. I got away, you see. I got away.'

She said nothing, staring at him, at the face now even more pale, but with tight spots of colour in each cheek so that he looked doll like. 'I have to think of that, you know. I have to think of that all the time. I went to the organization and I told them I must get out and there was a chance now after Arnhem. Oh! God, but I am tired!' He peered at her, his eyes gleaming a little in the lamplight. 'So tired. I left them there. Henk taken by the Germans, and Charles in the little room in Kaisersgracht, on his own. I could stay no longer, so I left my friends. You hear me? I left my friends. Such a friend for such men to have.'

To her amazement she felt a sudden stab of pity for him. She did not believe what he was saying, could not believe, yet she felt sorry for him.

'And then on the little herring boat, sick as a dog on the North Sea there was a man, a sailor, and he told me the same tale. He had heard it from a seaman who had heard it in Hamburg. It isn't only that place in Saxony. There are others, full of Jews and gipsies. Full of Jews and gipsies ... '

He was very drunk now, standing swaying a little there in the middle of her drawing room and she thought, he's going to be sick on my carpet. He's going to be sick all over my carpet, and suddenly that mattered more than anything else. She got to her feet, awkwardly as usual because of her stiff ankle and said firmly, 'You must go now.'

He peered at her a little owlishly and then, very solemnly, nodded. 'Yes. I have told you, and I must go. Charles said I must tell you. He said he will hope to see you again soon. Holland will soon be liberated everywhere, not just the south, and he will return to London, he said. I have given you the message and now I must go.'

To her surprise, he did. He put down his glass, now empty again, and moving with the studied care of the very drunk walked to the door and along the passageway outside to the front door and let himself out. By the time she reached the door after him, leaning on her stick, he was gone, walking along the pavement with his back very straight and very controlled, lifting each foot a little higher than was necessary, as drunken men do.

She watched him go, leaning heavily on her stick and thinking only of the way he was walking, and wondering, vaguely, whether he would fall over. But he reached the corner safely and turned it, disappearing into the greater blackness of the King's Road as the moon, once more, slid behind a cloud.

26

She tried very hard, to pretend nothing had happened. When Cissie and Florrie came home full of talk of the film, she behaved just as they expected her to, listening, smiling, making them their hot cocoa, saying goodnight, going to bed. But she lay awake a long time forcing herself to think of the work she had in hand. Mrs Jean Goldman's coat that she was making out of a pre-war brocade curtain, and Barbara Cohen's parachute silk wedding dress, anything to blank out the images that Gerhard De Jongh had etched in her mind.

But it was not possible to pretend it hadn't happened, that he had been just a madman, come out of nowhere, gone back to nowhere, leaving no more than a wraith behind. Everyone she looked at in the succeeding days seemed to be over-shadowed by that cadaverous face with the deep dark eyes; every thin child she saw in the street made her think of the children he had described in Belsen, every bent old man shuffling along the pavement made her recall the old men who had thrown themselves on the high tension wires.

Florrie and Cissie worried about her, asking anxiously whether her ankle was playing up again, whether she was sleeping, nagging her because she seemed not to have her usual appetite until, uncharacteristically, she lost her temper and shouted at them and there had been days of stiffness and unhappiness about the house, until she managed to coax them back into being comfortable again. But the old peace was gone; the shutting out of the war that they had managed

201

for so long had failed and she knew it.

Eventually she did what she had always done when she was distressed. She went to Uncle Alex.

His seventy-five years sat lightly on him. He was just a little more lined and perhaps a little fatter, but not much. His hair was as white and crinkled and as thick as ever, his clothes as natty, and his tongue as sharp. He still spent half of each day at his Pall Mall office, keeping a close control on every aspect of his business. Theatre trade had fallen off in London because of the flying bombs, but was brisker than ever in the provinces and he had three tours traipsing the country with Rudolph Friml revivals and Priestley plays and was making money hand over fist. Even the restaurants were doing well, in spite of the continued shortages of food and in spite of his determined refusal to seek extras on the flourishing black market.

'It ain't so much I got an excess of virtue, dolly,' he told her earnestly. 'It's just that it's bad business. Sooner or later these shysters get themselves caught and then what? If I do it, I get labelled as another lousy Jew profiteer. Not me. I'll give 'em what I can get for the restaurants and they'll have to settle for that. It can't last much longer, this war. Then the food comes back again. The people want fun again and my restaurants make money again. Meanwhile I got this idea I might start a few dance halls. I think dance halls is where it's going to be, you know?'

She had listened and laughed and told him yes, maybe he was right, dance halls were a good idea, and he had launched himself happily into plans for them. Now, when she went to see him, she found him surrounded by eager bandleaders all trying to convince him that theirs was the one and only outfit that could possibly open his brand new place near Tottenham Court Road.

She stood in the doorway of his office leaning on her stick and he looked up and waved jovially at her and opened his mouth to say something and then looked more sharply and said to the men clustered round him, 'Later, fellas, later. Right now I got some urgent family business.' They had looked at her curiously and gone away, leaving her there with him fussing over her, leading her to a seat, shouting for his secretary to bring her tea.

'So, dolly? Tell me what's happened.'

'How do you know something's happened?'

'How do I know? Fifty years you been my girl, dolly. Fifty years my niece, and she asks me, how do I know? So I look at your face, I see your eyes, I know. What more do you want? Diagrams?'

She smiled for the first time since Gerhard De Jongh had come into her life three weeks before. 'No diagrams. Yes, I'm – look, this will take time. Are you busy right now? Shall we meet later? If you've got business.'

'It can wait. Business never comes to no harm you keep it cooking a *bissel*. Those fellas, they want me more'n I want them, so they'll sit out there and they'll stew a little and that'll improve their flavour and make 'em cheaper. Talking to you'll be good business. So talk, already.'

She talked, haltingly at first and then more fluently, telling him what had happened, and, eventually, all that Gerhard had told her. That had been hard to start with, hard to get the words out of her mouth, but gradually, as she reproduced those painful images, she began to feel better, and she realized, suddenly, that letting it all out was having a cathartic effect.

'I – I'm beginning to think his telling me helped him,' she said. 'I thought he was mad, vicious, imagining it, trying to make me ill, unhappy, but now ... Please, Uncle Alex, tell me I was right. That this man *was* crazy? That for some reason I don't know he was making it all up?'

Alex was silent, sitting behind his big polished desk and staring down at the cigar between his fingers.

'You know, I remember the last time, 1914. The stories they put around then. About Germans bayonetting Belgian babies, killing pregnant women, raping nuns, burning hospitals. You remember. And everyone talked about it, everyone said it was dreadful and told everyone else. And then, afterwards, we found it wasn't true. Atrocity stories, all to get us stirred up. Not true. So, slowly, everyone tells everyone else it ain't true and nobody believes it no more. You remember any of that?'

She shook her head impatiently. 'I don't know – what does it matter what people said in 1914? It's now I'm talking about.'

'It matters, dolly. You see, people don't forget that easy. Last time it was atrocity stories all made up? Then,' he shrugged, 'it's the same this time. That's what I said. At first.'

She was silent for a long moment looking at him carefully, her forehead creased, but he did not look at her. 'Uncle Alex! Are you saying – what are you saying?'

Now he did look at her, his old eyes a little rheumy and then managed a tight little grin.

'I wish you got about a bit more, dolly. Got to meet some of the refugees, you know? The ones that came here the past five years or so, the ones still managing to slip in. I meet 'em, you know? I'm on one of these committees, give a few shows for 'em for raising money – you get the picture. And I talk to them, and they tell me things, about camps, about killings, about Jews being gassed, and I go home at first, and I say to myself, ach, Belgian babies on bayonets, that's what this stuff is. *Boobahmeisers*, old stories told by sad people! Lost their money, lost their homes, got no one to look at them and say there's a rich important man, so they got to make themselves look important. This is what I tell myself at first. But then ... '

He was silent and she leaned forwards, pulling on his hand on the desk.

'Then?'

'Then I get it from the others. Refugees in Liverpool start telling me the same stories I get from refugees in London and in Cardiff and everywhere else I go to give them shows, and I begin to think. Alex, I think, you're being a fool. Maybe last time it was stories and there weren't no atrocities like the papers was full of, but maybe this time it's different. Maybe it did happen already, these terrible things. I don't see these *nebbish* refugees getting together planning fancy stories to tell everywhere! These are ordinary people that have suffered so much they're angry. They sometimes hate each other as much as they hate the people they left behind and the people here they have to rely on. They don't plot together, I say to myself. So I reckon the stories I hear are true. Got to be true.'

'You knew,' she said. 'You knew? And it's true?'

'I knew. And I told you. I think it's true.'

'And you did nothing *about* it? My God, Uncle Alex, you heard all this, and from the people who'd been there and you did nothing about it?'

'Don't be a *shlemeil*, Hannah! What do you want I should do? Go get myself a train, a ship, hop over to Berlin, knock on Hitler's door say, "Adolf, *boobalah*, you shouldn't do such unkind things to my *landsleit*"? You want I should do that?'

'But to say nothing, to hear such things and say *nothing*?'

'Others heard the stories, others here who know the refugees, they heard them too, and what do they do?'

'I don't care what they did! What about you? Couldn't you have – '

'*Oy vey is mir*, what does she want of my life? Sure I tried! I went to the papers, right? I tell the newspapers and much good it does me. They listen to me sure, these fancy editors. I'm Alex Lazar, so they listen and they nod and they tut-tut and they say, "Well, Mr Lazar," they say, "I agree if it's true it's a terrible terrible thing, but is it true? That's the question," they say. "You bring me evidence and then we'll publish in our pages! But we got to have proof. You must understand this." And I ask 'em what proof they want, there's the refugees, go talk to them. And they say, "Oh, refugees," they say, "damaged people, they get a little mad in the head from their loneliness, they suffer a little, they tend, poor souls, to exaggerate. Remember the atrocity stories from last time," they say. So what more can I do? Go around telling you, telling my family, listen, in Germany the Jews are being exterminated like bed bugs? Much good that will do. And anyway, as the editors say, and I have to listen to them, where's the proof? I seen no pictures, no papers, no *proof.* Just angry lonely people talking of what... Ach, what can I do?'

They sat there silently for a long time and then she said, 'Then this man, this Gerhard – '

Alex made a little grimace. 'He sounds like the real thing. Another refugee. It's always the same, dolly, in every generation. Jews suffer, and some get over it and use it, and some are destroyed by it. Me and you, we were lucky. The ones that are here from Germany now, they're the sort that can't do it. Most of 'em.'

They sat there for a long time in the darkening office, neither speaking. Hannah could hear the rattle of a typewriter from outside, a mournful yet comfortable sound and beyond that the traffic in the street below. She thought of her house in Paultons Square and Gerhard De Jongh's dark eyes gleaming at her in the lamplight and thought of Charles in a small room in one of the tall houses that fringe the canal on the Kaisersgracht in Amsterdam.

'Uncle Alex, what about Charles? Is there anything we can

205

do? Anything at all? The south of Holland is liberated. Is there any way you know of we can find out what's happening in Amsterdam? Maybe get him out, somehow? De Jongh got out, maybe we can get Charles out too?'

He sighed and leaned forwards and switched on his desk light. The room sprang into brilliance.

'I'll see what I can find out,' he said heavily. 'The refugee committee, they can do a bit, maybe. But only a bit. Don't count on it.'

'No,' she said. 'I won't count on it.'

He got up and went to the window and began fussing with the blind although it wasn't quite blackout time yet. She watched him dully, feeling very tired now. It was as though she had spent the last hour running up hills rather than sitting in this luxurious office, just talking.

'People should know,' she said abruptly. 'If it's true. They should be told.'

'So who will believe it, hey? Like I said, where's the proof? The word of a few disgruntled refugees?'

'I don't believe it,' she said loudly. He came back to the desk and stared at her sombrely for a moment and then shook his head.

'I'd rather not believe it either,' he said. 'I'm trying hard not to.'

'It's not because I don't want to...'

"Never mind, dolly, never mind. Listen, I'll try to find out from Amsterdam, if I can, but don't count on it, and I'll find this Gerhard too. Talk to him myself, match his stories with the others I heard. There's a place in Poland they talk about, Ausch something. I wrote it down somewhere. I'd like to talk to this De Jongh fella. Where do I start?'

'Start?' She blinked at him. 'How do you mean?'

'Where did he say he was staying?'

'He didn't.'

'That of course makes it easy. He didn't confuse us with the facts, hey?' He grinned at her like a nursemaid coaxing a smile from a fractious child. 'Okay, okay, I'll see what I can do. Keep your chin in the air, dolly. It's the only place for it. And remember, bad as it feels at the moment it's no worse than it's been the past five years. You never knew where Charles was then, what he was doing, maybe you don't know now. Remember that.'

206

She tried to, but each day she woke to the thought of Charles, seeing him in that small room in Amsterdam as surely as if she had actually been there. Each day as she sat and sewed and the wireless blared and Cissie sang and Florrie brought the endless cups of tea, she thought of Gerhard De Jongh, walking away into the darkness of Paultons Square and hating herself for letting him go.

And each day, behind those thoughts, were others. Guilt and anger and helplessness as she let Uncle Alex's words march through her mind over and over again. The Jews suffer in every generation. Some get over it and some are destroyed by it. We're the lucky ones, the lucky ones, the lucky ones.

The words went on pleating themselves in and out of her thoughts as Uncle Alex, week after week, reported failure. No news of Charles, no news of Henk and no news at all of Gerhard De Jongh, even though he must be, had to be, somewhere in England, if not in London. He threw all his considerable energy into the search, sending people from his office to comb the refugee societies' files, badgering the Home Office for news of aliens, going to refugee clubs in every town he happened to be in as he stumped about the country looking after his tours and his actors and musicians. But it was as though De Jongh had never really existed and as the year turned into a hopeful spring and everyone was telling everyone else that it was almost over, it couldn't be long now, peace would come, she began to believe it had never happened. That night last October had been a nightmare, a figment of her war weary imagination. No young man with a thin face and dark eyes had come to get drunk in her drawing room and tell her mad stories. She had dreamed it all up because of her anxiety about Charles.

Then, the talk about the war ending became more than hopeful gossip and changed to certainty, and the newspapers were filled with accounts of allied soldiers fanning out over Europe so fast that even the most dedicated of readers could hardly keep up with it. And at last soldiers marched into Buchenwald and Belsen and the pictures arrived.

It was a sunny day in high summer and Hannah had come limping down to breakfast to find Florrie standing in the hallway with the *Daily Mirror* open in her hands and her face stiff with shock.

'What is it, Florrie?' Hannah had said, as she safely negotiated the last step. 'What's happened? You look as though the cat's got your – '

Florrie looked up and tried, clumsily, to fold the paper, to stuff it in her apron pocket. Hannah stared at her, puzzled.

'Florrie?'

Florrie shook her head again and then, slowly, obviously realizing the absurdity of trying to hide such a thing as a newspaper, gave it to her and Hannah leaned against the banisters, propping her stick beside her, and smoothed the crumpled pages as Cissie came down the stairs behind her, humming under her breath.

And there they were, the pictures, the words, the proof that they had asked for, she and Uncle Alex and all the others who had listened to the tales of the refugees and not really believed them. The pictures of starved bodies piled like garbage in a field, of faces staring out from behind barbed wire fences, of gas ovens and heaps of discarded spectacles and false teeth and shoes and bodies, bodies, bodies. They stood there, the three English women in the sunlit hallway of a pretty house in Chelsea, with the scent of their morning coffee in their nostrils and read over each other's shoulders of the deaths of millions. Florrie turned and ran, stumbling a little as she went up the stairs, and they could hear her vomiting in the bathroom.

27

In some ways it was harder to recover from the second world war than it had been from the first. Hannah had thought then, back in 1918, that she was at the very nadir of her life with Peter dead and Judith dead, and she alone to bear the burden of living on. But there had been the children then, two urgent reasons for getting up each morning and trying to get through the day. And she had been younger, and with more essential power still in her, though she had not realized that at the time.

But this time she realized full well how drained she was. Physically, she was deeply weary, eroded by the constant arthritic pain in her leg and hip, legacy of the injury to her ankle. She learned to stand as tall as she could, to use her stick at all times, and to control her pain by not thinking about it. When it got too bad to allow her to sleep, she took aspirin, but that was all. She would not see doctors, however much Cissie and Florrie nagged her to do so, determined to cope with her state as best she could, knowing it to be permanent.

The effect could be seen on her. Not only did she move with a rigidity that was a marked contrast to her old lithe easiness, but her face had changed. Her mouth had become tighter with the corners downturned and there were lines cut between them and her nostrils. The copper colour of her hair had faded, and was now tinged with white, though it was as thick as ever, and she flatly refused to do as Cissie did and have it dyed. Cissie was marching through her sixties triumphantly, a vision of New Look clothes and waved hair and lavish makeup while Hannah was heralding her fifties, it seemed, by displaying her age rather than fighting it.

But it was the emotional burden that was the heaviest. For the first two years after the war was over she went on hoping, forlornly, though she knew she was absurd. Of course Charles was dead, it could not be otherwise. Maybe, she would tell herself in the long dark nights, maybe one day someone will turn up who will know what happened to him. Maybe Henk will come to the door and tell her that Charles was well, alive and well and living in some remote country suffering from amnesia, his past driven from his memory by the hell of a particular present. She drifted back into the comforting fantasy habits of her childhood, weaving complex stories in her head to explain away the pain of reality, making elaborate story structures in which Charles triumphed over and over again, all culminating in Charles coming home to her.

Uncle Alex went on trying but a tide of displaced people was unleashed in Europe and in all the chaos and recriminations and confusion tracking down the fate of one Englishman who had lived in Amsterdam was a herculean task. At last he did find the facts and that was a bad day for Hannah. For Charles had died not a hero's death, fighting the injustices and hates that had fuelled him for so long, but a pointless wasted one, alone in a charity ward coughing his tubercular lungs into a chipped enamel bowl.

For weeks after that news reached Paultons Square Hannah walked taller and straighter and more grimly than ever, and Cissie stopped singing. Her own TB had been cured, leaving her with a safely calcified spot on her right lung. She, sixty-five years old, was alive; Charles, who had been little more than thirty, was gone, and that shamed her. So Hannah had to comfort her too. Bad days, bad days.

And not helped by the silence from Marie. Lammeck Alley moved back into gear slowly, picking up the threads of business as the world shook itself and returned to normal living, and it took some time for Hannah to identify the person most likely to help her. Peterson had long since retired, grateful for a little peace at last. He was succeeded by a Damont cousin who was quite uninterested in past family history, and took little trouble to advise her. But, by means of persistent letters and phone calls, she at last persuaded him to give her what news he had.

It was scant. Mrs Rupert Lammeck had gone on drawing her income until 1944 and then stopped. No more had been heard of her. There was now an accumulation of funds in her name, although of course the amount could not be divulged to anyone, even Mrs Rupert Lammeck's mother.

'Dammit!' Hannah shouted at the smooth faced boy reciting this at her. 'Dammit, do you think I care about her money? I only want to know where she is, is she well? What about her child? That's all.' But he just shrugged; he knew no more.

She considered hiring a private detective, but Uncle Alex talked her out of that.

'It's a big country, dolly, and she was always on the move. Forget it, look it in the face and forget it. She don't want to know you no more. Sure it hurts, but who promised you a life with no hurts in it? Anyone did, he was a liar.'

She wrote long letters to her brothers in New York, asking them to see if they could find news of her, not because she really thought they could but because it was better than doing nothing. They wrote back, short scrappy little letters full of their own doings on the fringes of the boxing world that made it clear they could not find their niece and wouldn't know where to begin looking. And Hannah tried to do as Uncle Alex advised and live with her pain.

The early post war years were hard for all of them, quite

apart from any personal distress. Food was in shorter supply than it had ever been, and rationing seemed to be a permanent feature of British existence. Women who could get their hands on black market cloth came to Hannah but most of her work was the dispiriting making over of old garments, lengthening skirts to approximate Christian Dior's New Look, remaking lingerie so that every possible use was made of every scrap of fabric. But at last the forties died miserably and became the fifties and people began to talk more of the future and to plan for it instead of looking back over their shoulders.

As the years of austerity eased and money became more available, it sometimes seemed to Hannah that the new young people had forgotten all the pain that their predecessors had suffered for them. Who cared any more about her Charles, about Marcus and his bitter loss, and her and her constant pain, who gave a damn? She would look at the young ones strutting about the streets in their full skirted dresses and drainpipe trousers, lugging their portable radios around and bawling their ugly noisy songs and was filled with a resentment and anger that tightened her mouth even more. For a long time Hannah disliked herself and her world sorely.

In 1955 Cissie at last took the plunge about which she had been talking for years. She had said, when Lenny and his Nina had gone to America to bring their children home and had decided instead to stay there, that she would follow them, would make her future there. Somehow she had never found the courage. But when she heard that her oldest grandchild had become engaged, she could bear it no longer. She would go – and what was more, she would go by air.

How they ever got her into the cab and out to Heathrow to get on her plane Hannah never really knew. The excitement in Cissie was so high it was almost hysteria, and Florrie started crying over breakfast and didn't stop all day, and Hannah was tight lipped with misery, for Cissie was her dearest friend.

They said little when they parted, just hugging each other, and Hannah sat beside a still weeping Florrie in the cab going back to Paultons Square and asked herself dully why she bothered to go on living at all. It seemed so pointless now. What was left of all the hopes and plans of the early years?

What was there in this new world for which her Marcus and Charles had died that was worth living for? Nothing at all, she told herself, nothing at all.

Cissie wrote regularly at first, twice a week. Her letters punctuated Hannah's dreary days with interest, but as the years moved on they became fewer and scrappier. It was not that Cissie had forgotten Hannah, but she had a new purpose in her life now, Hannah supposed, and was too busy to write.

Hannah was genuinely glad for her, but it underlined her own lonely uselessness. What good was she to anyone? Uncle Alex, old as he was, was still vigorous, still busy though not with business. Now an indefatigable committee man, he spent all his waking hours raising money for the infant state of Israel, an activity which seemed to have injected him with ever more energy, if that were possible. Certainly he had no need of Hannah. As far as she could tell, her only use was as someone for Florrie to fuss over, someone to give purpose to *her* life. That she had none in her own seemed irrelevant to everyone.

Until one evening in June 1957. It had been a hot day though not as hot as the previous weeks had been; the country had sweltered in one of the hottest summers on record, and Hannah, like many people, was drained by it. She had been to a wedding at Edgware. One of Reuben and Minnie's great brood had married, and Hannah had sighed when the invitation had come, wearied by the thought of yet another family party, for they were a burgeoning and busy clan, the Lazars. Weddings and brisses and Barmitzvahs seemed to happen with every rising of the moon, interspersed with house warming parties as the young ones prospered and moved on, shaking the dust of the East End from their well shod feet for the lusher pastures of north west London.

It amused her sometimes to contemplate them, business men and accountants, factory owners and shopkeepers, with their befurred and scented wives and sulky faced expensively educated spoiled youngsters, talking earnestly to each other of University for young Sandra and Lawrence and Andrea and Vernon and Debra and Ivor. They who had left their schools at fourteen were going to see to it that their children would have a better life in this better new world. Being Jewish in London in the nineteen fifties was a comfortable and safe thing to be, for was there not, at last, a safe haven available in case anything went wrong? When the State of Israel had been born in 1948 some of the more politically minded of them shook their heads, worried about the long term outcome, but most of them breathed deep and told each other how marvellous it was and set about fund raising as part of their social lives, and generally felt good.

So, when invitations to weddings and parties came Hannah sighed and accepted. It would be hurtful not to, but she never wanted to go. Their closeness with their children and grandchildren underlined too painfully her own solitude. And today had been no exception.

Florrie was away, gone to visit Bet in Whitby for her annual summer holiday, having left Hannah with long lists of emergency instructions, so she was alone in the house. The street outside was still shimmering with heat, even though it was now seven in the evening, for the day had sweltered. The reception had been a tea dance – tea dances were more fashionable now, because they were less ostentatious than the old East End style parties with mountains of food and hours of dancing. Those were considered vulgar, too reminiscent of the olds days in the *shtetls*. English Jews today aimed to be as English as they could be. Which meant control, and an awareness of what was high class behaviour and what was not. Really rich people (and the father of the bride as a record shop owner was becoming exceedingly rich) could make these more stylish modest parties without being thought cheapskates by the older generation while adhering to their own notions of what was proper. Hannah for one was grateful. And also grateful to be home.

She showered slowly, letting the water run over her, feeling some of the pain ease from her hip, and then went limping into the bedroom, not bothering to dry herself. Letting the water evaporate on her skin was cooling and she needed that. She caught a glimpse of herself in the dressing table mirror as she went past it and stopped to stare. The silence in the house enveloped her and for a moment time seemed to slip. It wasn't now, but long ago, when this room had been newly decorated, and she frowned sharply at the image in the mirror. Who was that, so tired looking and lined? Whose body was that with drooping breasts and thinning hair? What had happened to her? Inside she felt as she always had, but on the surface was a total stranger.

She shook her head and closed her eyes. When she opened them again the moment had passed. Just for a second it had seemed as it used to, with a small watching Hannah sitting in the corner of the room jeering at her, commenting cruelly on her, making her feel like a totally different person. She could not cope with that feeling again now; she would not. She moved away from the mirror purposefully and put on the cotton housecoat in which she was most comfortable.

At first she thought she imagined it when the bell rang downstairs. With Florrie away, there was no one who would call on her at seven on a Sunday evening, and for a moment she felt a surge of fear, a memory of that night thirteen years before when Gerhard De Jongh had come.

'Silly,' she said aloud, and pushed her feet into her slippers and began the slow painful descent of the stairs.

The bell rang again, impatiently, a double ring, and she said aloud, 'All right, all right! I'm coming!' even though she knew she could not be heard. She could see a shape against the stained glass insets on the door and she squinted a little, trying to identify who it might be, but the shape was ill defined, refracted by the shattered light.

She stood in front of the door for a moment and then opened it cautiously a few inches.

The light was lowering now as the sun moved further down the sky and the figure in front of her was hard to see. She squinted again and said carefully, 'Yes?'

'I'm sorry to bother you, ma'am.' It was a soft drawling voice with an unfamiliar accent, a high voice. Hannah looked closer, puzzled. The figure was wearing trousers and a shirt and had a cloth cap on its head and she had thought, just for a moment, that it was a man. Now she could see the face, and relaxed a little. A round face, soft and young. A girl's.

'Yes?' she said again.

'I'm looking for a Lady Lammeck? I was told that this was the Lammeck home and ... but you are, aren't you? You're Lady Lammeck. I can see you are.'

Hannah frowned and stepped back a little, pushing the door almost closed.

'What d'you mean, you can see I am?' she said, sharply. 'You can't see me properly at all.'

The girl smiled widely, showing very white teeth. 'I can see your hair, ma'am. Red hair. Like mine.' She lifted her

214

hand and took her cap off and a tangle of hair fell over her shoulders, red coppery hair, just as Hannah's own had been.

She stood there for a long moment, listening to her pulse beating thickly in her ears, staring at the thin girl in her shabby shirt and trousers and with a mass of red hair framing her face, not daring to think, not daring to hope, only daring to breathe slowly, regularly, counting each breath. One, two, three.

'I'm Lee,' the girl said. 'Lee Lammeck. I said I'd come and find you, ever since I was a kid. And now I have. Do I call you grandma, or would you prefer something else?'

28

Lee was sitting on the floor, her knees hunched up and her arms hugging them, while Hannah sat very upright in her high backed chair on the other side of the fireplace. The small table with the remains of their supper stood to one side and Hannah looked at it and thought, I ought to clear that up. But she did not move.

Lee had been quite calm about it; she had come to London to find her grandmother, and she had every intention of staying with her, now that she had found her.

'You've got room, haven't you? Or would I be trouble to have around? I'm not usually. I'm used to living in other peoples houses.'

'No trouble at all,' Hannah said. 'And yes, I have room. Too much room.'

'I can see that.' She looked around consideringly. 'I was told you're rich, and you sure are. Looks like you're loaded, in fact.'

Hannah frowned a little at that. 'I don't talk about money,' she said stiffly.

Lee nodded. 'That sure as hell proves you got a lot of it. You can only ignore it when you're loaded. When you're not it sort of pushes itself at you, know what I mean?'

'I know,' Hannah said. 'I was born in the East End.'

'Oh? Where's that?'

'Where poor people are born.'

'I was born in San Francisco,' Lee said after a moment. 'Or so I'm told.'

Hannah took a deep breath. So far she had hardly dared to speak to the girl at all. Her own feelings were in far too great a turmoil to be able to say much and the girl herself seemed so contained and remote, somehow. So, she had offered her supper and Lee had accepted calmly and helped her make omelettes for them both, and chattered on about her journey, about how long it had taken her to save the money to buy an air ticket by working as a waitress and in a summer camp and as a baby sitter, and how dramatic the world looked from so far up and Hannah had listened and watched the girl's face and the way the light played on her hair and lit it to that familiar bronze sheen that used to look back at her from her own mirror.

And now she could wait no longer.

'Lee,' she said. 'Your mother. Tell me about Marie.'

The girl looked up at her. swinging her head so that the mass of hair covered half her face and she could hide behind it. All Hannah could see was one eye staring watchfully at her.

'What about her?'

'Where is she? Why hasn't she been in touch with me all these years? And Rupert, your father, what about him?'

'Oh, he's dead,' Lee said easily and looked away, staring at the window which the summer twilight was now deepening to a dusky blue.

'Oh,' Hannah said blankly, and felt a little chill inside her. Was this child as cold as she seemed? 'I'm sorry.'

Lee shrugged. 'Why should you be? I mean, from my point of view, gee, I never even saw him! He was gone before I was born, they told me, and I never knew anything about him till after he died.'

'They told you – who told you?'

'Aunt Pearl,' Lee said. 'I lived with Aunt Pearl, you see. In Sacramento. She took me after ... when I was four. I lived with her ever since, till she died last year. They tried to put me in a Home then, you know? In California they've got all these crazy laws about how old kids have to be to be left in peace to live on their own, and they tried to put me in a Home, like I'd done something, and I never did a thing I shouldn't! Aunt Pearl would'a killed me if I had. So when she died, and they started talking about a Home I thought, hell, no, and I lit out.'

'Lit out?'

'Went to New York. Hitched, y'know? Wow, it was tough sometimes. Some of these truck drivers think that just because you want a ride you're ... well never mind, Anyway, I got to New York and – '

'But Marie. Your mother,' Hannah said, holding onto the thread tightly. There was a lot to hear about Lee, but first things first, she told herself. First things first. 'Marie?'

Lee sat silently staring out at the dark square, then said abruptly, 'I'd rather not talk about her.'

The silence between them lengthened and then Lee said angrily, 'Oh, hell! What can I do? You were her mother so I guess ... She took coke, okay? So Aunt Pearl said, anyway. Got into a whole coke bit and that did it.'

'I don't understand,' Hannah said carefully. 'I'm sorry, but I don't understand.'

'What don't you understand? That your daughter was a lousy addict? Spent most of her time so stoned she couldn't even talk, let alone take care of a kid? I remember it, you know that? I remember being in that apartment and she lying there breathing so loud I could ... and so goddam hungry I didn't know ... Aw, hell, she's dead, okay? And Aunt Pearl was her friend and she found her dead and took me in and that's all. Now, can we lay off my mother? I know you had to be told, but it ... I just don't like to talk about it. I told you what I know, now leave it alone already.'

Hannah said nothing. There was nothing she could say. She sat in the darkening drawing room remembering and trying not to, seeing Marie in a high chair, Marie in a frilled white dress going to a children's party, Marie and Charles in blue holland overalls painting at the big nursery table.

'I'm sorry,' she said then. 'Sorry for you, sorry for me. Sorry for Marie. I don't know what I did wrong, but I ... her father died when she was a baby, I ... I did my best. But it wasn't enough.'

'Listen,' Lee said and there was a rough anger in her voice. 'I'll tell you what Aunt Pearl told me, okay? That some people are born to it, you know? Born to misery, I mean. That it is no one's fault it happens, that you can be the best friend that person ever had, the best kid, the best parent, I

217

guess, but no matter what, they just don't make it. Aunt Pearl was the greatest friend anyone could have had. What she did for my mother, well, I'll tell you she was the greatest, fantastic. And she learned not to blame herself and she taught me not to blame myself, and now I'm telling you. None of this had anything to do with anyone except my mother, okay? You don't own people just because you care about 'em. You do what you can and the rest is up to them. That's what Aunt Pearl said.'

'Aunt Pearl sounds very special,' Hannah said quietly.

'She was. The best there was. She died bad, too, didn't deserve it. She had cancer in the breast. Awful.'

Lee stretched suddenly and yawned, opening her mouth wide and Hannah saw the gleam of her teeth in the darkness. 'And here I am. I got here! I always said I would. Aunt Pearl told me I had this high toned family back in London, and if I ever needed any help, go find 'em. So here I am. Jeeze, it wasn't easy, you know that? Getting a passport and all. I had to lie like crazy but I got it, and I raised the money and I kept out of their goddam Home and I made it! And from where I'm sitting that sure is something!'

'Indeed it is,' Hannah said, and felt a sudden warmth for this strange sharp girl. It wasn't just that she looked so like Hannah herself at her age. It was the determination in her, the strength in her that made Hannah feel good and whole again. Without thinking she put out one hand and said, 'I'm so glad you did. Glad you made it. I think I've been waiting for you.'

Lee sat still in the darkness for a moment and then she put out one hand too and took Hannah's in her rough young fingers.

'It's okay, then? You want me to stay?'

'I sure do,' Hannah said, and laughed softly in the dark room, enjoying her moment of affectionate mockery. 'I sure do.'

'Thanks most awfully,' Lee said with a neat imitation of an English voice. 'Thanks most awfully *awfully*.'

And so it was that at the age of sixty-four Hannah started to live again. It seemed to her sometimes, over the next ten years, that this was what she had been born for, what all the sad and painful years had been leading to, making a haven for

218

this tough little scrap of a girl who had, in her own way, suffered as much as her grandmother had. Nurturing her and teaching her and protecting her and loving her, watching her lose, slowly, her defensive edginess and become a laughing relaxed and happy person. That was what life was for. Even Florrie seemed to have a new lease on life with a young one in the house. She nagged less and sang more, and fussed over both of them with ill concealed delight.

Together they explored the East End where Hannah had been born, for Lee had a hunger for information about the past that was almost insatiable, and, slowly because of Hannah's arthritis, they walked through the Whitechapel Road and Commercial Road as Hannah told Lee stories of the old days, and how it had been to live in these tight, mean, hungry streets.

Many of them were gone now of course; where Antcliff Street had been there were now great tower blocks of flats set at angles in rough litter-covered grass. Sidney Street was still there and so was Jubilee Street, though largely rebuilt on the bombed sites of long dead houses and little shops, but Bromehead Road and Bromehead Street had gone, and the market stalls had gone. Now there were black and Asian faces where once had been Jewish side curls and old women in *sheitels* and men with their prayer shawls dangling beneath their waistcoats.

Lee stared and listened and asked questions and Hannah found herself, to her own surprise at first, talking about Charles and how he had come to these streets to fight for a better world for the people who had lived in them. How he had fought with the blackshirt marchers, how he had burned out his young life fighting, fighting, fighting. Lee had lifted her chin in exaltation at his story, and at last Hannah stopped mourning for the loss of Charles and was able to celebrate the fact that he had lived. So his life had been short? What matter when it had been so important and so well used? True, he had died alone and lonely in a foreign country. But what matter when he lived on now in this granddaughter of hers whom he would have loved as much as Lee had come to love his memory? Charles lived again, and lived well, because of Lee.

Lee and Uncle Alex took to each other with a delight that made Hannah want to weep with sheer pleasure. The old man, now almost ninety, would sit in his armchair when they went to visit him, and laugh and tease Lee as though he were still a sprightly sixty, and she teased him too, asking him why he had never married, just for the joy of hearing him giggle wickedly and tell her that he had been too clever.

'I tell you, dolly,' he would say in his thin old voice. 'I tell you, I had such girls! They were crazy for me, but I had my Hannah to worry over so what did I want with wives and more children? I had my Hannah and now she's got you. It all comes out in the wash, hey? That's what my Momma Rivka used to say, in the *heim*. It all comes out in the wash.'

One of Hannah's greatest delights was to discover that Lee had inherited her grandmother's gift for design and sewing. She told Hannah very quickly after arriving that she had no notion of being a layabout.

'I'm going to get a job,' she said. 'I'll find something to do. I gotta be independent, you know? I don't take no handouts from no one. I worked for Aunt Pearl, soon's I left school and I'll work now.'

'You don't have to, Lee,' Hannah said, tentatively. 'I don't mean I'll take care of you, though I would, gladly, but you've got your own money. Marie, your mother, only drew the income from hers. The capital's considerable by now, I imagine. All you have to do is go to Lammeck Alley. Once they know you're Marie's daughter, then, there it will be. You'll have all the money you need.'

'To hell with that,' Lee said, her voice flat. 'To hell with that. Much good it did my mother to have it. She didn't work for it, so she used it for junk. She killed herself with it. Didn't she? Not me. Not nohow, not ever. I'm going to work for my money. Anyway, I don't give a good goddam for money, not for itself. It's what you *do* that matters. What you create with your own head and your own hands. No handouts for me. I'm going to get work of my own.'

The work she got was in a dress shop and after listening to her and watching for a year, Hannah suggested, tentatively, that maybe it would be an idea to have a shop of her own.

'Not a handout,' she assured Lee hastily. 'I promise you not a handout. It's something that interests me, too, and maybe you could design your own, just as I did when I was Mary Bee Couturiere.'

And so it happened. By the time Uncle Alex died sweetly and contentedly in his sleep just after his ninety-first birthday, Lee had her shop just around the corner from Paultons Square in King's Road.

'Not the smartest place in the world, I grant you,' Hannah had said when they found the premises. 'But if you do good things people'll come to you, and districts change. You never know. King's Road could turn out to be a good place to have a shop.'

She was right, of course. By the time Lee's twenty-fifth birthday came, her boutique was regarded as one of the best in London. She had her own workshops behind it and was turning out clothes that every magazine wanted to write about and every smart woman wanted to wear. Never mind Courrèges and Quant, it was Lee Lammeck clothes they all wanted. And bought and talked about and feted Lee and she and Hannah laughed over the way it was all happening again.

Lee found a particular delight in tracing the similarities between herself and her grandmother's history, telling every interviewer that her grandmother had been to the 1920s what she, Lee, was now, forty years later.

And aged seventy-two, with her hair now completely white and her back as stiff as ever and her arthritis gripping her ever more tightly, Hannah found herself once again a person of fashion. It amused her immensely and when she planned a special birthday party for Lee, she made up an invitation list that was starred with famous names. Pop singers and photographers, actors and politicians, everyone who was anyone was invited. It was the biggest party of the year, one of the highlights of the Swinging Sixties world that London had become.

But Hannah did not invite only the rich and famous, any more than she had all those years ago when she and Marcus had entertained the Prince of Wales in their house in Paultons Square. She invited her cousins and their children too, though this time the difference between the children of Lazar and Rivka and the new aristocracy of England was difficult to see. For they came to the party in Paultons Square in their Bentleys and Mercedes, dressed and bejewelled as richly as anyone else, and spoke in the same voices with the same sort of words, expressing the same sort of sentiments. The differences had melted away in three generations. The poverty, the loneliness, the alienation of the immigrant East Enders were all gone.

One of the guests was Adam Lazar, the son of Lionel. A tall, quiet young man with a passion for learning that Hannah found very reminiscent of his long dead grandfather David and David's father, her Uncle Benjamin. He had been away working in America for the past five years and he and Lee had not met before.

Hannah watched them talk and laugh and dance together at Lee's twenty-fifth birthday party and knew that a new phase was about to begin, that a new generation was waiting to take the stage. And somewhere deep within herself she knew that the seeds of a new loneliness were being sown for her. And she was right, because in May 1967 Lee Lammeck married Dr Adam Lazar at the New West End synagogue at the smartest wedding of the year. Their shared relation, grandmother and great cousin Hannah was the most honoured guest. She sat at the top table as the other guests danced and ate and drank and danced again and watched them and thought her quiet thoughts. She was to be alone again, for Adam had an important research job to return to in California, and Lee was to accompany him. Hannah, almost seventy-five, could have gone with them; both begged her to, but she shook her head and patted their cheeks and told them, no.

'I belong here,' she said. 'Born and bred a Londoner, you know that. My parents and my grandparents had to wander, you have to wander. But me, I'm one of the few who stay put. So, I'm staying here. Come and visit me when you can. The house will always be here and I'll always be in it. *G'ey g'zint.*' And she smiled at herself for speaking Yiddish for she never had. But it was necessary, for that was what Uncle Alex would have said to them. '*G'ey g'zint.*' Go in good health.

And they went, with a good heart, Lee weeping a little, but glowing with the joy of having her Adam beside her. Hannah watched them walk through the departure gate at Heathrow Airport and turned away and went home to Florrie, now almost as arthritic as Hannah herself, alone, but not lonely. Lee might not be with her, but she was there in her world, and always a part of it. She had given Hannah reason to live and the reason was still there wherever Lee happened to be. So Hannah told herself as her taxi drew up outside the house in Paultons Square, and she went in tranquilly to make some supper for Florrie.

EPILOGUE

Returning

March 1980. A cold and blustery London morning with last year's leaves blowing along the gutters in little flurries and cars spraying up water as they swished past, their windscreen wipers working frantically. One of them, a big red one, spattered the small girl in the raincoat with muddy water and she squealed. Her mother looked at her and shushed her gently.

'You have to be quiet and polite this morning, honey,' she whispered, and pulled the rainhat more closely over her ears. The child wriggled and made a face.

Cars arriving, more cars, and people collecting in little groups, talking quietly. People in heavy black coats and ladies in neat hats and furs, all smiling small smiles, the sort that you smile when you want to but mustn't, or don't want to but must, the small girl decided. She tried not to yawn. If squealing was not polite, yawning must be worse.

People talked to her, were introduced and she smiled and nodded, not understanding who they all were but knowing she must be polite as Daddy pushed her gently forwards to shake hands. 'I'm ten years old,' she told them. 'Ten years old,' as they went on and on asking her, one after the other and smiling the way they did, small and tight.

And then there was praying and talking and she stopped listening, looking out at the sky that she could see through the high windows of the tall building they had all gone into and thinking how it would be tomorrow, going on a plane again. Three planes in three days. No one else in her grade at school at home had ever gone in three planes in three days, she was sure of that.

Walking again along muddy paths, all the people walking together, so close together that she could not see much more than the legs of the people in front. Anyway she didn't want to see. She knew what they were doing, for Daddy had told her, and it wasn't all that interesting. Or nice.

At last, they came back along the muddy paths, and the people were smiling more widely now, their shoulders less stiff, even laughing a little, as the men washed their hands at little fountains and nodded at each other.

And then it was over and they were ging back to their own car, the one Daddy had hired for today and there was someone calling after them.

'Lee? Adam? I knew it was you! I haven't seen you for, oh, years! How *are* you both? It's good to see you. I just wish it had been on a happier occasion.'

'Yes,' Mommy said, and the child looked up at her mother, a little surprised because she wasn't one who cried much and she was crying now. 'Yes.'

'You were close, I know,' the man said, and patted Mommy's hand. 'You'll miss her, but she had a good life, a good life. How old was she? Eighty-seven? And died peacefully in her sleep, just like old Uncle Alex, *alava ha-sholom*, you remember him? I tell you, we got good genes in this family, we live long, if we live in peace. And who is this? You haven't told me who this is.'

The child looked up at the man in his thick black overcoat and he smiled at her and she thought, I like his face, and she smiled too. He took off his hat and bent towards her, and wanting to be as polite as he was, she did the same, glad to pull the thing off anyway, for it made her ears itch. Her red hair came tumbling out and was blown about her face by the wind and she smiled at the man and said, 'Hi! I'm ten years old.'

He laughed. 'I was about to ask. And what do they call you?'

'Sukey,' she said. 'It's short though. Short, for all my name.'

'And what is all your name?'

Mommy and Daddy were smiling now. She could feel them standing there smiling at her, and she looked up at them and they nodded. It was all right to talk, to chatter on. The sad bits were over, now.

'Susannah Tamar,' she said. 'My name is Susannah Tamar Lazar, and I'm going to live in Jerusalem with my Mommy and Daddy, because he's going to work in a hospital there. Isn't that exciting?'

'Very exciting,' the man said, and Sukey pulled away from her Mommy's hand and went skipping along the path towards the car, leaving them to follow. Another airplane tomorrow, to go to Jerusalem. Very exciting. She began to sing.

Alav ha sholom: Literally, 'Peace to him or her'. Used whenever speaking of someone who is dead.

Ashkenazi: Jews of the Central and Eastern parts of Europe, most especially those of the Pale of Settlement, and Germany. (*See also* Sephardi.)

Bagel: A circular roll with a hole in the centre made of white flour and yeast, the dough being poached in hot water before baking, to make it particularly crisp.

Barmitzvah: Literally 'son of the commandment'; the rite of passage through which Jewish boys pass at the age of thirteen to permit them to join the community as full members.

Bimah: The central dais in the synagogue.

Blinis: Stuffed pancakes, sweet or savoury. Also known as blintzes.

Bissel: A little. (A *bissel* here, a *bissel* there – a little here, a little there.)

Bobbelah: A term of endearment, generally feminine of use, but, on occasion, directed at men. Derives from Russian Yiddish, as diminutive of buba – 'doll'.

Boobameiser: A grandmother's story (an old wives' tale).

Boychick: A small boy. Used sometimes to define a man with boyish ways.

Briss: Ritual circumcision of a baby boy.

Broigus: Offended, angry.

Chanukah: The Feast of Lights. An eight-day celebration observed in December and frequently coinciding with Christmas in the Christian calander. It commemorates the victory of the Maccabees, Jewish warriors who defeated the Syrians in 167 BC (See the Apocrypha, Book of the Maccabees I and II.)

Cheder: Schoolroom, where Hebrew is taught, only to boys in the old days but now to girls too.

Choleria: Literally cholera, but usually meaning a curse of some kind or another. ('A choleria on him' means 'May a plague fall on him and destroy him'.)

Chuchum: Clever – a show-off sort of person.

Chumash: First five books of the bible (Pentateuch).

Chutspah: (many different spellings) Impudence, outrageous effrontery. Best defined by telling a story, e.g. 'A man killed both his parents and at his trial for murder begged for clemency on the grounds that he was an orphan'.

Dreying your kopf: Literally 'banging your head' – upsetting yourself.

Farbissen: Embittered, sullen, sour. Can be used as a noun – e.g. *farbissener*, an embittered man (for an embittered woman *farbissenah*).

Ferstinkener: Smelly. Used as an epithet to describe a disliked person, as well as literally to describe a smelly object/place.

Gefärlich: Busyness – doing.

Gefillte fish: Literally stuffed fish. A mixture of chopped white fish, onions, eggs, sometimes ground almonds or chopped apples, and seasoning, originally used to stuff carp before it was poached, now often poached or fried in small portions. Usually eaten with beetroot-flavoured horseradish sauce (chrane) and considered a great delicacy.

Gelt: Literally gold. Money.

Giveh: Showing off – swank.

Goldeneh medina: Literally the golden country. Usually used to define the USA to which the majority of the Jews of the Pale wished to emigrate.

Gonif (plural *gonovim*): Thief.

Gornicht mit gornicht: Literally 'nothing with nothing'.

Gott se dank: Thank God.

Goy: A gentile, a non-Jew.

Gunser macher: 'A big noise' – a busy person, either in reality or his own opinion!

Guteneh shumah: Literally a good person.

Gy gesund: Literally 'go in health' and by implication 'with a good heart and with a blessing'.

Haggadah: The collection of Jewish history, fables and folk-lore, assorted rabbinical writings, prayers – a whole library of Jewish culture.

Heim: Literally home. Often used to describe the place from which immigrants came to London (*see also* shtetl). Hence *heimish* or *heimisher* – homelike or in the style of the old

229

home.

Halevai (sometimes pronounced 'aleavai', with a dropped aitch): Literally 'Please let it be so'.

Kaddish: A special prayer. The prayer at the end of the Sabbath service is a kaddish. Mourners say a kaddish for the dead. (Kiddush is another prayer used to sanctify the Sabbath and Holy Days and said before meals).

Kishke: Literally intestines. Guts.

Kopf: Head.

Kosher: Literally fit for use. Usually describes food prepared according to Jewish dietary laws.

Koyach: Strength.

Ladino: A vernacular used by Sephardi Jews (q.v.) deriving from Spanish, Portuguese, French, just as Yiddish (q.v.) derives from German and Russian.

Lavoyah: A funeral.

Lobbus: Lovable rogue.

Lockshen: Thin noodles, vermicelli. Traditionally served in chicken soup.

Lundsman (plural *landsleit*): Properly, land's man – one who comes from your land. A fellow Jew from the same *shtetl* in the *heim* (q.v.).

Magen David: The star of David. The symbol of Judaism.

Marrano: A converted Jew, from the Spanish word for pig.

Maven: Literally an expert. One who knows a great deal about a specific subject.

Mazel: Literally luck. Also part of the traditional greeting and congratulation, *mazel tov*.

Mechulah: Finished, without money. A person who goes bankrupt is *mechulah*.

Megillah: A long rigmarole, a spun-out tale, a false story. Originally for the Book of Esther which is a very long *megillah* indeed.

Mensch (plural *menschen*): Literally man, or men. But now used to describe a person of character, of stature or obvious worth. 'A real *mensch*' is a respect-worthy person.

Meshuggah: Literally mad. Used also as a noun *meshuggenah* – a mad person. Also *misheggass*, a madness, a crazy act.

Mezzuzah: A small container carrying a tiny scroll with the verses Deuteronomy vi, 4–9, xi, 13–21, and fastened to the doorposts of a house occupied by pious Jews.

Midrash: A collection of over a hundred books of Biblical

commentary.

Mishnah: One of the two parts of Talmud (the other is the Gemorrah). Contains the Law.

Mohel: A person who performs ritual circumcision (*see* Bris).

Mumser (plural *mumserim*). Literally bastard. So a bad person.

Nachus: Pride – especially in the doings of one's children.

Nebbish (also *nebbach* and other spellings): Pathetic. A pathetic person is a *nebbish*. When a person is ill, *nebbish*, he doesn't feel well. Widely used in many contexts to define a sad situation or person, but also a helpless person (a mentally handicapped individual is *nebbish*).

Oy vey is mir: Literally 'Oh woe is me!' A traditional Jewish cry of distress.

Putz: The male generative organ – expressed as a diminutive. (More insulting with the same meaning is *schmuck*.)

Rachmones: Pity. To show compassion.

Rosh Hashonah: The New Year festival, falling at the end of the growing and harvesting year, i.e. September, October.

Sairchel: Common sense, wisdom.

Sephardi: Jews deriving from Spanish and Portuguese communities. Often French nowadays. The old 'aristocracy' of Jews in some people's eyes. All, however, Ladino speaking (q.v.).

Shabbos: Sabbath. From sunset Friday to sunset Saturday.

Shachris: Evening prayers.

Shadchan: A matchmaker, active in the *heim* (q.v.).

Shaygets: A non-Jewish youth.

Shayne Mensch: Literallly 'pretty man' – a handsome person.

Sheitel: Wig worn by pious Jewish women who shaved their heads when they married, since a woman's hair is her 'crowning glory' and has erotic connotations which may no longer be allowed to be displayed once a girl marries.

Shidduch: A 'match', an engagement.

Shivah: The seven days of ritual mourning for the dead observed by the immediate members of the family.

Shlemeil: An idiot.

Shlep: Literally to drag, to carry on a long journey, a heavy load. Anything which gives a lot of trouble and takes a lot of effort.

Shmaltz: Literally fat. Used to describe cooking fat, especially chicken fat, but also for soft speech, and cooing talk.

Shnorrer: A beggar.

231

Shoin fertig: 'Make it,' finished, done.

Shprauncy: Fancy, showing off.

Shtetl: Literally a small town, a village. Used to describe the close-knit Jewish communities of the *heim* (q.v.) where the *landsleit* (q.v.) came from to enter their new homes in Britain and the USA, etc.

Shul: Synagogue.

Simcha: A happy occasion, for example a wedding.

Tallis: Prayer shawl, worn by men in synagogue.

Talmud: A collection of some sixty-three books encapsulating the Law, the customs, everything that matters to Judaism.

Tochus: Behind, bottom, arse, whichever you like.

Torah: The Five Books of Moses.

Tsitsis: Fringed garment worn at all times by orthodox Jews.

Tsorus: Literally trouble, suffering, unhappiness.

Was machst du: Literally 'What are you doing?' How goes things? How are you?, etc.

Yachner: A gossiping woman.

Yarmulkah: Skull cap worn by pious Jews, who keep their heads covered at all times.

Yenta: A vulgar woman. Often a *yenta* is also a *yachner* (q.v.).

Yeshivah: A Hebrew college, like a university when compared to a *chedar* (q.v.).

Yiddish: Diminutive term for Judisch-Deutsch, the vernacular developed by Jews living and working in Germany in past centuries, now used in other parts of the world, as the Jews dispersed even more widely.

Yom Kippur: The Day of Atonement. The most important Fast in the Jewish Year, occurring early in each New Year (*see* Rosh Hashonah).